GREENWILD
THE
WORLD BEHIND
THE DOOR

Praise for *Greenwild: The World Behind the Door*

'If you don't believe in magic, you will after you've read *Greenwild*. It's phenomenal.' – A. F. Steadman, author of *Skandar and the Unicorn Thief*

'A spellbinding, enchanting read full of wildness and beauty.' – Hannah Gold, author of *The Last Bear*

'A glorious, page-turning adventure . . . Thomson has created a gorgeous, utterly believable world as magical and magnificent as the Amazon rainforest itself. I adored this book!' – Aisling Fowler, author of *Fireborn*

'*Greenwild* is a thrilling adventure that takes seed in your imagination and runs wild!' – M. G. Leonard, author of *Beetle Boy*

'I fell utterly in love with this sharply beautiful, contemporary adventure.' – Cerrie Burnell, author of *Wilder Than Midnight*

'A wonderfully whimsical story with a beautiful world – and lots of mystery and adventure – for readers to immerse themselves in.' – Aisha Bushby, author of *A Pocketful of Stars*

'Wildly thrilling and beautifully written, *Greenwild* is the most special type of adventure!' – Carlie Sorosiak, author of *I, Cosmo*

'I adored this wild and wondrous adventure!' – Maria Kuzniar, author of *The Ship of Shadows*

'A rare and wondrous treasure that had me spellbound from first page to last.' – Catherine Doyle, author of *The Storm Keeper's Island*

'A wildly inventive adventure, bursting with beautiful detail and a satisfying plot as twisty as magical vines . . . I loved it!' – Tamzin Merchant, author of *The Hatmakers*

'A spellbindingly magical book full of adventure, hope, and lessons for us all to learn here in our world.' – L. D. Lapinski, author of *The Strangeworlds Travel Agency*

'A beautifully realised eco-fantasy that will open a door in readers' hearts.' – Chris Riddell

GREENWILD
THE
WORLD BEHIND
THE DOOR

PARI THOMSON

Illustrated by Elisa Paganelli

MACMILLAN CHILDREN'S BOOKS

First published 2023 by Macmillan Children's Books

This paperback edition published 2024 by Macmillan Children's Books
an imprint of Pan Macmillan
The Smithson, 6 Briset Street, London EC1M 5NR
EU representative: Macmillan Publishers Ireland Ltd, 1st Floor,
The Liffey Trust Centre, 117–126 Sheriff Street Upper
Dublin 1, D01 YC43
Associated companies throughout the world
www.panmacmillan.com

ISBN 978-1-0350-1574-0

1 3 5 7 9 8 6 4 2

A CIP catalogue record for this book is available from the British Library.

Printed and bound by CPI Group (UK) Ltd, Croydon CR0 4YY

For my parents, Adam and Fariba

Prologue

The sandstorm arrived like a leopard on the hunt: fast and very wild.

Daisy held her breath as sand glittered through the air. It was biting her cheeks in bright painful dashes, but she couldn't take her eyes off the storm.

'This way!' Ma had to shout over the wind. 'Now!'

A great zigzag of lightning struck the top of the nearest dune and Daisy leapt back, mouth suddenly dry with fear. She could see scarves of sand rising like ghosts in the wind, the flash of her own white knuckles, the grim expression on Ma's face. The sand made the air flicker, and then the storm was on them: outracing them over the ridges of the desert until there was sand in Daisy's teeth and between her eyelashes, and she couldn't see much further than her own fingers.

After that, several things happened very quickly. Ma skidded to her knees and pressed one hand into a dip in the dunes. The air went still. And a ring of bright white orchids rippled out around them like water.

Daisy's mouth fell open in astonishment and rapidly filled with sand. She was still spitting furiously when a fresh squall swept in and blinded her. But an after-image of the

orchids stayed burned onto the inside of her eyelids. They had been the snowy colour of cotton socks, fat-petalled and thickly veined with silver – and sending out threads of light that streamed together like a pale, shining dome over their heads.

Inside the dome, the sudden silence rang loud in her ears, broken only by their panting breaths. Daisy crouched low beside Ma, trying desperately to see past the grit in her eyes. She thought she could make out the blurred ring of orchids and – through the curtain of silver threads – the sandstorm raging silently through the red night.

By the time Daisy's eyes had recovered, the worst of the storm was over. The dome, if it had ever existed, was gone.

'We got lucky,' said Ma the next morning when the wind had cleared and the air was cool and crystalline in the pale-blue light. 'That valley between the dunes, it kept us safe.'

'But,' said Daisy, 'I thought I saw . . . flowers. White flowers.'

'Flowers in the desert?' said Ma. She laughed and ruffled Daisy's sand-crusted hair. 'My rascal, whatever will you think of next?'

Chapter 1

Six months later

Daisy Thistledown didn't have a home in the ordinary sense of the word, but there was something about London that always made her feel particularly happy. They had arrived that morning from Rome, where Ma had been writing an article about some disreputable politicians, and they'd had to leave rather quickly after it was published. Here in London, the December sky was a dazzling blue above the rooftops, and there was a glittering, festive feeling in the air. They were in town for a meeting with Ma's new editor at the *High Herald*: a man called Mr Craven who had a brilliant reputation and a fondness for toffees, which he kept in a jar on his desk.

Mr Craven had only been at the *High Herald* for three months – since just after Daisy's eleventh birthday – but people already spoke about him as if he was someone extraordinary. He was very tall and charming, with pale green eyes and a mouth that smiled on one side. He'd spent many years in the field, but had retired from active service after an unfortunate incident involving an angry hippopotamus.

'Rather *too* exciting,' he explained as he ushered them in, smiling lopsidedly and laughing in a way that showed his teeth.

As well as toffees, Mr Craven's desk also boasted a gleaming computer screen, a hostile-looking cactus and a framed photograph of himself shaking hands with the prime minister.

'A brilliant woman,' he said to Daisy, adjusting the gold cufflinks of his crisp white shirt, and revealing a cluster of five moles on his left wrist. They were arranged in a stretched-out W shape that reminded Daisy of the constellation Cassiopeia. 'Quite brilliant. She's going to take this country places, I can tell you. She called me just the other day to say —'

He broke off, staring at something. 'Why, what an unusual necklace, Mrs Thistledown. Wherever did you find it?'

'Just an old trinket,' said Ma, looking self-conscious, and tucked away the daisy-shaped pendant on its fine gold chain. 'Now, Mr Craven. About my next trip. These attacks in the Amazon rainforest . . .'

For a moment, Daisy caught an odd expression in Craven's pale eyes, as if he was staring at a great cinema screen that no one else could see. Then he blinked and

smiled, and she
wondered if she'd
imagined it.

'Ah yes,' he said
smoothly. 'Peru. You
mentioned that you were
thinking about covering
the story. Tell me . . .'

Daisy slunk into the
corridor, opened up the
creased book she kept in her
rucksack for occasions like these, and
settled down to wait.

Daisy was good at waiting. It was necessary, if you had
a mother as extraordinary as hers. Leila Thistledown
was a journalist and travelled all over the world chasing
stories. Daisy loved this expression: *chasing stories*. She
liked to imagine Ma waving a butterfly net through the
air and scooping up flighty headlines and unruly articles:
news about kings and anarchists, barrel bombs and jewel
thieves, rigged elections and rare monkeys with golden
eyes.

'Good journalism is like electricity,' Ma would say
when she was asked for the secret of her success. 'It should
make you sit up and *yelp*.' And she would grin the grin
that made her look more like a mischievous ten-year-old

than an internationally-renowned reporter. Daisy went everywhere with Ma, and at moments like this she felt like a partner in her world-changing enterprise: the sidekick in Ma's diamond-bright conjuring act.

Ma would shake the stories from their net and write them up on a travel-scratched laptop that clattered and battered its way through the night as Daisy tried to sleep. The stories were sent back to the newsroom of the *High Herald* to appear in thousands upon thousands of papers all over the country each day. They were read by bespectacled doctors with black briefcases and lawyers in immaculate suits, by apple-sellers and jazz musicians, avant-garde artists and moustachioed diplomats, by curious schoolchildren and

feather-boa-ed night-club dancers. *Everyone* read Leila Thistledown's articles in the *Herald*.

People always looked surprised when they discovered that Leila Thistledown had a daughter. Then they would be charmed. 'Why, she's just like you,' they would say, laughing. 'A little Leila doll.'

Daisy would scowl, pulling down her eyebrows in a way she hoped looked forbidding. Everyone always assumed that because she looked like Ma on the outside, she must be the same sort of person on the inside as well: wild and adventurous and brave. But Daisy didn't feel like any of those things. She was quiet and watchful, and not brave at all.

Now, she heard Ma's laugh from inside Craven's office, and the sounds of the meeting coming to an end. She closed her book, ready to go.

This was her life: Ma's headlong energy, the momentum that took them from city to city, from continent to continent – rootless, dauntless and always chasing the next big story.

Daisy's place was with Ma, and she was – Daisy told herself firmly – perfectly content.

She poked her head round the door of Craven's office just as Ma was gathering her bag to leave.

'Stay in touch,' Craven was saying, shuffling a large stack of papers. 'And don't take any unnecessary risks.' A page slipped from his hands and floated to the floor at

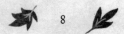

Daisy's feet. It was a map, the sort of thing you can't help bending down to stare at: beautifully detailed, covered in spiky handwriting and printed with a single bold word along its top edge: *PERÚ*.

'Thank you, Daisy,' said Craven, his voice suddenly steely. He leaned forward and took the map from her fingers, and in a moment, it had vanished into a drawer in his desk. His green eyes glinted, and he nodded at Ma. 'Safe travels, Mrs Thistledown.'

After the meeting, they walked out into the bustling streets that ran along the river, where Christmas lights shone like diamond bracelets, and the rolling Thames lapped against the stone walls of the embankment. The afternoon was dusky and cold, and filled with parakeets flashing across the sky like bright green needles through blue silk. The first time Daisy had spotted them, she had been astonished. But now she knew that London was full of the birds, and had been for years. They perched jauntily on lampposts and posed in the treetops like tropical Christmas decorations. According to Ma, some people thought the parakeets had escaped from London Zoo and multiplied in the wild. Others said they'd vanished from a film set. Either way, the city's frosty streets were teeming with glamorous green birds. It made Daisy feel as if anything was possible: as if all manner of unexpected and extraordinary things might be just around the corner.

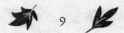

Ma checked the time on her phone, then turned and looked at Daisy with bright eyes.

'How about a quick trip to Kew?'

Chapter 2

An hour later, they were walking through the curling iron gates of Ma's favourite place in London. 'Royal Botanic Gardens, Kew', read the sign at the entrance. 'Welcome to the most biodiverse place on earth.'

The gardens were full of booted and mittened visitors, and the famous glasshouses were misted with condensation where their tropical warmth met the chilly air. Outside, the trees were bare and the flowerbeds empty, but inside the Palm House the air was rich and heavy, like a sauna. Daisy breathed deeply and sighed. She never got tired of the earthy way it smelled. All around them were swaying palms with leaves as big as tablecloths, and looped vines that twisted around the lacy Victorian ironwork of the glasshouse. It was like standing in an indoor rainforest.

'Look!' said Ma. She pointed at a five-petalled flower like a pink starburst. 'Madagascar periwinkles. They're used to make cancer medicines. Isn't that amazing?'

Daisy grinned. Ma knew everything there was to know about plants.

'And this palm tree,' said Ma, 'is called a suicide palm, because it only flowers once – when it's fifty years old – and then it dies.'

Ma reached out a finger and touched its bark. Daisy could have sworn that the great palm waved a leafy frond, but then she blinked and shook herself. It was nothing more than a coil of warm air passing through the glasshouse.

She tipped her face upwards, noticing a spray of monkey-brush vines, a cluster of yellow flowers like ear-trumpets and a bunch of tiny pink bananas that grew upwards instead of down. Ma had been bringing her to Kew since she was old enough to crawl, and the sheer variety and oddity of the greenery always made her fingertips tingle.

Daisy had always loved plants, even if they did sometimes behave in strange ways around her. Once, she had been so bored while waiting for Ma to finish an interview with a sherpa (they'd been on a mountain crag in the Tibetan Himalayas at the time) that she'd gone wandering off by herself, and hadn't seen the edge until she'd slipped over it. The fall should have killed her, but an outcrop of laurel trees had burst into wild leaf and shot their branches out sideways, catching her mid-plummet.

Another time, she had been playing football in the street (this was the April they'd spent in Delhi, during the last elections), and she'd seen a thick-necked boy called Bruce trip up the smallest girl on the other team three times in a row. He was a bully – she'd seen him do it before – and she had felt something boil over inside her, like a pan of water left too long on the stove. Then suddenly Bruce had been screaming, writhing on the pavement, his skin covered in big puffy red welts.

'Poison ivy,' she heard the doctor whisper as the boy was taken away, limping. 'Goodness knows how it grew through the pavement like that.'

And then there was the time Ma had taken her to dinner with a very grand lady in Paris, who had served them fresh lobsters and boasted about how her chef boiled them alive. The polished cherry-wood table at which they'd been sitting had sort of *shrugged*, and the next minute their dishes and bowls were soaring through the air, trailing dramatic arcs of lobster bisque behind them. Ma had marched Daisy out in double-quick time while their translator strewed abject apologies in their wake.

Today, though, was a perfectly ordinary day. Pulling a leaf out of her untidy braid, Daisy headed deeper into the glasshouse, barely noticing the commotion as a passing tourist turned to look at Ma and walked straight into a palm tree.

But then she saw something unexpected out of the corner of her eye. She thought at first that it was another vine – but vines are not black and white and furry.

Without pausing to think, Daisy darted after it, just as the thing whipped out of sight round the nearest corner. She followed, hurrying, ducking under a low-hanging branch, which seemed to lift itself a few centimetres out of her way.

There! Half hidden behind an ancient and tufty dwarf palm. It was a tiny cat. A scrappy black-and-white creature,

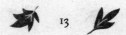

about as big as her foot, with a curling tail in domino colours.

'Hello,' she said, crouching down. The cat – more of a kitten, really – surveyed her with silver-green eyes, and sharpened a claw on her shoe. It had a warlike expression, with teeth like little needles, and whiskers that were long and very ticklish. Its ears were small and fierce and pointed, and it looked slightly lost and very grumpy.

Daisy frowned. 'What are you doing here?'

She checked for a name tag, but the kitten's neck was bare. Pets were not allowed at Kew Gardens, and there was no sign of a worried owner. In fact, no one was paying any attention at all to the illegal cat in the Royal Botanic Palm House.

Daisy glanced around. 'Ma!' she called. 'Come here. I've found—'

But when she turned back, the cat was gone.

'I'm not making it up,' said Daisy as they sat down to tea at the café some time later. 'There was a cat. Right there in the Palm House! It was there one moment, and then it disappeared. Poof!'

It had vanished without a trace. *Well, almost*, thought Daisy, glancing at the scattering of black and white hairs on her coat.

'I believe you,' said Ma lightly. 'Cats are sneaky like that.'

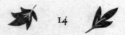

The café was filled with the clatter of forks and teaspoons and the warm hum of conversation as happy visitors dug into large slabs of carrot cake.

'Do you think it will be all right?' she said, still thinking of the cat. It had been so *small*.

Ma didn't reply. Her head was bent and she was busy arranging an enormous plate of scones, clotted cream and strawberry jam, and pouring out tea from a large red pot. Ma had been distracted all day, which usually meant she was thinking out a new article in her head, and that they were about to set off for somewhere new.

The cat had probably run back to its owner, Daisy told herself firmly. It would be fine.

She focused her attention on the scones, selected the nearest and spread it so thickly that her first bite left toothmarks in the cream. She took another bite and sighed happily.

Ma had taken a scone too, but she didn't seem to be hungry.

'What's wrong?' said Daisy, trying to lick Devonshire cream off her elbow. Then she saw Ma hesitate, and felt a chill despite the warmth of the room.

'Nothing,' said Ma. 'It's just – how would you feel about boarding school?' She glanced up, and added hastily: 'Only for a little while, of course.'

Daisy looked at her, eyes wide. 'Boarding school? Isn't that just for people in books?'

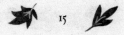

'Not always,' said her mother in the oddly casual voice Daisy had heard her use when she was interviewing someone tricky. 'Wouldn't you like to meet people your age? Make friends?'

Daisy felt a swoop beneath her ribs, as if she'd taken a step into very sticky quicksand.

'I don't need friends,' she said quickly. 'And I meet lots of people my own age.' It was true. From Rome to Russia, and from street markets to fancy hotels, Daisy ran wild with the children she met, always keeping an ear out for anything that might be useful for Ma's writing – a scrap of local gossip, complaints about the rising price of bread, a strange tale overheard.

Ma was a political correspondent – but more and more these days her articles focused on the climate too, which meant that Daisy knew more than most eleven-year-olds about floods in India and bushfires in Australia. She could tell you anything you wanted to know about endangered leopards in snowy Russia, and rare, whiskery black-bat flowers in tropical Burma. Daisy had taught herself to read using Ma's books and travel guides, spelling out long words like 'latitude' and reciting sentences like, 'When in the bush, it is always wise to carry with you a coconut.' She knew how to identify Somalian songbirds by their calls, and seven ways to say hello in Inuktitut, and how to tie ten different types of sailing knot. She could do long division and read maps, handle a slingshot, pick pockets (though Ma didn't know about that particular trick) and steer a course by the North Star. She was also the unofficial spitting champion of three US states, and could spit with greater force and accuracy than most llamas or teenage boys.

'I don't need to go to school,' she said, struggling to keep the panic out of her voice.

Ma was now crumbling her scone to pieces between her fingers.

'I know, joonam.' The word meant 'darling' in Farsi. 'But the truth is I'm chasing a new story, and it's somewhere that isn't safe.'

'The Amazon?' said Daisy, remembering what Ma had said to Craven.

'That's right.' Ma chased a crumb across the table. 'You already know that the rainforest is one of the wildest and most astonishing places on earth. But –' she paused and picked out her next words carefully, as if they had sharp edges – 'each year it becomes more and more of a battleground. The people who have always lived there have to fight every single day, to protect it from illegal logging and mining and fishing. From people who want to slash and burn it to the ground.' She hesitated. 'And . . . innocent people are disappearing.'

'Disappearing?' said Daisy, frowning. Somewhere nearby, a toddler wailed, and the red-haired man at the next table took a sip of coffee.

Ma nodded, and her lips were very pale. 'Someone needs

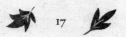

to find out what's happening. The world needs to know.'

Daisy took a deep breath. 'I could come with you. I could help—'

'No.' Ma's voice was rock-hard, and final. 'This time is different, Daisy. It's not like anywhere else we've been. It's no place for a child.'

Daisy felt fear stick in her throat like a knuckle. 'What about you?' she managed to choke. 'What if something happens to *you*?'

'I'll be perfectly safe,' said Ma firmly. 'I'll have a guide, and protection. And it's not for long, I promise. Two weeks at most.'

'Two *weeks*?' They had never been apart for more than two days.

Ma's forehead wrinkled and her mouth made a strange shape. 'I'm sorry, joonam. I wish you could come – I really do. But I need to know that you're looked after while I'm away – and since we don't have any family to take care of you, Mr Craven has recommended a girls' boarding school called Wykhurst where he's a trustee. They've agreed to take you on as a temporary student.' Ma gripped Daisy's hand, which was sticky with strawberry jam. 'Two weeks, that's all. I'll be back by Christmas, I promise.'

Daisy felt hot and prickly all over.

'But I *can't*,' she said, discovering that her cheeks were wet. She wiped her eyes furiously with the ends of her hair.

'You can,' said Ma fiercely. 'Courage, joonam.'

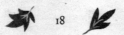

'But—'

Ma just looked at her. There was a terrible silence, and Daisy watched as a parakeet soared through the open doors of the café and then flitted back out into the darkening sky. A single green feather drifted down to land in the space between them.

'How will you manage?' Daisy asked finally.

Ma was terrible at map-reading and keeping track of her deadlines and remembering to eat. Daisy was the one who navigated them from A to B and made sure they didn't forget their passports. She was the one who tipped the hotel porters and bought extra supplies of biscuits for Ma when she was writing.

'Oh, joon-e-delam,' said Leila. The words meant 'life of my heart' in Farsi, and she called Daisy by that name only when she was very sad. 'I don't know. But I do promise it won't be for long. I'll catch this story as soon as I can.'

There was another silence, and Daisy heard the rustle of a newspaper from the red-haired man at the next table, and the friendly stir of a nearby family as they gathered up two toddlers and a pushchair in readiness to leave. She wondered, briefly, what it would be like to be part of a normal family, with a real home to go back to at the end of the day. She imagined a room that was hers, with the same bed each night and a shelf for her books, and felt a tug of longing in her chest.

Then Ma said, 'If anything goes wrong – anything at all –

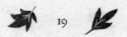

I want you to have this.' She reached into her bag and took out a small box. Inside was something round and glittering. It was a glass paperweight, about the size of Daisy's clenched fist. She took it and leaned so close that her nose touched the cool surface. A perfect dandelion clock was trapped in the glass, like a soft silver moon inside a bubble.

'It was your father's,' said Ma. 'He wanted you to have it, when you were old enough. He would be so proud of you, you know.'

But for once Daisy wasn't distracted by the mention of Pa.

'What do you mean, if anything goes wrong? I thought you said you'd be safe!'

Ma swept a few stray crumbs off the table. 'And I will be. But if – by some vanishingly distant chance – something does happen, then I want you to come back here to Kew. Bring that,' she said, lifting her chin towards the paperweight. 'Help will come. Oh, and don't show it to *anyone*. Keep it safe, and secret.'

'I don't understand. Why? What do you mean, "help"?'

But Ma was already stacking their plates and fastening the straps of her bag.

'Come on,' she said. 'We have lots to do.'

Chapter 3

The next day flashed by in a flurry of preparations. Since Daisy would only be at the school for the last two weeks of the winter term, she wasn't expected to bring her own uniform or buy the monogrammed Wykhurst suitcase recommended for new pupils. Instead, she shoved her clothes into the small, battered case that had once belonged to her father. It still had his initials on it – H. T., for Henry Thistledown – and was plastered over with faded stickers from his travels: boats from Tangier, flights to Chile and India and Greenland. Over the years, Daisy had added a few of her own. But her favourite sticker was the blue one on the corner, torn and faded now, that had marked her father's most important journey. The one from England, where he was born, to Iran, where he had met Ma and they had got married and lived happily ever after.

Until they hadn't.

Along with her clothes, Daisy stowed into the case a stash of biscuits, a pair of scarlet-laced hiking boots from Ma ('To remind you to be wild,' Ma said with a wink), an envelope of money ('for emergencies'), a box of old photographs and a pile of dog-eared books that had already accompanied Daisy halfway round the world.

Ma had also wanted Daisy to take the mobile phone she'd been given on her last birthday, so they could stay in touch, but they had been told firmly by Mrs Daggler, the school matron, that phones were not allowed at Wykhurst. ('Very unsettling for the girls, Mrs Thistledown, and so distracting. She'll be far better without.') Somehow, this made the looming separation feel even worse. *It's only two weeks*, Daisy told herself sternly as she closed the suitcase for the final time.

And after the goodbyes and the promises to write, this was what she was left holding onto, as Ma drove away to catch a story that might be dangerous. She stood at the entrance of Wykhurst School, and tipped her face back to the sky so that the tears didn't fall out, and clutched her father's case as if it was her only friend in the whole world.

'Well,' said the matron as Ma disappeared round the bend of the long drive. She was a tall, angular woman with arms like a praying mantis, and something about her eyes reminded Daisy of a giant trout: the dead kind you see fishermen posing next to in photographs. She gripped Daisy by the top of her arm, and surveyed her as if she was a particularly repellent flea. 'I can see I have my work cut out.' She marched Daisy beneath the grey parapets of the school and straight to the lost-property office, so she could be outfitted with a full set of Wykhurst uniform.

'But Ma said I wouldn't need to wear—'

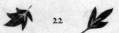

Matron narrowed her eyes and spoke in a matter-of-fact voice. 'Forget what your mother said, Miss Thistledown. You're at Wykhurst now, and you'll do as I tell you.'

She grabbed an armful of clothes from the lost property box and tossed them at Daisy to try on: two navy-blue skirts (so long that Daisy almost vanished beneath them), three striped shirts with threadbare cuffs and fiddly buttons, a navy jumper that itched abominably, a bundle of knee-high socks that smelled like pickled onions and, finally, a lacrosse stick with a small net at the top that was nothing like a butterfly net.

Matron surveyed her from head to toe, and then held out an imperious hand. 'Black hair ties only,' she barked. 'Hand it over.'

With shaking fingers, Daisy untied the red ribbon from her hair. It had been a parting gift from Ma, and she felt shivery without it, as if someone had forced her out of a warm coat.

Matron nodded curtly. 'Let's go.'

As they walked up the stairs, Matron enumerated the laws by which Wykhurst was governed. No running indoors, no laughing in the corridors, no chocolate, no spitting, and especially no pets. 'Nasty dirty things,' she said, sniffing.

They turned left at the top of the stairs and entered a dormitory with dull brass bedsteads ranged in two long rows against blank walls. Daisy's suitcase was dumped at the foot of a bed in the corner, her new uniform tossed on top of it.

'The other girls are at dinner,' Matron informed her. 'I assume you've already eaten?' She smiled unpleasantly and

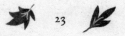

turned to go without waiting for a reply. 'Sweet dreams, Miss Thistledown.'

The door shut after her and Daisy collapsed onto her mattress, stomach rumbling. She could feel hot tears rising up again in the corners of her eyes and she turned to her rucksack to distract herself. There was a chocolate bar in the inside pocket, which would do for her dinner. It would be her first act of rebellion against Matron's hateful regime.

When she opened the bag, however, all thoughts of food left her mind. For there, curled up on top of Daisy's favourite T-shirt, was the cat from Kew Gardens.

Daisy barely noticed the watery grey porridge that was slopped in front of her in the dining hall the next morning. This was unsurprising, since her mind was on the small cat that was currently kneading his claws against her chest beneath her school jumper. He had curled up next to her all night like a tickly hot-water bottle, unseen by the whispering girls in the nearby beds. And that morning, after the others had left for breakfast, he had refused to stay in the dorm, determined to follow her no matter how many times she told him to stay put. He had turned his silver-green eyes on her and meowed furiously.

'Oh, all right,' she said. 'But you can't be seen. Matron does *not* like animals.'

Luckily, the cat was easy to conceal. He was so small he could sit on the palm of her hand, and barely made a lump beneath her shapeless school jumper. She stole him a large kipper from the breakfast table, and made a mental note to find a flowerbed for his litter.

Daisy's mind whirred as she followed the other girls out of the dining hall. He must have climbed into her bag that day in the Palm House – which would explain why she had searched the glasshouse from top to bottom without finding him, never thinking to look in the bag on her own back. He must have stayed hidden through the whole day of packing in London, and travelled with her all the way to Wykhurst: a misguided stowaway sneaking his way into the most depressing place on earth.

She noticed a group of girls tittering as she headed to her first lesson.

'Have you *seen* the state of her uniform?' she heard one of them whisper.

Daisy clenched her fingers around the paperweight in her pocket, and kept walking.

That day, the cat accompanied her through the school like a shadow. He was so small and sneaky that none of the teachers or other students noticed him. But Daisy knew he was there: admiring his reflection in the lacrosse trophies at the far end of the sports hall as she attempted gymnastics, combing his whiskers behind the sofa in the damp common room, licking his fur clean again and again as he hid under her lonely lunch table and sneezing furiously as she took her place in the dusty History classroom.

'What was that?' said Miss Lamprey, the History mistress, glancing around.

'Er – just a tickle in my nose,' said Daisy. 'Achoo!'

By bedtime, the cat had made himself at home on her pillow, and condescended to drape himself round her neck like a tiny, imperious shawl. He licked her cheek.

'Humph,' said Daisy. 'I suppose you can stay.'

And he did.

She called him Napoleon, because he was small, but incredibly vain.

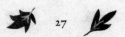

Chapter 4

Napoleon made everything bearable. Suddenly, she had an ally, and it made all the difference in the world.

Even so, the next two weeks were the hardest of Daisy's life. She hadn't realized what it would be like to miss someone so badly. She felt all shrivelled up with missing, like a tree starved of water.

Meanwhile, she was expected to sit still in lessons and run fast in lacrosse and follow the rules. Matron stalked the halls, looking around at the students – and especially Daisy – with a disdain so glacial it deserved its own iceberg. She disapproved of people being different, and anyone suspected of this crime was hauled into her office for a stern talking-to. Daisy, with her 'foreign' mother and 'exotic' eyes and home-schooled background, was more different than most.

Matron would have been horrified by Ma, Daisy thought, with a rebellious spark of satisfaction. Ma had five ear piercings and sported an assortment of pens, feathers and sparkly pins in her hair at all times. She dressed in rough combats when she was chasing stories, and flamboyant beaded ballgowns when she was celebrating their success. She drank tar-like coffee in the morning and sparkling champagne at night, and when an article was going well, she would take Daisy out dancing, or for giant eclairs, light as whipped cloud and covered in chocolate. When Ma walked into a room, the lights around the walls seemed to shine brighter, as if they were absorbing her energy. Even the hotel plants seemed to respond to her, greedily drinking up water and growing by inches when she was around, as if to say, 'Here is someone who makes us feel alive.' Ma bought potted orchids and geraniums wherever they stayed, and they always flowered extravagantly, miraculously, as if she was their own personal sun. Daisy knew how they felt.

Sometimes Ma would wake Daisy up in the middle of the night when the moon was clear and spin her around beneath it. 'We're moon-bathing! We're moon-dancing!' she would cry, as if the moonlight was pouring down around them in liquid drops like mercury. 'Ah! Magic!'

On other nights, though, Daisy would hear sobs from her mother's bed and know she was thinking of Pa. Before he had died, they'd lived in a house in London with a cheerful red front door and friendly, creaky wooden floors. The house had had a very particular smell, of dusty sunlight and roses and happiness, that Daisy had never quite been able to recapture in memory. Pa had been a news photographer, and he and Ma had worked together, laughed together, built a life together. Then the car crash happened.

Two days after the funeral, Ma sold the cheerful red front door and everything attached to it. She packed the remnants

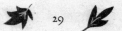

into two small trunks and took herself and three-year-old Daisy on the road, following one breaking news story and then the next, and writing, writing, writing. Since Pa's death, Daisy and Ma had been on the move – but whether they were chasing something, or running away, Daisy was never quite sure.

Still, they'd built a new life for themselves, day by day, story by story – a life where they were the heroines: a conspiracy of two against the world. Ma worked tirelessly, and began to be spoken of in high-up places. But no matter how busy she was, or how successful she became, the moments before bedtime belonged to Daisy. They kept a supply of biscuits in an old tin painted with three solemn-looking corgis, and each night they would sit down and select their favourites. Gesturing with a custard cream, Ma would tell Daisy fairy tales from her own childhood in Iran: stories about wandering dervishes and sly wolves and magical birds with rainbow tails. Sometimes she would talk about growing up near the city of Shiraz, with a garden fringed by pear trees and jasmine.

'In the summer,' Ma would say dreamily, 'my grandmother would grow roses and basil, and the scent was like witchcraft. We'd sleep outside on the porch, and I'd spend all day reading in the branches of the almond tree. My favourite story was about a magical pomegranate, with one ruby seed that had the power to grant a single wish.' She laughed. 'I used to eat pomegranates until I felt sick, staring at every last seed in case one of them was magic.'

'Did you get a wish? Did you?' the tiny Daisy had asked eagerly.

Ma had ruffled her hair. 'No one has found a magical pomegranate in a very long time. But I got my wish anyway. I have you, don't I?'

So, it didn't matter, really, that they moved around too often for Daisy to make friends, because Ma was the best friend you could imagine: funny and kind, and always on her side. True, Ma wasn't always *there*. She sometimes left Daisy at hotels with long-suffering concierges, or with one of her many glamorous and disreputable friends – or once at a seaside cottage on the Isle of Skye with a disapproving fisherman's wife. Daisy had spent hours surrounded by gold-buttoned doormen, or Ma's gossiping fellow journalists, or salt-crusted fishing nets, longing for her to come back.

So Daisy knew about waiting. But these two weeks at Wykhurst were harder and longer than she could have imagined. How could she be homesick if she'd never really had a home? She was person-sick; she was sick with missing Ma and it was even worse than the terrible flu she'd had one winter in Jerusalem. She felt tired all the time, worn down by a constant, physical ache in her chest, as if there was an elastic band that connected her heart to Ma's wrist, and being apart pulled it tight enough to draw blood.

Chapter 5

Ma's first postcard arrived a full week after it had been posted, smothered in airmail stickers and looking as if it had been gnawed by a rabbit. Daisy read it ten dozen times, and put it under her pillow. The next one described eating a tarantula for a bet ('surprisingly chewy'), the third detailed an interview with a dancer in a sparkly headdress, and the fourth reported a boat trip down the Amazon in which Ma narrowly avoided getting her toes bitten off by a piranha while taking a swim.

The postcards were a lifeline that sustained Daisy through the lonely hours and crawling minutes to the end of term – until at last the longed-for day drew close. Tomorrow, Ma would come, and together they would leave Wykhurst behind for good.

Daisy's suitcase was packed in readiness, her books stowed away, and her lacrosse stick pushed into the dustiest corner beneath the bed. She had considered ritually burning it, but hadn't been able to think of a way to do it without Matron noticing. She reached into her pocket for the twentieth time that day and her fingers closed on Ma's last postcard, creased with rereading and anticipation. It was postmarked from Peru, and it smelled like ink and jasmine and possibility. Daisy knew what it said by heart.

14 December
Daisy, joon-e-delam. At last, this story is finished.
I'll pick you up from Wykhurst station at 1 p.m. next
Friday. And then what fun we'll have!

*

'Ten more minutes,' said Daisy, scrambling on top of her suitcase for a better view. She gazed over the heads of the passengers, scanning each face as crowds jostled off the gleaming train and onto the platform. 'I know she'll come.' The December rain lashed against the high glass roof of the station, and Miss Peckmore sniffed.

'She wasn't on the last *three* trains,' the bony house mistress said, clutching her scaly black bag closer to her chest. 'She's not coming.'

But Daisy wasn't listening. Instead, she was trying to balance on one foot, craning her neck over a gaggle of overexcited schoolboys and a pair of delivery men carrying a Christmas tree covered in flashing lights.

Surely now, Daisy thought. Surely, at any moment Ma would come dashing down the length of the platform, would catch her up with inky fingers and swing her round, surrounding her with a flood of explanations and the scent of jasmine.

The last passengers had left the train. Two plump ladies passed by, chatting gaily, their arms filled with brightly

33

wrapped presents that looked like giant sweets. Then a group of teenage girls, playing music on their phones and laughing. Then an elderly, white-haired man, consulting his pocket watch. But Leila Thistledown was nowhere to be seen.

The station emptied. Daisy slumped down off her toes. Slowly, her face went grey. The echoing space was quiet once more: all she could hear beyond the spatter of the rain was the imperturbable ticking of the great station clock. Each slow, inevitable tick-tock reverberated with the same awful message: not-here, not-here, not-here.

'Come,' said Miss Peckmore into the not-silence, gathering up her black bag and affixing a fussy hat to her blonde curls. 'If your mother decides to join us, she can collect you from the school, like the other parents.' Like the *normal* parents, her voice seemed to say. She sniffed again. 'You will return to your dormitory tonight.'

The spiked gates and grey crenellated battlements of Wykhurst looked even more dismal than usual in the icy winter rain. Daisy could feel the dampness trickling down her long braid and soaking the back of her coat as they passed through the dim, cavernous entrance hall, strangely eerie now that the other girls had left for the holidays. It smelled sunless, as if the whole world was being shut out.

With a great effort, Daisy lifted her chin and squared her shoulders. Then she heard a grating voice from the top of

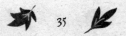

the stairs, and her resolve faltered.

'Ah, Miss Thistledown, you're back.' Matron's voice was cold, and she gazed down at Daisy with flat, thin-lidded eyes. 'Into my office,' she said, turning on her heel. 'Now.'

Daisy suppressed a shiver and trailed after her.

Matron's office smelled of damp and rot from a row of sinister-looking plants lined up on the windowsill, and she had an odd expression on her face, like a fish that had swallowed a tasty bug.

'Sit,' she said.

Daisy sat.

'I'm afraid, Miss Thistledown, that I have Bad News.' She swelled with trout-like self-importance, and if she'd had gills they would have been waving with mock solemnity. 'Your mother —' here Matron wrinkled her nose – 'has been reported missing, presumed dead.'

Daisy's heartbeat pounded in her ears, but Matron was still speaking. 'She took a flight into the Amazon rainforest five days ago, and hasn't been heard from since. There has been no communication from the plane or the pilot. It looks like the plane went down in a storm. No survivors have been found.'

Chapter 6

The rest of the day was blank. Daisy couldn't remember what she'd said to Matron, or even whether she'd eaten dinner.

Alone in the darkness of the icy dormitory, she lay down and stared at the wall with dry and itchy eyes. She felt as though there was a great weight crouched like a lizard on her chest.

At last, moving very slowly, she sat up, flicked on her torch beneath the thin, scratchy blankets and buried her face in Napoleon's fur. Then she reached into the suitcase at the foot of her bed to pull out Pa's paperweight, which she had carefully wrapped in a knobbly pair of socks. She watched it glimmer in the torchlight like an unshed tear.

Daisy felt around in the case again and brought out what Ma had always teasingly called her Magpie Box, because she used it to store shiny scraps and interesting things she wanted to keep. Amidst a mass of sea shells, train tickets, rhinestone hair-slides, sweet wrappers and clippings of Ma's articles, she found what she was looking for: a small pile of photographs.

She looked at them in the torchlight, with Napoleon peering over her shoulder. There she was as a baby, scowling and strapped in a sling across Ma's chest on a trip to Albania to interview a colony of beekeepers. Here she appeared as a toddler, clutching Ma's hand as she met with bushy-eyebrowed explorers in deepest Chile, and again on a puttering motor-scooter on the streets of Delhi, pursuing the story of a reluctant heiress who wanted to become a goat farmer. Here was Daisy, wind-burnt and wild-haired on the decks of a battered yacht that had taken them all the way across the Atlantic the year she turned eight. Ma tried to avoid flying because it was bad for the environment, which meant that their journeys were often just as interesting as the stories at the end of them. Daisy flicked to the next picture and smiled. Here she was again, older now, looking untidy and wide-eyed on camel-back next to Ma in the deserts of Jordan, the day before that great sandstorm. Ma's camel had spat on her about three seconds after the photo was taken, and Daisy could still remember their shrieks of laughter. She looked down at the photo, her stomach twisting like a worm on a fishing hook.

No. It wasn't possible. If Ma was really dead, she would know. She would feel it.

Daisy reached down into the bottom of the box with one finger and carefully prised out the last photograph, soft-edged and faded by time. It was her only photo of Pa. He had his arm round a younger version of Ma, who was laughing out at the camera, shaking back her long dark hair which, like Daisy's, glinted with red and gold flecks where it caught the light. Because Pa had died when Daisy was three years old, her memories of him were as faded as the photo in her hands. Mostly, she remembered him in dreams, where they were always in the garden of the house with the red door, and he was laughing, running his hands over the tops of the high flowers until they bloomed and grew so high that he disappeared behind them.

She remembered the rumble of his voice when she laid her head against his chest, and his smell of rain and sandalwood and old books. She remembered the white scar across his eyebrow that made him look like a pirate, and how he would toss her into the air: *whoosh! Whoosh!* How he could peel an apple in a single long spiral, like a magic trick. And how even though Ma was the journalist, it was he who had the gift of really noticing.

'*Look!*' he would say, and point out the shining tracery of a snail's path along a paving stone, or the astonishing colour of a gold-plated beetle, waving its small antennae. '*Look!*'

He didn't just look at things; he *saw* them. Daisy stared at the photo and tried to really see it. Pa was laughing, his eyes crinkled up and his head turning so that his face was slightly blurred. Around Ma's neck there glinted something bright: a pendant in the shape of a daisy.

Daisy had spent hours staring at this necklace over the years, though Ma kept it carefully tucked out of sight if other people were around. It was incredibly lifelike, as

soft-petalled as a real flower.

'So you'll always be next to my heart,' Ma would say whenever Daisy asked about it. Daisy usually rolled her eyes at this, but secretly she liked the fact that Ma never took it off.

Now, she glanced back at the sparkly debris of the Magpie Box, spotting a chipped enamel earring from Istanbul, a carved wooden elephant from Botswana and, finally, something unfamiliar wedged in the corner of the box. It was a tiny red envelope, about as long as her index finger. It felt light and empty as she pulled it out, and she turned it over to reveal a single, baffling sentence in Ma's untidy scrawl: *For use only in emergencies.*

Suddenly there was a creak outside the door – Matron! – and Daisy flicked off the torch. Once the clicking footsteps had moved away, she crept over to the ice-rimmed windows and opened the curtains. The night was dark and full of stars. By their light she could just see the flap of the envelope as she unstuck it. Something small and dry fell onto her palm.

Daisy nudged it, squinting in the moonlight.

It was a seed: narrow and reddish-brown, and no longer than an eyelash. But why had Ma left it in her suitcase? What possible use could it be in an emergency?

Daisy turned back to the photo of Ma and Pa as if it might hold the answers, but they smiled silently out at her, refusing to respond.

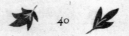

Come back, she thought with a sudden gulp of desperation. *Ma, I need you.* For a moment, she caught the scent of Ma's jasmine and Pa's blend of rain and sandalwood. She remembered the safety of her father's arms round her: the feeling that he was strong enough to hold up the whole sky. The paper buckled with the force of her wish, her thumb half covering Ma's face.

Help me, she thought. *Please.*

Her eyes were closed, so she didn't see the seed pulse like a flare, and then go dark.

That night, Daisy dreamed that she was climbing a vast apple tree, its branches filled with silver apples that hung like great shining stars. Perched in its branches, she felt as if she'd climbed out of her old life and into the heart of a spiral galaxy.

When she woke, she was lying in her cold bed at Wykhurst, and the weekly bin collectors were tipping out the glass into a recycling truck outside the dormitory window. The moon had set, and the pre-dawn light was as grimy and used-up as an old grey dishrag.

But something about the dream reminded her of the way she felt with Ma: as if something miraculous and unlikely was just around the corner. As if anything was possible.

She rose that morning with a burning conviction.

If Ma was lost, then it was up to Daisy to find her.

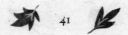

Chapter 7

Daisy waited impatiently for an hour after lights-out before creeping out of her dorm and down the corridor, Napoleon skulking at her heels. She tried the door of Matron's office. Unlocked! She pushed it open cautiously, wincing as it creaked, and then again at the electronic hum as she turned on the computer. She went straight to the internet and looked up 'Leila Thistledown disappearance'. Hundreds of results came up immediately, and she clicked on the top one:

<u>Famous journalist Leila Thistledown among those who vanished in Amazon rainforest</u>

The four people who vanished when a small plane crash-landed in the Amazon rainforest in Peru included award-winning journalist Leila Thistledown, 36, officials have said. Yesterday, Peruvian emergency services chief Luis Gonzales named those who disappeared on an unexplained exploratory mission into one of the most uncharted areas of the rainforest. 'We do not know the purpose of their journey,' Gonzales told reporters. 'It was a private plane. This is a very great tragedy for our country.'

The other victims were photographer Willem
Oaksure, 45, translator Sebastien Carlos, 31, and
the pilot, Calla Walker, 52. The plane was not
discovered until five days after the presumed crash,
due to the remote location of the disaster. Rescue
workers with machetes hacked through the jungle
to search for bodies in the wreckage, but found
no trace of the four passengers. It is believed that
they ventured away from the plane to seek food
and shelter, but although multiple search-and-
rescue missions have scoured the surrounding area
nothing has been found. 'Not even a button,' said
Gonzales yesterday. 'We just have to keep looking.'
But authorities do not expect to find the passengers
alive. 'It is an exceedingly dangerous part of the
jungle,' said Peruvian forestry minister, Domingo
de Flores. 'Most people who venture into it don't
survive.'

There was a windswept photograph of three people standing
in front of a small plane: the uniformed pilot, two men – one
short, one tall – and then Ma, grinning, swinging herself
into the cockpit, her hair swirling around her head and
the daisy pendant shining at her throat. The caption read:
*Tragically lost: Oaksure, Carlos, Walker and Thistledown,
minutes before boarding the flight that would end in their
disappearance.* The article continued:

> Leila Thistledown is a well-known journalist who has worked for the *High Herald* for the last eight years. She is the holder of the Foreign Reporter of the Year award for the last three years in a row, the Martha Gellhorn Prize for Journalism and . . .

Daisy stopped reading and turned off the computer with a stab of her finger. *Authorities do not expect to find the passengers alive.*

Suddenly, she heard a noise behind her and flinched, glancing over to the row of putrid potted plants ranged along the windowsill. She could have sworn that one of them had blinked at her with evil red eyes. Either she was imagining things, or Wykhurst's rat problem was worse than she'd thought.

Moments later, Daisy heard the unmistakable sounds of Matron on her midnight round of the building. Napoleon meowed, and she only just managed to fling herself into the broom cupboard in the corner before Matron threw open the door to her office and glared around it suspiciously. Daisy watched her through a crack in the cupboard door, trying to still the sounds of her own breathing. It was several minutes before Matron finally swept out, taking a ring of keys with her.

Daisy looked down at her hands, and saw they were trembling. She waited half an hour before staggering back

to bed, words chasing each other round and round in her head.

Most people who venture into it don't survive.

She lay awake for a long time that night, gazing out of the window beside her bed while Napoleon curled up imperially on her stomach.

I know you're alive, Ma, she thought. *I know it.* The stars winked back at her, tracing out their cold patterns in the endless dark.

It rained on Christmas Day, and term began again two days after the new year. Once more the corridors were filled with chattering students, and Napoleon hid himself in the collar of Daisy's coat. Word of Leila Thistledown's disappearance had spread, and Daisy couldn't bear the suppressed excitement of the girls who thought it was thrilling to have a famous, vanished mother in the news. Daisy ignored them all and spoke only to Napoleon, who was a good listener because he seemed utterly indifferent to whatever she had to say.

That night, he curled comma-like into her side, hidden by blankets. She woke sometime after midnight to find him gone, and crossed to the window to see him prowling the gardens like a black-and-white ghost: the tiniest bodyguard in the world.

But even Napoleon couldn't keep Mrs Daggler at bay. The next day, Daisy came back to the dorm at break time

to find Matron rummaging through the suitcase at the foot of her bed. Her clothes were tossed across the floor, the blankets stripped from her mattress. Pages had been torn out of her dog-eared copy of *The Secret Garden* and her Magpie Box had been smashed open, the photographs trampled across the floor and Ma's postcards dirtied and ruined.

No, no, no.

Daisy scrabbled at the floor, almost sobbing as she gathered up the fragments, barely noticing Matron staring at her with nostrils flared. The hummingbird on the front of Ma's latest postcard had been torn in half, so that its beak seemed to have been snapped in two. Daisy's throat hurt as she swallowed, and she felt abruptly furious.

'Why would you – what are you doing?'

Matron stared at her, gaunt and unmoved.

'I've had reports of contraband chocolate hidden in the dormitories,' she said coolly. 'I'm performing . . . spot checks.'

But as Matron turned and stalked away downstairs, Daisy knew she had been lying. None of the other beds had been searched. She looked at the chaos of second-hand uniform and torn paper strewn across the linoleum. Matron had been looking for something, that much was clear. Something far more important than a forbidden chocolate bar.

'It's time,' Daisy told Napoleon, 'to do some investigating of our own.'

As usual, he was already five steps ahead of her. As she turned to leave the dorm, he pounced on something on the floor, pinning it down like a jungle cat. Moments later, she found herself staring at a piece of paper with seven words scratched across it in black ink.

10 p.m. Tuesday. Have the Thistledown girl ready.

Tomorrow night. Daisy felt a chill that seemed to darken the edges of the room. *Ready for what?*

'It must have fallen out of Matron's pocket,' she said slowly. The writing was spiky and ornate, with sharp dashes that she'd seen somewhere else recently. But where?

Daisy slipped out of the dining hall before the end of dinner and paused as she passed Matron's office. There were voices coming from behind the closed door. Quickly, she knelt down, pretending to tie a shoelace, and applied her eye to the keyhole. She was confronted by Matron's back, which blocked most of the light from the lamp on her desk. Opposite her, his face partly obscured, sat an elegant gentleman with fox-coloured hair. He looked familiar; Daisy was sure she'd seen him somewhere before.

'What's taking so long, Maud?' he was saying.

'I've been trying,' said Matron, her words heavy and frustrated. 'I think she must carry it with her, in a pocket. I can't find it anywhere among her things.'

'Ah, well. No matter,' said the man. His voice reminded Daisy of a snake in the sun: lazy and dangerous. 'We'll be

able to take it once we have her in our custody.'

All at once, Daisy knew why he looked familiar. He was the red-haired man who had sat calmly reading his newspaper in the café, that day at Kew Gardens: the day when Ma had given her the dandelion paperweight.

She felt for its comforting heaviness in her pocket, where she carried it with her like a lucky charm. And suddenly she knew what Matron had been looking for that morning.

Matron spoke again, her voice hushed and conspiratorial. 'Everything's ready?'

'As arranged,' said the man. 'Ten o'clock tomorrow night.'

Daisy shifted, and a floorboard creaked softly.

Matron lifted her head, as if scenting the air.

'What was that?' She moved towards the door. But by the time she reached it Daisy had already darted silently away into the shadows.

Chapter 8

Ten minutes later, showered and sitting in bed, Daisy replayed what she had heard, and felt the hairs rising up on her arms. It wasn't good.

Napoleon butted against her elbow.

'We're getting out of here,' she told him quietly. 'Tonight.'

Daisy hadn't tried running away before, but she had thought about it often enough over the last few weeks to feel that she was going through a routine she had practised a hundred times. Before, she had been stopped by the knowledge that Ma would return for her. Now, there was nothing to keep her, and every reason to go.

'If anything happens,' Ma had said, 'I want you to come back to Kew. Help will come.'

She glanced at her watch. Ten minutes until the other girls returned from dinner.

Calmly, she opened her old rucksack and placed into it three books, two apples, a London tube map and a clean T-shirt. In the zipped front pocket, she stowed her pack of photos, Ma's torn postcards, the dusty seed in its red envelope and her stash of emergency money.

She got into bed fully dressed that night, and she woke before dawn. In her pocket was the dandelion paperweight;

on her feet she wore Ma's scarlet-laced hiking boots; and in her hair, defiantly, was the red ribbon Matron had taken from her, and which she'd stolen back from her office along with a useful-looking train timetable.

She cast one last look at Pa's battered suitcase and swallowed painfully. It was too big to take with her. Then she tiptoed out of the dormitory and slipped into the dark corridor. She stole silently down the stairs, pausing only when she reached the big doors of the grand entrance hall.

With infinite contempt, she spat
on the threshold. The spit landed
dead centre, like a bullseye.
Then she took a deep breath,
zipped Napoleon into the
V of her jacket and hurried
into the grounds.

By the time Matron noticed
that Daisy was missing at
breakfast, Daisy had already
snuck out of the school gates,
caught the train to London and
was trundling through the city
on a double-decker bus bound
for Kew Gardens.

She gazed out of the
window as they passed along
the embankment and spotted
the *High Herald* building towering at the end of the street,
like a giant steely lipstick. It was hard to believe that it was
only a month since she had been here with Ma, that the city
was the same as ever, when her whole world had changed
beyond recognition.

Then suddenly Napoleon meowed, and Daisy pressed
her nose against the bus window. There was a familiar
figure on the street corner. There was no mistaking the

height, the dark hair, the immaculate suit with the flash of gold cufflinks. It was Ma's editor, Mr Craven, and he looked agitated, gesturing with one hand and speaking urgently into his phone.

Without stopping to think, Daisy pressed the bell for the next stop, zipped Napoleon more firmly into her jacket and leapt out onto the pavement before the bus had fully come to a halt. Craven was Ma's editor, after all. Surely he would know more about what had really happened.

She approached cautiously, seeing that he was deeply absorbed in his conversation.

'Yes, vanished,' he was saying. 'I know. Looks like she's run away from school. Pity she hasn't got a phone, or we could track her location.' There was a pause, in which Daisy felt a chill scuttle like a spider down her spine. 'Oh, we'll catch her,' Craven continued, and Daisy froze. 'We'll get it off her. And then Mallowmarsh will be finished. We're talking dust and ashes.' He paused, and suddenly Daisy knew why the note that had fallen from Matron's pocket had looked so familiar. It had been in Craven's handwriting: the same writing she'd seen scribbled on the map of Peru in his office.

Craven was still speaking. 'Fine. Good. Yes, I'll keep you updated.' He hung up, and as he turned away Daisy saw him shove something into his pocket. It had been clasped in his hand and flashed as it disappeared from sight.

Daisy felt fear coat the roof of her mouth like glue. She had to move before –

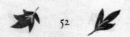

But it was too late. Even as she turned to run, Craven looked up and his eyebrows rose in shock. For a single frozen moment, their eyes locked – and then Daisy lunged past him, feeling the fine cloth of his suit jacket against her fingers. Then she was beyond him and running.

'Oi!' She heard his furious cry as he began to sprint after her. She skidded round the corner of the street and glanced down just long enough to confirm what she already knew.

There on her palm, liberated from Craven's pocket in the split second she'd rushed past him, lay a daisy on a thin gold chain, as lifelike as a living flower.

It was Ma's necklace. The one she never took off.

Chapter 9

Daisy stared, then shook herself. There was no time to waste. Already Craven was coming around the corner – and beside him was the fox-haired man from Kew Gardens.

She pivoted and ducked through the revolving glass doors of a nearby hotel, sprinting through the crowds in the grand lobby as Napoleon yowled in protest. Then – there it was! A fire-exit, like the beacon to a promised land. She pushed on the release bar and skidded out into an alleyway, slamming the door behind her and pressing her back against the skeletal ivy on the outside wall. She looked wildly in both directions, sending up a frantic prayer for more time.

Which way?

Already, Craven was pounding the door from inside the hotel – but something was stopping him from following her out. Daisy turned and saw with astonishment that the ivy was spreading in thick snaky vines across the outside of the door, sealing it shut.

'It's stuck,' she heard Craven shouting. He swore. 'Circle round from the front. And watch all entrances to the underground station. She won't get far.'

Daisy didn't have time to think about the vines, which were now spread so thickly across the fire-exit that it had

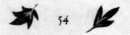

almost disappeared. Only one thing mattered, and that was getting to Kew.

It was too far to run; the bus wasn't safe, the underground was out of the question, but –

The idea came to her: mad and probably impossible. But it was her only chance.

She took a breath and plunged round the corner towards the river, pelting down the long street, half sliding on the treacherous, rain-slicked ground and scattering tourists and shoppers in her wake. The water shone beyond the embankment, grainy and glittering like a promise, if only she could reach it.

A boat, she thought, desperately. *Let there be a boat.*

'Stop, thief! Stop that girl!' Close behind her was Craven, puce with fury, followed by two security guards. Daisy cut down a side street, darting through the crowds and vaulting over a tiny Pekinese, which yapped after her.

She ran, desperately now, and felt something leap from her jacket onto the ground.

'Napoleon,' she cried, her voice ragged. 'Come back!' He streaked ahead and she sprinted headlong after him. She could hear her pursuers getting closer, their ranks swelling.

'Stop her! Stop that girl!'

She had almost reached the river – and then there was the fox-haired man, blocking the way. Before she had time to think, she saw Napoleon leap at his shins, raking claws across his knees so that he doubled over, swearing – and

in that split second she darted past him, sprinted along the edge of the embankment, searching for what she prayed would be there – and threw herself towards the water and into the open air.

She landed hard on the deck of a heavily loaded barge and, seconds later, felt Napoleon land beside her. She yanked a length of sacking over the two of them, and tried to swallow her panting breath.

Her pursuers hadn't seen her jump: they were looking around in confusion, running back the way they'd come.

'This way,' one of them shouted. 'She must have doubled back towards the *Herald*.' Their voices receded, and were lost.

The barge puttered its stately way onwards up the river, and Daisy felt her breathing slow. She could just see the boat's small crew through the stairwell leading down to the cabin: three old men in sou'westers, blissfully unaware of the drama playing out above their heads. Daisy could hear one of them singing along to something by the Beach Boys on the radio.

She kept her eyes narrowly on the shore as it passed, searching for the right place. The minutes passed like hours, and it felt like a new century by the time they reached the stretch of river that ran directly along the back of Kew Gardens. Here were the back gates, coming closer, closer, beckoning.

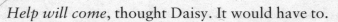

Help will come, thought Daisy. It would have to.

She took a deep breath, braced herself and jumped into the icy water. Napoleon clung to the top of her head, meowing furiously and trying to keep his tail above water. The river was high and fast, and the cold of it numbed her

legs and snatched fistfuls of air from her lungs as she kicked towards shore. Then she was being buffeted against the slippery and moss-slicked wall that divided the river from the towpath on the other side. She was scrambling, cursing, tearing her nails for purchase – and then she was over. She landed on the towpath like a small beached whale.

The air was very cold: much colder than it had been before she'd jumped into the water. Her breath was making desperate puffs of steam around her head and Napoleon was trembling in her arms, mute with cold and outrage. But they couldn't enter Kew yet. The fox-haired man had seen her here with Ma, had probably overheard Ma telling her to come back here for help. *No.* The best thing would be to hang on until nightfall, and to make her way inside under cover of darkness.

She hid herself in the undergrowth near the car park and settled down to wait, teeth chattering with cold and exhaustion.

She must have slept, because when she woke it was very dark and her limbs were icy and stiff. Napoleon licked the inside of her ear, and she raised herself with a groan. The gates of Kew were locked, the car park deserted.

Good.

She stretched, and spat on her palms. Then, grip by painful grip, she shinned her way up the metal bars of the gate, teetered dangerously over the spikes along the top and

finally dropped down into Kew. She landed in a crouch and heard Napoleon meowing from inside her jacket, as if to say the coast was clear.

The gardens were eerie in the darkness, and a high wind was stirring the trees. An owl screeched from somewhere nearby, and Daisy jumped. She closed her eyes, then opened them again.

Courage, joonam.

She closed her fingers on the dandelion paperweight in her pocket.

Then she pulled it out, and gasped.

It was shining in her hand: a great diffuse glow that slowly narrowed into a single beam of light that swung around like the silver needle of a compass before settling on the path ahead. Daisy stared, and turned from one side to another. The beam stayed fixed on the path, like a compass pointing north.

Daisy took a deep breath, and followed it up the long avenue towards the Palm House, and past the lake that lay before it. The water shone blackly under the starless sky, dark as an oil slick.

Now the beam from the paperweight swung round, laying out a thin silver path that led towards the towering glass doors of the Palm House itself. She turned, hesitating – and then she heard movement and shouts coming from the main gates. She recognized the voices of Craven and the fox-haired man. They must have been lying in wait. She felt fear rise up again, so powerfully that it was hard to move or even think.

Then Napoleon darted along the compass-beam of light towards the Palm House – towards the voices.

'No! Come back!' Without stopping to think, she sprinted after him, cursing under her breath. They were all converging on the Palm House now. Craven had spotted her, she was going to be caught and –

The paperweight flared like a silver torch, and light lanced between her fingers like the filament of a dazzling lightbulb. She lifted it high and turned her face away, and there were shouts as Craven and the other man fell back, blinded. Then Daisy yanked open the door to the Palm House and darted inside after Napoleon.

Chapter 10

The light of the paperweight dimmed to a soft glow, barely more than a glimmer, as if it knew they needed to keep hidden. Daisy ducked low, moving stealthily through the dim shapes of the palm trees, following the thready beam of light that traced out a faint path ahead. Napoleon darted along it, confidently leading the way between the roots of the trees – and then vanished behind a cascade of vines.

She could hear Craven at the entrance to the glasshouse. The door seemed to be jammed, and he was arguing with the other man.

Daisy glanced around and pushed after Napoleon, feeling waxy leaves brush against her cheeks and catch on her clothes in her haste. Even as she ducked through the curtain of vines, she heard glass shattering as Craven broke his way into the Palm House.

'Watch the exits, Fleish.' His voice was harsh, and she saw him draw close to her hiding place. 'She must be in here somewhere.' Daisy's breath felt stapled to the back of her throat. Her fear was so palpable she was surprised he couldn't smell it, like a bloodhound.

'Here, girl,' said Craven. 'Come out now. We won't hurt you.'

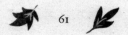

Yeah, right, thought Daisy.

Her back was pressed against a large tree, and she crouched down to make herself smaller. And then she saw it: a small door in the heart of the foliage.

It was low and gleamed with silver light round its edges, and above it shone a coat of arms in finely worked glass: two crossed dandelions above an oak tree. The handle of the door was cool and silver, and it turned soundlessly, like something in a black-and-white film.

Napoleon leapt across the threshold, just as Craven drew closer once again. Daisy hesitated, then followed, shutting the door silently behind her.

Immediately, all noises ceased. Ahead of them was a forest of towering oak trees, twined with thorny roses. It was dim within the forest, and round lanterns were strung between the trees, scattering light like gold sequins across a narrow and winding path. Napoleon was poised just ahead of her, looking back as if to say, *Hurry up, then.* The roses were the size of dinner plates, and their scent was overwhelming, like a perfume with spikes. Plumed birds, electric blue and yellow and rainbow-coloured, glided from branch to branch, and shimmery green moths trailed from flower to flower, looking for nectar.

One thing was certain: they were no longer in Kew Gardens, or not in any part of it that Daisy knew.

She stepped forward slowly. Any moment now she'd wake up and find herself back in Kew, probably with a nasty concussion. She pinched a giant rose petal between thumb and forefinger. It was velvet-skinned and soft, and the thorn next to it, when she tested it, was sharp enough to draw blood.

'Ouch!'

Was it possible to hallucinate pain?

The paperweight shone softly in her hand, lighting the way through the forest, which seemed to grow and rise up around them. The path began to curve, and then with a sudden turn a little hut came into view, its light shining out like a star amidst the trees. As they drew closer, Daisy saw that the hut was topped with the same coat of arms she'd spotted above the silver door: crossed dandelions above an oak tree. And standing at the entrance was a squat man dressed in red overalls with gold epaulettes, like a cross between a soldier and a gardener. There was a parakeet on his shoulder and he was leaning on a sharpened pitchfork that glinted in the light.

'Hold,' he called out. 'Who goes there?'

'Um,' said Daisy, glancing around. 'Do you mean me?'

'I most certainly do,' said the man. He brandished his pitchfork. 'Don't you know that inter-side travel is illegal for unaccompanied minors? Where's your grassport?'

'What?'

'No grassport,' said the man, rolling his eyes in despair. 'Give me strength. Where are your parents?'

Daisy swallowed. 'That's just it. My father is dead, and

64

I don't *know* where Ma is.' To her horror, she could feel tears burning in the corners of her eyes, and she scrubbed them away ruthlessly with the back of her hand.

'Oh dear,' said the man, looking discomfited. He lowered his pitchfork with a small cough. Now that it was out of the way, Daisy noticed that he had bright black eyes and a beard that came down to his belt buckle.

'I'm afraid that you are in breach of section 402 of the inter-side travel code: there's no getting away from it.' He sighed. 'I'll have to take you to the commander.'

Then Napoleon appeared from behind Daisy's ankles, and the guard leapt as if he'd been electrocuted. 'Why, you little blighter! So you're back!' Napoleon was licking his tail with lofty unconcern. 'Don't play innocent with me,' said the man, waggling his pitchfork threateningly. 'Seven sausage rolls you filched from my lunchbox, and then disappeared – for weeks! I call that poor behaviour. Very poor indeed.'

Daisy looked between the man and the cat. Napoleon had started on a hind leg, and was looking as if butter wouldn't melt in his mouth.

'Erm,' she said. 'Do you know each other?'

'Know each other?' said the man. 'I've been worried sick about that cat – he's been missing for weeks. Always hanging around the guard house, he was, always after my food. I told the commander, I told her, it's only a matter of time before he goes and sneaks out through the door, but does she listen, *oh no . . .*'

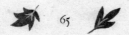

Napoleon leapt onto Daisy's shoulder and curled there, gazing at the guard with narrowed green eyes as he continued to mutter to himself.

'Well,' said the man at last. 'This is most irregular. You'd better come with me, Miss, ah—'

'Daisy Thistledown.'

'Hm. A good name,' he said grudgingly. 'Captain Malarky, at your service.' He coughed again, awkwardly. 'I'm afraid I'll have to clap you in vines – Mallowmarsh protocol, you understand, nothing personal; we have to do the same for all unauthorized travellers. You can't be too careful in the Greenwild nowadays.' As he spoke, he unwound a vine from his belt, and it wreathed itself around Daisy's wrists like a pair of leafy green handcuffs. They were immovable as iron.

Mallowmarsh? thought Daisy. Hadn't she overheard Craven using that word on the phone? And what – or where – was the Greenwild? But Captain Malarky was already ducking into the guard house and shouting to someone inside. 'All right, Corporal Smedley? I'm taking an unaccompanied minor to the commander. Guard the fort and I'll be back in a jiffy.' A spotty young man in ill-fitting red overalls came to the door and saluted smartly.

'Right you are, Captain.' He shot a curious glance at Daisy as Malarky adjusted his uniform and turned back to her.

'Right,' he said. 'Off we go.'

Chapter 11

They began walking, Daisy stumbling from exhaustion, and more convinced than ever that she was dreaming. She could feel Captain Malarky gripping the top of her arm, and she could smell something like candyfloss on the air. There was a sound like fireworks, and music, and people cheering: like the best party you could ever imagine, unfolding just around the corner.

A moment later, they came out of the trees, and Daisy realized that this was exactly what was happening. They had emerged onto a vast sloping lawn edged by yew trees that blazed with candles, and the space was filled with people, grown-ups and children, all wearing brightly coloured clothes, laughing and singing and moving about. A spry old man in sky-blue overalls and a top hat was tossing back a drink the colour of a sunset. A pair of women with red hair and bracelets of ivy snaking halfway up their bare arms were laughing uproariously. A group of children were flying kites that glowed in the dark, and a boy around Daisy's age with a tangle of brown curls ran past, dragging his gleaming kite behind him like the moon on a string. At the centre of the lawn was a great, shining palace that glittered in the light of a hundred torches and sparklers.

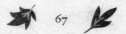

'*Oh.*'

Daisy looked in wonder.

It was a glasshouse, but quite unlike anything at Kew Gardens. Its smooth, bright walls were made of sparkling glass that soared three times as high as Kew's Palm House. The roof rose and fell in dozens of glass domes and towers that fluttered with cheery pennants bearing the same coat of arms: crossed dandelions above an oak tree.

The guard chuckled, looking at her face. 'I'm guessing this is your first visit, Miss Thistledown. Welcome to Mallowmarsh, the finest garden in the Greenwild.'

A couple of the revellers spotted Captain Malarky and came towards him with cheers of greeting.

'Happy Twelfth Night, Captain,' called the man in sky-blue overalls. He swept off his top hat and bowed to Daisy. 'And Good Dozentide to you, child.'

Malarky grinned back at him. 'Happy Twelfth. What a night, eh?'

'Your shift is over at last?' said a cheery, round lady with eyes like bright raisins and a chirruping French-accented voice. 'Let me get you a drink.'

'Can't, I'm afraid, Madame Gallitrop,' said the captain, looking regretful. 'I'm still on duty. Have you seen the commander?'

'She is about to speak,' said the lady. She was almost spherical, and so short that she barely came past Daisy's shoulder. '*Alors*, there she is!'

A woman with silver hair was climbing onto a platform at the end of the lawn, and a great cheer went up from the crowd. She was wearing a pair of emerald-green velvet overalls, and her long silver hair fell past her elbows. Judging by her hair and the criss-cross of fine lines across her pale skin, she was quite old, but she radiated a sort of bright energy, as if she'd swallowed a lightbulb for breakfast.

'Friends,' she called, her voice echoing around the space. 'Fellow Botanists of the Greenwild! Today our Yuletide celebrations come to an end, and we celebrate the Twelfth Night: the night of misrule, when beggars are kings, and children run riot –' here a great cheer from the children with their kites – 'when the nights are dark, but the candles shine brightest –' here the candles flared up blue and silver on the yew trees – 'and when seeds sleep in the earth, and gather their green sap to rise again in the spring.'

She lifted her arms and the cherry trees around the platform burst into riotous blossom that scattered like wild confetti across the whole lawn, dancing on the wind and swirling in wild pirouettes until the branches were bare once again.

'So, without further ado, I step aside and I give the night up to the children – the best of us – and this Twelfth Night celebration.'

The roar this time was deafening, and then fireworks shot up into the sky: golden chrysanthemums of light, and great crimson pinwheels shimmering and unfolding like

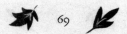

dragons' wings. Daisy was dazed, stunned by the light and the noise, and she barely noticed as the captain nudged her towards the platform and the silver-haired woman jumping down from it.

'Happy Twelfth, Commander,' he called.

'Ah, Captain Malarky. Happy Dozentide to you. Enjoying the celebrations?'

'Yes, Commander White. That is – ahem. I'm here to report an unaccompanied minor.' He stepped aside so that Daisy became visible behind him. 'Name of Daisy Thistledown. She turned up at the door as bold as brass – and brought Fluffkin back with her.' Napoleon gave an outraged yowl at the name, and Malarky glanced at the commander with an embarrassed cough. 'Our runaway cat,' he added in explanation.

Commander White stepped forward and surveyed Daisy up and down with blue eyes that were very bright and piercing. Daisy felt as if they were looking inside her and reading her soul like a map.

'What brings you to our door tonight, Daisy Thistledown?' asked the commander. Her expression was a complicated mix of surprise and something else Daisy couldn't name, possibly because she was feeling very dizzy. Her insides were hollow and the world seemed to swoop around her as she remembered that she hadn't eaten since leaving Wykhurst – almost twenty-four hours earlier.

'Um,' she said. 'I was . . . I was—'

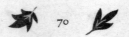

And then another firework unfolded through the darkness above, like a giant orchid made of stars. The stars filled her vision until she could see nothing else, and she staggered on her feet.

'Steady there,' said the commander. 'You're very pale; I'm not surprised you're feeling faint.'

'Don't be ridiculous,' muttered Daisy. She staggered again, and became aware that a small crowd of onlookers had gathered and were gazing at her with undisguised curiosity.

'Looks like she got at the plum wine,' said one of them sagely.

'All right, everyone,' said the commander. 'That's enough. Back to the celebrations. What the girl needs is space – and something to eat, by the looks of it. I'll take care of this.'

Commander White glanced at Captain Malarky. 'Before I forget –' she tapped at Daisy's handcuffs, and the vines unfurled elegantly – 'I'll return these, Captain, and let you get back to your post.'

'Right you are, Commander,' he said, saluting smartly. 'The Mallowmarshals are at your service.' Then he stowed the vines back on his belt, winked at Daisy and marched off, whistling.

'Now. Do you think you can walk?' asked the commander.

'Yes,' said Daisy, indignant. She was only slightly dizzy. 'I'm absolutely fine.'

'Of course you are,' said the commander kindly. 'Off we go.'

Then they were moving across the lawn and around the banks of a great silver lake. A couple of parakeets swooped joyfully ahead of them as they entered a frosty apple orchard where the long grass was tipped with silver. The trees were old and gnarled, with tiny crimson apples growing on them, and there was a stream somewhere filling the air with a sound like water gossiping.

Daisy paused. She felt bamboozled. 'Where are we going?'

'To the Roost, Daisy. My humble abode. Now come on. I won't have you fainting before we get there.'

They had reached a path lined with bluebells thickly coated in frost, ringing and tinging against each other like musical glass. At the end of the path stood a great beech tree that towered high into the sky. And held within its branches was the strangest house Daisy had ever seen.

Over the years, Daisy had stayed with Ma in Albanian log cabins and chalets perched precariously in the Swiss Alps. She had slept in fancy hotels at the top of skyscrapers, and Welsh castles with leaky roofs, and had once spent a week in an igloo. But she had never seen a treehouse rising five stories high, with six mismatched chimneys, four sweeping balconies and a

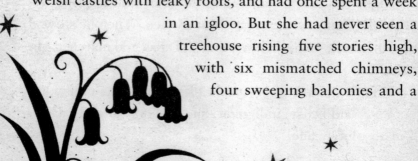

turret like something out of a folktale. There was a round, blue-painted door set into the roots, and gleaming round windows that winked from the trunk. Branches wove in and out of the beams and lintels, and the higgledy-piggledy roof was green with moss and scattered with poppies that waved cheerily on the night air. The whole thing was rambling and madcap and unexpectedly stylish: as if it were all sewn together by magic.

Daisy's eyes were wide as saucers.

'Come on.' The commander led her forward through the round blue door and up a spiral staircase, and then she was inside, sitting on a threadbare sofa in a warm round kitchen that smelled of burnt toast.

'Miss Tufton!' the commander called up the stairs, and a tiny old woman hurried in, bent and stooped with age. She looked old enough to be the commander's mother, with dyed black hair pulled back in a bun and a face like a shrivelled apple.

She took one look at Daisy and hurried to the stove. 'Hot tea,' she said, 'with lots of sugar, and a dash of snisky.' A delicate vine uncurled itself from the wall and lifted a blue china mug down from the dresser. Moments later she was pressing a steaming brew into Daisy's hands. 'There you are, child. Drink that.' She bustled out again, muttering something about a hot-water bottle.

Daisy drank, and felt warmth course through her veins. It felt as if every bone in her body was being hugged. She

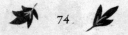

drained the mug and looked up, the kitchen coming into focus around her. There was a large, scrubbed table at one end of the room, and a wooden rocking chair beside an old-fashioned stove that radiated heat. Unlike the hotel rooms and rented apartments Daisy was used to, the space looked deeply lived in, with a pile of unwashed dishes heaped in the sink, a bright copper kettle warming on the hob, and a friendly chaos of chipped teacups, wooden spoons and colourful geraniums in mismatched pots. There was clematis looped around the inside of the windows, ivy climbing up the table legs and a pink gramophone playing in the corner, warbling overwrought opera music. At the centre of it all, a leafy tree was growing directly out of the wooden counter, its branches tangling with the roof beams.

Noticing her staring, the commander smiled.

'It's a larder tree. Very rare – I inherited it from my great-aunt.' She went over and placed a palm lovingly against the smooth, pale trunk. 'Plums, please,' she said. 'If you'd be so kind.'

A moment later the branches hung heavy with ripe purple fruit, shining in the light. Their taut skins were speckled with silvery freckles. Deftly, the commander plucked one and tossed it to Daisy, as Miss Tufton returned and began putting a meal on the table.

'Eat,' said the commander, pushing a plate of pancakes towards Daisy. 'You must be starving.'

Daisy ate. She closed her eyes. After a day without food,

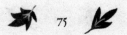

the taste made her lightheaded, almost delirious. After the pancakes there were hot scrambled eggs, and bread rolls filled with melted butter, and a sugar-topped cake she ate with her fingers. She finished with the plum from the larder tree, licking the sweet juice from the inside of her wrist. She couldn't remember the last time anything had tasted so good.

'Can you ask it for anything?' said Daisy when she'd finished, and was able to speak.

The commander nodded. 'As long as it grows on a tree. And as long as you ask politely.' She winked, and Daisy stared at her, wide-eyed.

'Ah, how rude of me.' The woman's blue eyes twinkled, as if she knew what Daisy was thinking. 'I'm Artemis White, the Commander and Head Mallow of Mallowmarsh. But, since you'll be staying in my house, you can call me Artemis.'

Daisy noticed for the first time that the woman's emerald-green overalls were embroidered with a pattern of purple vines, and she was wearing high-heeled boots with sparkling buckles shaped like pomegranates. Her silver hair was looped with thorny winter roses (Daisy wondered how she avoided getting scratched) and she radiated a sense of calm authority, like a very old tree with firm, settled roots.

'So . . .' said Daisy. 'I'm not a prisoner? I can leave if I want?'

'Of course,' said Artemis White. 'Though I don't advise it. It's not a safe time to be a Botanist in the Greyside.'

'I don't understand.' Daisy was no longer dizzy, but the

tea was wearing off and she felt terribly tired and cold, still damp from her dip in the Thames and covered in mud from her dash through Kew in the dark.

'We can talk later,' said Artemis. 'What you need now is a good hot bath and then bed.'

'I *can't* stay. You don't understand.' Daisy got up and began pacing. 'I have to get back, to look for –' But she had reached the back window, and what she saw there stopped her in her tracks.

Outside the window was a meadow of light, brimming with great shining globes that glowed in the dark. Daisy raised a hand to her eyes, dazzled. At first, she couldn't puzzle out what she was looking at. Then she understood.

They were dandelions, with stalks as tall as trees, and fat gossamer puffs as big as carousels. They filled the meadow in their hundreds, bobbing like round silver boats on a dark sea. They were radiant, luminous, as if they'd been sprinkled with a watering can full of moonlight.

Daisy thought of the coat of arms she'd seen everywhere: crossed dandelions above an oak tree. Her fingers closed round the dandelion paperweight, cool and hidden in her pocket, and she felt something fall into place.

Ma had *meant for* her to come here. Ma had given her the paperweight because, somehow, she knew it would bring Daisy to safety.

Help will come, Ma had said. And it had.

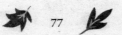

Chapter 12

Daisy woke to sunlight and the feeling of something tickling her nose. She sneezed and sat up in bed, pushing Napoleon's tail away from her face. Sunbeams were streaming through the skylight above her, and golden dust floated in the light that fell across the cool sheets.

Gradually, the details of the previous night came back to her. She remembered the commander leading her higher and higher up a set of winding stairs and into a softly carpeted tower room. She remembered how Miss Tufton – the tiny old woman with the shrivelled-apple face – had reappeared, grumbling to herself as she ran a steaming hot bath, and turned back the shining white sheets on a freshly made bed.

And then, there had been nothing but sleep, pulling her under like a smooth wave.

Now, swinging her feet out of bed, Daisy discovered that she'd slept in a white nightgown that made her feel vaguely Victorian. Her own clothes had been washed and pressed, and were folded neatly on a squashy armchair. She stepped across the soft green carpet and realized as she did so that it was, in fact, moss, starred with white flowers and small ladybirds she had to be careful not to step on. There was also a wisteria vine growing across the inside of the wall, curling around a bright mirror that reflected back her own startled face. There was a scrape on her forehead and another on her hand, which she sucked as she looked around the room. There weren't many items of furniture apart from the armchair and the soft, high bed, but there was a curious collection of shells, pebbles, feathers and ammonites scattered around the shelves, a stack of books piled on top of a chest of drawers – and, best of all, a long, rusty brass telescope poking out of the skylight, aimed at the invisible stars.

Below it was a large, round window like a ship's porthole, which looked out across the frosty apple orchard. Beyond that lay the lake, wide and blue and shining, and then the vast green sweep of the grounds and the great glittering glasshouse beyond. High above, flocks of parakeets filled the sky, settling on the trees like green glitter in a snow globe. Napoleon stood beside her with his paws upon the windowsill, and meowed.

So, thought Daisy, *I didn't dream it, after all*.

Barely pausing to do up the last button of her skirt, she scooped Napoleon onto her shoulder, and ran down the stairs.

The sounds of loud opera music and clattering pans led them down the spiral staircase and on to three successive landings. The first revealed the bathroom with the claw-footed tub in which Daisy had bathed last night, surrounded by piles of fluffy white towels and great stacks of rainbow soaps that reached the ceiling. The second opened onto a grass-carpeted corridor scattered with anemones, leading towards two closed doors that Daisy guessed were bedrooms. And the third led down again to a broader set of stairs that revealed the big, warm kitchen.

The commander – Artemis – was sitting at the table with a mass of papers spread out around her, taking a bite out of an enormous cheese scone.

'Ah, Daisy, at last!' She looked pleased. 'Come, sit. Did you sleep well?'

'Yes,' said Daisy, feeling suddenly timid. 'Thanks.'

Artemis beckoned her forward, and Daisy saw that there was a boy perched on the opposite end of the table: the one she'd seen last night with the glowing kite. His dark hair was even more curly and tangled than before, and he was demolishing a large and sticky slice of fruit cake. He had a look of rabid curiosity in his large brown eyes, and a parakeet perched on his head.

'Morning,' he said with a grin. 'I'm glad to see you're conscious.'

'More or less,' replied Daisy, her voice sounding uncertain even to her own ears. Then there was a clatter from the stove as Miss Tufton came into view. Her dyed black bun was skewered in place with a sharp knitting needle.

'Awake, are you?' she grumbled, but her eyes were bright. She had six missing teeth (Daisy counted them), and the sides of her slippers were cut away. 'To make room for

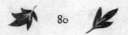

my bunions,' she said, catching Daisy's fascinated stare. 'Terrible pain I suffer, night and day. Oh, I'm a martyr to my feet, but then I never complain.' She heaved a weighty sigh, and plonked an enormous tureen of soup on the table.

'Thank you, Tuffy,' said Artemis sweetly. She turned to Daisy. 'Miss Tufton is my housekeeper. And this is young Podsnap,' she added, waving a hand towards the boy. She spoke with the air of one introducing a tiresome dog who nevertheless has the run of the house, and he gave an ironic salute.

'Indigo Podsnap,' he said. His eyebrows were winged at the tips, Daisy noticed, and his skin and eyes were both the same gold-brown colour, like raw amber when you hold it up to the light. He was wearing moss-green overalls with muddy knees, and a satchel filled with apples was slung on the back of his chair.

'Do you live here too?' she asked, barely managing to grab Napoleon's tail as he made a leap for the boy's parakeet.

'Me? No. Me and Jethro –' he indicated the bird, which was chattering furiously at Napoleon – 'live near the Mallow Woods. We're just here for the food.' Miss Tufton, passing by with a bowl of potatoes, clipped him on the side of the head. 'Ouch! AND the charming company.'

Artemis snorted, and pushed a steaming bowl of tomato soup towards Daisy, along with a pile of hot buttered scones. The boy called Indigo was already tipping up his soup bowl to his face and lowering it to reveal a ginger soup moustache. 'Neither of my dads are great cooks,' he said, as if this explained his hunger.

'Nor sticklers for table manners, apparently,' said Artemis with amusement, as Indigo reached for another scone with a grubby hand. She eyed him and he hesitated, then speared it with a fork instead, shoving it into his mouth.

'Mmmff,' he said apologetically.

Daisy took a spoonful of soup and looked around, keeping one eye on Napoleon to make sure he didn't make another attempt to pounce on the boy's parakeet. Next to the stove was a teetering shelf overflowing with books, most of them battered and well thumbed. She squinted at the spines. They had titles like *The Herbomancer's Guide to Practical Botany*, and *The Compleat Botanist: From Alfalfa to Zinnia*, and *The Trouble with Tulips*. A row of copper pots hung on hooks from the ceiling, along with bunches of rich-smelling herbs: rosemary, lavender, thyme and a few others she couldn't identify. A pot of ivy on the floor was sending crafty tendrils over Indigo's foot.

'Pass me that wooden spoon, please, Daisy dear,' said Artemis, who was now using a pile of books as a stepladder to coax a spiky, reddish vine down from where it was curling around the knobs of the spice cabinet. Daisy handed her the spoon and watched as Artemis cajoled the vine towards the others twining around the wooden roof beams. Indigo was feeding his parakeet with the stray crumbs of his fifth scone, a scowling Miss Tufton was supervising as a leafy vine stacked clean plates in a cupboard, and an enormous potted palm was waving its leaves in time to the music still blasting from the pink gramophone.

'I don't want to seem nosy,' said Daisy, 'but where am I, and what is going on?'

Chapter 13

Indigo and Artemis turned to look at her. Miss Tufton sniffed loudly.

Daisy flushed.

'I mean, I'm not in Kew Gardens anymore, obviously.' She gestured around at the room, and the potted palm leaned down and patted her consolingly on the shoulder with a giant leaf.

'You really don't know,' said Artemis slowly. 'It's extraordinary.' She paused, weighing her words. 'This house is called the Roost. And you are in Mallowmarsh, the biggest Botanical garden in the Greenwild. You came in through the door from Kew Gardens. Although how you managed it is a mystery to me if you claim to know nothing about us.'

'I don't,' said Daisy, making a snap decision not to mention the paperweight. 'I only found it because of Napoleon – my cat.' It was true that he'd led the way. She gestured to where he sat grooming himself magnificently on the kitchen counter, waiting to be noticed.

Indigo's eyes widened. '*Your* cat? That's Fluffkin! He belongs to the guard house! Captain Malarky thought he'd escaped through the Mallow gate.'

'Well, he's mine,' said Daisy, curling her arms protectively around Napoleon as he leapt into her lap, almost upsetting the cream jug. 'And I'm his. And his name,' she added with dignity, 'is *Napoleon.*'

'Don't worry, Daisy. No one's going to separate you.' Artemis's blue eyes twinkled. 'Though we really should tighten up on security. We can't have unauthorized animals slipping out into the Greyside like that.'

'Greyside?'

Artemis beamed at her. 'That's right. The Mallow gate is a crossing-place between the Greyside and the Greenwild: that is, between your world and ours.'

'Ri-ight,' said Daisy.

Artemis looked deadly serious. The potted palm belched.

'Well, either way, I need to go back to, um – there. My mother is missing, and I have to find her, and I don't even know if she's alive and—'

'Slow down,' said Artemis. 'Start at the beginning. We may be able to help.'

Daisy hesitated. Then she remembered the dandelions from last night, and her conviction that Ma had *meant* for her to come here.

She met Artemis's eyes and found them regarding her steadily, as if she was worthy of the greatest attention. No one had ever looked at Daisy like that except Ma.

'Well,' she said finally. 'It started with Ma going to Peru.'

She explained about Wykhurst and the plane crash, about

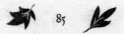

running away and being chased through Kew Gardens.

As she spoke, Artemis's gaze never left her face, and the movement of the rocking chair by the fire slowed as Miss Tufton leaned forward to listen. Indigo managed to stay quiet for most of it, but he was clearly bursting with questions.

'So Craven had your mother's necklace?' he blurted out as she finished. 'But how? Why?'

'I don't know,' said Daisy, pulling it from her pocket. As always, the pendant looked like a living daisy: golden hearted and fringed with white petals. 'Ma never took it off. She was wearing it when the plane left Lima. I think someone must have taken it from her after the crash.'

Artemis frowned. 'It sounds like this man Craven is our main suspect – him, or someone working for him.' Daisy suppressed a shiver at his name, feeling fear like pins and needles over her whole body. He had wanted the paperweight. He had wanted her captured. Where would she be now, if she hadn't stumbled into Mallowmarsh?

Miss Tufton hobbled over to examine the necklace, perching a pair of purple cats' eye glasses on her crooked nose. 'Ah,' said the housekeeper, peering closely. 'Some of Annibeth Ashley's finest work, if I'm not mistaken. I always said she was the best jeweller in the Greenwild.' She prodded the pendant with a gnarled finger and the petals furled up like a miniature umbrella, then curled open again, shimmering slightly.

Daisy's mouth dropped open in shock.

Artemis turned to look at Daisy, her silver hair falling around her face.

'So,' she said, 'your mother is Leila Thistledown, the journalist who disappeared in Peru last month? And this belongs to her?'

Daisy nodded.

'You're not here by accident, Daisy.' Artemis's eyes were very bright. 'Your mother is a Botanist. And so are you.'

Chapter 14

'Wait – a what?' Daisy shook her head. 'Aren't botanists people who study plants?'

'Well, yes,' said Artemis. 'That's true in the Greyside – in the so-called non-magical world. But, here in the Greenwild, Botanists are people who use green magic.'

'But—'

'Why do you think that cat adopted you?' The commander nodded at Napoleon, who was curled on Daisy's shoulder like a miniature sphinx. 'He recognized you as a Botanist and hoped you'd bring him home.'

'What are you talking about? What on earth is green magic?'

'Wait.' Indigo stared at her in astonishment. 'Are you telling me that you don't know anything about . . . anything?'

Daisy scowled. 'I know plenty about *lots* of things.'

She was forced to break off as a sharp ringing noise cut through the air like an alarm, and Captain Malarky came striding through the door of the Roost. 'Security alert, Commander,' he panted. 'We've had reports of an intruder near the Sighing Forest. You're needed there, fast.'

Artemis was already on her feet, coiling a length of vine round one wrist and nodding to Miss Tufton, who

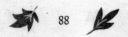

was palming a pair of murderously sharp knitting needles. 'Tuffy, secure the perimeter of the Roost. Indigo, Daisy: you stay here.'

Ten seconds later, Daisy found herself alone in the kitchen with Indigo and about a hundred unanswered questions.

'What's going on?'

Indigo shrugged, looking uneasy. 'Dunno. We've had a few attempted break-ins in the last few weeks – people trying to slip past the Mallowmarshals. I've heard people saying that it's –' he cast a nervous glance over his shoulder – 'the Grim Reapers.'

Daisy felt a chill, like a cold finger being dragged up the length of her spine. 'Grim Reapers? You mean like *the* Grim Reaper? The guy with the, er, long blade thing, who's supposed to represent Death?'

'Not exactly,' said Indigo. 'The Grim Reapers are a scary story for kids: a bit like ogres and goblins. In the old Greenwild fairy tales, Grim Reapers are evil giants who go around chopping down every tree in the world with their giant scythes, destroying green magic and cutting Botanist children in half. Dad used to say that if I didn't finish my broccoli, the Grim Reapers would come and get me.' He shuddered. 'They gave me nightmares.'

'So they're not real?'

'We-ell,' said Indigo. 'Like I said, they're supposed to be only a story. But I don't know . . . Maybe people are looking for something to blame for the disappearances.'

'Disappearances?' Daisy was suddenly alert. 'What do you mean?'

But Artemis and Miss Tufton chose that moment to come striding back in through the door. 'False alarm,' the commander was saying cheerfully. 'Nothing more sinister than an escaped sheep out for a morning adventure. Good greenness, it's freezing in here,' she added – and with a glance at the cold stove she pulled a handful of seeds from her pocket and flung them across the floor. Seconds later, a wave of thick stems shot up from the floorboards, topped with enormous sunflowers like big gold doubloons. They spread all the way around the table, beaming down soft rays of warmth, and in only a few minutes the whole kitchen was snug and toasty.

'That's better,' said Artemis, throwing herself down in a chair and turning her face up towards one of the flowers. 'Now, where were we?'

'Green magic,' said Indigo helpfully, as Daisy felt the warmth of the sunflowers begin to seep into her hands and feet. 'You were about to explain it.'

'Ah, of course!' Artemis beamed at them. 'It's another word for plant magic, Daisy: simple as that. The magic of the earth itself.'

Daisy grasped desperately for a scrap of logic, glancing between Indigo and the commander. 'Isn't that . . . nature?'

Artemis smiled, and her eyes sparkled. 'You're right, Daisy. Everything in nature *is* magic. Even the most ordinary

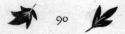

daisy or dandelion is its own small miracle. But there are also wonders here that most Greysiders can barely begin to imagine – plants that died out long ago in your world.' She paused, and her face seemed to light up. 'Mandrakes and talking trees, Daisy; magic beanstalks and forests of roses and seeds that can make you invisible. All of them exist here in the Greenwild, where the earth is rich with magic.'

Daisy stared at her. 'But—'

'Listen,' said Artemis, holding up a finger. 'Botanists are caretakers: custodians of a world of Botanical wonders. We can use green magic to help things take root and grow. Like this,' she said, passing a hand over a stray sunflower seed, so that it corkscrewed up and unfurled a bold gold flower. 'And we can harvest seeds, roots and leaves to make many thousands of different potions, poisons and salves.' She reached into another pocket and tossed Daisy a little pot. 'Chamomillion cream. It will help with that scrape on your hand.' Daisy twisted open the pot, dabbed a bit on her palm – and watched in astonishment as the graze knitted itself back together and vanished.

Artemis smiled. 'Most of all, being a Botanist means thinking about what *we* can do for nature – not just what it can do for us. That's the thing so many Greysiders have forgotten.' She stood and walked through the sunflowers to put her mug in the sink, and they shot up another foot as she passed, as if soaking in her energy. 'And that's why so many Botanists devote their lives to rescuing plants that are

endangered in the Greyside. Some of our "oddities", like this larder tree —' she patted it softly, and it curled a shoot into her hair — 'would once have been as ordinary in the Greyside as cabbages and turnips.'

Daisy was speechless. The sunflowers were still growing, and were now more than a metre taller than her head.

'We're not making it up,' said Indigo, reading her expression. 'It's true.'

'But . . . if this green magic really exists, wouldn't I have *known* Ma could do it?'

'Didn't you know she was different?' said Artemis. 'Deep down? You must have noticed she was unusual.'

Daisy hesitated. *Everything* about Ma was unusual. That's what made her the famous Leila Thistledown. And yet . . . She thought of the way that flowers always seemed to bloom higher and brighter when Ma was around. The way she could take a drooping hotel plant in a dried-out pot and have it flowering within minutes. The way she had — there was no denying it — called a ring of white orchids from the desert, creating shelter from a sandstorm. Daisy remembered the single astonishing glimpse she'd had before being sand-blinded: the fat white flowers sending out threads of light that had streamed into a pale dome all around them.

Flowers in the desert? Ma had said. *My rascal, whatever will you think of next?*

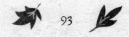

93

Yet, flowers could grow in the desert, Daisy knew – even orchids. So why had Ma laughed as if the idea was absurd?

'It's a knack,' Ma would say, when Daisy asked her about her way with plants. 'My mother had a green thumb too.'

But it had been more than that, hadn't it? It had been like –

'Magic,' she breathed.

Daisy turned to Indigo, remembering his words from earlier. 'You said something about disappearances? Other . . . Botanists going missing?'

Artemis nodded grimly. 'Botanists have been vanishing across the Greyside for months. Mostly in the Amazon.'

Daisy heard Ma's voice in her head. *Innocent people are disappearing*, she had said.

'I think Ma knew,' she said. 'I think she was going to investigate.'

Artemis nodded, her eyes grave. 'Someone is hunting down Botanists. And they've taken your mother too.'

There was a silence in the bright kitchen.

'Then what are we waiting for?' Daisy burst out. 'We need to go find her, *now*. Why are we hanging around?'

'That's exactly the right question,' said Artemis, getting to her feet. 'I've been trying for months to persuade the Bureau – that's the Bureau of Botanical Business – to investigate the disappearances. But they're like ostriches – heads buried up to their necks in the sand. No one wants to admit what's really happening, because it means facing

how much danger we're in. Botanists are vanishing *without a trace*. No bodies, no explanation. We need to launch a search mission, and for that we need the Bureau's support.'

'Why do we need their permission?' Daisy felt impatient. 'Why can't we just go? Now?'

Artemis sighed. 'The Bureau holds supreme power across every pocket in the Greenwild, Daisy. Without their authority, a journey to search for missing Botanists would be over before it began. Visas, border permits, grassport control – it's all nearly impossible without their co-operation. But your story could change things. It could convince them that we have a case: a lead to follow. I think we can help each other, Daisy. You can help us get permission for a search mission. And then we can help you find your mother.'

It was as if someone had lit a sparkler in Daisy's stomach, fizzing and painfully bright.

'Is it a deal?' asked Artemis.

Daisy's fist closed around the paperweight hidden in her pocket.

'Yes,' she said. 'It's a deal.'

Chapter 15

'Get ready,' said Artemis. 'Here we go.'

They were on their way to somewhere called Chiveley Chase, and according to Artemis the fastest way to get there was by boat. Or, rather, they looked like boats, but they were in fact enormous lily pads, scudding across the surface of the glittering lake and ferrying Botanists from one side of Mallowmarsh to the other.

'Lilypaddles,' Indigo whispered as Daisy stared at them, wide-eyed.

In theory, you just needed to pull one towards you as it came close enough to shore, leap in and float all the way to the other side. In practise, however—

'Make sure you jump aboard when I say,' said Artemis. 'And try not to fall in the water – the local alligator is hungry at this time of year. Don't worry,' she added, catching the look on Daisy's face. 'You'll be fine. It prefers fillet steak. Usually. Okay, ready?' She reached out and yanked an approaching lilypaddle towards the bank, holding it steady as it strained to escape. 'In you get! One, two, three . . . hup!'

Daisy leapt and landed with a bump, feeling Indigo and Artemis right behind her. The lily pad barely buckled as it swung out across the lake, sending up little frills of foam in its wake.

Daisy felt the wind in her hair and laughed. Napoleon, tucked into the V of her jacket, fluffed out his fur in disgust.

'Faster, please,' said Artemis, and the boat put on a spurt of speed. 'We've got lots to do.'

'Er – like what?' asked Daisy.

'Oh,' said Artemis vaguely, manoeuvring round a complicated knot of bulrushes, 'the school term starts in a couple of days, and we ought to get you kitted out.'

'School?' Daisy glanced uneasily at the commander, thinking of Wykhurst.

'You're eleven, aren't you? A good time to start on the basics of green magic. And it will keep you out of mischief while we organize the search mission.'

'The Mallowmarsh school goes up to age twelve,' explained Indigo. 'We start learning magic in our last year, to prepare us for the exams to get into Bloomquist. That's the best school in the British Greenwild,' he added. 'Botanists go there from across the whole country.'

'But . . . I can't do magic,' said Daisy. 'Can I?'

She remembered, suddenly, the mountain-top tree that had broken her fall that day in Nepal, the poison ivy that had burst through the pavement in Delhi, the vines that had saved her from Craven only the day before. *Had that been magic?*

Artemis smiled as if she knew exactly what Daisy was thinking. 'Come on,' she said, and they breezed towards the far bank and disembarked beneath a large willow tree,

which curved a possessive frond against Indigo's cheek and sent another probing into Daisy's nostril.

'Stop that,' said Indigo, batting it away. Then the willow branches rose and parted, and Daisy saw Chiveley Chase laid out in front of them.

It stood at the end of a long avenue, looking like a cross between a large abbey and a small citadel, with sandstone walls the colour of honey and thick vines climbing up its many towers. There were magenta bell-flowers tumbling from the enormous arched windows, and energetic trees sprouting from the chimneys. Ivy trailed in green ropes across the weathered stone, and a dozen roofs rose and fell against the sky, punctuated by a series of hothouse domes that looked like green glass bubbles.

'Here we are,' said Artemis. 'The Chase. This is where most of our Botanists live, eat and work.'

It's where you'll find the Seed Bank, the library, the infirmary, workshops, kitchens, bakeries and almost anything else you might need.'

Daisy looked around, taking in the great sweeps of emerald lawn in front of the massive building, the low trellises looped with sparkling frozen roses, and the raised flower beds crammed with extravagant peonies, irises and geraniums all sheathed in frost and glittering like mosaics. Hundreds of topaz-coloured tulips floated half a metre above the ground, bobbing up and down in the breeze.

'What are those?' she asked, pointing.

'Aerial tulips,' said Artemis. 'A gift from our friends in the Dutch Greenwild.'

Botanists in brightly coloured overalls and heavy boots hurried by with trowels hung at their belts and spades slung across their backs, greeting Artemis with cheery waves and calls of 'Good afternoon, Commander' as they passed. Most of them were heading up and down the avenue that led to the Chase, which was lined with hedges artfully clipped to resemble elephants and tigers and fearsome lions.

The jungle animals reminded Daisy of something she'd been meaning to ask. 'What's so dangerous about the Amazon? Why are the disappearances worse there?'

'It's the rainforest,' said Indigo, trotting beside her and Artemis as they headed up the avenue. 'It's the biggest storehouse of green magic left in the Greyside. We're trying to protect it, and so are thousands of Greysiders. But lots

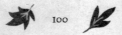

of the people fighting to stop the destruction tend to . . . disappear.'

Artemis nodded, looking troubled. 'It's not a safe time to be a Botanist.'

'Is it ever?' said Indigo, rolling his eyes.

'Is that why you've stayed secret?' asked Daisy. 'Why no one in the normal world – the Greyside, I mean – knows about . . . this?' She gestured around her, trying to encompass the oddness of everything, and accidentally knocked her arm against one of the hedge-lions. It shifted and growled in response, revealing a row of glittering incisors.

'GAH!' Daisy jumped, and a nearby hedge-elephant trumpeted and reared up before coming down with an earth-shaking swoosh of legs and leaves. Napoleon was clinging to her shoulder, spitting furiously.

'People fear what they don't understand,' said Artemis, ignoring the commotion and towing Daisy onwards. 'Botanists have often been called outsiders. For centuries, we were branded as hedge-witches and burned at the stake.'

'So,' said Indigo as strings of green drool fell across his shoulder from a nearby hedge-tiger, 'that's why the Old Botanists created the Greenwild as a safe place – somewhere the Greysiders can't find us.'

Artemis smiled. 'Imagine the Greenwild as a huge magician's cape. Mallowmarsh is in one of the many pockets: invisible from the outside, but big on the inside and full of interesting things.'

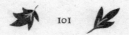

'So no one from my world – I mean, the Greyside – can get in?'

Artemis nodded. 'That's right. Only people with green magic can pass over the threshold between the two worlds. That includes you, Daisy.' She steamed on before Daisy could protest. 'The doors are so well hidden that an ordinary Greysider wouldn't even *see* one if it smacked them in the face. It's been that way for centuries: ever since the Old Botanists decided to split off from the Greyside, in order to survive. The Greenwild was – and continues to be – a sanctuary.'

Then she yanked Daisy out of the way as a hedge-lion swung a paw at her head, and another took a bite out of her coat-sleeve and began to chew. 'Don't worry,' she said. 'The topiary is quite harmless, just a bit hungry.' A woman came hurrying down the steps of the Chase, staggering under the weight of an enormous bucket of dripping raw steaks, which she began to fling at the hedge-creatures. Daisy watched, saucer-eyed, as they snatched the bloody meat from the air, snarling happily.

'Lovely day, Commander,' called the hedge-feeder.

'Superb,' agreed Artemis breezily, marching Daisy and Indigo on down the avenue and towards the worn stone steps of the Chase. Crowds of people streamed in and out of the great double doors, chatting and joking as if they were on their way to a party. By the time Daisy was back in control of her legs, Artemis and Indigo were already halfway up the steps and she had to trot to catch up.

Chapter 16

They came into a grand entrance hall topped by a soaring glass dome. There were throngs of Botanists toting wheelbarrows across the airy atrium and hurrying up and down a sweeping staircase lined with grand oil portraits. The floor was made of pink and black marble in the pattern of a giant rose, and from the ceiling hung an enormous chandelier in the shape of a crescent moon, glittering with thousands of milk-white crystals and beaming with silver light. Someone was playing a grand piano that looked like a giant black butterfly, and the music made Daisy feel giddy and light-headed.

Indigo pinched her, and she came back to herself.

'Ouch!'

'Sorry,' he said. 'Green music is one of the Botanical arts. The instruments are carved from magical wood and sometimes there's a floral orchestra too. The effect can be a bit overwhelming if you're not used to it.'

'Are there others? Botanical arts, I mean?'

'Oh, dozens,' said Indigo cheerfully. 'To start with, cookery, bookery, perfume-making, Botanical couture, arboreal architecture, interpretative dance and floral jewellery.'

'Right.' Daisy touched the necklace at her throat.

Artemis smiled and shook her head. 'I still can't believe your mother didn't tell you about green magic. It's plain irresponsible.'

'Ma is VERY responsible,' said Daisy, stung. She chose to ignore, at this moment, a succession of memories to do with Ma climbing mountains without harnesses, trailing mafia bosses in disguise and eating chocolate spread directly from the jar with a spoon.

The memories made her miss Ma desperately.

Then she spotted a figure hurrying over, gold epaulettes glinting in the morning light.

'Morning, Captain Malarky,' called Artemis. His pitchfork was strapped across his back today, and his beard looked wilder than ever. He was also holding a large potted plant in his arms, which was spitting purple seeds into his face.

'Good afternoon, Commander,' he said, quelling the plant with a glare. 'Everything is in order. Though we – erm – had an escaped puma in the Green Study this morning. No idea how it got in from the Great Glasshouse, but it's on its way back as we speak, and no harm done except to the upholstery.'

'Excellent,' said Artemis. 'I never liked those cushions anyway. Hideous colours.' She winked at Daisy. 'Malarky is Captain of the Mallowmarshals and head of security at the Chase.'

He grinned at them. 'Glad to see you looking better – Daisy, was it? And young Podsnap – no ferrets with you today?'

'That was a one-time thing,' said Indigo evasively.

'Glad to hear it.'

Daisy couldn't help noticing that the potted plant, taking advantage of Malarky's distraction, was now manifesting an orange mould that smelled strongly of rotten eggs.

'While I've got you, Commander,' he went on in a hushed voice, apparently oblivious to the stench, 'we've had a delivery of minim moss – arrived early this morning. Shall I have it sent to the Seed Bank?'

'Ah, finally,' said Artemis. 'Yes, that would be marvellous.'

There was a sudden flurry at the entrance of the Chase and a blonde woman staggered in with an enormous pink suitcase in each hand. Malarky hurried forward to help, and Artemis strode forward, arms outstretched in welcome.

'Marigold Brightly. At last.'

Daisy thought the new arrival looked like something out of a fairy tale, with a heart-shaped face and golden Rapunzel-like hair that went down past her waist. She was wearing sapphire blue overalls cinched in with a flowering gardenia vine, so that the scent swirled through the hall like perfume. Only her grey eyes were out of place: big and smudged with tiredness.

'Come in, come in,' said Artemis delightedly, clasping

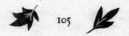

one of the woman's hands and drawing her into the hall. 'We were beginning to get worried. Daisy, this is Marigold Brightly, our brand-new Keeper of the Seed Bank. She comes to us from New York, replacing old Euphemia Grape, who left at the end of last term. Poor Euphemia,' she explained as Marigold Brightly put down her pink suitcases on the patterned marble floor, 'she was never the same after that venomous tulip attack last year – had to take early retirement.' Artemis shook her head sadly, then brightened. 'Still, we're delighted to have you, Marigold. How's your son, by the way? I heard he'd been unwell. Is he better now? Settling in well at Bloomquist?'

'Oh, yes,' said the blonde woman, passing a hand over her mouth. Her voice was sweet and scratchy, like honeycomb. 'Max is fine, and loving it so far. We were lucky they could find a place for him this term.'

'Wonderful,' said Artemis, beaming. 'I'll look forward to meeting him in the holidays. Captain Malarky here will show you to your suite, and I'll come and see you in the Seed Bank this afternoon so we can talk properly. We've just had some minim moss delivered: we can inspect it together.'

'Thank you, Commander,' said Brightly. 'I can't wait to get started.' Then she smiled at Daisy and Indigo, waved (just like a princess, thought Daisy) and followed Captain Malarky up the sweeping stairs of the Chase, her pink suitcases floating on a pulley of vines behind her.

You'll meet her properly next week,' said Artemis,

turning back to the children. 'She'll be teaching classes in Seed Craft when term begins. Speaking of which –' she glanced at Daisy's clothes – 'let's get you properly equipped.'

She sent Indigo back to the Roost, and took Daisy up the sweeping stone stairs to an enormous workroom dotted with palm trees, where a team of tailors were stitching away and sipping from cups of tea that were constantly being refilled by a teapot dangling at the end of a helpful grapevine. Artemis immediately disappeared to confer with the head tailor, and Daisy was left to look around at the bolts of shining fabric, hanks of soft wool and trays of buttons in the shape of mice and sparrows and pumpkins.

Gradually, Daisy became aware of an imperious voice floating towards her from the other side of a large palm tree.

'Really, my child,' said the voice, which (Daisy discovered by craning her neck) belonged to an elderly lady draped in a pearl-embroidered cape. 'Don't be so stubborn.' She was speaking (Daisy craned her neck further) to a girl around her own age, with a halo of dark hair and long eyelashes that bumped against the frames of her enormous spectacles. 'Ivy Helix is a charming girl, and by far the most suitable friend for you out of anyone here.'

'No thanks,' said the girl stubbornly. She was wearing a pair of faintly disreputable overalls with holes in the sleeves. Her brown elbows were very pointy, and her eyes were bright. 'She's horrible, Aunt Elspeth. She pushed Acorn into the lake last week and laughed.'

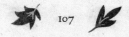

'Nonsense, child! All in the spirit of youthful fun, depend upon it. Ivy Helix comes from an old Mallowmarsh family, like ours. The Bellamys and the Helixes go back generations: all the way to the seventeenth century. You can't seriously mean you'd prefer to continue spending time with the Sparkler girl? And that horse-mad boy? You can do better than that. Although –' she surveyed the girl's overalls – 'if you persist in wearing those awful old clothes, I won't answer for the consequences. Now, if you'd agree to try on some nice taffeta and lace . . .'

Just then, Artemis reappeared with a tailor in tow, who used a floating vine to measure Daisy from head to toe, while an assistant held up different colours against her cheek. Half an hour later, she was staggering down the grand staircase in a brand-new pair of overalls, her arms heaped with soft cotton shirts embroidered with parakeets, dandelions and tiny red strawberries.

'And a trowel,' said Artemis, producing one from her belt and handing it to Daisy. 'Once you get the hang of things, we'll look at getting you one of your own.' Daisy felt an odd thrill at this, and stuck the trowel into the waistband of her new overalls. She was still smiling when they arrived back at the entrance hall, where someone was playing a jazzy tune on the big black piano. Then the notes faltered, and Daisy looked up to see a tall, gaunt man with narrowed eyes standing in the middle of the marble floor. He had a shock of bone-white hair, and his right hand was resting on the haunches of an enormous grey bloodhound, which growled menacingly, revealing a set of dripping yellow canines. As the man drew closer, the dog's nostrils flared, and then with a snarl it hurled itself across the marble floor – directly towards Daisy.

Chapter 17

Oh no oh no oh – Daisy barely had time to think, as a tonne of canine flesh and slavering teeth came hurtling towards her with the speed of a freight train. She had survived Craven – only to meet her fate in the form of a demon hound. She closed her eyes as the teeth came towards her and the great paws collided with her chest, knocking her to the floor. And then –

'Eugh!' The dog was licking her face, repeatedly and with a sort of delirious joy, wagging his tail like a puppy with a favourite new ball. Daisy struggled to sit up, soaked, heart still pounding as the dog licked her left ear with an expression of pure, blissful devotion. Napoleon was clinging to the top of her head like a Russian hat, every hair standing on end. Daisy laughed and then faltered as she looked up into the thunderous face of the dog's owner.

'Heel,' he barked. The dog stopped licking for a moment, as if it couldn't quite believe what it was hearing. 'HEEL, Brutus.' Brutus stood up and with a last, lingering look at Daisy, slunk back to his master. Clusters of Botanists had stopped in the hall to stare, while others whispered behind their hands.

Artemis laughed, eyes wide. 'I've never seen that before.

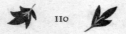

I thought Brutus was a dog without sentiment.'

'He is,' said the man, gritting his teeth. Brutus whimpered piteously, gazing at Daisy as if she was his long-lost love.

'Who is this girl?' asked the man, looking at Daisy with disgust.

She tried to wipe some of the drool off her face.

'Ah, how rude of me. This,' said Artemis, 'is Daisy, the daughter of Leila Thistledown, the Botanist who vanished last month in the Peruvian rainforest. Daisy arrived last night from the Greyside and I'm inviting her to stay on at Mallowmarsh until her mother is found. Daisy, this is Ferrus Sheldrake, the head of the Perilous Glasshouse.'

The man glared and yanked Brutus more closely to his side.

'So,' he said, looking thunderous, '*this* is the unaccompanied minor? The one without a grassport?'

'Indeed,' said Artemis sharply. 'Your point, Sheldrake?'

He scowled. 'My point, *Commander*, is that we can't trust her. She's an unlawful immigrant. For all we know, she could be a spy.'

Artemis looked exasperated. 'Ferrus, Daisy is not a spy. She's a girl who needs our help.'

'But—'

'Daisy is in danger in the Greyside,' said the commander, holding up a hand. 'We cannot in good conscience send her back.'

The air crackled with tension. Sheldrake's nostrils flared,

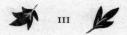

and when he turned back to Artemis, each word was deliberate. 'So be it, Commander. But –' he leant menacingly towards Daisy, his black gaze not leaving her face for a second – 'I'll have my eye on you, girl. I'll be making sure you abide by our rules.'

'Rules?' She fought the urge to step back.

'That's right.' He ticked them off on his fingers. 'No entering any of the glasshouses without express permission. No pilfering of seeds, leaves, petals or plant matter of any kind. And absolutely NO wandering around the pocket at night. Is that understood?'

Daisy nodded.

He stared at her for another moment, then turned on his heel and strode out of the Chase. Brutus trotted after him, snarling at everyone, but somehow managing to cast one last, longing look at Daisy.

'Well,' said Artemis, breaking the silence. Her blue eyes were almost mischievous. 'That was Sheldrake. My charming deputy.'

The piano started up again, breaking the tension. Someone laughed, and people began to mill once more across the hall, where Chef McGuffin had laid on pink lemonade and pyramids of wonderfully tasty cream puffs.

But as she walked with Artemis back to the Roost a little later, Daisy was left with a single image: the look of disdain in Sheldrake's sharp black eyes. *Unlawful immigrant*, he had called her. *Spy*. The words made her feel small as a gnat.

Chapter 18

Artemis disappeared upstairs as soon as they got back. 'To pack,' she said briskly. 'If I'm going to get to the Bureau tonight then there's no time to waste.'

Indigo was sitting at the kitchen table, looking disgustingly cheerful and digging into a waffle the size of his face.

'Owdigo?' he asked, through a huge mouthful.

'What?'

He swallowed, grinning. 'How'd it go? At the Chase?'

Miss Tufton was brewing tea at the stove, and she switched off the gramophone so she could hear all about it.

'That man!' she said, when Daisy had finished telling them about Sheldrake. 'He's paranoid, always has been.' The housekeeper stomped across the room, sharp nose just visible behind an enormous teapot. She looked even grumpier than usual, as if talking about Sheldrake made her bunions ache. 'A spy! What next? Ignore him, Daisy. He enjoys making people's lives a misery.'

'That's true,' said Indigo, who was feeding Jethro with seeds from his pocket. 'I wouldn't worry about it. He hates everyone. It's not personal.'

'So you believe me?' asked Daisy. 'You don't think I'm a

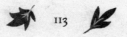

spy?' For some reason, the answer to this mattered a great deal.

'Of course I don't,' said Indigo firmly, and she felt something in her shoulders loosen. He had a smudge of butter on his smooth brown cheek, and a parakeet perched on his shoulder, which made him look like a cross between a pirate and a pastry chef.

There was a creak on the stairs and Daisy looked up to see Artemis thumping down with an old-fashioned suitcase in one hand. It was bound shut with a tough-looking vine.

'Wonderful,' she said, spotting a pile of cheese sandwiches on the table and taking one. 'I'll be lucky to get more than a stale biscuit where I'm going. Let's just say that the Bureau isn't renowned for its hospitality.'

Daisy leaned forward, and Napoleon pricked up his ears. 'Do you think it will work? Will they allow the search mission?'

'I think we have a good chance,' Artemis replied, spreading mustard energetically on her sandwich. 'As I said, Daisy, your story changes things. Speaking of which – is there anything more you can tell me about Craven before I go? Anything at all?'

'Ooh,' said Indigo. 'Was he horribly evil? With a sinister black cape, and eyes like pits of burning fire?'

'Well, no,' said Daisy. 'His eyes were green.' Indigo looked disappointed. 'And he always seemed, well . . . *nice*.'

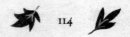

'Yeah, right,' he said, snorting. 'Until he tried to kidnap you.'

Daisy frowned. 'I mean, he was funny, and he liked toffees, and he always told these ridiculous stories. Like how once he'd interviewed a Highland sheep, or how he'd been chased five miles by an angry hippo in Ethiopia.' She remembered something else. 'Oh, and he had five moles on his wrist. I remember because they were in the shape of Cassiopeia: the constellation, I mean. Sort of like a stretched-out W.'

Artemis looked up sharply. 'His left wrist?'

'Yes, but—'

'You said he had green eyes? How old was he?' Artemis's voice was urgent.

Daisy frowned, considering. 'About forty, I think. And he had a way of smiling, you know, with one side of his mouth.'

Miss Tufton dropped the teapot she was holding, and it smashed all over the floor so that Napoleon leapt up, hissing, as hot tea splashed his fur. 'Cardew,' whispered the housekeeper. 'It must be.'

'What?' said Daisy, looking between her and Artemis, as Napoleon vaulted into her arms. 'Who is Cardew?'

But Miss Tufton was now loudly sweeping up the shards of the teapot, and Artemis was draining her mug and glancing at the clock above the door.

'Goodness, is that the time? I'm going to be late.'

Daisy stared at the clock. The minute hand was a spiky

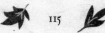

thistle and the hour hand was a pointy tulip, which turned from sky blue to cheery pink as the clock chimed the half hour.

Artemis, throwing on a startlingly purple coat over her lemon-yellow overalls, was already dashing down the spiral stairs. 'Behave yourselves,' she called over her shoulder. 'Miss Tufton will look after you till I'm back!' And then she was gone.

'That was weird,' said Daisy, glancing at Indigo. 'Miss Tufton, who's Card—'

But Miss Tufton had already vanished upstairs, muttering something about pruning back one of the wardrobes.

'Yeah,' said Indigo slowly. 'That was definitely weird. Cardew was – well. I've definitely heard of him. I mean, everyone has.'

'What?' Daisy's eyes went wide. 'Tell me!'

Indigo looked uncomfortable. 'He's . . . well, Cardew was a murderer.'

'Was?'

Indigo nodded. 'He killed three Botanists – about fifteen years ago, I think. Then he died himself. I'm not sure how, though. No one really likes talking about it.'

'Well, maybe he's alive,' said Daisy. 'Maybe he's out in the Greyside, working at the *High Herald* – calling himself Craven. And if that's true . . . then he's mixed up in Ma's disappearance.'

Indigo looked bright-eyed. 'This is a clue, isn't it? It could

help us find the missing Botanists!' He leapt up, glancing at the tulip clock, which was inching towards five o'clock. 'You need to come with me. There are two people you should meet. Come on, let's go!'

'Go where?'

But Indigo was already hurrying down the spiral staircase that wound through the trunk of the Roost, and out into the rambling front garden. It was filled with white foxgloves sparkling with frost, and little winding paths dashing off in different directions through the long grass. There was also a disreputable-looking goat cropping the grass next to a large paddock.

'Meet Silas,' said Indigo, as the goat spat at them.

Daisy leapt back and straight into the path of a trio of chickens heading towards a large hen coop. 'Watch out!' he cried, but it was too late: one of the hens had already opened its beak and was breathing out a dragonish plume of blue-tinged fire that ignited the end of Daisy's hair. She shrieked and plunged her braid into a nearby water trough, while Napoleon spat at them furiously.

'You wanted to introduce me to a goat?' said Daisy, as she straightened up, gasping. 'And a fire-breathing *chicken*?'

'No! Well, yes – but that's not actually who I meant.' Indigo murmured something to the hens and managed to swipe three eggs from the coop, which he set aside carefully for Miss Tufton. 'Salt hens,' he said, by way of explanation. 'Nasty tempers.'

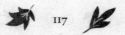

By the time Daisy had finished wiping water from her eyes and checking her new overalls for scorch marks, Indigo was already walking along the fence of the adjoining paddock and speaking to four huge horses on the other side, producing apples for them with the panache of a stage conjurer. He looked blissfully happy, wiping horse spit off his face as Napoleon twined around his ankles and three parakeets flew joyfully around his head. A hedgehog had waddled out of the long grass and was rubbing itself against his shoe like an enthusiastic bristle brush.

Daisy felt something fall into place. 'You're good with animals,' she said. 'Really good.'

Indigo shrugged, all hunched shoulders and winged eyebrows and charm. 'It's just a knack. Like juggling. Or licking your elbow.' Before Daisy could say anything, he turned and ran out through the apple orchard towards the shore of the lake, shouting over his shoulder. 'Hurry up! It's almost five o'clock.'

Daisy ran after him, scooping Napoleon onto her shoulder. 'What happens at five o'clock?' she puffed as Indigo commandeered the nearest lilypaddle, forcing her to leap after him. 'Who are we meeting?'

'Patience, Thistledown,' said Indigo. 'Everything will be revealed.'

Daisy humphed and sat back in the lilypaddle, deciding to give him the benefit of the doubt. 'I suppose this all seems normal to you,' she said, trailing her fingers in the

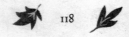

water and then remembering the alligator and removing them swiftly. 'How long have you lived here?'

'Oh, for years,' said Indigo as they swung round the fountain in the middle of the lake. 'I was born in Colombia – at Silvestrano, the largest pocket in the South American Greenwild. But Papa and Dad moved here when I was five.' He paused to wave at a Botanist passing on a neighbouring lilypaddle. 'They're away at the moment researching coral, but they'll be back next month. I'm still living at our house, over there –' he pointed towards a cluster of treehouses at the edge of the woods – 'but the commander said she'd keep an eye on me while they're gone, and I said I'd keep an eye on Miss Tufton's cooking. So it works out for everyone.'

Daisy laughed as they leapt off the lilypaddle and onto the far shore. 'Ma is Persian – from Iran. We've always travelled around a lot because she's a journalist.'

'So how come you have an English name?' asked Indigo, watching their lilypaddle skim back across the lake. 'If your mother's Persian, I mean.'

'Ma says I was named after my English grandmother – on my dad's side. My real name is Diana, but apparently I couldn't pronounce it when I was little, so it became Daisy instead.'

'It's a good name.' Indigo began leading them across the green expanse of the grounds, away from Chiveley Chase. '*Day's eye* – like the sun. And at least you got to travel. I've never even left the Greenwild.'

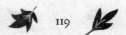

Daisy stroked Napoleon absently as they walked, thinking of the light in Ma's eyes each time she announced their next destination. *Goa! Caracas! Cairo! Lagos!*

It had been wonderful, but . . . 'Growing up in one place must be great,' she said. 'Growing up *here*.' She gestured around at the grounds, taking in the great bulk of the Chase behind them, its windows winking softly in the evening light. She felt a huge tug of longing, immediately followed by a rush of guilt. She'd spent her life feeling like a potted plant constantly being moved from place to place, never allowed to put down roots. What would it be like, to belong somewhere like this? To have a home here?

'Trust me,' said Indigo. His eyebrows were very fierce. 'You can have enough of one place. I can't wait to be out in the Greyside. Saving animals. Making a difference.'

Daisy frowned, thinking of Ma in Peru: searching for a story that had turned out to be just as dangerous as she had feared. She brushed her fingers along the top of a swathe of long, tufty purple grass, which sneezed. 'Bless you,' said Daisy absently. Then she jumped.

'Snodgrass,' said Indigo. He laughed, looking at her face. 'I keep forgetting you don't know this stuff. I've never met anyone who didn't grow up in the Greenwild.'

'How big is it?' asked Daisy, rubbing her nose. 'The Greenwild, I mean?'

'As big as the Greyside,' said Indigo carelessly. 'The pockets are tucked in everywhere – hundreds of them, all

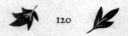

over the world, hidden just like the one in Kew Gardens.'

'Wait,' said Daisy, suddenly thinking of something. 'Do you have to come from a Botanist family to have green magic?'

Indigo shrugged. 'Most do – but some come from Greyside families. People who love nature so much it's in their bones: they usually find their way here, one way or another.' Then he grinned. 'Come on, you haven't seen anything yet! Race you to the trees!' He took off running, and Daisy sprinted after him, shouting indignantly.

They both stopped at the edge of the woods, panting and laughing.

'Beat you!' said Indigo.

'Not true! You had a head start.' But Daisy was grinning.

Indigo grinned back, revealing one slightly crooked tooth. Then a bell began to toll the hour across the grounds: five slow chimes.

'Five o'clock!' said Indigo, heading into the woods. 'Come on – it's time!'

Chapter 19

Entering the woods was like diving underwater. The trees swayed gently, and everything was dim and green and dappled. Jethro, who had been travelling on Indigo's head, launched himself into the air and swooped gleefully through the trees. Napoleon chased after him, meowing furiously.

Indigo held a finger to his lips as they passed a tall elm tree with a cabin perched at the top of it. 'Sheldrake's house,' he said darkly as they passed. 'He's lived in the Mallow Woods for years. Very antisocial.'

A shadowy pine forest stretched out to one side, deepening into an expanse of mysterious-looking slopes that generated mist in great sighing puffs. 'Aaaahhhh,' went the pines. 'Aaaahhh, aaaaahhh.' The pale mist rose upwards in gusts, veiling the treetops.

'The Sighing Forest,' said Indigo, waving uneasily. 'No one's ever managed to reach the end of it. If you go too far in you start thinking of all your regrets. Then you forget your own name and start sighing, and before you know it, you're the newest tree in the Sighing Forest.' He shrugged. 'It's a very bad idea to go in there alone. I tried once and almost didn't come out.'

Daisy shivered, and Indigo hurried them on.

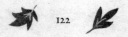

A few minutes later they came out of the trees and into a bright clearing, where a small, shabby glasshouse stood, overgrown with ivy and surrounded by purple crocuses. It was more of a glorified shed than anything else, but it had a pattern of diamond-shaped panes in red and blue and green that made it look like a harlequin's house: jaunty and cosy all at once.

And from within it came tumbling two excited figures in a hubbub of noise. A familiar-looking tall and skinny Black girl led the way, holding her spectacles to stop them falling off. And after her came a tiny round girl with freckly-pale cheeks and bright red hair, squeaking with excitement.

'You brought her! You brought her!'

'Indigo!' the taller girl cried. 'Come on, come inside.'

Five minutes later they were sitting around a rickety wooden table inside the shed, and Indigo was conducting formal introductions.

'This,' said Indigo, indicating the skinny girl with huge spectacles, 'is the Professor. We call her that because she's a child genius. She speaks twelve languages, including Latin and Greek.'

The Professor wrinkled her nose, and Daisy realized why she seemed familiar. She was the Bellamy girl from the tailoring workshop at Chiveley Chase: the one with the eyelashes and the bossy aunt. Her overalls, thought Daisy, were very fine, but clearly her aunt had lost the fight over ordering new ones – these had large holes in the elbows: rather in the manner of a grand aristocrat who hardly noticed what they wore.

'Welcome,' said the girl, crinkling her eyes at Daisy. She had an extraordinary smile like a flashbulb, and it lit up her whole face. 'We've been hoping to meet you practically since you arrived.' She was toasting and buttering teacakes on a camp stove in the corner, and began passing them around as she spoke.

'And this is Acorn,' said Indigo, taking a teacake

and gesturing with it towards the pint-sized girl with flaming red hair. She squeaked almost inaudibly when she was introduced, and put her elbow in the butter dish. Daisy could see that she was a few years younger than the Professor, and very excitable, with a snub nose and freckles that made her face look funny and nice. In fact, her face was almost more freckle than anything else, as if someone had painted a galaxy of fawn-coloured stars across her pale round cheeks and around her greenish eyes.

'Ahem,' said the Professor. 'Now we've all been introduced, I call this meeting of the Five O'Clock Club to order.'

She pulled out a battered logbook and declaimed as she wrote. 'Present: Bellamy, Professor (Chair, Secretary and Resident Genius); Podsnap, Indigo (Deputy Chair); Sparkler, Acorn (Treasurer and Junior Member); Alecky (Resident Tortoise).' She nodded towards a wizened creature at their feet, drowsing inside his emerald-green shell.

'Plus Thistledown, Daisy: New Member. Oh, and felines: one.'

Napoleon meowed loudly and leapt into Daisy's lap.

'And one caterpillar!' said Acorn. She pulled a matchbox from her pocket and opened it to reveal an incredibly fat and hairy brown caterpillar. She glanced up at the others.

'What?' she said defensively. 'Why can't Albert be part of the club?'

'We've had this conversation before,' said the Professor,

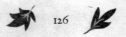

126

massaging her forehead. 'Caterpillars simply don't count as—'

But Daisy caught Acorn's wounded look, and hurriedly asked the first question that came into her head. 'Why is it called the Five O'Clock Club?'

'Ah,' said the Professor, who was now handing around cups of sweet tea brewed on the camp stove. 'That's because we meet at five o'clock every afternoon. The shed is where we exchange information.'

Acorn gave a tiny smile. 'Plus there are always snacks.' She nudged a morsel of teacake in Albert's direction.

'We pride ourselves on it,' added the Professor. With the tea distributed, she was now kneeling on the flagstone floor next to a teetering pile of books, watering a purple-leafed tree in a large ceramic pot.

'Wait,' said Daisy, looking at the liquid showering from the watering can. 'Is that *milk*?'

The Professor nodded, clearly pleased. 'It's a milk-chocolate tree. The more milk you add, the lighter the chocolate grows.' She reached up and picked a small chocolate drop from the nearest branch. It was about the shape and size of a blueberry. 'Try one.'

Daisy nibbled tentatively. 'Oh,' she said, and the Professor smiled. The taste of it was astonishing: purely chocolatey, rich and creamy and sweet.

'It's a hybrid species,' Indigo was explaining. 'The Professor – the Prof – created it by accident last year. Of

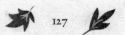

127

course, we're not *supposed* to be doing complex Botany yet, so that's why we keep it hidden here in the shed.' He grabbed five chocolate drops, and then a sixth for good measure. 'The best thing is that as long as we keep on watering – or milking – it, the chocolate keeps growing back.' He sighed blissfully. 'Free, unlimited chocolate! Mallowmarsh's best-kept secret.'

'That's not why you're here, though,' said the Prof, coming back to the table. She looked at him shrewdly. 'You can't sit still, which means you're worried about something. What's going on?'

Indigo stopped jiggling his leg, looking cross. 'I wish you wouldn't do that. I was *about* to tell you. In fact, I was just building up to it.'

Alecky emerged from his shell and blinked his shiny tortoise eyes. The Prof adjusted her spectacles and Acorn looked up from stroking Napoleon, who had migrated to her lap and was trying to climb her left pigtail.

Indigo cleared his throat. 'It's like this. Daisy's mother disappeared in the Greyside – in the Amazon – last month. And we think we might know who's responsible. And that means—'

'We might be able to find the others!' said the Prof, her glasses almost falling off her nose.

Chapter 20

The Prof turned to Daisy. 'The Five O'Clock Club have been investigating since last year – ever since my grandfather disappeared.' Her forehead puckered up and she looked suddenly very crumpled and tired. 'Grandfather is retired. Or he was supposed to be. He's not strong enough to go out into the Greyside like he used to. But with so many people missing he said it was his duty to go.' She swallowed, eyes bright with misery. 'He vanished along with two Canadian Botanists somewhere in the Chilean rainforest in the last week of November. No one has heard anything from them since.'

'Nothing at all?'

'Nothing,' said the Prof, shaking her head. 'Aunt Elspeth is convinced he's dead.'

'Oh,' said Daisy. 'Is that the woman you were with at Chiveley Chase yesterday?' She flushed, realizing she'd given herself away. 'Sorry, I didn't mean to overhear – she was quite . . . loud.'

'Yes,' said the Prof, looking mortified. 'That was my aunt: the biggest snob in the Greenwild. She lives at Bogbounty – the oldest pocket in Scotland – but she came to "take care" of me after Grandfather went missing.' She glanced at

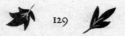

Daisy. 'He brought me up after my parents died. So you see I've *got* to find him, or I'll be stuck with Aunt Elspeth forever.' She tried to make this last bit sound like a joke, but it didn't quite work. She cleared her throat. 'Anyway. Whoever took Grandfather left no trace, and we've run out of clues to follow. Until now.'

Indigo nodded. 'Go on, Daisy. Tell them what you told the commander.'

The others stared at her as she recounted her story for the second time. Patterns of rose, amber and blue light filtered through the glass and onto their faces, illuminating Indigo's winged eyebrows and Acorn's astonished green eyes. The Prof was looking at Daisy fiercely, as if each word she spoke was a lifeline.

'Is that it?' she asked. Her gaze was piercing. 'You haven't forgotten anything?'

'No. I mean, yes, that's all.' Daisy blushed, uncomfortably aware that, once again, she'd left out any mention of the paperweight. The Prof nodded slowly, her dark hair like a halo round her head. 'Okay, then. It comes down to this: Craven, the man who probably kidnapped your mother, might actually be called Cardew: a convicted murderer who's supposed to be dead.'

Daisy nodded.

'But this is brilliant!' said the Prof, leaping to her feet. 'This is wonderful news!' She saw Daisy's face and sat back down. 'I mean, not good news for the missing Botanists,

obviously – but good news for our investigation. We finally have a lead.'

She frowned in concentration. 'I'm trying to remember everything I've heard about Cardew. Nobody really talks about him much. I mean, not in front of us, anyway. "*Not suitable for the children,*"' she said, imitating Aunt Elspeth's haughty voice. 'So I don't know who he killed, or how he's supposed to have died.'

'Well,' said Daisy, suddenly longing for the internet. 'We need to find out.'

'Agreed,' said the Prof, scribbling this down at the top of a list headed *The Five O'Clock Club Take Action*. 'What else?'

Daisy frowned. 'Maybe we can find out more about the other people who have disappeared, like what they were doing and when they vanished – to see if there's a pattern.'

'Yes.' The Prof nodded, making a note. 'We've already made a start on that.' She pulled a stack of paper out of an enormous folder and shoved it in Daisy's direction.

Daisy scanned through the pages, looking at the names:

Dianara Speedwell – last seen 16 August, Marau
   Peninsula, Brazil, near butterfly sanctuary.
Archibald Peagrim and Melanda Beechwise – last
   seen 19 September, Gran Chaco, Paraguay, near
   indigenous reserve.
Adalia Alcarraz – last seen 27 September, near

Serra dos Órgãos National Park, Brazil.

Felicity Wallop — last seen 2 October, Santa Cruz de la Sierra, Bolivia, near nature reserve.

Pandora and Wulliam Dingledrop — last seen 4 November, outside Buenos Aires, Argentina.

Arabilly Snifton, Milla Honeydew and Querkus Bellamy — last seen 28 November, near Los Flamencos reserve, Chile.

'Querkus Bellamy?' asked Daisy, recognizing the Prof's surname. 'Your grandfather?'

The Prof nodded grimly.

'And no one knows who's behind the disappearances?'

Acorn glanced up timidly. 'I heard one of the gardeners saying it was the Grim Reapers.'

'But that's ridiculous!' cried the Prof. 'Everyone knows they're just a story.'

Acorn blushed, and they turned back to the folder. 'So,' said Daisy, thinking furiously, 'we don't know who's behind the disappearances, but there are at least ten names here. And all of them have gone missing around the Amazon . . . or near other places that need protecting.' She frowned. 'I don't know much about how the Greenwild works, but isn't it odd that the Bureau aren't doing more to investigate?'

Acorn looked wide-eyed, but the Prof nodded briskly. 'That's exactly what I think too. We should try to find out

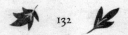

if they're covering something up.' She added a third bullet point to the list.

Then she allowed her pencil to travel back to the first thing she'd written. *Find out more about Cardew*, it read. 'Let's start here,' she said. 'There's bound to be something about him in the library.'

Chapter 21

Three hours later, however, it was clear that there was nothing at all about a man called Cardew in the whole of the vast Mallowmarsh library, where scores of towering oak trees held up a monumental roof and spread their branches over thousands upon thousands of shelves bursting with books of every shape and size. They had spent hours searching the indexes and scouring the stacks and been forced to give up shortly before midnight, when Miss Tufton had come stomping into the Chase with a loudhailer, embarrassing them all and turfing them into their beds.

Daisy lay in her room that night staring up at the stars through the skylight in her turret room. Knowing that Ma had been part of this magical world – and had kept it hidden from her – made her both sadder and angrier than she'd ever been before.

'It's different here,' she told Napoleon, who was shredding a corner of the quilt with his claws. 'And I don't just mean the magic.' She thought of the Five O'Clock Club and the way they'd welcomed her into their shed and their lives.

She found herself remembering the summer when she was nine, and she and Ma had lived in a sunshine-coloured house in Budapest. On their second day, the girl next door had taken one look at Daisy, curled up in the corner reading *Prince Caspian* for the seventh time, and said, 'I'm Anna. Come on. Let's go out.'

Anna was the leader of a band of kids who were waging determined war against the rival gang from the neighbouring district, and she made Daisy feel immediately welcome. They ran wild all day in the hot sun, planning ambushes, laying booby traps and slingshotting the enemy with balls of twisted paper and spit. Anna was a master strategist, a backstreet explorer, an extravagant liar. She told outrageous stories about gangsters and legendary treasure buried in the sewers, and involved Daisy in an intense, summer-long challenge that involved filching small coins from the pockets of hapless tourists. She was the one who taught Daisy to pick pockets with the ease of the Artful Dodger, to spit with the accuracy of an Olympic champion and to say at least thirty-six extremely rude things in Hungarian. She was a sister-in-arms: a friend.

Usually, Daisy lived in a constant state of alert for signs that the next move was coming. The increasingly loud clatter of laptop keys late into the night as Ma reached the end of a story, the endless cups of coffee, the sighs and screwed-up bits of paper, then the phone calls back and forth to London as Ma argued about the word count and whether a certain sentence deserved to stay in or out. Then Daisy knew it was about to happen again: the packing, the moving, the hurried goodbyes, and the odd relief in her mother's eyes as she slipped free once more, twisting like a gleaming fish from a net, back out into the wide sea of the world beyond.

But this time Daisy had let down her guard. She had been too busy with her new friend to pay attention. It had been two months, longer than they'd stayed anywhere else, and she had missed the signs.

'We're going tomorrow,' Ma had said casually after dinner one night.

'Going where?' said Daisy, distracted. She was worrying about whether to wear her new red shoes that weekend, or if they'd get ruined in the scavenger hunt Anna was masterminding.

'Mexico City,' said Ma, who was already hauling her suitcase out of the wardrobe. 'A new story. A new adventure.'

There was a long silence. 'We can't leave,' said Daisy. 'We just can't.'

But they could, and they did.

For the first time in her life, she had rebelled. She had sulked and shouted. But it was no use.

'She's your mother,' Anna said sadly. 'You have to go.'

Daisy didn't talk to Ma for a week after they left Budapest. She had tried to stay in touch with Anna, sending emails and long letters – but it wasn't the same. After a few months, Anna stopped replying. That was when Daisy decided that it was easier not to make any more friends. It

136

wasn't worth it when all you'd do was leave in the end.

Now she thought of Indigo and Acorn and the Professor, and wondered how long she would be in Mallowmarsh. Being treated as part of the Five O'Clock Club had been wonderful: like fizzy lemonade for the soul. But she couldn't lose sight of the fact that it was temporary. It had to be. Because she was going to find Ma, and then she was going to go back to the Greyside and the life she had left behind.

Carefully, she took the dandelion paperweight out of her pocket and placed it on top of the sheets, watching as it cast nets of silver light around the room.

Ma had told her to keep it secret. Craven had wanted it enough to chase her across London. But why? Surely not just because it was pretty and glowed in the dark. She couldn't see Craven sprinting across Kew Gardens for the sake of a glorified torch.

Suddenly, she remembered the shrivelled old seed in its red envelope. 'For use in emergencies,' Ma's note had said. She hadn't thought about it since leaving Wykhurst. But if green magic was real, then maybe –

'Maybe we should plant it,' she told Napoleon, rummaging in her bag and pulling it out. He meowed from the pillow, as if he knew what she was planning was a very bad idea. 'I have to,' she told him, yanking a coat over her nightgown and pushing the paperweight into the left pocket. 'If Ma going missing isn't an emergency, then I don't know what is.'

Moments later, she was padding down the spiral stairs and into the dark, empty kitchen, with Napoleon perched reluctantly on her shoulder. The larder tree rustled as she paused by the front door. If she was caught breaking the rules, Sheldrake would be furious. He might even throw her out of Mallowmarsh.

She hesitated for a moment longer, then slipped into the night.

Outside, the tall grass glittered with frost, and the sky was a wilderness of stars. An owl hooted like a sentinel from the high branches of the orchard, and the cold air smelled like peppermint.

Daisy slipped round the back of the Roost and into the meadow, where the giant dandelions glowed like velvety moons. She took out the dandelion paperweight and held it up: a moon in miniature.

'Yes,' she said to Napoleon. 'They really are the same.'

Next, she rummaged for the seed, glancing around for a good spot to plant it. But before she could pick one, she heard something unexpected.

A sobbing, stuttering noise on the night air.

She looked around, confused. The noise seemed to be coming from behind the solid ivy-covered wall that ran along one side of the meadow. She hurried over. It was darker here in the shadow of the wall, and she glanced behind her to check no one was watching before lifting the paperweight higher and shining it over the crumbling brickwork.

There! There was a wooden door in the wall, low and half hidden in ivy. The paint shone, the hinges gleamed, and there was a polished bronze doorknob in the shape of a pomegranate. Daisy glanced at Napoleon, who brushed against her ankles and meowed.

She pushed at the handle. For a moment it seemed to stick, as if it was much older than it looked. Then it clicked softly and turned beneath her hand.

Chapter 22

'Wow,' breathed Daisy. Napoleon's eyes were wide.

They were standing at the entrance to an overgrown garden. Cascades of white roses tumbled around the high walls, and the moonlight cast the scene in a vivid crosshatching of black trees and rippling silver grass. There was a sweep of lavender to her left, leading down to the shores of a silver pond that caught the moon in its centre like a pirate coin. The place felt delicious and full of promise.

On the other side of the door, it had been a frozen winter night, but here in the garden it was rich, full summer with the smell of night-blooming jasmine on the warm air and the stars spilled like glitter across the sky. She pulled off her coat and let it drop, the red envelope half falling out of her pocket and onto the grass.

There was a beat of silence, and then she heard it again: an odd, stifled sound: a clenched fist of a sob. As Daisy stepped forward, she saw a boy sitting in the crook of an apple tree, one leg looped around the trunk, and one hand picking ruthlessly at a loose piece of bark.

Daisy glanced at him quickly and then looked away. This was a very private sort of crying, and she knew instinctively that he had come here to do it without being heard. She turned her back, then stepped deliberately on a large twig, which cracked like a shot through the silence of the garden. The boy looked up, startled, and almost fell out of the tree. Daisy saw him scrub a hand angrily across his eyes before calling, 'Who's there?'

Daisy stepped out of the shadows, shivering as she saw the shining apples on the glowing branches.

It was the tree she'd dreamed of at Wykhurst.

'Oh,' said the boy, sounding uncertain now. 'Who are you?' He looked down at her. 'How did you get in here? No one comes here except *me*.'

Daisy stepped closer and looked up at the boy's uncertain face. His hair was pale and standing on end like a dandelion, and his eyes were dark smudges above his high, slanting cheekbones. He looked about her age, although it was hard to tell in the moonlight. He was very thin and wore a pair of corduroy shorts that showed his knobbly knees.

'I'm Daisy,' she said. 'Who are you?'

'I'm Hal.' The boy placed a pair of glasses on his nose and peered at her through the smudged lenses. Daisy saw that they were broken and had been stuck back together with a bundle of sticky vines.

'You don't live in Mallowmarsh,' he said. 'I'd know if you did.'

'I've only just arrived. From the Greyside, I mean. I ran away from school to look for my mother . . . and somehow I ended up here.'

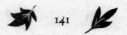

141

'Where is she, then, your mother?' asked the boy. He looked curious now, leaning down from his branch, distracted from whatever it was that had made him cry.

'I don't know, exactly,' Daisy answered.

'You don't know much,' said the boy, dismissive again.

'Well, neither do you,' said Daisy, stung, and feeling at a disadvantage standing on the ground while he sat loftily up in his tree. 'It's none of your business anyway.'

She turned away, indignant and suddenly very tired. She clearly wasn't wanted here.

'Wait. I'm sorry.' Hal's voice came from behind her, and she heard him scramble to the ground. 'My father says I'm stupid, and he's probably right.'

'Oh,' said Daisy. It felt important not to react to this.

'He can't stand me,' said Hal. 'He thinks I'll never be a good explorer.' His voice was unsteady, and he flopped down onto the grass with his arms spread wide, as if making a snow angel out of moonlight.

Daisy joined him, and they gazed upwards in silence while she tried to think of what to say. The grass was cool and slightly damp with dew, and the stars seemed closer than ever, like low-strung diamonds in a great necklace of light.

'Once,' she said, 'I was with Ma in the desert. We were stargazing. She told me how nomads navigated by using the stars, just like sailors at sea.' Daisy remembered sitting with Ma next to their campfire and gazing up at stars so thickly

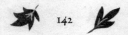

spattered across the sky that they looked like bright streams of silver.

'The stars will always show you the way,' Ma had said, 'if you know how to read them. Look up, and you'll find yourself.'

Daisy felt a tear trickle across her cheek and into her ear.

'The North Star,' she managed to say, pointing. 'And there's Orion's Belt, and the Plough.'

'That's *Persephone's* Belt,' said Hal, as if she'd just told him that the apples on the tree above them were actually tennis balls. 'Gosh, you really ARE ignorant.'

Daisy glared at him.

'All right, all right.' He rolled his eyes. 'No reason why you should know, if you've only just arrived.' He pointed. 'That's the Little Spade, that one's the Parakeet, and over there's the Great Marigold. I've never seen the stars in the Greyside . . . but one day I will, if I become an explorer. I'm going to see *everything*.' He glanced sideways at her. 'Have you really been to the desert in the Greyside? Where? Tell me . . .'

And Daisy found herself describing the contours of sand and the wind-shaped canyons, the shimmering heat and how she'd almost had her fingers bitten off by Ma's bad-tempered camel.

Hal's profile was stony, but something about his stillness made Daisy think he was listening very hard indeed. She remembered how Ma had challenged her to a camel race and charged across the desert shrieking like a madwoman, and felt a lump rise in her throat.

Noticing her silence, Hal turned his head to look at her.

'I don't know where she's gone,' she whispered. It felt terrifying to admit out loud.

'You'll find her.'

'How do you know?' she said.

'I can tell from the way you talk about her. You'll find her.' He sounded impatient, as if she was being stupid. Then he sneezed.

'Hayfever,' he said, wheezing slightly. 'It's like the universe is playing a big joke on me. A Botanist with hayfever! Hilarious.'

'Oh, stop feeling sorry for yourself,' said Daisy. 'You'll probably grow out of it.'

Hal harrumphed and sat up to blow his nose loudly on a filthy handkerchief.

Daisy plucked a spear-shaped leaf from the ground and closed her eyes. Hal was annoying, and yet something about him felt familiar. Even his sneeze sounded like something she'd heard before.

'What did you mean, when you said no one except you comes here?'

Hal ran his fingers through the grass beside him. 'Haven't you ever wanted somewhere that's just yours? Somewhere you can be alone?'

Daisy flushed self-consciously. 'Sorry,' she said. 'I can leave if you'd like.'

144

Hal grunted, and his next words were mumbled. 'It's fine. Just don't tell anyone else about this place, okay?'

'I promise,' said Daisy quietly. She felt the grass warm beneath her back and watched the stars wheeling above her. She couldn't say how much time passed before she heard, from somewhere far away, a bell tolling: six slow peals that rang across the garden.

'It's late,' she said, scrambling to her feet. 'Or early, I'm not sure which. I'd better go.'

'Will you come back?' Hal sounded prickly, as if he wanted her to know he didn't care.

'Yes,' she said carefully, picking up her coat. 'I will.'

Outside, dawn was just breaking above the meadow and the giant dandelions were wreathed in misty gold, like ghostly pompoms. She turned to creep back to the Roost, then froze.

There, in the distance, was a tall, rangy figure with white hair and an enormous hound padding by his side.

Sheldrake.

Daisy shrank back into the shadows, heart pounding like a drum. Napoleon was tucked into the front of her jacket and she could see his fur prickling on high alert as his chest rose and fell. She waited for a long time after Sheldrake had vanished round the lake before her feet were steady enough to take her back to the Roost.

Chapter 23

When Daisy finally got up the next morning, she thought her yawn might swallow her face. She'd had barely more than a wink of sleep after getting back to bed, where she'd lain thinking about Hal and the hidden garden, and wondering where Sheldrake had been going at that unsociable hour. He had looked almost *furtive*.

She was about to head downstairs for breakfast when she remembered the seed. She'd been interrupted last night before she'd had a chance to plant it.

Her coat was on the chair, and she turned out first one pocket, then the other. The crimson envelope was there, but –

'No, no, no,' she muttered, remembering the way she'd tossed down her coat under the apple tree, carelessly enough for anything to fall out. 'Please, no!' But it was no use.

The seed was gone.

'Someone called Hal?' said the Prof that afternoon in the shed. 'Around our age?' She wrinkled her nose in thought. 'There's no one at Mallowmarsh with a name like that. There *is* a boy called Harry, but he's about sixteen, I think, and he's away at Bloomquist.' She squinted at Daisy.

'Where did you say you met him?'

'Oh,' said Daisy, conscious of her promise not to tell anyone about the hidden garden. 'Outside the Roost last night.' It wasn't exactly a lie.

Indigo frowned. 'Maybe he's a visitor?'

'No,' said the Prof, shaking her head. 'New arrivals have to come through the Mallow gate. We would have heard if a visiting Botanist had brought a child with them.'

'Mmm.' Daisy chewed her lip. She was sure that wasn't it. Hal had spoken as if he'd lived in Mallowmarsh all his life.

Daisy half expected the door to have disappeared when she went back that night, but it was waiting quietly for her in the crumbling stone wall, the doorknob glinting softly in the moonlight. The bottom of the door swished over the long grass, and then she was inside, where the garden was wilder than ever, swarmed with rambling roses, wildflowers and weeds. Hal was crouched in the dirt, yanking a thorny vine from the ground and swearing under his breath. Daisy shrugged off her coat – like before, the air here was summer-warm, melting frost off her hood – and hurried forward to help.

'You came back!' He beamed hugely, and Daisy smiled at him before she could stop herself.

'I said I would, didn't I?'

Hal gave a last yank and the weed finally came free with

a puff of green dust that made him sneeze. He set it aside and tried to stroke Napoleon, who spat at him.

Hal cleared his throat. He was trying not to look pleased, but his cheeks were slightly pink. Something had shifted since last night, as if she'd proved something important by returning.

'So, you live here, right?' she asked, trying to sound casual. 'In Mallowmarsh, I mean.'

'Yep,' said Hal, smearing a bit of dirt across one blond eyebrow.

'But you don't know anyone called the Prof? Or Indigo? Or Acorn?'

Hal snorted and shook his head. 'What kind of names are those?' Daisy scowled at him, and he lifted his hands apologetically. 'There are probably lots of people I don't know. I've got a terrible memory for names. Now, can we talk about something more interesting?'

'Okay.' Daisy shrugged. 'Actually, I dropped something here yesterday – a seed. Right around there, I think,' she said, pointing to the overgrown tangle near the apple tree. 'Will you help me look?'

Hal sighed, but didn't argue. Half an hour later, though, it was clear that the seed was well and truly lost. Daisy's view of the garden went suddenly watery and she cursed herself.

Whatever Ma had meant for her to do with the seed, her chance was gone.

Somehow, Hal knew not to ask any questions. Instead, he tossed her a pair of gloves and turned back to his work. 'I've been clearing these nettlespurs,' he said. 'They're choking out everything else. There's a whole sapling buried under here.'

Daisy blew her nose inelegantly on a leaf (this was messier than she expected), and shuffled on her knees to join him.

'You've got to yank them like this,' said Hal, demonstrating. 'Sort of at an angle. Yes, like that.'

Slowly, the tangles came away, revealing the small sapling Hal had spotted. It was brand new and spindly, with a single webbed leaf. Daisy smiled, wiped her cheek roughly, and kept going.

She would have spent more time wondering about the mystery of the boy in the garden – but term finally started the next day, and soon she barely had time to think about anything else.

'What if I can't do magic?' she asked Miss Tufton that first morning. She'd spent an hour the previous day staring at one of the vines in the kitchen, willing it to move. Nothing had happened, and she was starting to wonder.

'You'll be fine,' said Miss Tufton, shoving a stack of hot buttered toast into Daisy's hands and chivvying her towards the stairs.

'But—' Daisy tried to protest, but Miss Tufton had already shut the door in her face.

Mallowmarsh, Daisy was learning, was a busy working Botanical garden that housed several hundred Greenwild families, most of whom lived in large and airy private apartments within the walls of Chiveley Chase, or in a small forest of eccentric and leafy treehouses at the north end of the Mallow Woods. While the qualified Botanists tended the gardens and woods and greenhouses, or ventured out into the Greyside for research and exploration, their toddlers went to a nursery in the grounds, while children between the ages of five and twelve attended a school that taught English, Maths, Botanical History, Greenwild Geography and basic non-magical Botany. In their final year, the students were finally allowed to start learning green magic, and Daisy found herself joining a class that was already a full term into their studies, which made her feel hopelessly behind – not to mention lost, as she tried to find her way around the grounds.

Luckily, she had Indigo to help. They started their day at the Intemperate House, which had a collection of transparent onion domes that made it look like an enormous, glittering Russian church. Daisy quickly learned that the glasshouses were much bigger on the inside than they appeared from outside. The Intemperate House seemed to go on for miles, filled with alpine meadows of white edelweiss, craggy peaks crowned with groves of aspen and moss-curtained marshes that shone with wandering creeks.

They found the class waiting at the edge of a small prairie, gathered round a near-spherical woman resplendent in scarlet satin overalls, who Daisy recognized as the cheerful French lady from the Twelfth Night party.

'That's Madame Potentille Gallitrop,' whispered Indigo. 'Head of the Intemperate House.'

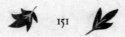

'*Alors*,' she said, waving them over. 'Indigo, nice of you to join us. And you must be Daisy.' She had an enormous bun studded with holly berries, and merry dark eyes that seemed to dance in her round face. 'Now, as I was saying, this term we will focus on pruning: starting with zither roots and working up to the baneful hellebore.'

She set them to work at a series of benches, where Indigo and Daisy found a spot beside the Prof. On the Prof's right was a pale boy with bright blue hair and a beech-leaf earring, who turned out to be called Septimus Bubble. On Daisy's other side was a pair of twins with gleaming black hair and matching gaps between their front teeth ('Ravi and Rishi Rowan-Rajan,' said the Prof, introducing them) and a girl called Kalissa Cantrip with confident shoulders and a mass of fine braids. 'And over there is Ivy Helix,' added Indigo in an undertone, nodding towards a smug-looking girl at the front with caramel-coloured hair, whose pointy nose was lifted high into the air.

Madame Gallitrop handed each of the final-year students a zither root, a plant that played beguiling music when the wind blew through it, and sent the nearby bumblebees wild with excitement.

'You have to be firm with them,' she said, turning away to help one of the other students, right as Daisy's root twined its strings around her head like a turban, twanging furiously.

'Ah, Indigo? A little help here?' Daisy felt panicky.

'Hang on,' said Indigo, looking a bit panicky himself. 'I'll just—'

'Don't worry,' said Kalissa, tapping the root sharply so that it dropped meekly back into its pot. 'You'll get the hang of it.'

On Daisy's other side, the Prof had already got down to work, wearing a pair of bright green gloves and an expression of fearsome concentration as she approached her root, deftly disentangling its harp-like strings from where they were trying to wrap around her neck like a musical noose, and neatly clipping its dead shoots.

'Bravo, Mademoiselle Bellamy,' said Madame Gallitrop, looking delighted. 'Bravo!'

Daisy spotted Ivy Helix scowling at the Prof as if she'd put her pointy nose out of joint.

'Come along, Ivy,' said Madame Gallitrop briskly. 'Back to work.'

The class settled down, and Septimus leaned over to Daisy, blue hair glinting. 'My parents were talking about you yesterday: everyone is. Is it true your mother was kidnapped?'

But before Daisy could think of a good reply, a snapping Venus flytrap made a bid for her necklace, yanking it from around her neck and swallowing it with a smack of its tiny jaws.

'No!' cried Daisy, blinking with shock.

'Greedy little things,' said Madame Gallitrop, coming

over. 'Here: something small and heavy usually does the trick.' She picked up a small pebble and flicked it into the flytrap's open jaws. It swallowed, then choked, coughed and regurgitated the pebble, along with Daisy's necklace. It was covered in green slime and the clasp was crooked, but it was otherwise unharmed. 'There you go.' Madame Gallitrop winked. 'No harm done – though I'd disinfect it before you put it back on.'

After that, they trooped across the lawn for a lesson in Seed Craft with Marigold Brightly, the golden-haired woman who had arrived during Daisy's first visit to the Chase.

'I'm the new Keeper of the Mallowmarsh Seed Bank,' Brightly explained, once they'd assembled in the entrance hall of the Chase. She was without her pink suitcases today, and her hair was wound like a crown around her head. 'I can tell you everything you want to know about the magic of seeds, bulbs and spores.'

She took the class to the edge of the woods, where she taught them how to distinguish between tiny black poppy seeds ('excellent in lemon cake') and their rarer cousins, which came only from pure white poppies. 'Dark night's delight,' she said. 'They allow you to control your dreams – people pay thousands for them on the black market. Or so I'm told.'

Then she set the class to planting daffotrill bulbs ('a musical variety'), and demonstrated by holding a bulb

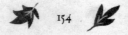

between her palms until it glowed like a tufty Christmas bauble.

'There,' she said, putting it into the earth. 'A simple bit of activation to make them good and strong when they flower in spring. They sound like a first-class brass band when the sun shines through them: very stirring. Now, you try.'

The rest of the class soon had their bulbs glowing – the Prof's was practically blinding – but Daisy's stayed stubbornly dull and brown in her palm.

Marigold Brightly placed a cool hand over Daisy's. 'Planting a seed is an act of hope,' she said. 'It means you have faith in the future. Think of that hope: hold it steady, and don't let go.'

Daisy tried, but all she could feel was her worry about Ma like an iceberg in her stomach.

'Never mind,' said Brightly, patting her shoulder. 'Maybe next time.'

By the time they stopped for lunch, Daisy was both dispirited and starving. She and the other students headed over to the Orangery, the glass-roofed dining hall of Chiveley Chase. It was one of several cafés and bakeries dotted around the grounds, and it was bursting with citrus trees and buzzing with conversation from big crowds of Botanists sitting at the long oak tables. Acorn was already perched at one of them and waved them over, beaming.

'How was your morning?' Daisy asked her as they sat

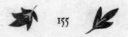

down and began tucking in to warm cheese turnovers, followed by thick slices of wild cherry and almond cake doused in pools of fresh cream. The floor beneath their boots was covered in springy grass and their table (which grew straight from the ground) widened itself generously so they could all squeeze around one end of it.

'Boring,' said Acorn gloomily. 'Two hours of Pastoral Poetry, and then double History. I can't wait until I'm old enough to start green magic.'

'It's not all fun and games, you know,' said the Prof darkly. 'There's a lot of pressure.'

'To do what?' said Daisy, who was still smarting from the contrast between the Prof's beaming daffotrill bulb and her own.

'To get into Bloomquist,' said the Prof. 'My parents were both top of their years, and my grandfather even used to teach there.' She swallowed. 'I *have* to get in.'

'You'll get in,' said Indigo, sighing as if he'd heard this speech a hundred times before. 'You're a genius, remember?'

The Prof shook her head as if trying to dislodge a fly. 'The first test is only a couple of weeks away. I can't afford to make any mistakes or get distracted. That's why it's good that Marigold Brightly is the new Seed Craft teacher. She's supposed to be the best. What she doesn't know about seeds isn't worth knowing.'

Acorn nodded. 'My dad says the commander was lucky to get her to come here.'

'And she's so pretty,' said Indigo. 'Like an angel.'

The Prof rolled her eyes and threw a bread roll at his head.

Acorn, though, was silent, chasing a pea around her plate.

'What's wrong?' The Prof peered at her in concern.

'Oh, nothing. It's just . . . History today was pretty horrible. We were learning about people being stripped.'

'Stripped?' Daisy looked around and saw that everyone had gone very pale. Even Albert the caterpillar looked peaky.

It was the Prof who spoke first. 'It's the worst sentence for criminals in the Greenwild. It means being stripped of your magic.'

Daisy's understanding of green magic was still hazy, but even she realized that this was bad. She thought of Artemis making sunflowers shoot up from the ground, Miss Tufton using vines like extra hands, Ma calling orchids from the desert sand.

The Prof was still speaking. 'Most people die of the shock, some go mad: not many people survive it.'

Daisy shivered. 'And this still happens?'

'No.' The Prof shook her head. 'It was abolished about eight years ago. There were lots of demonstrations and rallies to put an end to it – a bit like people protesting against capital punishment in the Greyside.' She glanced at Daisy. 'It's a horrible sentence. Living without the magic

you're born with, they say that it's . . . worse than death. A living death.'

After that, no one had much of an appetite, and they were relieved when the bells of Chiveley Chase tolled out two o'clock and signalled that it was time for their next lesson.

Chapter 24

Everywhere she looked, Daisy felt she was learning more about Ma and the world she had come from. She gazed at the giant mushrooms glowing like luminous blue parasols along the edges of the paths, the intrepid seedpods that took flight from the trees on fluttering green wings, the red sump-roses that hummed as they passed the rose garden and waved their petals as if tasting the air.

'It's . . . wonderful,' whispered Daisy, forgetting herself. For the first time, she felt the true meaning of the word in her bones. *Full of wonder*. It gave her a knotted and complicated feeling that was a bit like indigestion, for enjoying anything while Ma was missing seemed like the worst kind of betrayal.

All the same, she couldn't help the prickle of curiosity that rose up as they headed towards the Great Glasshouse and their final lesson of the day.

'The Great Glasshouse is my favourite,' said Indigo, skipping slightly as he walked. 'It has toucans and tarantulas and giant otters with white whiskers that make them look like grumpy old gentlemen.'

They were emerging onto the sweeping lawn lined with yew trees where the Twelfth Night party had taken place,

with the enormous glasshouse glittering at its centre. As they came closer, Daisy could see that it was filled with swaying palm trees and heavy purple flowers that pressed against the glass like starfish. Some of them seemed to have teeth. Above the canopy, a languid jaguar was lounging on a branch hung with what appeared to be blue pineapples.

Botanists were hurrying in and out of the great glass doors, and Indigo and Daisy slipped inside, joining Kalissa, Septimus, the Prof, Ravi and Rishi Rowan-Rajan and Ivy Helix, whose caramel hair was in a tight braid that somehow made her nose look even pointier than usual.

Daisy tilted her head back, gazing at the glittering dome above. It was like standing in a great glass cathedral. There were thin ladders bolted to the outside of the glass ('for cleaning' Indigo said), and palm trees towering overhead, with leaves the size of mattresses. Tiny hummingbirds sipped from scarlet flowers in the bushes and jade-bright parakeets circled beneath the crystalline roof. The sky outside was impossibly blue, but inside everything was greeny-gold: palm-shaded and sequinned with light.

'Well . . .' said Indigo, beaming. 'Welcome to the Great Glasshouse.'

Tiny blond monkeys with long tails were swooping beneath the canopy, calling brightly to each other. To her left, Daisy saw a leafy plant emitting large, bubblegum-blue bubbles that floated up and popped against the glass roof. To her right, she spotted a tribe of hot-pink porcupines

lazing under a rubber tree. ('Hedge-piglets,' said Indigo fondly, as one of them shot a quiver of spines towards his behind and he pirouetted out of the way.) Above them, one of the palm trees grew three metres in as many seconds, shooting up towards the ceiling. Daisy braced herself for a crash, but instead the glass stretched like toffee and formed a new dome with a satisfying pop.

Daisy was wide-eyed with wonder.

Indigo laughed, his tangled curls twice their usual size in the humid air. 'This is the oldest of the Mallowmarsh glasshouses, and the biggest.'

A figure materialized out of the foliage and clapped his hands. Daisy saw a sturdy Botanist with a leaf-green waistcoat and enormously bushy dark eyebrows that he quirked in their direction. He had a prosthetic arm, Daisy noticed, and there was something marvellous about the wood it was carved from, which was somehow supple and alive.

'Here we are again,' he said, polishing his monocle with a wooden thumb and forefinger, and wedging it under a bushy eyebrow to survey the eight students. 'And you must be Daisy,' he said, spotting her lurking at the back. 'The commander mentioned you'd be joining us. I'm Gulliver Wildish, head of the Great Glasshouse.' His bearing was fierce, but his brown eyes reminded Daisy of the beautiful ring-tailed lemurs she'd seen with Ma on a trip to Madagascar. She liked him at once.

'All of you, come this way,' he said, and the class traipsed after him.

'Wildish is famous,' whispered Indigo as he led them deeper into the glasshouse. 'He spent years researching rare medicinal plants in the Amazon rainforest. He lost his arm after he was attacked by a poacher, and made himself a new one from the wood of the flexilis tree – seriously advanced magic. Then he dismantled the whole poaching ring and rescued twenty-six trapped manatees – single-handedly.' His voice was reverent, and Daisy glanced at the sturdy Botanist with interest.

They were passing through a small clearing with Botanists hard at work on all sides, pruning, digging, harvesting, climbing up and down ladders, talking to each other and the plants. Daisy glimpsed a flash of red among the foliage high above, and stared. It was a tiny man about the height of her thumb, dressed in red overalls. He was rigged up to an elaborate miniature harness, and was abseiling his way into a small yellow trumpet flower.

'Ah,' said Wildish, and his bushy eyebrows danced gleefully up and down. 'We had a delivery of minim moss a few days ago, which means we can finally tend to some essential tasks that require a . . . lighter touch.' He turned to the class. 'Watch carefully, everyone!'

'Minim moss?' asked Daisy. 'What does it do?'

'Isn't it obvious?' said the Prof, appearing at her elbow. 'A single square will shrink you to a fraction of your normal

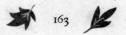

size. It only lasts for a few hours, of course, but it can be very useful.'

'Precisely,' said Wildish, nodding. 'Young Mr Foggit over there is helping to hand-pollinate those thimblewort flowers. A full-size human is too clumsy for the job: the flowers are so delicate that the touch of a careless finger could destroy them.'

There was a cheer as the tiny Botanist emerged from inside the trumpet flower with a dusting of pollen on the end of a minuscule paintbrush and began manoeuvring his way towards a nearby flower, where he deposited the fine grains on the orange stamen within it. Daisy glanced around and realized that half the glasshouse had gathered to watch. Several were exchanging pairs of opera glasses, as if they had front seats to a performance at the theatre.

'Bravo!' one lady cried.

'A little to the left, old chap,' advised another.

'Watch out for that hummingbird!' shouted a third. Then: 'Ooh!' There was a collective intake of breath as the miniaturized Mr Foggit took shelter behind a palm leaf. A tense silence followed as the bird winged past, and then: 'All clear,' came the Botanist's small voice from high above, and everyone breathed out.

Daisy watched, entranced, as Foggit pollinated six more flowers, and then abseiled down to the ground, where his tiny form was lost among the feet of the watchers. A few minutes later, she saw a broad red-overalled back rising

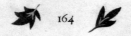

164

up from the floor, and the smiling Foggit – six feet tall at least – accepting a great round of cheers and backslaps, and calls of 'Good show!' and 'Nicely done!' from the watching Botanists.

Indigo looked almost sick with adulation. 'So. Cool,' he breathed.

Wildish smiled and led them onwards into the depths of the glasshouse. Daisy saw a flock of rainbow-coloured macaws overhead, and the glittering black scuttle of tropical spiders underfoot. Then she heard the roar of a river nearby, rushing its way through the heart of the glasshouse. Its surface was glass-green and covered in the glitter of sunlight and twirling specks of white foam.

'Look!' she cried. For there were pink river dolphins leaping high through the water, chirping and somersaulting for sheer joy. Indigo grinned at her, and she grinned back, before they hurried to catch up with the rest of the class.

The light was dimmer here, the canopy denser and wilder. The air was thick with vapour, heavy enough to part like a curtain, and humming with insects and bird calls and chirrups. Napoleon leapt up into the branches of a nearby fig tree, basking in the warmth like a tiny jungle panther. Daisy felt as though they had arrived in the heart of a lost continent.

Wildish paused next to a giant peach, roughly the size of a motor-taxi. It snapped a serrated leaf towards him, and he yanked his left arm out of the way just in time.

'We'll continue where we left off at the end of last term,'

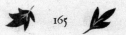

he said. 'Weaving practice: the Botanist's bread and butter.' The others lined up, and Daisy saw that there was a thin green vine laid out in front of each of them. One by one, they lifted their hands and the vines began to rise into the air. The Prof's shot upwards and soared into a neat loop, like a snake swallowing its tail, while Indigo's did a sort of wriggle before collapsing back onto the ground.

Daisy gazed at them in astonishment. 'Er,' she said, looking at Wildish. 'How—'

'Lesson number one for you,' he said, ignoring her. 'Pay attention.'

'I am,' replied Daisy.

'No, that's the lesson. *Pay attention* to the world around you. Nature is wilder and stranger than you know, more miraculous than you can imagine.' His eyebrows bristled. 'The best Botanists know that there's magic everywhere, in every molecule of the natural world. Even in the Greyside,' he said, pausing. 'Perhaps especially there, where it has to fight so hard to live.' He looked very fierce for a moment, like a figure on the prow of a sailing ship. Then he waved his right hand and sighed. 'But you'll have to learn that for yourself.'

'So . . . weaving?' Daisy asked. 'How do I . . . ?'

Wildish drew his eyebrows together like two brown caterpillars. 'Use your magic like a muscle, Daisy: an extension of yourself. Watch.' He raised a hand and a trio of vines lifted sinuously from the forest floor to coil round his left wrist like a many-looped bracelet. Then, faster than

Daisy could see, they snaked out around Indigo's ankle, yanking him upside-down.

'Argh! Let me go!'

'As you wish,' said Wildish peaceably. The vine released Indigo, and he landed in a pile of foliage with a soft *whump*. He surfaced, sputtering, and spat out a leaf.

'Now, you try,' said Wildish, turning back to Daisy. 'This is a nice friendly vine. Pay attention to it. Feel for it with the fingertips of your mind. Make it come to you.'

What did he mean, *fingertips of her mind*? Daisy frowned, and stared at the vine until she thought she might pop. *Come on*, she told it silently. *Move*. She focused so hard that a bead of sweat dripped off the end of her nose. But it was no use. The vine refused to budge.

Daisy heard a snigger from nearby, and turned to find Ivy Helix smirking at her.

'Something funny, Ivy?' said Indigo.

'Not at all,' said the girl. She looked Daisy up and down, from her scuffed boots to her tangled hair. 'There's nothing *funny* about being an unlawful immigrant – especially one who's probably a SPY. But at least we don't have to worry about *you* as competition for Bloomquist.' She smiled slightly, showing small and even white teeth. 'You don't even have magic.'

Before Daisy could think of a good enough response, the girl had turned back to her vine, which she looped into a complicated double knot in mid-air. Daisy's cheeks were

burning with humiliation. Wildish was speaking to a passing Botanist and had missed the whole exchange.

'Ignore her,' said Indigo, gritting his teeth. He looked furious. 'Ivy Helix thinks she's the Greenwild's gift to Botany, but she's just nasty. There's a reason we call her Poison Ivy.'

'It's okay. I'm fine. It's only a bit of dirt in my eyes.' Daisy rubbed at them angrily. 'What's so great about Bloomquist anyway? What did Ivy mean about competition?'

'Oh,' said Indigo, looking suddenly very tired. A three-toed sloth climbed down from a nearby tree and onto his shoulder, and he stroked it absently. 'It's the only school for green magic in the country. Terribly competitive. I mean, if you don't get in, you *can* go straight into an apprenticeship: loads of really good Botanists do. But if you want to be an Explorer, or a Botanical Healer, or an Arboreal Architect – or if you want to go into Greenwild politics and diplomacy at the Bureau . . . then you pretty much have to go to Bloomquist.'

Something in Daisy thrilled at his words. What would it be like to do one of those jobs? To be a Healer, or an Explorer?

Indigo traced the toe of his boot across the ground. 'My sister's at Bloomquist,' he said quietly. 'She's two years older than me, and she's always been good at everything. Not like me – I'm hopeless at Botany. I overheard Dad and Papa talking a few months ago and they're worried I won't be good enough to get in.' He ran a hand through his curls so that they stood up on end. 'It's exhausting, always being compared to her.'

Daisy reached out and squeezed Indigo's hand quickly. 'I understand,' she said. She knew what it was like to go through life with a person who shone so brightly they cast everyone else in the shade.

Then she looked at Jethro, who was kneading his claws happily into Indigo's shoulder, and at the sloth, which was now wrapping its arms about Indigo's neck. There was a dragonfly perched in his curls like an emerald hair-clip, and a trio of geckos curling their tails lovingly around his shoes.

'But you're not hopeless, Indigo. What you do with animals – that's its own kind of magic, even if people here are too focused on plants to notice.'

Indigo blinked, just as Wildish coughed and turned back at last. 'Ahem. Where were we? Ah yes, Daisy. Try again.'

The next hour was humiliating. Daisy stared so hard at the vine in front of her that it felt as if she was going to spontaneously combust, with Ivy making snide remarks each time Wildish's back was turned.

At last, Daisy kneaded her knuckles against her eyes. 'Maybe I don't have green magic.' Maybe all those times she *thought* she'd done magic, it had just been coincidence; or it had been Ma's magic at work, and not her own.

'Nonsense,' said Wildish. 'You have to have magic to—'

'To get through the door from the Greyside. I *know*. Well, maybe the Mallow gate made a mistake with me. I'm about as magical as a tea strainer.'

Chapter 25

The mood in the Five O'Clock shed was sombre that afternoon. They'd been asking around about Cardew, but no one had been willing to talk.

'He was a cold-blooded killer,' said Wildish when Daisy had plucked up the courage to ask at the end of that afternoon's lesson. 'That's all you need to know.'

'Marigold Brightly looked like she was going to have a heart attack when I asked her,' said Acorn, nibbling on a piece of shortbread. 'But then she pretended she had no idea who I was talking about.'

'I asked Chef McGuffin at lunchtime,' said Indigo, 'and he nearly decapitated me with a soup ladle.'

'Madame Gallitrop wouldn't tell me a thing,' said the Prof, taking a chocolate drop from the tree and rolling it thoughtfully between her palms. 'Just that he was dead and good riddance.'

'We've asked pretty much everyone,' said Daisy frustratedly. 'Except Sheldrake, of course. And I don't think asking *him* about Cardew is a good idea.'

The Prof snorted. 'He'd probably feed your cold remains to Brutus.'

They walked out of the shed and into the rustling of the

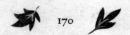

Mallow Woods. When she spoke, Acorn's voice was very small. 'My dad says Sheldrake's not as horrible as he looks: only unhappy.'

Daisy frowned, remembering how he'd cornered her in the entrance hall of the Chase. 'He seems pretty nasty to me. You should have seen the way he talked to the commander . . . it looked like he was trying to karate-chop her with his eyes. Like he really *hates* her.'

'Ah, so you noticed,' said the Prof, shooting Daisy her flashbulb smile. 'When old Bletherwick died six years ago, Sheldrake thought he'd be the new commander. He was *furious* when she was elected instead.'

'Yep,' said Indigo. 'And most people think she's the best commander we've ever had. Sheldrake's jealous. Spends his time stewing in the Perilous Glasshouse.'

'What *is* the Perilous Glasshouse?' asked Daisy, who had been wondering.

'It's where they keep the *really* dangerous plants,' said Indigo, with relish. 'The flesh-eating snapdragons, the giant Venus flytraps. Fanged foxgloves. Poison-spitting nightshade. It's out of bounds for almost everyone. I tried to break in once and almost got eaten by bloodberries.' He shuddered. 'Anyway, like the Prof said, Sheldrake's never really forgiven the commander for being Oak Bound instead of him.'

'That's what happens when you become the commander,' explained the Prof. 'Your magic is bound to the Heart Oak:

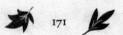

stitched into the fabric of Mallowmarsh.'

'What's the Heart Oak?' asked Daisy, feeling disorientated.

The Prof looked at her in astonishment, and even Acorn looked startled.

'Come on,' said the Prof. 'This calls for a field trip.' They were already emerging from the woods onto the great lawn, and following a path that took them past the Great Glasshouse and down to the shores of the lake, where a vast oak tree grew beside the water. Daisy had seen it before in the distance, but up close it was awe-inspiring. The tree was as wide as a truck and as tall as a lighthouse, its bark twisted and green-mossed, its branches twined with mistletoe and strung with hundreds of bright ribbons and trinkets. White squirrels chased each other up and down the trunk, field mice burrowed among the gnarled roots and tiny robins and goldfinches darted in and out of the twisting branches. It was like standing inside a wildlife palace.

Daisy watched Botanists pausing on their way around the lake, tying ribbons and coins and gold thimbles onto the tree's lower branches and pressing their foreheads against its trunk. Their faces reminded Daisy of the way she'd seen people look in old churches.

'The Heart Oak,' said Indigo, brushing his hand reverently against the bark. 'The Old Botanists used it to anchor the magic when this pocket was created. It holds Mallowmarsh together.'

The tree looked splendid: ancient and vast and very dignified. Daisy pressed her own hand against its wrinkled skin and felt her heart beating in her palm. The bark tingled, like muted electricity, and she shivered.

'People come here for weddings,' said the Prof, 'and funerals too, and if they want to make a wish for someone's safety.' She nodded at all the scraps of cloth tied round the branches. 'That reminds me.' She took a green ribbon from her pocket and handed it to Acorn. 'For your dad.'

'He left for Brazil last night,' explained Acorn quietly. 'He's a specialist in rare cycads and he's trying to protect them from loggers, but . . .'

She couldn't quite finish, but Daisy understood, now, why Acorn had been so pale and quiet that day. The sooner they solved the mystery of the disappearing Botanists, the better.

'So,' she said as Acorn, lips moving silently, finished tying her ribbon, 'the commander's magic runs through the tree? Only hers?'

The Prof nodded. 'That's what it means to be Oak Bound. And it runs both ways: the tree's magic is in her veins too. Sometimes when she's in a really good mood, the Oak sprouts acorns and catkins in midwinter.'

A cold wind whipped over the water, and Daisy watched the ribbons and coins of the Heart Oak spin and dance as a ghostly barn owl soared from its branches over the dark grounds.

'I'd better go,' she said at last. 'I'm late for dinner, and Miss Tufton does *not* like to be kept waiting.' Waving goodbye to the others, she scooped up Napoleon and hurried to catch a lilypaddle home to the Roost.

On the far side of the lake, she used the dandelion paperweight to light her way through the twisted roots of the empty orchard, wondering for the hundredth time what it was, and where it had come from. If it had belonged to Pa, did that mean he'd been a Botanist too?

Then she heard a twig crack behind her and spun round in time to see a sharp, pointed face in the gloom, and a pair of pale blue eyes fixed on the paperweight. Before Daisy could call out, Ivy Helix was gone.

Daisy was so worn out from her first day of lessons that she fell asleep at the table during dessert. Napoleon had to stick his tongue in her ear to wake her up long enough to get upstairs to her room.

She slept for two hours and woke at midnight to find the moon shining in through the window. Rubbing her face with tiredness, she staggered out to the hidden garden. Hal was already there, yanking up weeds, and for a few minutes they worked in a comfortable silence. Then Daisy lost her grip on a nettlespur and went flying, landing unceremoniously on her back.

'Nice,' said Hal, dissolving into wheezing laughter. 'One–nil to the weeds.'

'All right, all right, O mighty one. I'd like to see you do better.' She tossed a clod of mud at his head and he ducked, still laughing.

'I think we've done a pretty good job, actually.' Hal was sitting back on his heels and surveying the area in the centre of the garden. Their rescued sapling was spindly but upright, and, in the space they'd cleared, there were masses of violets unfurling like tiny flags across the grass.

'Mm,' said Daisy, glancing around. 'This garden must

have been beautiful once. I wonder why it was abandoned.'

'There are all sorts of forgotten corners at Mallowmarsh,' said Hal with a shrug. 'I expect someone long ago lost the key, or went away exploring and never came back.' He looked wistful for a moment, then shook himself. 'It feels sort of like we have a responsibility, though. Like maybe we should try to bring it back to life.'

'Yes.' Daisy nodded, swept up in that 'we'.

'Don't laugh, but . . . I want it to be a surprise for my mother,' said Hal. 'If I can make this garden good, maybe it will show her that Father is wrong: that I *can* do something worthwhile.'

Daisy was quiet for a moment. She felt as though she'd been handed a brightly coloured balloon, and that it was very important that she didn't let it go.

'Okay,' she said. 'What do we do next?'

Daisy left the garden near dawn, exhausted but happy, and promising to be back the next night. It was only when Napoleon meowed that she looked up and spotted a dark figure moving around the banks of the lake, beneath the frosty branches of the orchard. She saw him glance swiftly to each side, as if checking he wasn't being followed, before hurrying off again.

'Look,' Daisy whispered urgently, and Napoleon hissed.

Once again, there was no mistaking what she saw.

Sheldrake was on the move. And this time, she was going to follow him.

Chapter 26

She had to move fast to keep pace as the figure hurried past the Roost and into the Mallow Woods. He was heading for the Sighing Forest.

Daisy took a deep breath and kept going.

The woods were hushed and the earth seemed to swallow the sound of her feet as she walked. At last, Sheldrake stopped beneath the pines, and Daisy ducked behind a tree to listen. He was talking to someone who Daisy couldn't see; their face was lost in shadow.

'Aaaaah,' sighed the trees. 'Aaaaaah, aaaaaah.' They released great dragon-puffs of mist into the air, and their sighs obscured the sound of Sheldrake's voice. Daisy shifted closer, darting behind a giant leaf for cover, until she could just make out a few words.

'I've got her where I want her. She trusts me.'

The rumble of the other person's voice was lost amid the sighing of the pines, and then Sheldrake spoke again, sounding angry now, his voice louder:

'One more month, then we act. The Grim Reapers won't wait.'

And he turned on his heel and hurried out of the forest, passing within a few metres of Daisy. He was frowning,

too intent on his own thoughts to notice her giant leaf trembling in the gloom. Brutus sniffed twice at the air, but then Sheldrake called to him curtly, and with a last quiver of his nose the great dog disappeared after his master.

Daisy's whole body felt cold. Who had Sheldrake been speaking to? Had he really said *Grim Reapers*? She felt a drowsy numbness creeping upwards from her toes. If only she could get to the bottom of this. If only she had tried harder to stop Ma from going away . . .

'Aaaaaaah,' sighed the pines, and Daisy sighed too.

She felt very sleepy, and very sad, and lay down underneath her leaf. She just needed to sleep for a little while. The mist was very thick now, a soft white cloud blocking out the world.

She'd failed Ma, and it was no use fighting anymore. Daisy turned her face to the ground and felt something bright go out of her.

Then, slowly, she became aware of a scorching heat in her pocket. The dandelion paperweight was blazing like a beacon, or a white-hot star. Blinding light speared between her fingers: silver-bright, star-striped, incandescent. Suddenly her mind was clear and sharp as broken glass, and she could hear Ma's voice in her head. *Courage, joonam.*

She lurched to her feet, and then there was Napoleon yowling, and on his heels came a huge dog, licking her face from chin to eyebrows, and a tall man with white hair carrying her out of the forest.

Sheldrake dumped her on her feet as soon as they were out of the trees.

'What do you think you were doing?' His eyes glittered dangerously in the moonlight. 'Didn't I make it clear that wandering around the pocket at night is strictly forbidden?'

Daisy scrambled desperately for an excuse. 'I was only – I thought I heard—'

But Sheldrake's eyes had fallen to Daisy's left hand, clutched by her side. Too late, she remembered the dandelion paperweight. She tried to hide it behind her back, but Sheldrake was already lunging forward. He snatched it from her grasp and held it up so that it shone in the moonlight.

'Where,' he seethed, 'did you get this?'

'It was my father's,' said Daisy desperately. 'Please, it's mine. Give it back.'

'So! You're a thief and a liar, as well as a spy. Ivy Helix told me you were carrying something suspicious, and she was right.' Sheldrake slipped the paperweight into his pocket, and turned to leave. 'I'll take this, girl. It will be safe in the Perilous Glasshouse.'

'*No!*' cried Daisy. The word seemed to fill her whole body, and half the sky. 'It's mine!' It was the only thing she had that had belonged to Pa.

'Not any longer,' said Sheldrake. He was almost snarling. 'Back to the Roost, now. Or you'll be thrown out of here

faster than you can say "thief".'

Daisy swayed, and when she opened her eyes, he was gone.

She didn't think things could get much worse, but she was wrong.

'Let me get this straight,' said the Prof the next day. She looked furious, and her elbows looked particularly sharp. 'Craven chased you through London because of a mysterious *paperweight* your mother gave you? And you didn't bother to tell us?'

'It's not like that,' said Daisy. 'Ma wanted me to keep it secret. I thought if anyone found out they'd take it away. And I was right! Ivy saw it and told Sheldrake.'

'Ivy's different,' said the Prof impatiently. 'Everyone knows she's a snake. But you could have trusted *us*; we wouldn't have told.'

Daisy's pause was just a moment too long.

'Oh,' said the Prof, her spectacles glinting dangerously. 'So that's how it is! Well, maybe Ivy's right. Maybe you are a spy, after all. You're certainly good enough at hiding the truth.'

The words hit Daisy like a slap. Being called a spy by Sheldrake or Ivy was one thing, but hearing it from the Prof felt like being knifed in the back. The Prof was already stalking out of the shed, grabbing Acorn's hand and towing the smaller girl behind her.

Indigo looked stricken. 'She didn't mean it,' he said quietly. 'You didn't have to tell us about it right away – you only met us a few days ago. The Prof's worried about her grandfather. She'll come round, you'll see.'

Even so, Daisy lay sleepless for a long time that night, hearing the Prof's words in a loop in her head. She turned over restlessly, and this time she heard the words Sheldrake had spoken in the Sighing Forest.

The Grim Reapers won't wait.

Hadn't Indigo said the Grim Reapers were storybook ogres, made up to scare small children? She shivered. Something in Sheldrake's voice had made them sound very real indeed.

Chapter 27

The following day was her fifth in Mallowmarsh, and the worst since she had arrived. The Prof wasn't talking to her, and studiously ignored her in their lessons that day. It was raining sideways, Artemis still wasn't back from the Bureau and Miss Tufton's bunions were making her even grumpier than usual. On top of this, Napoleon seemed to have caught a cold and kept sneezing miserably into Daisy's ear from his perch on her shoulder.

To add insult to injury, Daisy's second lesson in the Great Glasshouse had been even worse than the first. No matter how hard she'd tried, her vine remained stubborn and unmoving. There had been one glorious moment when she thought she'd made it move – but it had turned out to be nothing more than a dung beetle surfacing for a snack. Ivy Helix had been watching, and her snickers had haunted Daisy for the rest of the day.

Everyone else had moved on to something called Binding, which was the opposite of Weaving. It allowed you to stop the movement of a magical plant, and was, according to Wildish, an essential skill for any Botanist. He demonstrated on a fanged tulip, freezing and unfreezing its tiny jaws at will. Daisy looked on dully, feeling more useless than ever.

Worst of all, though, was the loss of the dandelion paperweight, and the knowledge that she had failed Ma. Her pocket was cold and empty, and she felt as if a small mouse was gnawing at her heart.

Alone in her room that afternoon, Daisy paced back and forth for a few minutes before collapsing onto the bed. She looked at the room upside-down, her hair trailing back onto the floor. That was when she saw it, lying in the dust under the bedside table: a pile of books with dog-eared edges.

There was one called *When Roses Roamed: Travels in Central Asia*, another titled *The Age of Orchids: A Journey Across Botanical Bhutan* and a third emblazoned with swirling letters that read *The Adventures of Ajax von Halle: through Byzantium on a Bicycle*. The turned-down pages all had illustrations, as if their owner had lingered over the pictures and skipped the words altogether. Last was an old notebook with a battered leather cover. It was full of smudged pencil drawings: sketches of leaves and flowers and butterflies, along with some that were more improbable: pumpkins with teeth, and trees with eyes, and porcupines sketched in hot pink. She flipped to the front page and noted the year pencilled on the faded flyleaf: thirty years ago. Beneath it was a name, written in an adult's smooth, looping hand: *The Logbook of Hal White, age twelve and a half.*

Daisy stared for a moment, then shook herself. 'Hal' was

probably a common name in the Greenwild. The Hal she knew from the hidden garden was her own age, and the owner of the notebook would be grown up now: forty at least, and probably off exploring somewhere.

She glanced at Napoleon. 'It's just a coincidence,' she told him sternly. 'It doesn't mean anything.'

All the same, she had to know. She found Miss Tufton in the kitchen, clattering pans at the sink and listening to something operatic on the pink gramophone. Daisy tried to sound very casual as she asked her question.

'Have you ever heard of someone called Hal White, Miss Tufton?'

'Hal?' Miss Tufton looked as if someone had trodden on her foot. She took a long time to answer. At last she said, 'Hal White was one of the most famous Botanical explorers in history.' She paused. 'And he was the commander's son.'

'Was?' Daisy felt her heart pounding.

'He died, many years ago now. Killed by his best friend.' Miss Tufton's weathered face wrinkled up, and Daisy saw her wipe away something that looked suspiciously like a tear. 'He was the one who called me Tuffy.'

'Oh.' Daisy didn't know what to say. 'So . . . there's definitely no one called Hal who lives here now?'

'No.' Miss Tufton sounded very sad. 'Not for thirty years.'

Daisy drew in a breath. Suddenly, there was no time to waste. 'I'll, um, be right back!' She sprinted down the stairs,

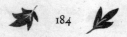

whipping past the larder tree and upending a bowl of broad-beans on the counter.

'Sorry!' she yelled. She had to check; she had to see. She ran to the crumbling wall in the dandelion meadow, running her hands back and forth across it until she found the door. Except it wasn't the fresh, shining door that had always greeted her before. It was lichen-stained and rust-hinged and – she yanked at the handle – completely impossible to open. It looked ancient and forgotten, swollen shut, as if it hadn't been used for decades.

Daisy staggered back to the Roost, feeling dazed. Could it be true? Could Hal – her Hal of the hidden garden – be the same boy who'd filled that notebook with sketches? Could he be Artemis's son? She remembered the writing on the flyleaf: *The Logbook of Hal White, age twelve and a half* – and below it, a date thirty years in the past. But why hadn't the door opened for her just now? Did it only open at night?

'This can't be happening,' she muttered, glancing at Napoleon. He stared back at her impassively and licked his left paw. 'How is it even possible?' She looked down at her shaking hands, and realized that she had thirty-year-old dirt stuck under her fingernails.

She hurried back up the stairs to her room, grabbing the notebook and flicking desperately through its pages, looking for confirmation.

Then – wait. *What was that?* She flipped back, smoothing the page open with her palm. There, beneath a drawing of

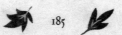

a monarch butterfly, was a quick pencil study of a boy's loosely curled hand. And there, on the left wrist, was a pattern of five moles in the shape of a stretched-out W.

Daisy stopped breathing.

She closed her eyes, then opened them again slowly.

Cardew, here at Mallowmarsh, thirty years ago.

Daisy shut the notebook with a snap. It was the clue she'd been waiting for. She had to ask Hal what he knew about Cardew. Ma's life could depend on it. She needed to go back to the hidden garden, now: as soon as possible. She braided back her hair, shoved her feet into their boots and waited for night to fall.

Chapter 28

BOOM! BOOM! BOOM!

Daisy had never heard anything like it. Thunder rolled through the air, peal after peal, like a great bell tolling underwater. Rain lashed against the turreted roof and she could hear the wind howling outside the windows of the Roost.

'Storm!' came Miss Tufton's voice from the landing. Daisy, who had been sneaking down the stairs, froze in place.

'Ah, Daisy! Good, there you are,' said the housekeeper, peering up at her. 'You won't want to miss this.'

She hurried away before Daisy could ask what was going on. She glanced at Napoleon, who twitched a whisker at her. Then, together, they hurried into the kitchen.

BOOM! The whole treehouse was swaying violently and lightning flashed outside the window. According to the tulip clock, it was just after midnight. Miss Tufton was looking impatient, and barely paused before bundling Daisy into a pair of fluorescent yellow wellies and a matching raincoat and sweeping her out through the door. Daisy tucked Napoleon inside her jumper, hoping that the waterproofs would keep him from getting too wet. She wasn't sure where they were going, but it was clear that her trip to the hidden garden would have to wait.

Outside, the rain was driving sideways, icy and vicious. The wind whipped the trees and a thin moon cut through the racing clouds like a knife.

Miss Tufton had to roar over the noise of the storm. 'THIS WAY.'

A bolt of lightning broke the sky, and three seconds later came the deafening rumble of thunder. Miss Tufton was hobbling towards the woods, into the heart of the storm. Dimly, Daisy could make out the shapes of other Botanists converging and could hear the uproar of shouts and calls and crashes. At the head of the crowd was the unmistakable form of Madame Gallitrop. Gradually, Daisy realized that the shouts weren't panicked but highly organized.

'HELLO!' came a voice in her ear. She looked round and saw Indigo, soaking wet and grinning. Just behind him was Acorn, red hair bound back in two tight pigtails. The Prof stood by Acorn's side, carefully ignoring Daisy.

'What's going on?' Daisy shouted. Glittering snakes of lightning split the sky, sending out forked tongues of electricity.

'Lightning-seed harvest!' yelled Indigo, shoving a bucket into her hands. 'Collect as many as you can.'

Daisy saw that the gathered Botanists were sprinting in all directions, holding out buckets to catch thick showers of blue sparks as they fell. Madame Gallitrop was busy

directing proceedings from halfway up a tree. In the brief lull after the thunder, she raised her voice.

'Three, two, one . . . ready everyone . . . NOW!' As she yelled, the next fork of lightning thrashed down from above, blindingly white. The whole scene appeared frozen for a moment, and then everything was in motion again as the blue sparks rained down and the Botanists sprinted after them. A tall, long-haired man caught a seed and yelled in triumph. Daisy could see Indigo racing after another, skidding on his knees and catching it in his bucket just before it hit the ground.

'YES!'

Daisy looked about wildly as the sparks showered down like blue fireworks, fizzling out where they hit the earth. She saw one soaring over her head and ran after it, boots squelching, ears filled with the roar of the storm. She heard Napoleon's furious meow in her ears and lifted the bucket over her head, hardly able to keep up with the skidding of her feet. And then: 'Oof!' She felt something heavy hit the bucket and staggered to stay upright. There inside it, shining against the black rain, was a single seed of lightning, hissing and crackling with electricity. The next moment, someone knocked against her so hard that the seed leapt out like a fire opal against the darkness, and sputtered out on the earth.

'Oops, clumsy me!' It was Ivy Helix, caramel hair coiled sleekly beneath her hood. 'Poor Ditzy Thistledown, can't even catch a single seed.' She sighed tragically, and her voice

was sugary when she spoke again. 'You don't belong here, Greysider. Go home.'

Then came the next lash of lightning, further to the east this time, and she vanished into the dark as the Botanists scattered once more, slipping and whooping as they chased the storm.

Daisy was boiling with rage. *Go home.* The words echoed like thunder in her ears. She didn't *have* a real home. Home was nowhere in the world except by Ma's side, and that had been taken away.

A thought came to her unbidden: if she didn't belong here, then it wouldn't matter what she did next. She felt a rush like static through her bloodstream.

No one was watching. She could stick to her plan and go to the hidden garden. Or . . . She glanced around, thoughts racing. She wasn't far from the Perilous Glasshouse. And what she wanted more than anything right now, with Ivy's words stinging in her ears, was to take back her father's paperweight: the one thing Ma had told her to keep safe.

She would never have a better chance.

Slowly, she put down her empty bucket and slipped away into the woods.

Daisy had never been to the Perilous Glasshouse, but she knew where it was – everyone did. It lay at the heart of the woods like a great glass castle, ringed by a battlement of thorny brambles that rose as high as a house. She paused, looking up at them. Then she took a breath, stepped

forward – and jerked to a halt. Someone had grabbed the back of her jacket.

'Stop!' hissed a low voice. 'Are you completely insane?' It was the Prof, dressed head to toe in waterproofs. Her curls were held back by a headband patterned with tiny acorns.

'What, are you following me now?' asked Daisy, outraged. 'Keeping an eye on the spy?'

'I saw you slip away,' said the Prof. 'Do you have any idea what those are?' She gestured towards the brambles, which glittered dimly with fat dark berries. 'Carnivorous bloodberries. I knew you were stupid, but do you actually have a death wish?'

'Look,' said Daisy hotly. 'I have to get the paperweight back. I can't explain now, but it's important.'

Acorn and Indigo appeared behind the Prof. 'What's going on?' asked Acorn in a small voice, glancing between them. 'Are you fighting again?'

Daisy looked at the younger girl, and saw that her eyes had filled with tears. Something inside her pinged, like a rubber band against her heart.

'We're not fighting,' she said. The Prof snorted. 'We're, um, having a discussion about getting into the Perilous Glasshouse.'

Acorn gave a little gasp. 'But it's against the rules! The Perilous Glasshouse is—'

'Perilous. Yeah, I grasped that. But Sheldrake stole my paperweight, and I want it back. And I've been wondering

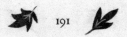

why Craven wanted it so badly. If we know that, it could help us work out how he's connected to the disappearances.'

She turned to the Prof, closing her eyes as she spoke. 'I'm sorry I didn't tell you about it sooner, but Ma made me promise to keep it secret, and I'd only just met you, and –' she hesitated – 'I'm not very good at the whole friendship thing.' She looked away, cheeks burning. 'Now, if you could go away and pretend you didn't see me, I have a job to do. I can do it alone.'

'No!' said the Prof, looking furious. 'I forbid you.'

Daisy prepared to push past her.

Then the Prof took a breath. 'I forbid you . . . to go in there alone. If this paperweight is a clue, then I'm coming with you.'

'What?'

'You heard me. There's no way you can break into the Perilous Glasshouse without my help. It would be like sending a bush-baby into a snake-pit. You need me.'

Daisy stared at her, speechless.

Then: 'I'm coming too,' said Indigo.

There was a tiny pause. 'Me too,' said Acorn in a shaky voice.

'All right.' The Prof nodded and looked around. 'I'd say we have an hour before the storm blows itself out, which means we need to move fast. First things first, we need a diversion. Something to distract the bloodberries.'

'Luckily, you have me,' said Indigo smugly. 'It's not for

nothing they call me the Para-King.'

'Honestly, Ind,' the Prof said, rolling her eyes, 'that is *never* going to catch on.'

'Just you wait.' Indigo whistled, and a flock of parakeets soared through the air and landed on the branches of a nearby tree like rustling green leaves. 'I can ask them to create a distraction.'

The Prof gave a tiny smile and nodded. Then she looked around at them. 'The glasshouse is called Perilous for a reason. We've all heard the stories. There are some seriously nasty things in there. We'll need to get in, find the paperweight and get out as fast as we can.'

Daisy nodded shakily. Acorn tightened her pigtails, and together the four of them walked towards the brambles.

'Ready?'

Indigo whistled through his fingers and the parakeets soared above the bramble thicket. The bloodberries swarmed up towards them, searching for blood as the birds flew nimbly out of reach.

'Go, go, GO!'

As one, they sprinted into the space left by the surging bloodberries. It took less than sixty seconds for the brambles to notice them, and then they were under attack, thorns latching onto their limbs with tiny vampiric teeth. Daisy felt herself assaulted from a hundred different directions, felt thorn-fangs fastening onto her arms and legs, bouncing off her jacket, tangling in her hair. She stepped on a swollen

berry and dark red liquid squelched out.

She opened her mouth to scream, and felt a thorn hook itself into the tender inside of her cheek. *No,* she thought. *Get off.* She yanked herself free as the thorns gave way around her and she half ran, half fell into empty space. Seconds later, the others came stumbling after her, blood-streaked and gasping.

They were through.

The Prof had a vicious scratch across one cheek. Indigo had a chunk of hair missing, and Acorn was swallowing back tears. But they had done it.

'Right,' said Daisy, fighting for composure and wiping her bleeding palm against her leg. She turned her back on the bloodberries and squared herself to face the glasshouse. It looked like a medieval fortress built from glass. Each of the clear walls was three feet thick and completely impenetrable. Daisy strode up to the door and pressed her hand against it. It was smooth as a mirror and cold to the touch.

There was a keyhole in the shape of a wolf's mouth with

snarling fangs. It was carved from pure white wood that glimmered so that the wolf's eyes seemed to blink.

'What now?' Daisy glanced around.

The Prof drew in a deep breath. 'It's a blood-key door,' she said quietly, moving towards it. 'It opens when it's given blood.'

Daisy moved in front of the Prof before she could get any closer. 'I'll do it.'

Carefully, she angled her bleeding palm towards the lock so that three drops of blood splattered across the fangs of the wolf's mouth. The miniature jaws widened, exposing a set of needle-like teeth that lunged for her hand. She leapt backwards, but it seemed that her blood had been enough. With a snarling click and a sigh of cold air, the teeth retracted and the door swung open.

Chapter 29

Daisy wrapped her hand in her scarf, blinking against the pain. Then she glanced at the others. Indigo gave a small nod. Acorn was gripping onto the Prof's wrist. Together, they stepped inside.

The Perilous Glasshouse was very beautiful, in the way a knife is beautiful and bright in the moment before it cuts you. The air was hushed and still, and all around were tall, knotted trees with leaves and flowers that glowed in the dark. The flowers were ravishingly lovely, fat silver magnolias that shone like starlight fallen to earth. They were giving off a scent that was like a Sunday afternoon in heaven. Daisy staggered. She blinked slowly, then listed to the side.

Blink. *What was she doing here?*

Blink. *Where was she?*

The smell was flooding through her, a sweet piercing shock that stole sensation and obliterated memory.

Blink. Daisy opened her eyes to see the Prof bending down and gesturing to her frantically. She was pushing some kind of putty into her nose, and trying to make Daisy do the same. At last, Daisy understood. She pressed the putty into her nostrils, blocking out the scent of the flowers.

196

She breathed through her mouth. Slowly, her head cleared. She stood, staggered and looked around.

'Sobby about dat,' she said. It sounded like she had a nasty cold.

'Dob't wubby,' said Indigo, who was already moving forward. 'Reaby?'

Acorn wrinkled her plugged-up nose, looking determined. The Prof adjusted her spectacles. Daisy nodded, and the four of them moved forward into the glasshouse.

Beyond the magnolia grove was a beautiful knot garden laid out in an elegant geometric pattern, with hemlock hedges surrounding beds of herbs and flowers – some frothy and white like lace, some with flowers like bronze bells, others with big purple flowers like stars. Just as Daisy was thinking how pretty they all looked, the Prof lifted her chin. 'Poison garben,' she said, her voice still indistinct. She pointed. 'Deably nightshabe. Snakeroot. Hemlock. Each one's enoub to kill you fibty times ober.'

On one side of the knot garden was a grove of giant cacti, each one twice the height of a man, spines bristling; on the other was a colony of enormous Venus flytraps, ten times the size of the one that had swallowed Daisy's necklace, with huge fangs that opened and closed lazily.

And in the centre of the knot garden, sitting in a silver cage, was a beautiful orchid with a hundred flowers.

Its petals were pale and shimmering, slicked with shifting, unsettling patterns that seemed to absorb all the light. The

197

plaque on the outside of the cage read: *GHOST-MOTH ORCHID*, and a Botanist in the red and gold uniform of a Mallowmarshal stood beside it, leaning on a sharpened pitchfork. It was Corporal Smedley, the spotty young man

who'd been in the guard house when Daisy had first arrived through the Mallow gate. He appeared to be dozing on his feet, his chin dipping dangerously close to the pitchfork as he snored, and then jerking up again as he caught himself, before beginning to nod once more.

Daisy and the others ducked down before he had the chance to wake and spot them.

'What now?' whispered Indigo as the guard shifted and coughed. They were far enough away from the magnolia trees to remove their nose plugs, and Daisy dug hers out with a finger before shaking her head despairingly.

'I didn't realize there would be a guard. What's a ghost-moth orchid anyway?'

The Prof glanced at her. 'I'll tell you later – if we ever get out of here. We need to focus on the paperweight, remember?'

'Right.' Daisy nodded. 'If we go round that way –' she indicated the side of the knot garden – 'we'll be shielded from view by the cactuses.'

'The cacti,' said the Prof. They stared at her. '*Cacti*, not cactuses.'

'Are you serious?' Indigo looked incredulous. '*That's* what you're worried about right now?'

Daisy rolled her eyes – and that was when she spotted the dandelion paperweight. It was nestled in the fanged mouth of one of the gigantic Venus flytraps. She stared at it, mind racing. To get it out, she'd have to reach an arm

right into its glistening jaws. Unless . . .

'Prof, can I borrow your headband?'

The Prof looked confused, but handed it over. Daisy hunted around until she found a Y-shaped stick among the tree litter, and twisted the fabric around it to fashion a slingshot.

'I need something small and heavy,' she hissed. Indigo rummaged in his pocket and eventually extracted an enormous and slightly sticky gobstopper. 'Will this do?'

'Ick! Indigo!' She paused. 'All right, all right. Hand it over.'

Moving slowly and with infinite care, she placed the gobstopper in the slingshot and lined up the flytrap in her sights. She drew back the sling, breathed in, and – THWOK!

The gobstopper soared through the air and into the open jaws of the Venus flytrap. The plant gave a convulsive hiccup, shuddered – and then spat out the gobstopper in disgust. Along with it came the dandelion paperweight, covered in corrosive green slime. Using her sleeve, Daisy picked it up carefully and wiped it off. She grinned. 'Got it.'

She lifted her hand and the paperweight shone out like a star, glinting off the Prof's spectacles. Anyone watching from outside would have seen the whole glasshouse glowing like a silver lantern.

'I think I know what this is,' whispered the Prof. 'There are illustrations in Grandfather's books, but I never thought I'd see it in real life.' She reached out and touched it, eyes wide. 'It's a dandelight.'

The others looked blank, and the Prof sighed, exasperated. 'The story goes that one of the Old Botanists made it from one of the Mallowmarsh dandelions when they were first planted. The art was lost centuries ago, so this must be . . . really old.' She glanced at Daisy, still whispering so as not to wake the corporal. 'According to the story, this Botanist – Sir Robert Chiveley, the man who built Chiveley Chase – fell madly in love with a Greysider, and created the dandelight so she could visit him whenever she wanted. It works like a compass, you see, magnetized to the Greenwild – always leading you towards the door of the nearest pocket.'

Daisy nodded, remembering the way its beam had swung like a compass needle, leading her towards the entrance to Mallowmarsh.

Indigo frowned. 'But no one without magic can get through the gates – or even see them.'

'That's the point,' said the Prof quietly. 'The dandelight is also a key: it allows the holder to cross the threshold, *even if they don't have magic themselves.*'

Suddenly, there was an odd noise from behind them: something like a dog choking on a bread roll. Daisy turned, and drew in a deep, shocked breath.

Slumped on the floor was the limp form of Corporal Smedley, with blood trickling out of his nose.

And the ghost-moth orchid was gone.

Without stopping to think, Daisy sprinted over to the guard's body. His face was very pale, and when she shook him he didn't respond.

'What do we do?' Indigo's voice was panicky.

'We have to raise the alarm,' said Daisy. Smedley needed help, that much was clear. They would have to call for it, even if it meant being caught themselves.

'This can't be happening,' the Prof was muttering. Her voice rose to an anguished squeak. 'We are going to be in *so much trouble.*'

Then there was a noise from the door, and Sheldrake came bursting into the Perilous Glasshouse.

With one glance, he took in the scene: the four children,

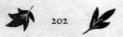

pale faced and trembling; the guard, unconscious on the floor. And the priceless ghost-moth orchid: gone.

He looked straight at Daisy, his voice laced with menace. 'You, girl. Come with me.'

Chapter 30

The next few minutes were a kind of nightmare.

Sheldrake marched the four of them towards the Roost, his expression tight, and his grip around Daisy's upper arm even tighter.

When they emerged into the kitchen, Miss Tufton was standing by the stove wearing a hideous purple dressing gown and matching slippers. Her expression was as fearsome as the knitting needle harpooning her hair. And beside her was –

'Artemis!' cried Daisy. 'You're back!' All her worry about Ma and the search mission came rushing in like a great wave. 'What did the Bureau say? Did they say yes?'

Artemis ignored her questions. 'Where have you been?' she demanded. She was standing very still, worry making sharp lines around her mouth. 'Miss Tufton told me you disappeared from the storm harvest.'

'We, er . . .' Daisy stuttered.

Sheldrake cut in. 'The ghost-moth orchid has been stolen. I found these four in the Perilous Glasshouse.' He spoke with grim satisfaction. 'Caught red-handed.'

'What? No!' Daisy whipped her head towards Artemis. 'That's not true. I mean, we *were* in the Perilous Glasshouse,

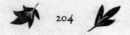

but we didn't steal the orchid. We looked away and it was just – gone. And Corporal Smedley was out cold. Someone attacked him.'

Artemis's lips were white with anger. 'The Perilous Glasshouse? What on this green earth possessed you to go there? You could have been *killed*.' She brought a hand down on the table, and the potted palm curled up its leaves in distress. 'You KNOW the rules. Bellamy, I especially expected better of you.'

The Prof stared at the floor and didn't say anything.

'It's not her fault!' cried Daisy, pushing a rain-soaked length of hair away from her face. 'It was my idea.' She took a deep breath and placed the dandelight on the table. 'I was going to get this back, after Sheldrake confiscated it. Ma gave it to me. She told me to keep it safe.'

Artemis's eyes widened in shock, and she glanced at Miss Tufton. 'I see,' she said, almost to herself. 'I see.'

'That child is a liar,' said Sheldrake, looking furious. 'She stole that dandelight, and I say she stole the orchid too.'

'Honestly, Ferrus!' Artemis threw up her hands. 'What would Daisy – or any of these children – want with the ghost-moth orchid? And how do you think she managed to knock out a fully-grown Botanist? As for the dandelight—'

'A clear case of theft!' snarled Sheldrake.

'I didn't—' said Daisy at the same time.

Artemis banged her hand on the table again, silver hair spilling around her face. 'That's enough,' she said, slipping

205

the dandelight into her pocket. 'I will take care of it from now on. We should count ourselves lucky, Ferrus, that Daisy got to it before the thief did. They could easily have swiped it along with the orchid.'

Sheldrake glared murderously at Artemis, grinding his teeth. 'Be that as it may,' he managed, 'these children have disobeyed the rules. They *must* be punished.'

Artemis sighed. 'A demerit on each of their records will be punishment enough, I think.'

Daisy heard a horrified gasp from the Prof, but the commander was still speaking, turning to look at each of them in turn. 'For now, the most important thing is to remain vigilant. The theft of the orchid means there's someone here at Mallowmarsh we can't trust.'

Miss Tufton's face was creased tortoise-like with worry, and Indigo was gazing at the commander with huge, fearful eyes. Daisy, though, was staring at Sheldrake, and remembering his secret meeting in the woods. *'I've got her where I want her,'* he had said. *'She trusts me.'* What if he had been talking about Artemis? Should she tell the commander what she had heard?

Daisy opened her mouth – but Artemis was still speaking.

'Ferrus, I'd like you to speak to the Mallowmarshals about upping security. I know I can count on you.'

Daisy closed her mouth. She would wait, she decided, before making any accusations.

*

Ten minutes later, Sheldrake escorted Indigo, Acorn and the Prof away in disgrace. Daisy felt hot with guilt as she watched her friends leave, a bedraggled and chastened trio. She caught Indigo's eye from the window as they boarded a lilypaddle back to the Chase, and saw him mouth, *Don't worry*.

When they were gone, Artemis turned to Daisy. Her mouth was a grim line.

'I'm sorry,' said Daisy miserably. 'I'll leave, if you want.' She swallowed, remembering Ivy's words. 'I don't belong here. I can't do green magic.' Now that she knew about the dandelight, everything suddenly made sense. She'd cheated her way through the Mallow gate with a magic key. No wonder she hadn't managed to weave so much as a pea shoot.

'Leave Mallowmarsh?' Artemis's nostrils flared. 'Absolutely not. The last thing I need is for you to be kidnapped by Craven, on top of everything else.' She sat down heavily at the table, untangling a leaf from her hair. 'It wasn't good news from the Bureau, Daisy. They refused to grant permission for a search mission. They claimed it would be a "waste of resources".'

'Dunderheaded earthworms!' Miss Tufton marched over and slammed down two mugs on the table. 'Blue-bellied barbarians!' She sloshed hot tea into the mugs, and the potted palm cowered as she stomped back to refill the teapot.

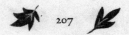

'A waste of resources?' Daisy looked at Artemis incredulously and felt a wave of anger that made her stomach burn. Even her hands felt hot, and she placed a palm on the table to steady herself.

'I know,' said Artemis. 'My feelings exactly. And that is why we're going to launch the search mission without –' she paused delicately – 'official permission.'

Daisy felt a lurch behind her belly button. 'But I thought you said it would be impossible without the Bureau's support.'

'I said *nearly* impossible,' said Artemis, with a glint in her eye. 'It will be tricky, and unorthodox. But we no longer have a choice.'

'So when do we leave?' Daisy leapt to her feet. 'Now? Tomorrow?'

Artemis shook her head slowly. 'First, we need to find out exactly where the vanished Botanists are being held. I've got Mallowmarsh agents out in Peru, following a number of leads. We'll plan to set off the moment we have news of a firm location. Without it, it would be like searching for a needle in a haystack. I can't ask my Greenwilders to defy the Bureau – and risk their lives – until we have as much information as possible.'

Daisy swallowed at this, then nodded reluctantly. 'Okay,' she said, and then plucked up the courage to ask the question she'd been wanting to ask since arriving at Mallowmarsh.

'Artemis?'

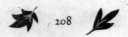

'Mmm?'

'Why didn't Ma tell me about the Greenwild? Why did she keep this –' she gestured around, and a vine swooped down to catch the teapot before it went flying off the table – 'hidden from me?'

Artemis examined the cuffs of her overalls, which were embroidered with green oak leaves. 'I wondered the same thing, Daisy. I asked some, ah, discreet questions while I was away, and managed to get hold of the Persian ambassador to the Bureau. It seems that your mother was born in the Iranian Greyside. Her parents were killed during the revolution, and she lived in a state orphanage until she was eight years old.'

'An orphanage?' Daisy tried to imagine it, and flinched.

'Quite,' said Artemis. 'But somehow, when she was eight, she found her way to a pocket of the Iranian Greenwild called Pardisa. She lived there happily for many years. Then, when she was nineteen, Pardisa was attacked by black-market traders – Botanists gone bad – who murdered her whole adopted family. She escaped with her life, apparently with the help of a visiting Englishman. That must have been your father.'

Artemis glanced at Daisy, who felt pinned to her chair. The whole kitchen looked shocked and pale in the starlight from the window. 'It's no wonder she kept our world a secret from you, Daisy. In her mind, being a Botanist was dangerous. She wanted to keep you safe.'

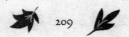

209

'So that's why . . .'

'That's why she left you behind when she decided to investigate the disappearances. She wanted to help the Greenwild, without putting you in danger.'

Twenty minutes later, Daisy crept halfway down the stairs, hoping to slip out to the hidden garden. But Artemis and Miss Tufton were talking softly in the kitchen, the dandelight shining on the table between them. Daisy watched as Artemis said something and the housekeeper nodded. Then the commander stood and pressed a hand to the ivy-covered wall beside the stove. A heavy tracery of vines unspooled itself like a green lock to reveal a loose brick that Artemis removed from the wall. Behind it was a small safe, and within a moment the dandelight was inside, the brick restored, and the ivy allowed to grow back into place.

Daisy stood very still, watching. Then she heard a scrabbling noise behind her and jumped. It was coming from the window on the landing. Napoleon leapt onto the windowsill, hissing out into the night like a scalding teakettle on the boil.

'Shh!' she said, tiptoeing over to look. But there was no one outside: only stars and empty darkness.

She slept fitfully, and woke puffy-eyed at dawn, to find Napoleon's tail in her ear. The kitchen was empty when

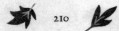

they came downstairs a little while later, but they found Miss Tufton outside feeding parsley to Silas the goat. The sky was very clear and blue after the storm, like a sapphire washed clean by spring water.

'Morning,' grunted Miss Tufton as the goat spat on Daisy's shoes, and Napoleon spat back. 'How are you feeling?'

'Fine,' Daisy lied, ignoring the blood-bramble scratches on her cheeks. She tried not to think of her lack of magic, or the loss of the dandelight, or what she'd learnt about Ma's family.

Miss Tufton looked at her silently, and handed her a bunch of parsley for the goat.

Chapter 31

The Prof was dressed in funereal black overalls when they met later that day, with tattered black lace at the cuffs and a black cloth headband. As part of their penance for breaking into the Perilous Glasshouse, they'd been assigned to griffin-dung-delivery duty for the foreseeable future, and were assembled at the manure heap on the edge of the Mallow Woods.

'Who died and made you chief mourner?' said Indigo, snorting at the Prof's outfit.

'I'm in mourning for my chances of getting into Bloomquist,' the Prof said with a sniff.

'What? Why?' asked Daisy, glancing between them.

'Weren't you listening to the commander last night? This,' said the Prof, gesturing at the dung heap and the teetering piles of manure in their wheelbarrows, 'isn't our real punishment.'

'It isn't?'

'No. It's the demerit on our records for getting into Bloomquist, of course. Three demerits and you're disqualified from entering, no matter how well you do in the tests.'

'Ah,' said Daisy, suddenly understanding. She didn't care

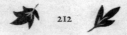

about herself: there was no way some snobby Botanical academy would want her. But it was different for the Prof. Bloomquist meant everything to her.

'I'm really sorry,' she said quietly.

The Prof shrugged stiffly. 'I'll just have to be extra careful from now on,' she said, hefting her wheelbarrow and wafting a lungful of stinking air into their faces. 'No more rule-breaking. No more sneaking around.'

Daisy nodded, and they pushed their barrows of dung across the quiet grounds as flocks of parakeets streamed past overhead.

'So,' said Indigo, when they finally got to the shed. 'What did the commander say about the Bureau?'

Daisy explained about the Bureau's refusal to allow a search mission, and the plan to set out for the Amazon as soon as they had confirmation of where, exactly, the missing Botanists were being held. *If they're still alive*, she added silently, before banishing the thought.

The Prof's eyes were wide. 'The commander is going to defy the Bureau? But that's—'

'Seriously cool,' finished Indigo, grinning.

'Well, while we wait for her spies to come up with the location, I think we should keep investigating. Here at Mallowmarsh, I mean. Especially because I think Sheldrake –' Daisy took a deep breath – 'I think Sheldrake is working for Craven. Hang on, hear me out,' she protested,

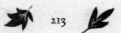

as the Prof tried to interrupt. 'I didn't have a chance to tell you before, but I overheard Sheldrake talking to someone in the Sighing Forest, right before he caught me with the dandelight. He said something about the Grim Reapers – as if they were real.'

'That's impossible,' said the Prof at once. 'Everyone knows they're only a story.'

'I know that,' said Daisy impatiently. 'But what if someone is using the name? What if it's a group that wants to attack Botanists? Isn't that what the Grim Reapers do, in the stories? What if Craven is a member, and Sheldrake is helping them from inside Mallowmarsh?'

'I don't know, Daisy.' The Prof looked uncomfortable, but Daisy forged on.

'Look, I think Sheldrake stole the ghost-moth orchid. Why else was he so close by when we called for help?'

'Let me think,' said the Prof, putting a finger on her chin. 'Oh, yes. Maybe because it's HIS glasshouse?'

'Actually,' said Indigo slowly, 'Daisy has a point. It was the middle of the night and, as far as he knew, the glasshouse was guarded. What *was* he doing there? He could easily have stolen the orchid, taken it outside, stashed it somewhere safe and then returned to "discover" that it had been stolen. It would be the perfect way to make himself look innocent.'

The Prof huffed. 'I don't know – it's definitely fishy. But it isn't proof that he attacked a Mallowmarshal and stole a priceless orchid. There are hundreds of Botanists at

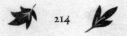

Mallowmarsh. It could have been any one of them.'

Acorn piped up from the corner, blushing as she spoke. 'My mum works in the infirmary. She told me Smedley woke up this morning and said he didn't see who attacked him.'

Daisy exhaled. 'So it really could be anyone. We'll just have to keep our eyes open.'

After everything that had happened, Daisy was dying to get to the hidden garden that night and finally ask Hal about Cardew.

But when she came towards the apple tree, it was to see Hal looking at her with something like annoyance.

'Where have you been?' he asked, taking off his thick glasses and polishing them vehemently on his shorts. 'You haven't come in ages, and I've had to do everything on my own.' He gestured around him, and Daisy saw that all the remaining weeds had been cleared and new shoots were sprouting around the base of the trees like silvery snowdrops.

'I'm sorry,' said Daisy. 'I only missed two nights.'

Hal shook his head.

'It's been almost two weeks.'

Daisy noticed brand-new leaves on the trees, and saw that the clematis climbing the old stone walls had begun to flower. He was right: all this couldn't have happened in a single day. Somehow, time was speeding up in the garden.

'I'm sorry,' she said. 'I came as soon as I could. Things have been – odd.'

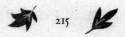

'Odd how?' Hal didn't say he'd accepted her apology, but he handed her a pair of gardening gloves and a trowel, and she knew she'd been forgiven.

'Well,' she said, beginning to dig near the roots of the apple tree, 'I think we might be getting closer to finding out who's behind Ma's disappearance.'

'Really? That's brilliant!'

'Yeah.' Daisy stuck out her bottom lip and blew a strand of hair off her face. 'Have you ever heard of someone called Cardew?'

'Of course I have.' He grinned at her, and Daisy's heart leapt. 'He's my best friend. Apart from you.'

Daisy stared at Hal, hearing Miss Tufton's voice in her head.

He died, many years ago now. Killed by his best friend.

Impossible as it seemed, she was talking to someone from the past, who no longer existed in her own time. The thought made the hairs rise up on the back of her neck.

'What?' Hal prompted. 'You look like you've swallowed a bug.'

Daisy opened her mouth. She tried to say, 'Watch out for Cardew. He's dangerous. One day he's going to try and kill you.' But nothing came out. She tried again. It felt like someone was choking the air from her lungs. She paused, wheezing.

'Nothing,' she said at last, and now the words came easily. 'I was just curious.'

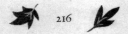

216

The atmosphere in the Five O'Clock shed the next day was electric.

'Holy Hollyhocks!' Indigo looked shocked. 'Cardew killed Hal White? The commander's son?'

Daisy nodded. 'Even though they were supposed to be best friends.'

'Wait,' said the Prof sharply. 'How did you find this out? Did someone finally crack?'

Daisy opened her mouth to tell her about the hidden garden. She didn't want any more secrets. But it was exactly like when she'd tried to warn Hal. The words wouldn't come out. 'I—' She battled to speak, and felt she might faint from lack of oxygen. It was like doing jujitsu against a high wind: pointless and possibly dangerous.

'Miss Tufton let slip,' she said at last, panting. This time, the words came smoothly, and she frowned. The hidden garden seemed to be acting like a time-capsule with the lid screwed tight. She couldn't tell Hal about the future outside it, and she couldn't tell anyone else about the past within it.

'Hal White!' The Prof's spectacles were glinting with excitement. 'This changes everything. He was one of the most famous Botanical explorers in history. He discovered the phosphorescent mango and the mimosa periculosa. And –' she paused significantly – 'the ghost-moth orchid!'

'*What?*' Daisy sat up.

'Exactly.' The Prof adjusted her spectacles and puffed

out her cheeks. 'Everything is starting to connect.'

'What else do we know about this orchid?' asked Daisy.

The Prof took a deep breath. Her hair was a halo round her head, and her elbows were poking out of her jumper so that she looked more than ever like an elegant philosopher-aristocrat.

'I've spent most of today in the library, finding out everything I can.' She pulled out a green leather-bound book called *L'Orchidée Interdite: Une Histoire Triste*. 'It's in French, but basically what it says is this: the flowers of the orchid are edible. For each flower you consume, a year is added to your life. But at the same time, a year is taken from the lifespan of the person you love most in the world.' The Prof read from the book, translating as she went: '*It is a beautiful and terrible plant, and eating even one flower is an imprisonable offence.*'

She looked around at them.

'Grandfather told me that people used to think it was a myth: no one really believed it existed. Then, on an expedition to the Amazon rainforest, Hal White *actually found* the orchid. It was the discovery of the century, but he was killed before he could bring it home. And no one ever talks about who was responsible, though Grandfather said they were caught.'

'So Cardew killed him,' breathed Daisy. 'On that expedition?'

Indigo nodded slowly. 'It makes sense. Cardew probably

wanted to claim the discovery for himself. He must have been wild with jealousy.'

'That's awful,' said Acorn quietly. 'No wonder nobody wants to talk about him.'

The Prof leapt up, as if she'd sat on a pinecone. 'Great greenness! Why didn't I think of it before! If Cardew was a convicted murderer, and this happened, what, eight years ago? It would have been before the abolition of the stripping penalty. So—'

Acorn completed the thought, her voice tiny. 'Cardew would have been stripped of his magic. Most people don't survive that.'

Daisy felt understanding and dread slip like twin ice-cubes down her spine.

'But Cardew *did* survive, didn't he? He's back, and he's calling himself Craven. That explains why he wanted the dandelight. If it's really a key to any Greenwild door, and if it works *even if you don't have magic* . . . it would be the only way for him to get in.'

The Prof's eyes were wide with horror. 'Forget about kidnapping one Botanist at a time: Cardew would be able to attack any pocket in the whole Greenwild – including Mallowmarsh. Nowhere would be safe.'

Acorn squeaked, and clutched Albert's box to her chest.

Daisy knew how she felt. 'That conversation I overheard – it makes sense now. Craven said, "Mallowmarsh will be finished . . . we're talking dust and ashes."' Her whole being

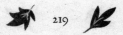

revolted at the thought. The idea of even a single snowdrop being harmed made her want to kick something, or throw up. 'And in the meantime, he's attacking Botanists in the Greyside.'

Acorn's green eyes were like golf-balls in her freckled face. 'As some sort of revenge for taking away his magic?'

The Prof nodded. 'So,' said Daisy, taking a deep breath. 'It comes down to this: Craven is kidnapping Botanists. And he's planning to attack Mallowmarsh. So, until the search mission is ready, it's up to me to do something.'

'No,' said the Prof, looking at her. 'It's up to *us*.' Her eyes shone, and she looked like the leader of a revolution. 'That's what the Five O'Clock Club is for, right? One of the reasons we're friends –' Daisy felt a jolt at the word – 'is that we each have parents out in the Greyside. Acorn's father is protecting cycads in Brazil. Indigo's dads are researching coral reefs in the Indian Ocean. Daisy's ma has vanished, and my grandfather is missing. This is about *all* of us.'

'So . . . you'll keep helping?' Daisy looked around at their bright faces.

'Of course,' said Indigo, nodding so vigorously that Jethro took off from his shoulder and flew screeching around the shed.

'Absolutely,' said the Prof, pushing her spectacles once more up the bridge of her nose.

Acorn's squeak of agreement was almost ultrasonic.

'That's settled, then,' said the Prof. 'So. What next?'

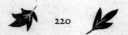

220

Chapter 32

Daisy came back to the Roost that evening to find Artemis sitting at the kitchen table in plum-coloured overalls that matched her painted nails. She watched as the commander pulled a large leaf from the vine above her head, and bent to write on it with a bamboo pen.

For a moment, Daisy longed to tell her about the hidden garden. But even thinking about it made her gasp for breath, just as it had when she'd tried to tell the Prof. Instead, she dropped into the nearest chair, massaging her throat.

Artemis whistled and a parakeet soared down from the roof beams to perch beside her. Daisy realized that there was a whole row of birds up there, camouflaged by the leaves and leaving little mounds of poo all over the floor. Taking the rolled-up leaf in its beak, the first parakeet launched itself unceremoniously out of the window. The process was repeated about six times with the remaining letters, until the kitchen was bird-free but covered in droppings.

'Instructions to our Greenwild agents in Peru,' said Artemis. 'I've told them to ramp up the search for any trace of the missing Botanists. No stone will be left unturned.'

Daisy watched the parakeets soar over the lake, diminishing in size until all at once they flashed out of existence.

She blinked. 'How –?'

'Birds – and some butterflies, I believe – are the only creatures that can come and go directly through the walls of the pocket,' explained Artemis. 'As far as post goes, we find that parakeets are best for the job – even better than carrier pigeons. They're a magical variety, specially bred for intelligence and endurance.'

'Will they really get to South America?' asked Daisy.

The commander's eyes sparkled. 'Oh, they'll get there, Daisy – and bring back answers. Parapost is more reliable than human post, and twice as fast. One of the main mailing offices is in London, and birds fly from there across the two worlds.'

Daisy thought of the parakeets that had filled the skies above London on that long-ago winter day with Ma. It looked like she'd finally discovered where they came from.

'Stop, stop!'

'No, you stop!'

It was late that night and Daisy was in the hidden garden, collapsed beside the small pond that shone like a silver penny. Hal had started it, splashing her with a handful of water – but she had finished it, tipping him headfirst into the pond. He had surfaced, water streaming from his nose, his face a picture of outrage.

'Why you—' He hooked a hand round her ankle, pulling her in after him, and a happy water fight commenced, ending

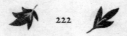

with both of them freezing cold and gasping on the bank.

Daisy gathered the long rope of her wet hair in both hands and wrung it out like a washcloth, aiming the icy water at Hal's feet.

'Enough! I surrender,' he said, and laughed, shaking his head like a wet dog so that the droplets flew out in a bright arc around them, catching the moonlight.

'Come on,' said Daisy, scrambling to her feet as Hal peeled off his dripping socks and hung them on a nearby branch. 'Don't we have work to do?'

They worked side by side for an hour, and as they weeded Hal asked for more stories of Daisy's travels with Ma. She told him about India, where she had seen people riding on elephants as big as double-decker buses (Hal didn't know about buses, which meant a digression into public transport in Greyside London). She told him about visiting the Red Fort in Lahore, where the flagstones of the courtyard had been so hot in the summer sun that they had burned the soles of her bare feet. She told him about celebrating the Persian New Year each spring, wherever they were in the world, and how Ma would grow dozens of hyacinths, and they would eat as many sweets as their stomachs could hold.

'One day, I want to go to the Shah Mosque in Isfahan,' said Daisy dreamily, yanking up a particularly recalcitrant bramble. 'Ma says that the patterns on the dome are blue and gold, like looking at heaven.'

'I'm going to go there one day,' said Hal, looking

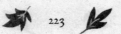

determined. 'I'm going to go *everywhere*.'

Daisy glanced at him, suddenly seeing the explorer he would become.

'You will,' she said. 'I know it.'

Indigo and the Prof spent the next few days frantically preparing for the first Bloomquist test, which had somehow snuck up on them and was now only a couple of days away. Acorn, of course, was too young, and Daisy didn't bother trying to practise – it was pointless. They'd been told that the test would evaluate their skills in Weaving and Binding, and that the latter would involve tackling some form of dangerous plant.

'I bet it's a vampire orchid,' said Indigo, feeding Jethro a handful of pumpkin seeds. 'That's what it was two years ago when my sister was applying.'

'Or a termagant blood-oak,' said the Prof. 'I've been researching the history of the tests and they've come up at least six times in the last twenty years.'

Daisy was silent: she knew that whatever the challenge was, she had no chance of passing it. She'd asked Artemis if she could be spared the humiliation of trying, but the commander had refused. 'Every Mallowmarsh student must take part,' she said firmly. 'No exceptions.'

Whenever they weren't practising for the test, the Five O'Clock Club were piecing together clues.

'As I see it, there are three mysteries,' said the Prof, putting down a slingshot (she had insisted Daisy teach her, and was getting quite good). She ticked them off on her fingers. 'One: the disappearing Botanists. Two: the theft of the ghost-moth orchid. Three: the indifference of the Bureau. Craven is connected to the first two. Does he have something to do with the third?'

Indigo looked thoughtful. 'We could, um, arrange to overhear the next council meeting. I bet they'll be talking about it.'

The Prof looked scandalized. 'Eavesdropping?'

'It's not eavesdropping if you just happen to be passing by. The kitchen storerooms are right next to the council room, and there's a larder there with my favourite biscuits.'

That was how Daisy found herself squashed in a cupboard with three friends, one grumpy cat and a parakeet, straining her ears for the sound of a conversation just beyond the wall of shelves. So far, the talk had been dull: they seemed to be discussing when a crop of feverfew would come into flower, and there was something about black-market trading getting worse. Then she heard the word 'Bureau', and felt Napoleon prick up his ears.

'I'm afraid you were right, Potentille,' came Artemis's voice, low and emphatic. 'The new Bureau head isn't sympathetic to tales of missing Botanists. We knew this already, of course, but something was different on this visit. Bertram Deeproot had been dismissed, and Elvira Elmlock had been moved to a different department.'

There was a murmur of surprise from beyond the wall.

'Both of them spoke up about the need to investigate the disappearances. It feels as if there's something systematic going on.'

Wildish said something Daisy couldn't quite hear, and then Artemis's voice, closer, answered. 'Exactly. We were wise, I think, to start feeding them false information about the precise whereabouts of Mallowmarsh explorers in the Greyside. I'm surer than ever that there's a leak in the Bureau, which is why—'

Indigo trod on Acorn's foot, and she squeaked.

'What was that?' It was Sheldrake's voice, coming closer.

'Mice in the snack cupboard again, I suspect,' said Artemis. 'I'll get Chef McGuffin to look into it this afternoon.'

Moving as silently as they could, the four of them left the cupboard, Indigo's pockets weighed down with ginger biscuits.

The day of the test dawned bright and chill, with frost glittering and crunching underfoot like sugar. Daisy, Indigo and the Prof met outside Chiveley Chase after breakfast. The Prof was tight-lipped, and Indigo looked queasy. Every time she thought about the test, Daisy felt as if a party of snakes was dancing the tango in her intestines.

A large enclosure made from holly boughs had gone up

overnight on the lawn in front of the Chase, and it felt like half of Mallowmarsh was crowded around it to watch the coming event. Daisy swallowed, feeling sick. She didn't care about getting into Bloomquist, but she was dreading the moment when everyone would finally learn that she didn't have magic after all.

She said a small prayer of thanks that Artemis had been called away to an urgent meeting of the Fungi Preservation League and wouldn't be there to witness her humiliation. But she spotted a scowling Sheldrake in the crowd, as well as a tired-looking Marigold Brightly and a beaming Madame Gallitrop, who was waving a red handkerchief at them and calling, '*Bonne chance, mes enfants!*' Acorn was jumping up and down at the front, holding a large GOOD LUCK banner covered with real four-leaf clovers. Daisy only just managed to summon up a small smile for her benefit.

The other students were already inside the enclosure, standing around nervously while a hearty-looking woman with muscular calves ticked off their names on a clipboard.

'The Bloomquist examiner,' whispered Indigo, nodding at the woman, who had thick braids looped around her ears, and the sort of voice that is well-suited to yodelling from alpine peaks.

'Greetings, Mallowmarshers,' she boomed. 'Another year, another fresh crop of young Botanical talent!' She breathed in deeply, like an Olympian athlete surveying mankind from the top of Mount Everest. 'My name is

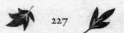

227

Honoria Plume, Bloomquist examiner and outreach officer. We're here today for the first of three Bloomquist entrance examinations. Those who succeed in passing each of the three tests –' she beamed around at the students – 'will have the honour of joining the school in September.' Someone in the crowd whooped, and Miss Plume clapped her hands as the bell tolled out nine times across the grounds. 'Right on time! Let us begin.'

Wildish had prepared his students well for the first part of the test, which involved Weaving a length of specially provided vine into a series of complicated sailing knots. The Prof passed with flying colours after executing a superb cleat hitch, and everyone else managed well enough, even if Indigo's bowline knot came out more like a squiggle. Daisy's vine, as she had expected, remained slumped on the ground.

'Time's up!' called Miss Plume, who was pacing up and down the line of students and making notes on her clipboard. 'Jolly good, Miss Bellamy!'

Daisy shifted uneasily. 'Can you hear that?' she whispered, turning to the Prof. 'It sounds like . . . hissing.' The Prof gave a tiny nod and turned Daisy to face the other half of the enclosure, where a huge, indistinct shape writhed beneath a giant green tarpaulin.

Daisy gulped. 'That's it, isn't it? The dangerous plant we're supposed to . . .' She trailed off, and the Prof nodded again, looking slightly sick.

'And now,' Miss Plume was booming, 'for the fun part. The Binding task!' She strode across the enclosure and whipped back the green tarpaulin with a dramatic flourish. The crowd gasped and leapt backwards as one.

The uncovered plant hissed, a susurration of sound that seemed to double and redouble across the enclosure. Slowly, Daisy began to piece together what she was seeing. It was a plant the size of a tank, with dense interconnected roots and scaly vines that swarmed upwards like muscular pythons: fifty of them at least, each as long and sinuous as a fire hose, with cold amphibian eyes and unhinged jaws.

Miss Plume beamed at them. 'A venomous hydra,' she said, rubbing her hands together and looking inordinately pleased, as if this was a treat she'd arranged specially. 'It arrived yesterday from the wilds of the Greek Greenwild. The international task force who subdued the plant said it was terrorizing a small Botanical community outside Athens, and we immediately earmarked it for today.'

The Prof was gazing at the hydra, eyes wide with a mix of terror and fascination. There were a few uneasy murmurs from the crowd.

'Your task,' called Miss Plume heartily, 'is to bind as many of the heads as you can at one time. The more you bind, the more points you will earn.'

'But, miss . . .' Kalissa raised her hand, looking doubtful. 'Isn't it dangerous?' One of the hydra's many heads snapped and a passing pigeon vanished with a terrible squawk.

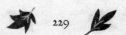

'That,' said Honoria Plume, making a note on her clipboard, 'is why you mustn't go past the white line by your feet.' She pointed and they looked down to see a thick line drawn in chalk across the middle of the enclosure, at a distance of about twelve paces from the hydra. 'The plant is firmly rooted, so as long as you don't cross the line, you'll be safe, Miss Cantrip. Now, I'll ask each of you to come up in alphabetical order by surname.' Slowly, they lined up along the perimeter as the hydra lunged and snapped forward with a hundred flickering tongues, yanking wildly against its roots. Daisy could see beads of poison glistening on the tips of a thousand fangs, and shuddered.

The Prof was first in line, and drew gasps of admiration from the crowd by immobilizing a total of nine snake-vines in one go. They froze in mid-air, each petrified into a furious S with open jaws. Septimus was next (four heads), then Kalissa (five), before Ivy managed to bind eight simultaneously. Her shout of triumph rang out across the enclosure, and Indigo scowled. To everyone's astonishment, however, he managed to bind seven when his turn came. 'I just pretended they were real snakes,' he whispered to Daisy, as Ravi and then Rishi stepped up (six heads each). Daisy was last, and she approached the white line with a feeling of grim resignation.

'Nothing, Miss Thistledown?' asked Miss Plume five minutes later. She looked genuinely disappointed. 'Nothing at all?'

Ivy gave a small snigger that made Daisy want to hit her, though it wasn't quite loud enough for the examiner to hear. 'No surprises there. Unlawful immigrants don't have magic.'

'Stop it,' said the Prof, jaw clenched.

'What was that? Did *the Professor* say something?' Ivy murmured the words from the side of her mouth. 'You're no more use than your grandfather, Bellamy. It's no wonder he went missing, everyone knows he was too ol— ARGH!'

The Prof had lunged at Ivy with her spade, eyebrows pinched in fury. For a moment, the pair of them teetered on the white line, and then they plunged over it: into the waiting jaws of fifty poisonous snakes.

Chapter 33

'NO!' cried Daisy. The world seemed to slow, and she watched in horror as Ivy and the Prof fell towards the hydra. At the last moment Ivy squirmed away, using the Prof as a shield, and the nearest snake-vine lunged forward and fastened its jaws savagely round the Prof's arm. The Prof screamed, a pure high noise that seemed to dissolve thought and block out feeling. After that, everything happened very quickly.

Daisy felt her palms tingle and grow cold with fear, and saw Miss Plume gasp and raise her arms above her head.

The hydra froze.

Fifty snakes, petrified like Medusa's hair, stood out against the vastness of the sky. Without stopping to think, Daisy lunged forward and stabbed the nearest frozen snake-vine with the side of her trowel until its teeth ripped free from the Prof's arm. Then she grabbed the Prof and yanked her back over the white line. Ivy tumbled after them and they landed in a heap of arms and legs at the edge of the enclosure just as the hydra began to move once again, seething and twisting in thwarted fury.

Someone in the crowd was screaming. Ivy was whimpering with terror, while the Prof sobbed with pain and shock.

There was blood on Daisy's clothes, on the grass, all over the Prof's arms. Wildish was hurrying forward, pulling a pot of chamomillion cream out of his overalls.

'Out of the way,' he called. 'Give her space.' He slathered the whole pot of cream onto the Prof's arm, as a team of Mallowmarshals fought their way into the enclosure to contain the hydra. Honoria Plume dashed to help them, brandishing her clipboard like a javelin.

Wildish glared at the Prof and Ivy, and his voice was quiet with suppressed rage. It was the first time Daisy had ever seen him angry. 'I have *never* seen such foolish behaviour,' he said. 'A demerit for both of you. That will teach you never, EVER to ignore a dangerous plant again.'

'But—' The Prof stared at him as if this punishment was worse than nearly being eaten by a rampaging snake-plant. 'You can't! It wasn't my fault!'

'No arguments,' said Wildish. 'Miss Bellamy, you'll need an anti-venom treatment immediately. To the infirmary. Now.'

'I'm so sorry,' said Daisy, sitting by the Prof's bedside that night. The Prof had been given a tisane of steeped scorpio leaves in the infirmary to combat the poison, and sent up to her own room in the Chase to recover. The chamber was small and cosy, the walls packed with overflowing shelves of books in a dozen different languages, and on the bedside table was an old photograph of the Prof as a toddler riding piggy-back on the shoulders of an elderly Botanist who shared her flashbulb smile and had to be her grandfather. Beside it was a portrait of a young couple with a tiny black-haired baby in their arms: the Prof and her parents.

Daisy was uncomfortably aware of Aunt Elspeth next door, muttering about the Prof being a disgrace to the ancient name of Bellamy. 'Good luck getting into Bloomquist now, my girl,' she had said grimly, sucking her teeth as Daisy brought the Prof up to bed. 'Two demerits . . . Well!'

'She doesn't need to remind me,' said the Prof bleakly. Her eyes looked distant and wintry as she gazed at the photo of her parents. 'What have I done?'

By the following night, there was still no news from Artemis's spies, and Daisy was getting impatient. She brooded on the delay as she hurried around the edge of the lake with Indigo and the Prof. They'd been given special permission to stay up late in order to help with the planting of lightning seeds from the storm harvest, and had been told to arrive at the Intemperate House at midnight.

The waxing moon was rising behind the Heart Oak as they passed, and Daisy noticed that the tree was looking a bit subdued tonight, almost . . . sickly. Its branches drooped and one whole bough looked as if it was rotted through.

'It's a bad sign,' said the Prof darkly. 'Aunt Elspeth says it means there are traitors at Mallowmarsh. I hate to agree with her, but she's probably right.'

Daisy shivered, and a chill wind whipped glittering black spray off the surface of the lake. She couldn't help thinking of the head of the Perilous Glasshouse.

'*Not* Sheldrake,' said the Prof, reading her mind. 'But still . . . not all Botanists are good. There's a dark side to the Greenwild, just as there is to the Greyside. People who aren't so scrupulous about how they use their magic.'

There was a grim little pause before the bells of Chiveley Chase began to toll out midnight.

'Come on,' said Indigo, and they hurried onwards to the Intemperate House, slipping inside the doors to join the crowd of gardeners, under-gardeners and apprentices standing near the alpine meadows. Daisy spotted the other final-year students clustered at the back, and headed over, waving to the twins. She was learning to tell them apart now: Ravi was quieter, with a sweet smile and a freckle underneath his right eye. Rishi was the joker, with a wicked sense of humour and the miraculous ability to lick his own elbow. He was swapping jokes with Septimus and Kalissa while Ivy loftily ignored them, her pointy nose in the air.

'Which plant is always cold?' asked Septimus.

'Go on,' said Rishi grinning.

'A chilli!'

The others groaned, and Kalissa turned to Daisy, Indigo and the Prof. 'Thank greenness you're here – I'm not sure I can take one more terrible pun.'

Luckily, Madame Gallitrop chose that moment to clap

 235

her hands. 'This way, everyone,' she called cheerily, leading them to the centre of a grove of lightning trees, which gave off their own unearthly blue glow. 'The moonlight is strongest here.' The trees were as tall and slender as aspens, their pale branches covered with shining, electric-blue leaves. There was, the Prof whispered, a fine mesh of copper wires beneath the soil that conducted raw electricity from their roots to a central grid that powered all of Mallowmarsh.

'Why do we have to plant the seeds by moonlight?' Daisy hissed, as Madame Gallitrop began handing around the sparking lightning seeds in small buckets. The seeds clearly didn't want to be planted and leapt about wildly, exploding themselves like miniature bombs whenever they were dropped or jolted.

Daisy tried to grab one and – ZAP! She was thrown onto her back. There was the smell of singed hair, and she touched her eyebrows to make sure they were still attached to her face.

The Prof looked at her kindly, as if forgiving her for being an idiot.

'You know how Greyside plants grow by photosynthesis? Turning sunlight into energy that they use to grow?'

Daisy nodded.

'Well, magical plants do that too – but they also use lunarsynthesis. They turn moonlight into energy and use it to generate magic. Planting when the moon is near full means that the seeds have the best chance of strong magical

growth.' The Prof slipped a seed into the earth with a competent pat. 'Lots of magic only works at night.'

'Ohhh,' said Daisy, thinking of the hidden garden and feeling something fall into place. That would explain why the door only opened at night and stayed rusted shut during the day.

'And of course,' the Prof was saying, 'that's how Moonmarket works too.'

Daisy glanced up. 'Moonmarket?'

'Right,' said the Prof. 'It's a market that happens once a

month on the Moonriver, starting at midnight on the night of the full moon.'

'What's the Moonriver?'

'It's a sort of in-between place,' said Indigo. 'Once a month, it lets Botanists travel between different pockets in the Greenwild.'

'Using moon magic,' added the Prof.

'So that stuff about witches brewing potions by the light of the moon . . . ?'

The Prof rolled her eyes. 'There are no witches,' she said. 'But yes – Botanists often plant and gather by moonlight. It strengthens the green magic.'

Daisy sat back on her heels, thinking about this, and remembering those nights of moon-bathing and moon-dancing with Ma.

Ma, of course, had known about the power of moonlight. She had revelled in it.

Chapter 34

The next morning was chill and grey, with sleet needling past the windows of the Roost and stripping gossamer from the giant dandelions. The gramophone was playing in the warm kitchen and Miss Tufton was stirring porridge at the stove, but Daisy was worrying about Ma. Another day, and still no news.

She frowned and glanced sideways at Indigo, who was using a leather-bound book as a plate while buttering several thick slices of toast. Daisy recognized Artemis's copy of *The Compleat Botanist* and distracted herself by reading some of the entries as he scattered crumbs across the W section.

At the top of the page was an entry for a Whimbuckle gourd (calabash family), which could be ground into a tisane to promote truthful visions. (*Warning: known to cause severe flatulence.*) Then there was an entry for something called a Whipple (also known as the Vanishing Tree), a tropical evergreen that was only visible at dawn and dusk. Its seeds, said the book, were completely invisible and thus difficult to source: but they could induce temporary invisibility for up to three hours in a full-grown adult. (*Warning: excessive consumption can induce exhaustion, paranoia and permanent vanishing.*)

Daisy's eyes stopped at the last entry on the page:

*Whishogg (also known as anar-e-arzu, from the
Persian meaning 'wishing pomegranate').*
*Native to Iran, and famous for its rarity, the whishogg
is the fruit of an unusual deciduous tree said to take
root only where true friendship exists. Uses: each fruit
contains one ruby seed that will grant a single wish.
The other seeds are an exceptionally good source of
vitamin C. Warning: be careful what you wish for.*

'Oh!' Daisy thought of Ma's stories about a magical
pomegranate and knew this was what she'd meant. She
spoke without thinking. 'Tuffy, could a –' she glanced down
at the page – 'a whishogg really grant *any* wish?' Her head
swam with visions of bringing Ma home.

Miss Tufton looked at her, surprised. 'No one has found
one of those in decades, Daisy. And even if they did . . .' She
sighed. 'It wouldn't be able to grant the only wish I care
about.'

'Oh?' Daisy glanced up, trying not to look too curious.

'The one thing magic can never do is bring a person
back from the dead,' said Miss Tufton, and Daisy knew,
suddenly, that she was thinking of Artemis's son. 'That is
beyond the power of even the greatest Botany.'

*

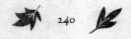

The hidden garden was very still when Daisy slipped through the door that night. The long grass was greeny gold, with fireflies embroidering their threads of light against the darkness. She could hear someone humming gently, and found Hal kneeling on his knobbly knees next to the great, shining apple tree.

'Oh good, you're back,' he said, looking pleased. He glanced at her. 'You look happier this time.'

It was true. At some point in the last few days, Daisy had begun to feel like a seed taking root. She was insect-nibbled and wind-ruffled and elbow-skinned. Her hair was full of twigs, her fingernails were filthy – and every part of her felt hungry and alive. It was an astonishing feeling: like finding a shining daffotrill bulb where her dull heart had been. Even if she couldn't do magic, it couldn't stop her from trying everything else in Mallowmarsh.

From Madame Gallitrop, she was learning how to trim and prune, how to mulch and fertilize (*lots* of griffin dung), how to wield a pair of gardening shears and how to tell if a plant was under the weather just by looking at the pattern of its roots.

From Marigold Brightly, she was learning the names and uses of dozens of different plants and seeds: from feverfew (good for headaches) to sneezewort (for toothache), and from baneful hellebore (for cursing the toenails of one's enemies) to monkshood – queen of poisons.

From Wildish, she was learning how to move so quietly

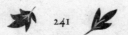

that she could sneak up on the hummingbirds in the Great Glasshouse. She had watched as they dipped their long beaks into the scarlet bassoon flowers, wings beating too fast to see. After they had flown away, she surreptitiously licked the nectar and found it was sweet as honey.

It was Miss Tufton, though, who had done more than anyone to make her feel like a Mallowmarsher. Daisy had come upstairs a few days earlier to find a copy of *The Compleat Botanist* on the end of her bed, along with a pair of new pruning shears and a blue velvet waistcoat embroidered all over with green vines and tiny gold stars, which she had taken to wearing everywhere, even to bed. She was wearing it now, with Napoleon perched on her shoulder like an imperial raja.

And yet . . . She swallowed, feeling like a fraying rope pulled in two directions. She loved Mallowmarsh, but it didn't make her worry about Ma any less frantic. It didn't make Mallowmarsh *home*. Home was with Ma, and the only thing that really mattered was finding her.

She felt her face grow stiff and uncertain, and Hal wrinkled his nose at her. 'It's not against the law, you know, to feel a little bit happy sometimes, in between the intense brooding.' Then his nose twitched again and he gave an almighty sneeze. 'Oh, botheration!' His eyes were streaming with hayfever, and Daisy tried not to laugh as he fumbled for a handkerchief. Looking at him, with his broken glasses and his knobbly knees, it was impossible to imagine that he'd grow up to be the great and adventurous Hal White, the most famous explorer of the century. Or that he'd be killed at the hands of Cardew.

'What is it?' he asked, looking at her face. 'You look kind of . . . feverish.'

'Gosh, thank you,' she said, trying to act normally. Then she turned, picking up her trowel. 'Things are finally happening. There's going to be a search mission for Ma.'

'That's great!' Hal's voice was full of excitement. 'You'll be able to go and find her!'

Daisy stuck her trowel in the soil, and Hal glanced at her face. 'What?'

'I still don't know where she is,' she cried, feeling desperate. 'I know she disappeared in the Amazon rainforest, but she could be anywhere now. I'm just so, so –'

Tired, she thought.

She yanked at a spiky weed with a sort of suppressed savagery.

Once, when she was about six years old, she'd got lost at a funfair that Ma had taken her to as a treat. They were supposed to go on the rides together, but within minutes of arriving Ma was interviewing one of the contortionists, completely absorbed as she always was when she discovered a new story to chase.

Annoyed, Daisy had stamped over to a nearby candyfloss stand. She was mesmerized by the fairy-tale puffs of spun sugar. When she turned back in the whirl of the fair, Ma was gone. Vanished. She still remembered the empty, cold splash of terror, like a bucket of ice water had tipped over inside her stomach and trickled down her legs.

She had wandered around for what seemed liked hours, until the sky went black and the lights turned creepy and the shadows grew claws. Ma had gone – left her – and Daisy had cried silent tears that coated her face in salt water and snot, while the air rang with the eerie laughter of stragglers leaving the fair.

Ma had found her at last hiding under one of the caravans, and she had cried almost as much as Daisy.

'Thank greenness,' she kept saying, holding Daisy so tight it hurt. 'Thank greenness you're all right.' Ma had never used the expression before or since, but in the extremity of that moment Daisy hadn't even noticed. She'd been giddy with relief, but also something unfamiliar that might have been anger. How could Ma have disappeared like that? How could she have left Daisy behind?

It was the same strange, angry knot of desolation she felt now. It took her straight back to that night at the funfair, her face tight and gritty with salt, and then to that first day at Wykhurst, when she had stood on the gravel, clutching her suitcase, and watched Ma drive away.

She blinked very fast and dug her spade furiously into the soil. The whole time, Ma had been keeping this great glittering secret: this other world full of wonder and magic, this place where they could have belonged.

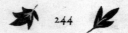

She felt Napoleon butting his head softly against her leg.

'You're right,' she murmured to him absently. She had found the Greenwild. She had Napoleon and Hal, and Indigo and the other members of the Five O'Clock Club. She had a mother who might still be alive – and who needed her – and that was what mattered.

Hal was silent, but she could sense that he knew some of what she was feeling. That was one of the nicest things about him: they didn't always need to talk to understand each other.

Instead, he sat back on his heels, laying aside a clump of thistles and dusting his gloved hands on his muddy shorts.

'Come on,' he said. 'I want to show you something.' He got up and led Daisy through a bank of newly flowering lavender that swayed coolly in the moonlight. 'Over here, look! Capersnip flowers.' He pointed to a carpet of tiny blooms that looked like pale purple pom-poms, bobbing up and down as if they were dancing for joy. Along the walls grew cool green figs and bushes filled with glitter-cherries, and the grass was dense with golden-eyed marguerites and fat peonies.

'The whole garden is coming to life,' he said. It was true. As Daisy looked around, she could hear a night bird singing on a branch above and smell the warmth rising out of the soil. The sapling they'd unearthed was taller and covered in green, with a single red fruit starting to grow on one of the branches. There was white jasmine coming into bloom and climbing through the boughs of the trees, which flickered with new-minted leaves. Daisy closed her eyes and felt the green magic beating like a pulse in the bark beneath her fingers, sending out steady surges of energy beneath her bare feet and into every corner of the garden.

'It's funny,' she said at last. 'My whole life, Ma told me stories of magic – Persian fairy tales where red roses had power and pomegranate seeds granted wishes, and magical birds raced through the sky. But I never thought things like that could happen in real life. I thought they were, well – stories.'

'Who says what's magic and what isn't?' said Hal. 'There's only what *is*. You wouldn't call it magic when a sunflower turns its head to follow the sun, because there's an explanation for it. In a way, *everything* is magic. The magic is in the sunflowers and the trees and the grass, in the dandelions and the parakeets and earthworms. Even –' he wrinkled his nose – 'in Brussels sprouts. It's in me and you and Napoleon too: in all of us.'

Yes, thought Daisy. The Greyside, with its mountains and rainforests, tigers and turnips, pumpkins and pangolins, was the opposite of grey. It was utterly full of magic. People had just forgotten how to see it. The whole world was brimming with wonder, if only you looked closely enough.

Chapter 35

Daisy was just sitting down to breakfast the next morning when there was a loud rustling noise and two parakeets came swooping in through the open window. The first landed on the table and deposited a squirming brown-paper parcel, which fell open to reveal a tiny monkey that darted behind the toast rack. Napoleon leapt onto the table, scattering toast everywhere, and Daisy hurriedly scooped up the monkey, which gazed out between her clasped hands with bright black eyes. It was about the size of a pat of butter, and weighed no more than a lemon, and she could feel its heart whirring against her palms. It was astonishingly beautiful, with brownish-gold fur flecked with glints of light, and a curling tail smoke-ringed with black. It rotated its neck one hundred and eighty degrees to stare at Daisy, and began to gnaw on her overalls with pointy incisors.

There was a note in the remains of the shredded parcel, which read: *I'm sending this pygmy marmoset to Mallowmarsh for safe-keeping. Home destroyed in the Greyside. Regards, Cuthbert Quirk.*

'Honestly,' said Artemis, rolling her eyes as the monkey made a bid for the roof beams. 'This goes against all the regulations. Cuthbert always was irresponsible – he should know it's illegal to send living creatures by parapost. Plants, fine; animals, definitely *not*.'

Once they had chivvied the marmoset out of the rafters and deposited it in the Great Glasshouse with a small colony of its fellows (Daisy watched as it flung itself ecstatically into a stand of bamboos, chattering with joy), their next stop was Chiveley Chase, where their morning lesson in Seed Craft was to be held.

'In the Seed Bank,' said Indigo excitedly, as they swept through the entrance hall and beneath the sparkling milk-white chandelier. It was no longer crescent shaped, Daisy noticed, but an imperfect circle: like a ball with a bite taken out of it.

'It matches the phases of the moon,' explained Indigo. 'It's almost full now, and it'll be a crescent again in a couple of weeks. Then there's one day a month when it's really dark and we all have to use candles.'

The Seed Bank lay down a flight of stairs and beyond a heavy oak door at the end of a dim passage. Inside was a dark, cavernous space that shone with rich and muted colours. The air was sweet and spicy, and on the polished wooden counter stood an array of scales in all shapes and sizes. There were miniature golden scales, just the right size for weighing an acorn, and enormous cast-iron scales, with weighing baskets big enough for a lion to take a nap in. There were bronze scales piled high with sacks of seeds and spices, and one that was weighed down by something very heavy but completely invisible.

The other students were already inside, and behind the counter stood Marigold Brightly, beckoning them forward. With her golden hair falling around her like a cloak, she looked more than ever like someone from a fairy tale. Daisy half expected a flock of bluebirds and dancing mice to begin serenading her.

'Today, we focus on value,' she said, looking around at the expectant faces of the class. 'Who can tell me what these are?' she asked, indicating a pile of tiny pearlescent nuggets.

'Oh!' said Kalissa. 'Seed pearls! My aunt planted one in her garden and the tree grows ten enormous fresh pearls every year.'

'Very good,' said Brightly. 'They're worth a king's ransom. It's the same here,' she added, indicating a pile of magnificently blood-red moss, speckled with little gold dashes that glittered like tears. Alongside it was a note that read: *Fresh minim moss, Tanzania. Plant moss within one month. Spores store well for up to five decades. Regards, Cuthbert Quirk.*

He certainly gets around, thought Daisy.

'It's strong stuff,' Brightly was saying. 'Incredibly valuable. A square centimetre of moss will shrink the eater to the height of my thumb joint – for an hour or two.'

Daisy nodded, remembering the Botanist they'd seen at work in the Great Glasshouse. Indigo was clearly thinking the same thing, eyes wide with longing.

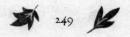

'Over there, it's the opposite.' Brightly turned away from them to indicate a towering set of scales braced against the wall, where a gigantic hairy pink coconut quivered gently. 'The bravarub,' she said. 'As heavy as a car, but not terribly powerful. The milk is good for calming anxiety, though. Wonderful in cocktails.' She winked.

Daisy nodded, vaguely aware of Indigo behind her, sneaking something into his sleeve. She sensed that Brightly was about to turn round and spoke quickly. 'So, how come you have to weigh the seeds?'

'Ah,' said Brightly. 'The scales measure both weight and magical strength. Once we know how powerful a new seed is, it can be deposited into the appropriate vault of the seed bank.' She gestured towards a huge circular metal door in the wall behind the counter. 'Who can tell me more about it?'

'It's the largest Seed Bank in the world,' said the Prof, looking reverent, 'with wood enchanted to keep the seeds fresh for centuries.'

'Excellent,' said Brightly, scooping the seed pearls into a jar. 'Extinction is sweeping the Greyside like a virus, but every seed means a chance to regrow and rebuild. Every seed is a toe-hold in hope.' Then she clapped her hands and set them an exercise in weighing various seeds and recording their findings. Daisy's scales were close to a framed photograph on the counter, which showed a boy with jet-black hair and big dark eyes. He had a port-wine birthmark below his right eye and a dimple in his left cheek that exactly matched Brightly's own.

'Is that your son?' she asked as Rishi scribbled away beside her, tongue poking out between his front teeth.

Brightly nodded, eyes distant. 'I wish he could see all of this. He's just a year older than you, you know.'

'Oh?' said Daisy. 'Didn't the commander say he was at Bloomquist? He'll be back for the holidays, right?'

'That's right,' said Brightly. She looked suddenly exhausted. 'For the holidays.'

The rest of the lesson was uneventful, but Brightly paused on the threshold as they filed out, and looked at Daisy with her large grey eyes. The others were already out of earshot, but Daisy heard her words perfectly.

'Watch out for Sheldrake,' she said. 'He's dangerous.' Then she turned, and was gone.

Chapter 36

Brightly's words rang in Daisy's mind all afternoon, until her head hurt. She heard them as she went about her chores, tramping from the Intemperate House (where a confused hoopoe needed rescuing from the depths of the marsh) to the banks of the lake, where extra hands were needed to help with the snodgrass, which had come into flower and taken to squirting noxious-smelling goo over anyone who came too close. By the time Daisy got back to the Roost, she was weary, aching and covered in blue slime. Worse, she had accidentally stumbled across Ivy Helix behind the potting shed. She was being shouted at by a tall man who had her light brown hair and pointed nose, and her face was small and pinched.

'But I tr—'

'That's not good enough.' The man banged his fist against the back of the shed. 'It might as well be your middle name. Ivy *Not-Good-Enough* Helix. Bloomquist will demand the best, and that Bellamy girl already has you beaten.'

Ivy was silent, and Daisy hurried away before she could hear anything else. She knew Ivy would hate her even more if she knew what she'd seen.

*

Nearly a week had passed since Artemis had sent out her letters asking for renewed action from her Mallowmarsh agents in the Greyside.

'Nothing,' said Artemis at dinner that evening, throwing down a letter. 'Both Petronella Mimble and Cuthbert Quirk say the same thing – there's no trace of where the missing Botanists are being held.'

Daisy rested her head on her knees as she sat in the claw-footed bath that night, her chest hollowed out by worry. Even using most of a bar of snoozefloret soap hadn't helped to calm her nerves. The clock was ticking, Ma was still missing and the rescue mission wasn't going to set out: not without knowing more about where the lost Botanists were being kept. They needed directions, a map of some kind –

Then she sat upright with a yelp, splashing bathwater across the room and making Napoleon yowl with disgust. She was remembering what she had seen in Craven's office, the day she had visited with Ma.

'That's it!' She looked at Napoleon, her heart pounding. 'I know what we have to do.'

Daisy strode up and down inside the shed at five o'clock the next day. She could only fit in about three steps before she had to turn around, but pacing felt important.

'We need to know exactly where the missing Botanists are being kept. And I know how to find out.' She explained about the map of Peru she'd seen falling to the floor of

Craven's office, scrawled with his notes and annotations.

'It's the answer,' she said. 'I only wish I'd remembered sooner.'

The Prof looked doubtful. 'Shouldn't we tell the commander? She'll be able to send someone to the Greyside.'

'No.' Daisy shook her head. 'Nobody else knows the *High Herald* like I do. I know where to look. And we can't afford to waste time trying to convince the grown-ups to investigate. They'll probably think it's another dead end.'

'But . . . that would mean going into the Greyside,' said Indigo, with an expression that made Daisy think of a skydiver standing on the edge of a cliff. 'There's no way we'd get past the Mallowmarshals at the door.'

'*That's just it*,' said Daisy. 'We wouldn't go through the Mallow gate.'

'Then what are you proposing?' asked the Prof, looking at her suspiciously.

'It's simple,' said Daisy. 'We go by parapost.'

Chapter 37

'*What?*' Indigo stared at her.

She looked back at him levelly. 'You have a square of minim moss, don't you? I saw you sneak some into your pocket at the Seed Bank, when Brightly wasn't looking.'

The Prof stared at him, and Indigo looked shamefaced. 'I wanted to try it,' he said sulkily, pulling out the square of blood-red moss. *It was only a little squashed,* thought Daisy, *and pocket fluff didn't really count as dirt.*

'Well, this is your chance.' She could hardly sit still. 'We're going to use it. We're going to shrink ourselves – and fly out of Mallowmarsh by parakeet.'

'You're joking.' The Prof was staring at her in horror.

'No,' said Daisy. 'I thought at first it would be impossible, but then I remembered the pygmy marmoset. Artemis said it was illegal to send living creatures by parapost, *but not impossible*. There's no reason why we shouldn't be able to pass through the walls of the pocket, if we're travelling by parakeet.'

The Prof shook her head. 'No. We *can't*. Have you forgotten how much trouble we were in last time we tried sneaking around? If we were caught, it would mean a third demerit for me. And no Bloomquist. My family – I can't.

And you can't, either,' she said, glaring at the three of them. 'I won't allow it.'

'But, Prof,' pleaded Daisy, feeling guilty even as she asked.

'No,' said the Prof, her voice fierce. 'It's too dangerous. We're not doing this. We can't.' And she walked out of the shed.

There was a short silence as Daisy stared after the Prof's retreating back, trying to ignore the hot, stinging feeling behind her eyes.

It was Indigo who spoke first, his eyebrows drawn together very tightly. 'I think you're right, Daisy,' he said quietly. 'Even if we have to go without the Prof. We have to get that map.'

Acorn, who had been silent up to this point, quietly reached for a battered copy of *The Compleat Botanist* in the shed's book pile, then flipped to the M section and read carefully, her freckled face creasing as she spelled out the long words. 'It says here that any inanimate object you're in contact with when you swallow the moss will shrink with you. So, clothes, shoes – maybe even backpacks, if we do it right.'

Daisy looked at Indigo, cautious. 'What do you think?'

'It's outrageous,' he said. Then he grinned. 'So outrageous it might actually work.'

'We'd need parakeets,' said Acorn hesitantly.

'Well.' Indigo looked smug. 'It's lucky you're friends with the Para-King.'

There was a pause as they waited automatically for the Prof to roll her eyes and tell him to shut up.

But the Prof wasn't there. There was only silence.

Daisy barely had any appetite that evening, and even Indigo only managed three helpings of sticky toffee-apple pudding. As soon as she heard the tulip clock chime midnight, she crept down the stairs and out of the Roost. Ten minutes later, she was hurrying away from the Intemperate House with four stolen lightning seeds tied up in an old scarf. A few minutes after that, she was assembled with Indigo and Acorn in the Five O'Clock shed.

'Ready?' said Daisy quietly.

They both nodded, and Acorn peered into a book on aerodynamics, hesitantly reading out last-minute advice on lift and wind direction, while Indigo munched a fortifying handful of chocolate drops straight from the tree. Napoleon was winding himself anxiously around Daisy's ankles – she had told him firmly that he'd have to stay behind in the shed – and even Alecky the tortoise looked wide-eyed and alert.

'Right,' said Daisy. 'Synchronize watches! I make it twelve-sixteen a.m. The book says the effects of the minim moss will last up to three hours: a larger dose could be dangerous. So, no matter what, we need to start the return journey at two a.m., in order to be back here by three a.m. Allowing for an hour's travel each way, that gives us forty-five minutes to search Craven's office. Understood?' Indigo and Acorn nodded, and Daisy felt the sort of organizational thrill she hadn't experienced since arranging Ma's travel itineraries.

They hurried outside and Indigo gave a great whistle, summoning three emerald-green birds down from the heights of the nearest tree. Daisy recognized Jethro, his orange beak jaunty and his black eyes glittering with intelligence. Next to him was a slim jade bird with a sweeping tail, and another that was a bit bedraggled, with feathers that looked as if they'd been pulled through a hedge backwards.

'Cleopatra and Bob,' said Indigo proudly.

'Bob?' Daisy gazed at the unkempt parakeet in fascination.

'Short for Sir Bobbington.'

Acorn giggled and stroked Bob's wing.

'Okay, Indigo,' said Daisy, refocusing. 'The minim moss.'

Carefully, Indigo pulled the square of moss from his pocket and tore it into three pieces, each about a centimetre across. Daisy's sat innocently on her palm, small and innocuous-looking. But something about it felt *alive*, as if it was humming, breathing . . . waiting.

Indigo was looking slightly sick. Acorn hiccuped solemnly. Daisy felt the absence of the Prof keenly. It seemed wrong to be doing this without her, but she also felt sure that they had no choice.

'Well – cheers,' she said at last. She took a deep breath, and ate the square of moss. It was very chewy and tasted bizarre: a mix of marzipan and something slightly fishy, like caviar.

Gradually, Daisy became aware of a shrinking feeling in her chest and the tips of her fingers, as if a helium balloon was slowly deflating inside her ribs, taking her skin with it. She felt herself sinking towards the ground, saw the world grow around her, the trees rising up to monstrous proportions, the tiny shed becoming a gigantic structure like a cathedral, until at last they stood among blades of grass that rose as high as trees above their heads. There was a ladybird near Daisy's foot that looked as big as Brutus.

Daisy glanced around and saw the other two standing beside her with dazed expressions.

'This had better wear off,' said Indigo, shaking his head. Then he whistled again, and three enormous birds swooped down towards them from a branch that now seemed as high above them as a church tower. Each one was as big as a winged horse.

Indigo was the first to mount his parakeet, settling his legs behind Jethro's wings and murmuring to him to keep still. Then Daisy settled her legs uncomfortably behind the wings of Cleopatra, while Acorn scrambled onto Bob's back, where she was barely visible behind a mass of untidy feathers.

Daisy felt the smooth ripple of her parakeet's pinions beneath her, and the bird's heartbeat whirring. The view of the world at this scale was extraordinary. She could see each one of a thousand shimmering feathers on Cleopatra's neck. She watched the wind ruffle the microscopic filaments on the back of a fallen leaf, and the mathematical precision of petals unfurling from a huge and gaudy chrysanthemum high above their heads. Below Cleopatra's talons was a cushion of moss that looked like a thick fairy-tale forest.

How had she not noticed it before, the marvellous detail of everything? She felt it now like a swoop in her stomach, like a magic spell, or a helter-skelter ride.

'Hey!' She heard a painfully familiar voice from behind the shed.

It was the Prof.

Daisy looked at the others, panicking. The Prof was storming closer, big as a giant, each foot as tall as a house. She had seen them. 'You can't do this!' she cried, her voice strangled. 'It's too dangerous. Acorn! No!'

'We've got to go! Before she stops us!'

'I'll go first,' said Indigo, speaking quickly. 'Jethro will follow my directions, and the others will take his lead.'

Daisy's heart clenched like a fist.

'Let's go,' she heard herself say.

'Stop!' cried the Prof. 'I command you to stop!'

Then Indigo gave another great whistle, and in a whoosh of wings that sent her hair in every direction, Daisy was airborne, with two shapes rising with her: up, up, up, into the starry wilderness of the sky. There was a deafening rush of air and movement – Daisy's stomach seemed to have remained behind on the ground – but when she opened her eyes a moment later, she was flying: really and truly *flying*.

She saw a flash of the Prof's anguished face beneath her, and she swallowed painfully, tasting guilt on her tongue. She hoped, desperately, that the Prof would forgive them, that she wasn't about to run and tell Artemis where they'd gone.

They soared above the Mallow Woods, across the lake – Daisy glimpsed three emerald shadows pass across its moonlit surface as they flew – over the Great Glasshouse and Chiveley Chase with its windows lit up against the night; and then with an audible *pop*, all of that was gone.

They had passed through the barrier.

Daisy's hair whipped around her, and her parakeet swerved, buffeted by enormous winds. It was a stormy night in the Greyside, and below them stretched the great dark expanse of Kew Gardens, surrounded by streets like necklaces of light.

'This way,' she shouted against the wind, seeing the others out of the corner of her eye, and then the glimmer of water in the distance. 'We need to follow the river.' Indigo picked up the direction immediately, steering his parakeet in a great curve, and Daisy felt the world tilt below Cleopatra's wing as Indigo called out, 'The *High Herald*! Quickly!'

The three parakeets screeched in unison and launched themselves forward. London spread out beneath them in a thousand arteries of gold and silver light, street-lamps and car headlights winking far below them like drops of quicksilver running though the veins of a giant. They followed the dark, glimmering expanse of the river, wind slapping their faces like an angry spirit. Daisy heard Indigo give a great whoop of delight from beside her and glanced over to see him leaning forward, teeth bared at the thrill of it. Acorn looked wide-eyed with disbelief, her squeaks rising above even the roar of the wind. She was hanging onto Bob for dear life as her bright red hair whipped out behind her.

Daisy began to recognize landmarks lit up along the river: Battersea Power Station hulking on the banks, the London Eye like a diamond ring turned on its side, and finally the great stone loops of Waterloo Bridge, where the parakeets turned as one and began heading inland, over a maze of streets and finally towards the great bulk of the *High Herald*'s massive edifice.

'Sixth floor,' she called to Indigo, who steered Jethro and gestured to the others to follow. They flew up the sheer concrete face of the building, and at last came to rest on the ledge outside the window of Craven's office. Then she saw the smooth expanse of glass, and felt despair grip at her insides. It was shut tight as a fist.

Chapter 38

'How are we going to open it?' hissed Indigo. They hadn't planned for this. Daisy glanced at her watch, which had shrunk along with her wrist. Time was surging forward and it was already past 1.20 a.m. She dismounted from her parakeet and ran along the ledge towards the seam of the window, pushing against it with all her tiny might. The glass towered as high as a skyscraper above her, locked and immovable.

'Hang on,' she said, thinking furiously. 'Right, I'm going to try something.' She climbed back onto Cleopatra. 'Indigo, can you direct her up to that lock – there.' She pointed to a spot halfway up the edge of the window. Indigo murmured and the parakeet launched into the air and hovered level with the lock so that Daisy could peer through the glass. The room beyond was dim, but she could make out the shape of Craven's desk, and the closed door behind it. She reached into her backpack. Everything in it had shrunk to match her own size, and with careful gloved hands she pulled out a tiny lightning seed.

'Stand back, everyone,' she said, and pushed it against the lock.

The seed exploded on contact, sending up a puff of smoke

and the odd acrid smell of burning metal.

Indigo and Acorn stared at her, open-mouthed, as the window to Craven's office swung open.

Inside was a realm of giants. The chair soared above them like a church. The desk rose like an enormous apartment block, standing solid and foursquare in the middle of the room, and the ceiling was so dizzyingly far above them that it was lost in shadow.

Still on her parakeet, Daisy flew up and landed on the desk, which was surfaced with green leather and a pad of rich creamy blotting paper that seemed as big as a swimming pool. A photograph of Craven glinted on the edge of the desk like an enormous billboard.

'Right,' said Daisy. 'He shut the map into one of the drawers of the desk the last time I was here.' She felt a clutch of uncertainty and prayed that Craven didn't take it home with him. But no – there had to be something valuable in this office: why else had the window been locked?

'We need to search the drawers,' she said.

Indigo uncoiled ropes – now thin as threads, but still sturdy – and looped them round the handle of the top left drawer.

'Everyone grab onto the rope and then fly backwards,' he called. They obeyed, and the rope strained in their hands. Then slowly, slowly, the drawer creaked open. Acorn dropped the rope and flew close enough to the open drawer to leap inside.

'Nothing in here but stationery,' she called. 'He *really* likes hole-punches.'

The next drawer contained monogrammed notepaper, and the next a stash of envelopes, but the next drawer they tried – the one at the centre of the desk – was locked. Daisy looked at Indigo and raised an eyebrow.

One exploded lightning seed later, and the drawer was open. Daisy saw the corner of a map and knew immediately that they'd found what they needed.

'Quick,' she said, dismounting, still panting from the effort of blowing up the lock. Together, each of them took a corner of the map and dragged it first out of the drawer, and then – reversing precariously – up onto the desk. Daisy stood at the centre of the map which stretched out around her, as big as a tennis court. She was standing on top of the word 'Cusco' – and, twenty paces away, she could see the dark green fringes of the Amazon rainforest. There was a trail marked through the forest, and there, in the heart of the jungle, a position marked with a cross. Daisy ran over the paper forest and stood with her feet over the cross. *G.R. Secure Facility*, read the letters, and she felt a chill shudder through her.

'There's something else,' called Indigo, and Daisy turned and ran back to the edge of the desk. They pulled a second sheet of paper out of the drawer, and Daisy stood and stared at it. It was slightly crumpled, ripped at the top as if it had been torn out of a notebook. *G.R. Fac – Inmates,* read the writing at the top – writing that Daisy recognized as Craven's. Then came a list of names.

Archibald Peagrim. Melanda Beechwise. Turford Grimroot. Dianara Speedwell. Emilda Spatchett. The names unspooled across the page, painfully familiar. *Felicity Wallop. Pandora Dingledrop. Milla Honeydew. Querkus Bellamy.* And there, at the bottom of the page: *Leila Thistledown.*

Daisy gave a cry and dropped to her knees on top of Ma's name. Her hand fitted precisely inside the O of *Thistledown*, and she saw the edge of the L of *Leila* smudge as tears dropped freely from her eyes.

'Ma!' she whispered. 'Ma!' She gazed up at Indigo. 'She's alive.' The words flooded through her like cool, clean water, washing away doubt. 'They're alive. The Botanists who've disappeared.' She imagined Craven tracking them one by one. 'We can still save them.'

Then Daisy heard something that chilled her blood. The noise of footsteps along the corridor outside.

She glanced frantically at Indigo and Acorn.

'Quick,' she mouthed. Together, bracing their feet against the green leather of the desk, they rolled up the two sheets of paper until they formed a single cylinder. Indigo used one of the thread-like ropes to lash the scroll closed, and then, each taking one end of it, they staggered to the edge of the desk, which dropped away like a cliff face beneath them.

Indigo whistled and the three parakeets swooped down

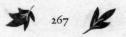

from where they'd been perched on the light fixture high above, and he and Daisy mounted.

The footsteps were getting closer now, nearer the door. The window seemed very far away, and – Daisy looked around wildly – where was Acorn?

She heard a squeak from inside the desk and saw Acorn's bright red hair emerging, then her body, staggering as if she'd knocked her head on the top of the drawer.

'Hurry,' urged Daisy. 'Come on.'

There was a jangle of keys, and then a hiss of surprise from the doorway. Whoever it was had spotted the open window and its broken lock.

'What the—'

Daisy knew that voice. She felt dread pool at the base of her spine.

It was Craven.

'Up,' whispered Indigo, and Daisy felt the rush of three sets of wings as they whooshed towards the ceiling. They were perched on the picture rail in the darkness, looking down as Craven walked into the room. Acorn was stranded down below, and Daisy watched helplessly as she ducked back into the drawer to hide.

Craven crossed to the desk in two huge strides. He looked as big as an ogre. Within moments, he'd spotted the open drawer and the missing papers. He swore under his breath and swiped his hands into the depths of the drawer. Daisy heard Acorn scuttle out of his way – he'd missed her by a millimetre.

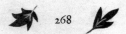

Craven was on his phone now, wedging the window shut with a bronze bust of the prime minister. Seconds later, an alarm began to blare through the building, so loud in Daisy's tiny eardrums that she felt they might burst. Then Craven turned and caught sight of Acorn's parakeet scrabbling across the blotting pad, desperately trying to get close to his invisible mistress. Craven brought down his fist, and Bob fell still, crushed on the desk.

Daisy stifled a cry of horror. The bird's iridescent feathers were crumpled, neck twisted at an odd angle. Craven's face was blank and empty.

Daisy felt her heart pounding like a lightning seed about to explode. Acorn was still trapped in the drawer, centimetres away from him. They had to escape. Any moment now, Craven would turn on the lamp and everything would be lost. She felt in her bag for the two remaining lightning seeds. There was only one thing for it.

'Indigo,' she whispered, almost noiselessly. 'I need to go down. Now.' There was a pause, a suspended second that seemed to last forever: and then Cleopatra swooped down like a fighter jet, and Daisy exploded a lightning seed ten centimetres from Craven's face. There was a great blue flash, the smell of singed hair and then – 'Acorn!' screamed Daisy. 'NOW!' Acorn rushed out of the drawer and Daisy grabbed her wrist with one hand and swung her up behind her onto her parakeet. Then they flew towards the closed window, Craven still pawing at his face, cursing, and Daisy exploded the last lightning seed right against the glass. It shattered with a noise like a hundred flower pots going through the roofs of a hundred potting sheds. Daisy felt a shard graze her leg, and the wet slickness of blood running down her calf. Then, with the others beside her, she flew out into the cold night.

The return journey was a blur of cold and pain and panic. Daisy could feel Acorn sobbing against her back. She was gripping on tightly with one hand to the feathers of Cleopatra's neck, urging her onwards, and hanging on with the other to one end of the scroll of papers.

London was silent and frozen beneath them, and Daisy could sense the parakeets beginning to flag. She felt, for a moment, the vertigo of the infinite dark sky above her, and the endless drop below.

'Just a little further,' she whispered desperately. 'Come on.' They needed to reach the barrier before the parakeets' strength gave out. And before the effects of the minim moss wore off and they returned to their normal size. How much longer did they have? There was the taste of fear like a sour coin in her mouth, and she could feel her arms begin to shake with the effort of holding onto the scroll. The stars were very large and close above her, and she could see with dizzying clarity how easy it would be to slip and fall into the glittering oblivion of the city below.

Don't think about the drop, Daisy told herself. *Think about Ma. You're doing this for her.*

At last Daisy saw the black expanse of Kew Gardens, the Palm House like a vast ghostly steamer ship against the night. *Almost there.*

It was beginning to rain, and each enormous drop burst against her body like a tidal wave. She battled for balance as Cleopatra wavered and sank.

'Come on,' she urged, closing her eyes, straining for the noise that would mean they had made it. The rain was thundering so loudly that she almost missed the pop when it came – but she *felt* the crossing in her bones, and then they were inside the barrier and soaring over the Sighing Forest and Mallow Woods, and the beautiful, glittering shape of the Heart Oak.

She gasped with relief – and then with horror. She felt her chest beginning to stretch, as if the helium balloon that had deflated within her a few hours ago was now beginning to expand again, filling the space inside her ribs. 'Down!' Indigo cried desperately to the birds, and she felt Cleopatra give a last, frantic surge towards the ground. Then, all at once, Daisy was her own size again and she was hurtling through the air and – OOMPH! She rolled end over end and came to a stop, panting, bruised, but in one piece. She saw Acorn beside her, and then Indigo falling out of the sky. He'd managed to direct the parakeets down in time and they only had a metre or so to fall.

For a moment, they lay there, panting. Then Indigo rolled over and staggered to his feet. He was covered in

orange goo, and Daisy realized that they had landed right on top of Mr McGuffin's prize pumpkins. Acorn was pale as milk, and Indigo was clutching the scroll – now easily circled by one hand – like a talisman. He scooped up the two exhausted parakeets and cradled them both in his palm, before placing them on his left shoulder. She could see tears on his cheeks and knew that, like her, he was reliving the sight of Bob, lying crushed and broken on Craven's desk. Daisy swallowed a sob. An innocent creature was dead because of her recklessness, and she wasn't sure she'd ever forgive herself.

Then they heard shouts coming from the guard house. Captain Malarky was running towards them, with the Prof beside him and several Mallowmarshals close behind.

Chapter 39

'There you are!' Malarky's voice was rough with fear and relief.

'Acorn!' cried the Prof. She sounded terrified.

Then Artemis appeared, and from the look on her face Daisy knew they were in deep trouble.

Once, when Daisy was four years old, she'd been standing beside Ma next to a busy highway in New Delhi. Someone had jostled her from behind, and her favourite toy, Blue Bunny, had fallen into the road. Daisy had run out into the traffic and then there was a screech of brakes and exhaust and noise and confusion. When she opened her eyes, she was in Ma's arms, bruised and too shocked for tears. Blue Bunny was crushed on the tarmac, unrecognizable. But what she remembered most clearly were Ma's eyes: wide and black with a fear that was a thousand years old: a fear that had made her shout at Daisy in a way she'd never heard before or since.

The way Artemis was looking at her now was something like that, only worse, because she didn't shout. Her voice was very low and quiet as she said, 'I didn't believe it when your friend told me.' Daisy glanced at the Prof and saw that her cheeks were burning with a mixture of shame and defiance. But Artemis was still speaking: 'I expected better from you, Daisy. You too, Acorn, Indigo. But I was wrong.'

Daisy made to speak, but Artemis held up a hand. 'I don't want to hear your excuses. Not this time. You've endangered our community and, even worse, you led your friends into a situation that could have got you all killed.' She turned away. 'Back to the Roost, please. I'll speak to you in the morning.'

Daisy ran the whole way back to the Roost, tears streaming down her face. Miss Tufton was standing at the counter when she came in, kneading candied hazelnuts into bread dough. Daisy stood in the doorway, chest heaving, and then Miss Tufton opened her arms, and Daisy rushed into them.

'Oh, Tuffy,' she sobbed. 'Artemis said . . . she said . . . Oh, what have I done?'

'Shh, shh, now, petal. It will be all right. Artemis was that worried about you. Whatever she said, she didn't mean it – you'll see.'

'No,' said Daisy. 'She's right. The Prof was right too. We could have been killed. Bob . . . and Acorn almost—' She heaved, unable to choke out the words, and the housekeeper stroked back her tangled hair until the crying stopped. Then she gave her a gigantic yellow handkerchief to blow into, and sat her down in the rocking chair next to the stove. While she blew her nose, Miss Tufton made her a large cup of tea with a good dose of snisky in it, grumbling in a way that Daisy found indescribably soothing: until at last she fell asleep in the hard wooden chair.

Someone was banging on the door. Daisy decided to ignore it. She was, she noticed, dimly, in her own bed; she remembered stumbling upstairs before dawn. She turned over and her memories of the night before loosed a rush of feeling like two rivers meeting and churning together in her chest. First came the flood of joy: Ma's name on the list. Imprisoned, but *alive*. Then came the surge of shame: the expression on Artemis's face when they'd got back. The risks she'd taken with her friends' lives. Bob, who'd died because she hadn't taken the right precautions.

The banging started up again.

'Daisy! Daisy! Come on, wake up!' It was Indigo.

'Go away.'

'Oh good, you're awake.' There was a pause. 'Listen,' said Indigo. 'I know you're upset. But Sheldrake is at Chiveley Chase, arguing against the search mission. We *need* to tell everyone what we found in Craven's office.'

Daisy sat up slowly, her muscles protesting.

'Otherwise,' said Indigo, 'all of it – what happened to Bob –' his voice cracked – 'will have been for nothing. They need to know the truth.'

Five minutes later, they had commandeered a lilypaddle and were sailing at full speed across the lake towards the Chase,

the scroll clutched in Indigo's right hand.

Up the avenue, past the roaring topiary lions, up the stone stairs they pounded. The bell was tolling ten a.m. as they came to a stop at the mighty oak doors of the Chase. The hall was full of Botanists, and there was a furious argument in progress, with some shouting for the search mission to go ahead, while others – led by Sheldrake – argued loudly against it.

Daisy breathed in like a diver about to go underwater, and pushed inside.

First one head turned, then another, and Daisy froze, pinned like a butterfly on the skewer of a hundred pairs of eyes. Then she felt Napoleon at her heels, and Indigo at her back, and she stepped forward.

'What's this about?' said Artemis, who was standing on the stairs, looking tired. 'Now isn't the time, Daisy.'

'No,' said Daisy, moving into the centre of the marble hall. 'I have to say this. We went into the Greyside last night, to the offices of Mr Craven – Cardew.' A murmur sprang up around the hall. 'We shouldn't have done it, and I'm sorry about that. But I'm not sorry about what we found there.' She took the scroll of paper and handed it to Artemis. 'I think everyone should see this. It sets out the names of all the missing Botanists – and tells us where they're being held.'

The murmur rose to a roar, and Artemis opened the scrolled papers and smoothed them out on the banister in

278

front of her. Her face was very white. Sheldrake, Wildish and Gallitrop craned over her shoulder to look, and Marigold Brightly gasped as she read.

At last, Artemis looked around at the hall, and the crowd hushed. She cleared her throat painfully.

'The children are right. Everyone needs to see this.'

The papers were handed around from hand to hand, and Daisy heard mutters and oaths echoing against the domed ceiling.

By the time the map and the list of names had worked their way back to the front, everyone was solemn and serious. Daisy saw the Prof, wide-eyed, at the back of the hall, and quickly glanced away. She didn't know which was worse: her guilt at not listening to the Prof's warnings, or her anger that the Prof had told on them.

Artemis mounted the stairs and spoke, looking around at the crowd.

'Friends, Mallowmarshers. The Greenwild has never been in so much danger. We know now that Cardew, a man we thought was dead, is involved in these disappearances – and at last we have a place to begin our search.' She paused and looked around, meeting the eye of each and every Botanist. 'I say we call a vote: right here and now. The people of Mallowmarsh will launch this search mission. So let the people of Mallowmarsh decide.' Her long silver hair shone in the light from the dome above, and even the portraits on the walls seemed to lean forward to listen. 'All those in favour, vote in red. All those against, vote in white.'

'What does that mean?' whispered Daisy out of the corner of her mouth.

'Wait. You'll see.' Indigo was tapping his feet with anticipation. There was a hush, and then a rustling began and an amazing scent gusted through the hall as a hundred red roses burst from the polished marble floor and rose towards the ceiling, far outnumbering the dozen or so white roses growing among them.

'Yes!' Indigo punched the air.

'Red takes the day,' said Artemis over the roar of noise in the hall. 'The vote is cast.'

It was done. They were going to find Ma.

Chapter 40

Daisy woke the next day with a flood of excitement rising in her like bubbles.

'Everything is going to be all right,' she told Napoleon. And she hummed as she dressed, putting Ma's red ribbon in her hair – for, she suddenly remembered, it was Acorn's birthday, and there was to be a party.

Their visit to the Greyside had earned each of them a demerit – the Prof had been right about that – but it *had* swung the decision about the rescue mission. Artemis had taken Daisy aside after the vote, her blue eyes grave. 'I'm sorry I spoke to you like that,' she said quietly. 'What you did was wrong, and VERY dangerous – but it must also have taken a lot of courage. I should have listened to what you were trying to tell me.'

Now, Daisy hurried outside towards where the lunch party was gathering on the shores of the lake beneath the Heart Oak, which was hung with fresh ribbons and charms. The air was cool and bright and filled with the laughs of apprentices playing tag and leap-frog, and the shrieks of Littlies – the youngest Mallowmarshers – being herded towards the Chase for their naps.

Daisy was hurrying past the potting shed when she heard a noise. At first, she thought it was an animal in pain. Then she peered round the side of the shed and saw the Prof sitting hunched with her back against the wall. She was trembling, pointy elbows pulled in as she clutched her chest. Her breaths were sharp and shallow as the stabs of a penknife, so that the air hardly went in at all.

'What's wrong?' Daisy rushed over to her, anger forgotten. The Prof glanced up, tears streaming down her face.

'Acorn,' the Prof gasped, chest heaving.

'What happened?' Daisy panicked. 'Where is she?'

'She's – fine. I – keep thinking – how she was – almost caught. Indigo – told me. My – fault.'

'Right,' said Daisy as firmly as she could. She crouched down and took her hand. 'You're going to be fine. Try to breathe. Slowly, in. Slowly, out. Close your eyes.' Napoleon placed a paw on the Prof's other hand where it lay clawed on the floor. 'Can you feel that? He must like you.'

The Prof nodded tightly. It took more than twenty breaths, but slowly her breathing began to calm, and she opened her eyes. When she spoke, her voice was shaky. 'She's like my little sister. I should have been there. I should have protected her. You were right, Daisy. I should have come with you. I shouldn't have worried so much about the stupid rules.'

'No.' Daisy shook her head so hard that her braid hit her

cheek. 'You were right, Prof. It was so dangerous. Craven – he killed one of the parakeets. He could have killed us too.'

The Prof closed her eyes. 'You did the right thing, finding that map. I saw Grandfather's name on the list. I'm sorry I doubted you. I'm sorry I didn't help.' She took a deep breath. 'And I'm sorry I told the commander what you'd done. It's only – you were gone for so long and I was so *worried*. You're my friends. If anything happened to you – oh, Daisy, I couldn't bear it!'

'I know,' said Daisy quietly. 'I feel the same.' Somehow, the mission to find Ma had grown bigger than herself. It was about every single missing Botanist. It was about protecting the first place in her whole life that had felt like home.

'Next time you get some harebrained idea in your head,' said the Prof, 'I'm coming with you, demerit or not. And Acorn is staying safe at home.'

Daisy nodded. She squeezed the Prof's hand, and the Prof squeezed back.

'There's something else I keep thinking about,' Daisy said at last. 'The map in Craven's office said "G.R. Secure Facility". I know it's impossible, but I wondered if it was G.R. like . . . Grim Reaper?'

'I wondered the same thing,' said the Prof, frowning. 'I saw the map. Maybe the Grim Reapers *do* exist. Not the ogres from children's storybooks, I mean, but real-life people – people who want to hurt the Greenwild.' She shivered.

'If they do exist,' said Daisy, 'we're going to find them, and we're going to stop them.'

There was a short, prickling sort of silence, and she decided to change the subject. 'Do you not mind being called the Professor?' she asked, voicing a question she'd been too shy to ask before.

The Prof laughed. 'You really want to know?'

Daisy nodded and the Prof looked down at their joined hands.

'When we were small, the other kids used to bully me because I was such a know-it-all. Plus I was an orphan and I'd been brought up by Grandfather. He's a great Botanist, but he's a bit . . . eccentric. He likes gardening at dawn without too many clothes on, and singing swing music on the roof at the top of his lungs. Anyway, it didn't exactly help me fit in. And if you think Ivy's bad now, you should have seen her then. I felt like I was going to die of loneliness. Then, when I was six, Indigo arrived and decided to be my friend. It changed everything.' Her smile seemed to light up her whole face. 'A few years later, Acorn started tagging along. She needs us, and it's a good feeling, being needed. Neither of them cares that I'm a know-it-all. So "the Professor" went from being an insult to a sort of honorary title. I've earned it.'

Daisy nodded. She understood, suddenly, that the Five O'Clock Club was a family, and that she was astonishingly lucky to be part of it. For the first time in her life, she had

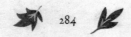

friends. Real friends. The feeling was like an espresso shot of pure joy, so powerful it made her blink.

'So,' she said, emboldened, 'what's your real name?'

The Prof groaned. 'That's the other reason I was bullied. It's Eggbertina.'

'Eggbertina?'

'Yep. It's a family name. If you ever use it, I'll have to kill you.'

Daisy laughed, and then, after a pause, so did the Prof, until their faces streamed with tears and their sides ached. They were still sitting there, hiccupping, when Indigo found them.

'What are you two doing? We're late for Acorn's party!'

The birthday party, it soon became clear, had morphed into an unofficial celebration of the vote's outcome, and Mr McGuffin and Mrs Marchpane (the pastry chef) had entered fully into the spirit of the occasion. There were great trestle tables laid out near the Heart Oak, groaning with platters of thyme-crusted bread and sweet pea soup and cheese tarts pulled from the ovens with long paddles. There was winter-strawberry fizz and dandelion cordial, and cloudberry pies with honey and twirls of cream. And at the end of the feast, Mrs Marchpane and two assistants came staggering from the kitchens with an enormous six-tiered chocolate cake set with candied plums, and nine sparkling candles for Acorn to blow out.

Acorn's mother, a plump woman called Ida Sparkler with hair as red as her daughter's, had brought out great terracotta pots filled with sunflowers, which beamed down pure sunshine and warmth and kept them snug in the wintry chill — a bit like heat-lamps at outdoor restaurants in the Greyside, thought Daisy, as she nibbled on a candied plum. Madame Gallitrop, meanwhile, had hung the trees with rainsap from the Intemperate House, so that the whole lakeshore was criss-crossed with rainbows like a miraculous light display.

With the vote decided, Daisy's mind shone with a single thought. They were going to search for the missing Botanists.

They were going to rescue Ma.

'How soon?' she had asked Artemis as they'd gathered for the party.

'Within the week,' said Artemis. 'Maybe sooner.'

Now, it was hard not to be swept up in the warmth of the celebrations as Acorn ended up with cake in her eyebrows, and Littlies ran around in sugar-induced delirium, and the older Botanists exchanged competitive stories of their past adventures. Everyone was there, even Ivy Helix, who sat at one end of the table glaring at everyone like a furious ice sculpture.

'Why is *she* here?' asked the Prof.

Acorn shrugged. 'Dad said I should invite her. It's not nice to leave anyone out.' She smiled. 'He sent me a birthday

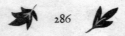

letter from Brazil – look!' The card was a hand-drawn self-portrait of a Botanist with a bushy beard and a big smile, waving wildly from a canoe. A speech bubble read: 'Happy birthday, Acorn and Albert!'

'He gave me Albert for my birthday last year,' Acorn explained, pink with pleasure.

Daisy spotted Marigold Brightly at the far end of the table, her golden hair curling around her face. She was laughing prettily at something Wildish was saying, but she looked, thought Daisy, rather exhausted, with purplish circles beneath her eyes. Daisy wasn't surprised when she hurried off early, claiming a headache.

But just as the plum wine came out and the rest of the company was beginning to break into off-key renditions of well-worn drinking songs ('Greensleeves' was a favourite, as was 'Ninety-nine Bottles of Snisky' and 'Barnacle Bill the Botanist') something happened that sent all thoughts of merriment straight from their heads. There was a squawk from above and a travel-worn parakeet toppled onto the table, collapsing into the remains of a rhubarb crumble.

Wildish leaned forward hesitantly and used his wooden hand to extract a scrap of paper tied to the parakeet's leg.

He opened it slowly, and Daisy watched as the colour drained from his face.

'What?' she asked. Dread coated her throat like tar.

'It's Bill Sparkler,' he said at last. 'He's disappeared from his research station in the Amazon. Gone, without a trace.'

After that, everything was chaos. Acorn gave a single heartbreaking squeak and staggered up from the table. Ida Sparkler ran over to her daughter, tears streaming down her pale, freckled cheeks. The Littlies, not understanding what was happening, began to cry too, until the air was full of wailing. Ivy Helix looked stricken, face pale and sharp with distress. At last, Artemis took Acorn and her mother to the infirmary to be treated for shock, and the rest of the party broke up, confused and muttering. There was fear in the air, as bitter and metallic as a bad penny. Daisy glanced up at the Heart Oak and saw that, despite its gallant ribbons and polished coins, the bough she had noticed before was almost rotted through.

The Five O'Clock Club gathered with unusual solemnity that evening. Acorn came in late, clutching Albert's matchbox, and the others made room for her silently. The Prof hugged her, hard. Indigo offered her a handful of chocolate drops, and Daisy reached over and squeezed her hand.

'This isn't good,' said the Professor, adjusting her glasses. She looked at Acorn apologetically. 'It means there's a spy at Mallowmarsh.'

'How do you know?' asked Indigo.

'Remember what the commander said at the council meeting we overheard? She's been giving the Bureau false information about the location of the Botanists because she was afraid there was a leak.'

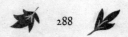

'And now it looks like there's a leak here at Mallowmarsh too,' finished Daisy miserably.

This was confirmed when Artemis came sweeping into the Roost that evening, brushing rain from her eyebrows.

'It's a spanner in the works all right,' she said grimly. 'It means our explorers are in danger – and it puts the whole search mission at risk. If the details are being fed straight to Craven, we'll be attacked before we're out of England.'

Suddenly, everything was in doubt. Artemis swept out again as soon as she'd wolfed down a sandwich, back to emergency meetings at the Chase.

Daisy and Indigo exchanged a wide-eyed look.

'You heard her,' said Daisy. 'No rescue mission unless this spy is found.'

'Well, then.' Indigo raised his eyebrows. 'We're going to have to do some looking.'

Daisy spent the next few days obsessed with thoughts of Sheldrake. All signs seemed to point to him being the spy. The sneaking around at night. The secret meeting in the woods. The way he'd been so close by after the theft of the ghost-moth orchid. Not to mention the fact that he disliked the commander so much.

'It's him. I know it,' she said stubbornly at the next meeting of the Five O'Clock Club.

Indigo wrinkled his dark eyebrows. 'He *is* on the council, so he'd have access to details about Mallowmarshers in the

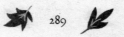

Greyside. Their locations, everything.'

The Prof nodded reluctantly. 'I can't believe I'm saying this, but . . . perhaps we should try to follow him, find out what he's up to.'

Acorn only looked miserably into her lap. Even the sight of Albert tucking into a particularly juicy cabbage leaf couldn't cheer her.

'Right,' said Daisy, straightening her spine. 'It's settled. From now on, we stick to Sheldrake like glue.' She paused. 'Very subtle, practically invisible glue.'

They spent most of the next two days tailing Sheldrake from one end of the grounds to the other, leaping behind hedges each time he turned around. Daisy was convinced that it was only a matter of time before they caught him doing something incriminating, but he spent much of his time in the Perilous Glasshouse – and they weren't about to try sneaking in there again.

'Who knows *what* he's doing in there,' Daisy said darkly. 'He could be running a whole criminal empire and no one would know about it.'

It was several days before she finally realized the obvious.

'I'm an idiot,' she said, smacking her forehead.

'We all know *that*,' said the Prof, grinning. 'Any particular reason the truth has finally struck you?'

'There's one easy way to find out what Sheldrake is up to. We should be intercepting his post.'

'But how?' Acorn frowned, fluffing up the leaves in

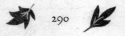

Albert's matchbox while he explored the back of her hand like a small roving moustache. 'He'd be *furious* if he found out.'

Daisy looked across the shed. 'Indigo? You're the bird whisperer. Couldn't you help?'

'I don't know,' he said. Daisy knew he was thinking of Bob.

'Come on,' said the Prof. 'You're the Para-King, remember? We need you.'

At last, Indigo looked up and smiled a little sadly, showing his wonky tooth. 'All right,' he said. 'We'll have to check everything that goes in or out, but . . . it's worth a try.'

Daisy felt a rush in her chest like a hawk on the wind. 'This is it. Once we have Sheldrake's letters, we'll know what he's planning – and we'll be ready to catch him.'

She stood on the end of her bed that night, gazing out at the stars through the rusty telescope that poked out of the skylight. Napoleon's whiskers brushed her ankles, and she felt again the eddy of sand against her skin as she'd watched Ma's profile tilted up at the Milky Way in the desert.

Look up, and you'll find yourself.

Tonight, Daisy couldn't find any meaning in the pattern of the constellations, except as a compass mapping the way towards Ma.

'I'm doing everything I can,' she said quietly. 'We're going to catch this spy – and then we're coming.'

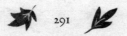

Chapter 41

'Have you ever been to Moonmarket?' Daisy asked Hal that night in the hidden garden. They were planting winter-flowering pansies, and she had been wondering if the market – which sounded like the biggest and most regular gathering of Botanists in the Greenwild – might hold any clues. To her, it sounded like exactly the sort of place a spy would take advantage of.

'We-ell,' said Hal, suddenly becoming very absorbed in polishing his glasses. 'Not officially. But sometimes I go – er – without permission. It's the best place to find rare plants, and it's run by the Moon Travellers. They're wonderful: they cross the rivers of Europe, going from market to market with their wares. My father was born into a Traveller family, not that he ever talks about it. I keep hoping that one day I'll bump into a cousin or an uncle at the market – and that somehow I'll *know*. But it's never happened. It's silly.'

'It's not silly,' said Daisy. She thought of the fantasies she used to have that Pa wasn't dead: that one day they'd arrive in a new city, and he would be there waiting. She felt, yet again, an enormous tide of longing to see and talk to him – even once. 'You should write to them. Your Traveller family, I mean. I bet you could reach them by parapost.'

'Huh,' said Hal. 'That's actually not a terrible idea.'

'You're welcome.'

'Actually,' he said, 'I've been going to Moonmarket a lot recently because . . . well, there's something I'm investigating.'

'Really?'

'Yes,' said Hal, sticking his spade into the earth and sitting back on his heels. 'Plants have been disappearing from Mallowmarsh. At first only a few, but now more and more. I think someone is stealing them and selling them on the Darkmarket.'

'What's that?' Daisy felt her heart pounding.

'It's the shady side of Moonmarket,' said Hal. 'It's nothing new – it's been around for centuries. But now I think they're buying and selling endangered plants and animals . . . And it's *wrong*. Just because someone is willing to buy a black rhino or a rare fire-lily doesn't mean humans have a right to sell them.'

'Have you told anyone about this?' asked Daisy.

'Yes.' Hal nodded. 'But my dad told me to stop making things up. I'm not, though! I've been going to Moonmarket for months; I've overheard all sorts of things. No one pays attention to the scrawny boy in the corner. I even know what the Darkmarketeers call themselves. The Grim Reapers.'

Daisy breathed in sharply, and Hal looked up. 'What?'

'Nothing.' She struggled to hide her shock. 'Only, do you

know what they want? The Reapers?'

Hal shrugged. 'Money,' he said, as if this was obvious. 'Power. Environmental destruction.'

'But why?'

Hal looked impatient. 'It's simple, Daisy. The rarer a plant or animal is, the more you can charge for it on the black market. Say the number of fire-lilies left in the wild drops from fifty to five. You can charge ten times as much for them: millions and millions of pounds. So destroying rivers and forests and habitats is a good strategy.'

Hal's voice was bitter, and his eyes were fierce.

'Someone needs to stop them. And that's what I'm going to do, as soon as I'm old enough. I'm going to become an explorer – but not an ordinary one. I'm going to travel the world and stop the Reapers stealing so much as another cactus.'

Daisy felt foreboding like a swoop to the stomach. Was this how Hal would be killed? Trying to save the ghost-moth orchid, the rarest plant of all? Would Cardew grow up to betray Hal by joining the Grim Reapers, and kill his friend to get his hands on it?

For the hundredth time, Daisy struggled to voice a warning. Instead, she was left gasping, hands at her raw throat.

'What's wrong?' asked Hal. 'Do you need a cough drop?'

'Nothing,' she rasped. 'Everything's . . . fine.'

'Good,' said Hal, and settled his glasses back on his nose.

Daisy returned to the Roost for tea the next day to discover a note from Indigo on the kitchen table. It read: *Para-King comes up trumps. See you at five.*

When she arrived at the shed, Indigo had a parakeet perched on each shoulder and he was looking very pleased with himself.

'It's working,' he said with a huge grin as soon as they were assembled. 'Tell them, Prof.'

The Prof nodded. 'You wouldn't believe all the letters that go in and out each day. *Hundreds* of them! Madame Gallitrop is addicted to seed catalogues, Mr McGuffin keeps ordering fancy vegetable peelers and Marigold Brightly sends about three notes a day to her son Max – you know, the one at Bloomquist.' She held up a stack of envelopes all addressed to '*Max*' in elegant cursive script: each one sealed with three kisses.

'That doesn't matter,' said Daisy impatiently. 'What about Sheldrake's letters?'

Indigo grinned. 'I thought you'd never ask.' He handed over a folded note, addressed in an impatient hand. '*Ferrus Sheldrake*,' read the scrawled direction.

She unfolded it and read aloud.

'*Moonmarket, 1 a.m. At the sign of the Dancing Salamander. Bring the item we discussed. M. D.*'

They looked at each other, wide-eyed.

'M. D.?' said Indigo. 'Who's M. D.?'

'That,' said Daisy, her eyes very bright, 'is what we'll find out. It's the full moon, which means Moonmarket is TONIGHT. We have to follow him and find out who he's meeting.'

She folded up the note and handed it back to Indigo. 'Make sure Sheldrake gets this,' she said. 'And intercept his reply too – to make sure he agrees.'

She watched as Indigo reattached the letter to the parakeet's leg and it vanished in an emerald flash towards the woods.

The Prof looked unsure. 'We're not allowed to go to Moonmarket by ourselves until we're eighteen. Shouldn't we tell the commander and see what she says? Then she can decide what to do.'

'Listen,' said Daisy, speaking urgently. 'I think the Grim Reapers started out at Moonmarket, running a black-market trading operation – and they've expanded from that into kidnapping Botanists. I think—'

But she didn't have a chance to finish, because that was when they heard the first screams. Then came alarm bells: first distant, then growing louder and louder as the warning was passed on from glasshouse to glasshouse, and shouts and cries filled the air.

'SLUG ATTACK! SLUG ATTAAAACK!' came the panicked voice of Captain Malarky through a loudhailer. 'All hands to the Sump-Rose Garden immediately. Repeat. All hands to the Sump-Rose Garden IMMEDIATELY. This is NOT A DRILL.'

296

The four of them ran, Napoleon at their heels, and encountered a terrifying sight.

Giant slugs, everywhere.

It was an invasion.

Enormous frilled orange slugs with razor-sharp teeth, crawling over the flower beds and leaving empty desolation in their wake. Dog-sized blue slugs with piranha teeth that absorbed plants like jelly and left them blackened and hissing like a chemical burn. Huge scarlet slugs as tall as horses, which bulldozed over everything in their path, leaving the sump-roses crushed and destroyed.

Within a matter of minutes, more than half of the glorious rose garden, pride of Mallowmarsh, pinnacle of centuries of cultivation, was an oozing graveyard.

The slugs were legion; they were unstoppable, and they were on the move.

Daisy lifted Napoleon out of harm's way and tucked him into the V of her jumper. Then she hurried over to a corner where Botanists were donning full-body suits, including a sort of pith helmet and visor, because, according to a panicked Prof, the slugs were partial not just to plant matter but also to human flesh.

'Don't hurt them!' cried Wildish, who was overseeing operations. 'We must remove them one by one.'

'How are we supposed to do that?' Daisy reared back from a nasty blue slug and almost slipped on a slick of slug mucus.

But Wildish was already organizing the Botanists into teams, directing them to use thick loops of vines to swoop down and truss the slugs like slimy prisoners, before catapulting them into the giant wooden pens that were being erected by the woodsmen at the edges of the garden.

'How – how could they have got in?' Daisy heard Madame Gallitrop moan to herself as she looped a vine round a particularly large scarlet slug. 'They must have come from the forest,' she muttered, casting dark glances in the direction of the Sighing Forest and Sheldrake's cabin. Sheldrake himself was nowhere to be seen.

An hour stuttered past in flicks and flashes, and then another: a blur of panic as they worked to stem the tide. At one point, a large orange slug chewed its way through the rubber of Daisy's boot and began nibbling on her toe.

'GAH! Get off!' She shook her foot desperately and sent the slug flying into the air, praying that the others wouldn't be attracted by the smell of blood.

Indigo dashed around intercepting slugs with a sort of manic glee, while the Prof wielded a vine like a cowboy, lassoing the giant molluscs with expert precision. The commander had several vines looped in each hand, and sent slugs careering over their heads with the regularity of an artillery cannon. Daisy did what she could by helping to bathe the surviving sump-roses with distilled water, washing away the remnants of grey slime from their petals.

Every Mallowmarsher was called to the task, and it was well past ten p.m. when the last slug was finally trussed up and the bulging pens were hitched to horses from the stables and sent trundling towards the forest so that they could be deposited back in their rightful homes. The ground was strewn with fallen rose hips, and Daisy bent down and cupped a handful in her palms. She put them in her pocket: perhaps, later, they could be replanted.

She was about to head back to the Roost when Ivy stopped her.

'What now?' said Daisy. She felt very weary. 'Come to accuse me of something else?'

Ivy shook her head. She had a smear of something unidentifiable across her forehead, and her usually sleek caramel hair was matted with slime.

'Well?' Daisy looked at her, suddenly impatient.

'I'm – I . . . I wanted to say I know you're not the spy. I know how much you care about Acorn. I know you'd never give away her dad's location.' She paused, struggling for words. 'He's a nice person, Mr Sparkler. He's always been kind to me, even when my dad . . . Well, anyway.' Daisy remembered seeing Ivy's father shouting at her, and unfolded her arms as Ivy continued. 'I know you've been, um, investigating things, and I thought you'd want to know – I overheard the commander talking to Wildish. She said that an entire jar of slugnip vanished from the Seed Bank this morning. It's a herb that's irresistible to slugs. I think they usually use it to lure them *away* from the sump-roses.'

'But . . . that means someone set them on the garden *deliberately*,' said Daisy, horrified.

Ivy nodded, her mouth a grim line.

'I've got to go,' said Daisy. 'Ivy, I'm . . . thank you.'

She turned and sprinted for the Roost.

Chapter 42

She'd never run so fast in her life. Someone had wanted to stage a distraction, and she could only think of one thing that was valuable enough to warrant such a drastic one.

The dandelight.

Daisy's legs burned as she mounted the stairs of the Roost to the kitchen two at a time, forcing herself onwards. Then she reached the threshold of the kitchen and stopped dead.

Plants lay mutilated on the floor, their pots shattered and leaves shredded. Plates were smashed and pages had been torn out of books and scattered across the floor. The vines had been yanked from the rafters, and the pink gramophone lay broken and silent, its needle circling empty space. And there in the corner lay a tiny figure in a purple apron, prone and lifeless on the floor.

'Tuffy!'

Daisy rushed towards her.

She lay with her eyes closed, her bun askew on her head. The ivy near the stove was wrenched onto the floor, the loose brick tossed aside, the safe behind it empty.

The dandelight was gone.

'Miss Tufton!' Daisy was trembling.

Artemis burst through the door and took in the scene. In

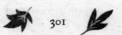

moments, she had her fingers on the housekeeper's pulse. 'She's alive,' she said. Slowly, Miss Tufton opened her eyes.

'What happened?' Artemis's voice was urgent.

'Someone. Couldn't – see them.' Miss Tufton spoke with difficulty, wheezing slightly as the words came out. 'Just heard them. Tried to – stop them.'

They looked at each other, speechless. Tuffy closed her eyes in exhaustion, and turned her face to the wall.

'Come on,' said Artemis. 'Help me get her upstairs.'

Daisy had never been inside Miss Tufton's room, but she noticed, in a distracted way, that the floor was carpeted in tangled long grass scattered with cornflowers, and that the walls were curtained with rambling roses and showers of ghost ivy, which glowed in the dark. Daisy stared at Miss Tufton, who lay on the bed looking impossibly small and still, her big fierceness gone.

Before she had time to say a word, Artemis grabbed Daisy's arms. 'I need to alert the Mallowmarshals,' she said. 'And call a council meeting. I need you to stay here and watch Tuffy.'

'I know who did this,' said Daisy. 'It's Sheldrake. It's—'

Artemis was shaking her head impatiently. 'No, Daisy, not Sheldrake. Listen, I need you to stay here. I've ordered a triple guard on the Mallow gate or I wouldn't leave you at all. I'm trusting you.'

Daisy opened her mouth to speak, but Artemis was already gone.

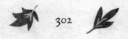

Daisy turned back to Miss Tufton and felt as if she was back in the Sighing Forest, surrounded by mists of regret and self-recrimination. *My fault*, she thought miserably. *All my fault*. If only she had told Artemis earlier about Sheldrake, none of this would have happened.

She stood for another moment, then hurried back downstairs. Indigo, Acorn and the Prof were standing in the kitchen, staring around in horror.

Acorn looked ferocious. 'Whoever did this is – is – *evil*.'

'It was Sheldrake,' said Daisy furiously. 'He wasn't there during the slug attack. It was a diversion, so he could come here and steal the dandelight.'

'It's gone?'

Daisy nodded. She felt terribly cold, as if she'd slipped into a deep, icy well.

It was Indigo who spoke first. 'Sheldrake is going to hand over the dandelight, isn't he? Tonight, at Moonmarket.'

Daisy nodded. '"*Bring the item we discussed*": that's what the note said! We have to stop him.'

The Prof protested. 'The rules—'

'Forget the rules.' Artemis's instructions to stay put no longer seemed to matter. 'This is more important.'

The Prof closed her eyes, then nodded slowly. 'All right,' she said at last. Her voice was quiet, and Daisy knew she was remembering their conversation behind the potting shed. She also knew what it was costing the Prof to risk this: a third demerit, and her future at Bloomquist.

'We'll go,' said the Prof, sucking in a breath. 'But Acorn stays.'

'That's not fair!' Acorn's freckles stood out starkly against her pale cheeks.

'No,' said the Prof. 'You're too young and it's too dangerous.'

'But—'

'She's right,' said Daisy quietly, meeting the Prof's eyes. 'It's not safe, Acorn. We need you and Albert here to hold the fort.' Acorn's expression was mutinous, but she stayed quiet.

Indigo glanced at the kitchen clock. The tulip hand was flowering an uneasy purple and pointing to eleven p.m.

'One hour,' he said. 'The moontide leaves at midnight, when the moon reaches its height.'

They settled down to wait.

The moon was full and huge, like a great silver ship setting sail across a dark sea. Daisy, Indigo and the Prof were crouched in the bushes behind the Roost, waiting, their eyes fixed on the margin of the woods, and the light in the window of Sheldrake's cabin.

Mallowmarsh was silent, exhausted by the slug attack. There were guard-lights visible from the Mallow gate, and Mallowmarshals patrolling outside each of the glasshouses. Daisy wondered, wildly, whether she should pull one of them aside and accuse Sheldrake. But she heard the commander's denial in her head, and she knew it would be no use.

She could hear Silas the goat snoring quietly on his patch, and felt a beetle creep over her foot. She suppressed a yelp, and shifted. Her knees ached from crouching.

Then, just as she felt she couldn't take another moment of waiting, they saw a movement from the woods, and the dark shape of Sheldrake as he slipped out of the shadows.

'*Now*,' whispered Daisy, and the three of them scattered out from behind the bushes, past the plum trees and silver birches that led down to the lake.

They could see Sheldrake standing on its banks, hesitating, a leather satchel thrown over one shoulder. Then he stepped deliberately into the moonlit water – and vanished.

Daisy inhaled sharply.

'Shh!' Indigo glared at her. 'Follow my lead and hold hands so we don't get separated. On the count of three, we step into the water. One. Two. Thr—'

At the last moment there was a squeak and a blur of fiery red hair, and Daisy felt someone grab onto her shins as she stepped into the lake and the sky somersaulted around her. There was a lurch, as if she'd been snagged like a fish and turned upside-down, and the world became a sick pinwheel of silver and darkness.

When everything righted itself, Daisy found that they were standing on a long wooden landing stage, where other people were appearing in puffs of silver steam. These

Botanists, for that was who they were, shook themselves off and adjusted their coats, before striding away towards a mass of pontoon boats that stretched down the length of a great silver river.

Beside them stood Acorn, breathing hard.

The Prof looked horrified. Indigo scowled.

'I had to come,' said Acorn, pushing back her blazing hair. 'Daisy's mother and the Prof's grandfather aren't the only ones missing. It's my dad too, and I need to do something.'

Daisy looked at the Prof and squeezed her hand. 'There's no way back to Mallowmarsh until moonset. We'll just have to be careful.'

Chapter 43

The river curved away from them as far as the eye could see, wide and glinting beneath a giant moon that swung like a stage prop in the theatrical sky. Spreading out from the landing stage was a city of boats on the water, lit with coloured lanterns and torches like fireflies. The swaying boats were linked with bridges and walkways and pontoons made from floating barrels, and they were hung with signs advertising every imaginable ware, from magic trowels to buoyant wooden rakes and poisonous nightcap mushrooms.

There were canal boats and vast ships with furled white sails, large flat-nosed barges and roly-poly tug boats, Japanese cutters and log boats, rusty steam ships, brigs and small barques flying the flags of different nations, and a Chinese junk hung with red dragon kites that soared in the night breeze. The market flickered and glowed over its own reflection, doubled in the shimmering water – and it was thronged with brightly dressed people, more Botanists than Daisy had ever seen or imagined.

'Moonmarket,' she whispered.

'Yep,' said Indigo, and she could hear the smile in his voice.

The Prof nodded. 'This is the main moonriver,' she

said. 'It's wider than a mile across, and it's a place between pockets – and a way to travel safely between them.'

Daisy remembered how Hal had explained it to her. 'Every pocket has a lake or stream or pond,' he had said. 'And on the night of the full moon, they become connected to this in-between space.' Once a month, from moonrise

to moonset, Botanists from around the world could come together to buy and sell and barter, to share news and flasks of snisky until the moon set and the moonriver vanished once again.

Indigo was already hurrying forward, but the Prof pulled him back. Sheldrake was visible at the far end of the landing stage, shaking his coat and checking that his satchel was safe. They ducked down behind a party of brightly dressed Brazilian Botanists who had just appeared from thin air, towing behind them several large jewelled lizards on gold leashes.

A bored-looking official was standing near the arrival point on the landing stage and reminding incoming Botanists that moonset would be at 5.30 a.m.

'Be back at the landing stage in good time, ladies and gentlemen,' the official called loudly, 'and you will be taken back to your lake, pond, river or stream of origin. If you are on one of the boats at moonset, you will return with it to that boat's place of origin. Stowaways are strictly forbidden. As always, we will ring a bell half an hour before moonset so that visitors have time to make their way back to the landing stage or their boat of origin in an orderly fashion. Latecomers will not be tolerated.'

'Right,' said the Prof. 'Remember, we're here to follow Sheldrake, find out who he's meeting and get the dandelight back. No getting distracted, no getting separated. If we *do* get separated, meet back here at five a.m. – that's half an hour before moonset.'

Indigo nodded. 'The main thing is not to get stuck on the wrong boat at the end of the night. That happened to my dad once and he ended up on a fishing vessel in the middle of the Atlantic.'

'Exactly,' said the Prof. 'And don't stray too far from the centre of the river, or you might end up in Darkmarket. You definitely don't want that.' She glanced at Daisy. 'Weren't you saying something about the black market, before the slug attack?'

'I think it has some kind of connection to the Grim Reapers,' Daisy explained, voice low. 'Remember I said that they started out as black-market traders? I think Sheldrake might be meeting with the Reapers – here, tonight.'

The Prof drew in a breath. 'I hope that's not true. But, either way, we need to be really, really careful.'

Daisy nodded, her eyes on Sheldrake, who had already begun moving away through the crowds.

'Quick,' she said. 'He's on the move. Let's go.'

Keeping their heads down, they darted after him, off the landing stage and onto the first barge. It was canopied with a red-and-white striped awning, so it felt a little like stepping into a circus tent. The air was spiced with the rich aroma of mulled wine flowing from tapped barrels, and the struts of the awning above were twirled with yellow flowers the size of umbrellas, giving off a scent that was almost electric.

Sheldrake was making his way down the barge, occasionally nodding at acquaintances but never stopping, refusing offers of wine or refreshment and moving purposefully forward, as if he had a clear destination in mind.

They crossed surreptitiously after him onto the neighbouring wherry-boat. Its mahogany decks sat low on the water, and the air was filled with rowdy cries: 'Winter strawberries, a moon penny a pound! Fresh purple mangoes, best white starberries! New season crumberries! Come buy!' Raucous and strident, the sellers' competing voices echoed across the decks in a happy cacophony of sound, their goods displayed in stalls piled high with tempting pyramids of shiny red pomegranates and glittering cherries, sky-blue apples and speckled black-and-white plums.

One stall was exclusively devoted to mushrooms and fungi: red and white toadstools, purplish chanterelles and tiny elfcaps that glowed an evil, phosphorescent green. Daisy stared.

'Doombell kingcaps, ten moon pennies a pound,' the seller cried, leering down at her and laughing. 'Go on, little girl, why don't you taste one?'

Daisy hurried to catch up with the others. Sheldrake was still visible ahead of them, moving forward neither slowly nor quickly, before ducking onto the next boat. This one was devoted to selling honey from all over the world, and Indigo had to be forcibly hurried along from the tasting jars lined up on one of the stalls – 'African song-bush honey!' he murmured. 'Ghoul-pepper honey! Hawaiian bronze-bean blossom . . .' The longing in his voice was palpable.

'No time,' said the Prof. 'We mustn't lose him.' They stayed as far away as they could while still keeping Sheldrake in their sights, tracing his progress through the maze of the floating market.

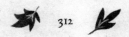

The next boat sold an array of oozing cheeses, the next a bewildering assortment of nuts and unusual seeds. But it was the boat after that which rendered them all speechless.

It was a floating sweetshop, the shelf-lined walls overflowing with jars of sugared rose petals and honeycomb crisps, scuttling chocolate beetles and starberry laces. There were sugar-frosted snowflakes and marshmallow mushrooms, chocolate-nut brittles and vanilla fudges. Daisy saw outcrops of edible buttercups filled with gold caramel, and gleaming red toffee apples growing on trees, each one the size of her fist. At the end of the room, releasing an amazing aroma into the air, thundered a chocolate waterfall from which you could scoop mugfuls of molten chocolate.

Acorn allowed a chocolate butterfly to perch on her ear, while Napoleon chased after a gang of frisky sugar mice and Indigo thrust his hands into a sack of glittering chocolate doubloons. Even the Prof was momentarily distracted by a display of Mexican jumping beans.

They almost lost sight of Sheldrake.

Which way had he gone? Daisy panicked and sprinted to the doorway, half tripping over a giant ball of blueberry bubblegum that was bouncing lazily between floor and ceiling. *There!* She saw a satchel whisking round the next corner.

'This way!'

They rushed through the cabin of a boat that shone with the light of lustrous, silvery mirrors and bright chandeliers.

Daisy caught a fleeting glimpse of gentlemen in green tuxedos and ladies in long, jewel-coloured evening gowns, the glitter of champagne and candlelight on shining silver forks. Eyes widened in astonishment as four ragtag children sprinted through the cabin; then there was laughter, and the orchestra played on.

They emerged, panting, onto the deck of a gaily painted river barge that boasted a gleaming selection of gardening tools – fortified spades that would do the heavy lifting for a year, silver trowels guaranteed to repel aphids, armoured gloves and boots impregnable even to the nastiest flesh-eating slug. Daisy felt her toe throb and wished she'd had a pair earlier that evening.

There he was!

Sheldrake had paused to examine the label on a jar of anti-sting ointment, exchanging a word and a nod with the stallholder. Then, between one breath and the next, he vanished. Daisy looked around wildly and spotted his shadow ducking through a low doorway behind the stall into the inner room of the barge. She glanced up and saw a painted sign above the door with a grand-looking lizard picked out in green and gold.

'Look,' she said, pointing. 'The sign of the Dancing Salamander! This is it.'

They had reached the bustling heart of the market, and they were jostled on all sides by eager buyers, families with overexcited children and groups of friends examining the

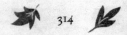

wares. They waited until the stallholder was distracted by a grey-haired couple looking for a miniature trowel for their grandson, then ducked through the dark doorway beneath the sign. Inside was a dim, busy room, lit by portholes and elegant bay windows along its length. There was a polished bar at one end, and several groups crowded around low tables – a pair playing chess, a trio muttering over sunken pints of ale, a rowdy gang clinking glasses and laughing uproariously. The tables were separated by solid, leafy chestnut trees that seemed to be growing directly out of the decks of the ship.

There was already a woman sitting there, alone and waiting. A cadaverous woman with arms like a praying mantis, and eyes like a dead fish.

Matron.

Chapter 44

Daisy's breath stopped. 'It's her! I *knew* she was working with Craven.'

'Who?' Indigo looked confused.

'Matron! From the school I ran away from. The woman who tried to steal the dandelight.' She took a breath. 'M. D. *Maud Daggler*. Matron.' She suddenly remembered the evil-looking potted plants in Matron's office. Could *Matron* be a Botanist? A bad one?

Things were clicking into place, but Daisy still couldn't quite see the full picture. She felt winded, but forced herself to keep still. Now was the moment they would see . . .

She watched as Sheldrake reached into his leather satchel and pulled something out, passing it to Matron beneath the table. It had to be the dandelight, thought Daisy.

Matron glanced down and closed her bony hand round it, stowing it in a bag before Daisy could see it. Matron's smile was as thin as a knife.

Sheldrake nodded. Then he was getting up, moving quickly – Daisy shifted further back into the shadow of the nearest chestnut tree – and he was gone.

Then there was a shout from the entrance of the Dancing Salamander as three men armed with truncheons stormed in, looking wildly about them.

'Daggler,' they roared, fixing their eyes on Matron and moving purposefully forward. 'We've got you – there's no getting away this time.'

'The moon police,' whispered Indigo, looking horrified. Daisy tried furiously to work out what to do, shrinking back as Matron rose and moved closer to where they were hidden behind the chestnut, close enough for Daisy to see the woven pattern of black thorns on her coat.

And then, as the police fought their way through the crowded tables, Matron reached out one long arm and yanked Daisy from her hiding place.

'Thought I hadn't seen you there, Daisy Thistledown?' she hissed, wrapping a hand around Daisy's neck. She raised her voice to the moon police. 'Come any closer and the girl dies.'

Daisy felt the chill of cold metal against her throat.

It was a knife.

She held her breath, shaking. She didn't dare move. She could feel Napoleon quivering with indignation against her chest. Indigo had been shouting, but now he fell silent. Acorn stood wide-eyed, out in the open. The moon police were gathered in an ineffectual ring: frozen by the gleam of Matron's blade. It was like standing in the eye of a tempest, in the eerie silence between turmoil and tide.

Matron was inching backwards, knife raised, dragging Daisy with her.

Think! she told herself. They were almost at the door. *Think!* She felt Matron shift her grip on her neck to tighten it, and then she didn't think – she acted.

She drew in a deep breath, lifted her foot and stamped her heel down *hard* on Matron's toes.

Matron roared and loosened her grip, and Napoleon leapt to the deck.

'Daisy!' cried Acorn, and rushed forward, as if to pull her to safety.

It all happened in the space of a finger-snap. In one smooth movement, Matron grabbed Acorn's wrist, pushed open the nearest bay window and was gone: taking Acorn with her. There was a great splash, and between two heartbeats they vanished beneath the silver water.

'No!'

Daisy dived after them.

The water was so cold that it seemed to gasp around her. She came up spluttering and then plunged under once more. There was nothing, either above or below the surface, except the seething chaos of the Dancing Salamander as the moon police began herding people out. Napoleon watched anxiously from the rocking deck as she dived again and again, searching the empty water until her arms were numb and she was forced to admit that Matron had escaped. Acorn was gone.

By the time she pulled herself back onto the deck, she was shivering uncontrollably as shock and cold took over

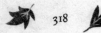

her limbs. She gathered Napoleon up into her arms and tucked him next to her chest for warmth.

Then she turned, tears streaming down her face, to look for Indigo and the Prof.

But they too had vanished.

Fear rising in her chest, clothes dripping, shoes squelching, she darted back inside the cabin of the Dancing Salamander, where the chestnut trees were reflected with dark menace in the wet slick of the damp floor. Empty.

She sprinted back outside and looked at the neighbouring decks, searching desperately for Indigo's corkscrew curls, the Prof's clever eyes behind her glinting spectacles.

Nothing.

They were gone.

The word echoed in her head like a hollow heartbeat.

Gone, gone, gone.

She ran onto the next boat, sprinting back through the tent of chandeliers and ballgowns, scattering champagne flutes and upending a hapless violinist as she went; through the boat of sweets, trampling buttercups underfoot and overturning a barrel of starberry laces as the sweet-seller shouted after her. She turned and ran through boat after boat, desperate now, turning at random.

This one was shadowy and dark, the beams hung with empty, gleaming snakeskins like shrugged carcasses, the walls glittering with slimy eyeballs and venomous flytraps that hissed as she passed. Shuddering, Daisy tried to turn

319

back, but the gangway was blocked by a knot of men with glittering eyes. Blindly, she made for the other exit, only to find a nightmarish stuffed alligator hanging across the doorway, its jaws bared over dagger teeth.

She felt fear rise in her throat. She was truly alone.

Chapter 45

The men were staring at her. So was the alligator.

How could she have been so stupid? The Prof had *warned* her not to stray too far from the central boats. She knew without being told that she was in Darkmarket. She had to return to the landing stage, to the meeting point at the heart of the floating city – but where was she? How would she ever find her way back?

'Got something to trade, girl?' One of the men had got up and was coming towards her. Daisy swallowed. Napoleon unsheathed his claws, but she could feel him trembling.

Then she saw a familiar figure standing at the other end of the boat, and she felt a surge of relief so powerful it was like a tidal wave.

That blaze of bright, gold hair, those quick hands and that reassuring smile.

It was Marigold Brightly.

Daisy ran into her arms.

'Why, Daisy!' she cried, astonished, pulling her close. 'What are you doing here? What on earth has happened?'

The men glanced at each other and sloped away, and for the first time Daisy was able to draw breath. She was safe. Brightly would know what to do.

They had been so foolish, Daisy thought, to think they could catch Sheldrake and fix everything themselves. It had all gone so wrong, and now the thought of handing over that responsibility was an indescribable relief.

'Here.' Brightly gave her a small lacy handkerchief, and Daisy blew her nose violently.

'Now, tell me what's going on.'

Brightly listened quietly as Daisy poured out her story: Sheldrake's duplicity, the meeting with Maud Daggler and the kidnapping of Acorn: Acorn who loved her caterpillar and was afraid of the dark, who had begged to come with them, and when they'd refused had come anyway because she couldn't bear not to.

'Thank greenness I found you,' said Marigold Brightly, hugging Daisy close, surrounding her with the smell of gardenias. 'We'll get you back to Mallowmarsh and then we'll rescue Acorn. Don't worry, my sweet – you'll be together again very soon.'

They were walking back across the maze of boats. Daisy's head was spinning with tiredness, and she barely noticed where she put her feet as Brightly led her through the labyrinth of ships and barges and walkways. Vaguely she noticed a row of cheese stalls packing up, the fruit-sellers and sweet-makers and brandy-wine merchants who were closing up shop for the night. The moon was setting in the sky like a punctured gold balloon as the air rang with tired calls, and Moonmarket came to a close. The river shrugged and murmured in the dim light, as sleek and polished as sealskin.

Dawn was coming. In a moment, when the moon sank beneath the horizon, the multitude of boats would disappear, each one back to its home river or lake or stream, each with its own cargo and passengers, to wait until the next Moonmarket. The crowd of shoppers on the landing stage would find themselves standing ankle-deep in the very same water they had stepped into at the start of the night. Daisy could already imagine splashing back into the lake at Mallowmarsh with Marigold Brightly and the others, how Napoleon would sneeze indignantly and how she would rush home to find Artemis at the Roost.

Home, she thought longingly. *Mallowmarsh*.

Artemis would be furious, but she would know what to do.

Daisy looked up from her thoughts, expecting to see the landing stage ahead, but instead found that they were walking across a small, dingy barge.

'This way,' Brightly was saying, with a hand on Daisy's elbow. 'It's just through here.'

Something was wrong.

'Wait,' said Daisy. 'Isn't it that way?'

'Don't worry,' said Brightly. 'Moonmarket can be confusing, but I know the best route.' They had crossed the gangplank onto another small boat, this one hung with grimy black sails. The market felt menacing again, with the

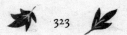

stalls all shuttered and the sellers in their cabins, waiting for the moontide to take them home.

Already, Daisy could see boat after boat beginning to vanish. It was happening in a sort of slow-motion wave, starting with the boats furthest away from the horizon as the moon sank below it and its beams shortened and retreated.

'We'll miss the moonset,' said Daisy, panicking. 'We won't be back at the landing stage in time.' She turned her head, desperate.

And then out of nowhere came a cloth clamped hard over her nose, and a cloying sweet scent so dizzying that it dissolved the whole world into blackness.

It was very cold when Daisy woke, and it felt like someone was trying to break into the top of her skull with an ice pick. She moaned and shifted, peeling her eyes open with effort. Even her eyelashes hurt.

She was in a small, shadowy cabin. There was a low bunk on either side, and crouched over her was a familiar form with a small, round face and blazing red hair.

'Acorn!' she croaked, and then coughed.

'Daisy,' sobbed the girl. 'You're awake!'

Daisy reached up, her arms and head aching with the movement. 'Don't worry,' she said. 'I'm here. It's going to be okay.'

It was not going to be okay, as far as Daisy could see, but she knew as deeply as she knew her own name that

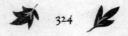

she needed to be brave for both of them. She looked around in the dimness, at the dark sky outside the single porthole window, far too small to escape through. The darkness meant it was after moonset: they had missed the moontide back to Mallowmarsh. It meant that they were now somewhere else entirely, for the black-sailed boat would have returned with the moontide to wherever it had originally come from – which, Daisy realized with a sick feeling in her stomach, could be anywhere in the world. She pounded at the door, which was locked and bolted, and then shouted to be let out. Nothing.

'I've tried,' said Acorn miserably. 'We're prisoners.'

Brightly must be imprisoned in another part of the boat. The only good thing was that Napoleon seemed to have escaped. With any luck, he'd have made it back to the landing stage with Indigo and the Prof. Perhaps they were sounding the alarm in Mallowmarsh at this very moment.

She could hear soft voices talking outside – the voices of their guards.

Staggering to her feet, she lifted herself until her chin was level with the tiny porthole. She strained to peer out, and saw the dark glow of night water and the ghostly foam of the ship's wake. They were moving fast, possibly down a river, with dark trees rushing past on either bank.

'There are two guards,' said Acorn. 'The woman who took me from the Dancing Salamander left right after you arrived.'

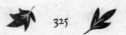

'Maud Daggler,' said Daisy. 'She works for Craven. Sheldrake gave her the dandelight, and she's probably passed it on to Craven by now. I bet we're just a bonus. Hostages.'

Acorn nodded. 'The two thugs take turns guarding the door – they're the ones who carried you in. And there's someone else steering the boat.'

Daisy's mind raced. They were outmatched: two children against three armed adults.

Then she heard the scratch of claws against wood and her heart leapt. She knew, without hesitation or doubt, that outside the door was a tiny black-and-white cat. A cat with the command – and the whiskers – of a major general.

Daisy smiled. They weren't outnumbered after all.

Chapter 46

Slowly, she began to think of a plan.

It was pitch dark. She could hear the rush of water against the hull of the boat and, more distantly, the pitch and fall of voices talking.

She rummaged inside her pocket and excavated several squished chocolate drops, only a little dusty, which she shared between her and Acorn. She felt warmth and courage flood back to her stomach at the taste. Dawn was breaking outside the porthole, and a ray of light flooded like pale honey across the cramped cabin, illuminating Acorn's scared eyes, the barred and locked door.

Daisy took a breath. There had been something else in her pocket: something that had given her an idea. It was mad and probably impossible. But it was their only chance.

She took off her shoes, scraping a biggish pile of dried mud and earth from the soles and packing it between the cracks of the rough wooden planks. Biting her cheek, she gave thanks for her heavy boots, and the fact that she hadn't had time to clean off the griffin dung they'd accumulated. The manure sparkled in the cool glow from the porthole.

'Yours too,' she said to Acorn. 'Come on, hurry!' Acorn fumbled to prise off her boots, which were still muddy after

the slug battle in the rose garden.

'Here,' she said, adding a healthy amount of mud to Daisy's and patting it down. 'But what are you going to do with it?'

Daisy didn't answer. She was busy spitting on the mud as hard as she could. It was difficult, because her mouth was dry with fear and exhaustion, and she hadn't had anything to drink in hours. But it was not for nothing that she had been crowned the unofficial spitting champion of three different US states. Now, she spat with fury, with determination.

Now, it was time to test her plan.

Three minutes later, a blood-curdling scream came from the locked cabin of the black boat. The two guards looked at each other. The cry came once more, ragged with terror. They looked at each other again.

'Oh heck,' said the taller of the two guards. 'We can't hold them to ransom if they're dead.' They hurried towards the cabin as another chilling scream came from inside.

As Acorn screamed behind her – she was very convincing, thought Daisy, admiringly – she knelt down on the ground. She breathed in, pressing her fingers into the mud piled on the boards of the boat – and, beneath the mud, the handful of sump-rose hips she'd saved in her pocket.

True, she hadn't managed to do magic before. True, the chances of it happening now were vanishingly small. *But*

not impossible, she told herself. She remembered the ivy snaking across the wall of the hotel in London and knew in her bones that she hadn't imagined it.

Pay attention, said Wildish's voice in her head. *Feel for them with the fingertips of your mind*. Daisy breathed in, and reached out with everything inside her. And there they were: the rose hips. Barely perceptible: mere threads of cool and incurious indifference.

I need help, she said. She felt their dreaming coolness, their furled mystery: their secret hearts. *Please*. Everything seemed to fade away, until she sensed only the threads of energy, silk-thin, coiling up from the mound of dirt.

She felt a jolt and sat up straighter. The feeling prickled all the way down her spine, until her skin hummed with it, as if everything from her fingertips to her eyelashes was tingling brightly.

Planting a seed is an act of hope, said Brightly's voice in her ear. *It means you have faith in the future. Think of that hope, and don't let go.*

Daisy thought of Hal and the hidden garden coming back to life. She thought of Artemis and the way she spoke to every plant as if it was a person. She thought of Ma's smile and her inky fingers and the way she said, 'Courage, joonam.'

Nothing. Then – something.

The feeling flooded her whole body, until her heart almost burst with it. She felt the rose hips split open and

watched as they scattered their seeds across the mud and into the cracks of the floor. She closed her eyes, and felt the tendrils of something new start to unfurl.

Outside, the two guards looked at each other again.

The screams were really quite alarming, as if one of the children was actually dying.

'Oi,' shouted the taller guard. 'That's enough of that.' The screaming continued.

'Stand back. We're coming in.'

The lock clicked – and then everything happened very fast. Out of the open door surged something enormous: a great, tangled mass of curling stems spiked with thorns like tiny knives. Red flowers bloomed and closed, and the smell of roses was overwhelming, a wall of pure glorious scent that sent them reeling backwards, half swooning, half stunned.

Daisy and Acorn burst out of the cabin in time to see the guards come to their senses. One was brandishing a tarnished pitchfork, the other a wicked-looking pair of secateurs. Marigold Brightly was beside them, holding a glittering knife. In a moment, it was against Acorn's throat.

Daisy stood dumbfounded. The sump-roses faltered.

'It was *you*,' she said, staring at Brightly. 'You're the spy! You stole the dandelight.'

For an instant, she was paralysed – and then she threw herself at the woman. The guards rushed towards Daisy,

shouting, and there was a yowl as a ball of spitting fur and claws flew out of nowhere, scratching across the taller one's cheeks and attaching itself to the other's head. In that instant, Daisy closed her eyes and *pulled* at the vines. They moved clumsily, but with enough force to knock the two guards off their feet and send Brightly sprawling on the deck

before pinning them down. Daisy poured her energy into the vines, sweating with the effort of it.

'I thought you said she didn't have magic,' said the taller guard, cursing.

'Quick,' Daisy called. 'Acorn. There's rope in the corner. Tie them up.'

Acorn ran to do as she said, swiftly lashing rope around three sets of wrists and ankles. The tall guard was swearing filthily, while the other struggled against the thick, thorny stems holding them in place. Daisy let go of the vines, panting, just as Acorn finished tying her last knot.

Brightly's clear grey eyes blazed up at her, bright with fury.

'Where's the dandelight?' said Daisy, struggling to control her voice. 'Where is my mother? And the other Botanists. Tell me. NOW.'

Brightly shook her head and Daisy glared at her.

'Tell me where they are,' she said fiercely. 'Or I'll throw you overboard, ropes and all.'

'I don't know,' said Marigold Brightly at last. Her voice was hoarse. 'Craven never told me – I swear it. He blackmailed me. He has something of mine: something precious. I had no choice.'

'What did he take from you?' said Daisy. *What could it be?*

Brightly tightened her lips and said at last, despair in every word: 'He took my son. Max. And he threatened to

kill him unless I did as he said.'

'But I thought—'

Brightly shook her head impatiently. 'Max was never at Bloomquist. He's been very sick for a long time – and Craven kidnapped him.' Her face contorted, and she glared at Daisy. 'I would do anything – *anything* – to save him. I would burn down the world for him. Don't you understand, Daisy? I don't care about any of it – only my boy. My Max.' A line of tears trickled from the edge of her eye and down through the ropes binding her, onto the deck.

'And the dandelight?' asked Daisy.

'Craven wanted me to steal it. But it was always with you, and then locked up in the Roost. Finally, today, I made a distraction, and I took my chance.'

Daisy remembered her visit to the Seed Bank, and how one set of scales had been weighed down by something heavy but invisible. With a feeling of pieces falling into place, she remembered a page in *The Compleat Botanist*, scattered with crumbs from Indigo's toast. *Whipple*, it had said. *Also known as the Vanishing Tree. Its seeds, although large, are completely invisible.*

Seeds that could also make a person invisible. She remembered the noise from outside the landing window on the night when Artemis had hidden the dandelight behind the loose brick.

Couldn't see them, Tuffy had said.

'You stole the dandelight,' said Daisy slowly. 'You

333

brought it to Moonmarket because there was a triple guard on the Mallow gate tonight – so this was the only place to hand it over. And you must have stolen the ghost-moth orchid too: Smedley never saw who attacked him. But why take it? So Craven could extend his life by a few miserable years?' She felt disgusted at the thought.

'No,' said Brightly. 'Not for Craven.' She swallowed painfully. 'For Max. Why do you think I agreed to come to Mallowmarsh, the one place I could get hold of the orchid? Max is dying and this . . . will give him all the years he deserves to grow up and *live* and grow old.'

Suddenly, Daisy understood.

'You've been sending Max the flowers of the ghost-moth orchid. But that means that the person he loves most—'

Marigold Brightly smiled sadly. 'The person he loves most in the world is me. And I would sacrifice every year I have left, to give him more time.'

Daisy remembered the piles of letters Brightly had sent, sealed with little rows of loving kisses. Not jolly letters to a boy away at school, but letters to her dying son, each one filled with a ghost-moth flower. No wonder she had looked so pale and drained every time they'd seen her in the last few weeks. She had been siphoning her life away.

'Craven has been holding him hostage, but after tonight I get him back, safe. That's the deal.' Brightly's voice was fierce. 'When Craven attacks Mallowmarsh, Max goes free.'

'When he attacks Mallowmarsh,' repeated Daisy numbly.

'Yes.' Brightly closed her eyes again. 'Mallowmarsh will fall tonight. I gave the dandelight to Daggler, and she's taken it to Craven. He's already on his way.'

And she turned her head, tears dropping onto the deck, her fists curled in despair.

Acorn looked at Daisy. 'We can't throw her overboard now, can we?' she said sadly.

'No,' said Daisy. 'We can't.'

Chapter 47

Daisy looked at the water rushing past the bow of the boat in the dark. Everything felt impossibly urgent.

'We need to get back to Mallowmarsh and warn them about what's coming.' She looked at Brightly. 'I'm sorry,' she said. Staggering slightly with the roll of the deck, she and Acorn carried her into the cabin. The next order of business was to deal with the guards, who were still bound and yelling furiously for help. They were far too heavy to lift, but after a bit of experimenting she and Acorn were able to roll them roughly across the deck and shunt them into the cabin. Their shouts faded as Daisy locked the door and put the key in her pocket.

Then she ran to the front of the boat and looked around, wishing she had the dandelight to pierce the darkness. The boat was veering wildly from side to side with no one at the helm, and a map fluttered next to the spinning ship's wheel. She glanced at it, and then at the shapes on the horizon. London. With a blaze of relief, she looked back at the map, and then she gazed into the sky and found the North Star, right where it had always been. She grabbed the wheel. And then she steered the boat towards Kew Gardens.

*

Half an hour later, they were inside the doors of the Palm House.

'Come on,' said Daisy, holding out a hand to Acorn. She cast a single backward glance in the direction of the river, where Marigold Brightly was locked inside the black-sailed boat moored on the banks.

Then, hand in hand, Daisy and Acorn stepped through a curtain of falling, tangled vines, and opened the silver door to Mallowmarsh.

The path was darker than the first time Daisy had walked it, but this time she could feel the oak trees around her and see their shapes with her mind.

Her magic was awake, and all about was an unfamiliar world of sensation, criss-crossed with skeins of energy that she could barely begin to untangle. It was like finding a new sense: as if she'd been blind her whole life and was suddenly able to *see*. It was as if she'd discovered that she could taste music, or hear colour, or touch smells with her fingers. She thought she could have walked the paths blindfolded, navigating by her green-sense alone.

As before, Napoleon raced ahead down the path. But this time Daisy had Acorn beside her, and she squeezed the younger girl's hand as they hurried through the wood. The scent of roses surged up on every side, and Daisy saw the lanterns glowing along the path and the window of the guardhouse twinkling like a little white star. Daisy felt all around her the unmistakable atmosphere of Mallowmarsh on the breeze: of cool water and silver birches and plum trees, the tang of rich and concentrated green magic that had built up in one place for centuries. She was almost dizzy with it. How could she have not sensed it before?

There was a strange murmuring amidst the branches, an uneasy shiver and stirring, as if the ancient oaks were tossed by an unearthly wind that made them whisper, *Hurry, hurry. Faster.*

Daisy began to run, pulling Acorn behind her. She had a terrible feeling of foreboding and her heart beat in relentless double-time inside her ears.

Boom-boom,
boom-boom.

Too-late, too-late.

Then they heard a scream, and a smash of exploding glass. The guard hut was abandoned. A figure in red overalls was lying utterly still on the ground outside it. Daisy didn't have to go closer to know that it was Captain Malarky. She stifled a cry, and sprinted towards the great lawn with Napoleon racing ahead and Acorn's hand clutched in her own.

The air smelled of fire and burning, with sparks streaming upwards into the night sky like swarming, fiery hornets, strangely beautiful against the dark.

Mallowmarsh was on fire.

Craven was already here.

They were too late.

The fire was racing across the great lawn, gaining force and scale like a great, ravenous mouth that consumed everything in its path and left only ashes in its wake. Gardeners and under-gardeners were running around in panic, sprinting with buckets of water from the lake towards the source of the flames, and shouts filled the air as the priceless aerial tulips around the Great Glasshouse became fiery torches, flaring up against the night. The lower panes began to buckle and warp in the heat that gathered from all sides.

As they came closer to the Great Glasshouse, Daisy saw the Prof at the edge of the woods, directing a squadron of apprentices with slingshots of stones and pebbles. The Prof's aim was unerring. The stones made contact with one of the attackers, who staggered and fell unconscious to the ground.

She spotted Indigo at the edge of the lake, helping frantic gardeners who were pulling buckets of water from the lake and splashing it over the fire. But it was hopeless, like spitting into a furnace. The water sputtered and steamed before it even reached the flames.

Finally, Daisy saw the man standing at the centre of the inferno. It was Craven, tall and smiling his charming lopsided smile. Daisy watched as he sloshed a bucket of petrol across the grass, and dropped a lit match onto the ground.

WHUMPH.

The figure opposite him went staggering back, and Daisy recognized the slight form of Artemis. She righted herself, weaving giant vines in her hands, calling snaking roots out of the ground at Craven's feet so that they erupted and tangled around his legs, and he was forced to slice at them with the knife in his belt.

'Enough, Cardew,' she called, her voice steady. 'It's not too late to make peace.'

'Make peace?' Craven jeered. 'You weren't so keen on making peace eight years ago, when they took my magic.' He dropped another match, and a wall of flame shot up into the sky. Daisy held her breath, but Craven was staring at something beyond the fire.

There was a terrible splintering noise like a howl of pain. Daisy turned to see the Heart Oak sway in the air, as ten figures wielding axes finished cutting through its massive trunk. She looked on in horror as the noble, ancient tree, the guardian of Mallowmarsh, pitched through the dark, ribbons streaming, and its great branches crashed down across the lake like the death of everything good in the world.

There was a great ringing stillness.

Daisy could feel the loss like a black hole in the air.

Mallowmarshers stood paralysed, despairing, leaving their positions undefended as a ghastly figure climbed on top of the trunk and began to laugh: a wild and empty sound.

It was Matron.

Daisy felt a rage such as she had never known before, as if an axe had sliced through her own chest and released a flare of magma. She was sprinting towards Matron. She was going to kill her. She was going to –

Then she heard a cry from behind her and turned to see Artemis crumple and fall to the earth, a sob of pain tumbling from her open mouth.

'NO!' Daisy turned and ran back. Artemis lay still and unmoving, cut off by a channel of flames. It was true: Artemis's life was bound to the Heart Oak. And now they were both gone.

Daisy looked at Craven through the flames, her face slick with tears that evaporated in the burning air. His eyes were flat and emotionless, like a shark's. She could see him lighting another match.

Then Sheldrake was running from the woods, dodging streams of fire and shouting in fury. He wove vines from his hands as he ran, and they erupted viciously around Matron's feet on the Heart Oak stump so that she toppled like a statue from a plinth and lay still. Sheldrake didn't even pause. He ran until he was standing in front of Artemis's body, shielding it from the flames.

'No need to look so upset, Sheldrake,' said Craven. 'I've barely started.' His eyes glittered, reflecting the firelight. 'Stand aside. Or I'll let this place burn until I can pick your beloved commander's bones from the ashes.'

'Over my dead body,' growled Sheldrake.

'With pleasure.' Craven dropped a match into another slick of petrol. Daisy could see lines of flame snaking out into the darkness, all the way to the edges of the Mallow Woods.

Sheldrake staggered back from another wall of fire. The smell of sulphur filled the air.

Daisy and Acorn edged forward, unseen, picking their way across a break in the flames. At last, they crouched behind Artemis's fallen body, hidden by billows of smoke. Napoleon was by her side, licking and licking Artemis's cheek.

Craven was still smiling. Daisy could see the bulge of the dandelight in his coat pocket. 'You forget, Sheldrake, that I have two hostages: children of Mallowmarsh. If you don't do as I say, they will die.'

What happened next had the unreality of a dream.

Daisy saw Artemis's chest move: the slightest rise, like the wing of a moth.

She bundled Napoleon into Acorn's arms. 'Keep each other safe,' she said.

And she stepped forward to face Craven.

Chapter 48

'You're wrong, Craven.' Daisy's voice rang out over the roar of flames.

He turned furiously, his face a mask of anger and disbelief.

'You!'

Daisy moved so fast that Craven didn't have time to react. She hissed as she brushed past him and pulled the dandelight from his coat with the lightness of a pickpocket. It was heavy and cool in her hands, like a crystal ball.

Craven gave a great yell of fury and snatched at her. But she was already beyond him, sprinting for the Great Glasshouse.

She saw his eyes widen. Then she placed one foot on the first rung of the ladder that climbed up the side of the Glasshouse to its towering roof.

'Bring it back, girl. Bring it here now, or everything will burn.'

'Everything's already burning,' said Daisy, surprised at the steadiness of her voice. She took another step further up the ladder. 'If you want it, come and get it.' And then she climbed up hand over fist, not thinking of the ground beneath her, thinking only of going higher, of drawing

Craven away from her friends, away from Artemis, away from the gardens.

She had a few seconds' head start, and then she heard a shout of rage as Craven dropped the petrol and sprinted after her, felt the ladder shift and tremble below her with his weight. Up and up she climbed, higher and higher, breathing fast at the effort, the dandelight tucked inside her jacket in the spot where Napoleon usually curled himself against her chest.

The ground dropped away and the air became cooler as she reached the level of the roof. All around her the night was lit up by a terrible red-white glow, spreading its desolation in an ever-widening circle across the grounds. She felt dizzy with vertigo and terror.

She pulled herself up onto the glass roof of the Great Glasshouse, where the ladder flattened out and became a horizontal track across its curving top. She glanced down through the glass and saw the highest palm trees swaying centimetres below her feet, and the solid stone floor forty metres below. She looked up quickly, staggered and almost fell. Her fear was thick enough to bite down on.

'Don't look down, Daisy,' she whispered. She breathed. In, out.

Courage, joonam.

She stood unsteadily and backed away as Craven's head cleared the roof and he clambered up to stand opposite her, breathing hard.

Now he was coming towards her, reaching into his

belt and pulling out something that gleamed sleekly in the firelight, alien and horribly out of place.

A knife: glittering with the blue electricity of a lightning seed embedded in the hilt.

'A toy from Darkmarket,' said Craven, grinning.

Daisy backed away further, panicking now, knowing that in seconds she'd run out of roof.

'Hand it over,' said Craven.

His voice was cool, fearless: he looked invincible. Daisy remembered, suddenly, that this was the man who had killed Hal.

There were frantic shouts and cries from below as people spotted the drama playing itself out above. Daisy could see the Prof's horrified face, Acorn running forward as if to help and Sheldrake, upright once more, pushing them both roughly aside and sprinting towards the ladder.

The knife shone coolly in the fiery night as Craven came forward and lifted it to Daisy's throat. It was very sharp, and she saw the play of electricity around it, just millimetres from her skin. There was sudden silence all around, broken only by the dull crackling of the flames.

'Nobody move,' he roared from the rooftop. 'Or she dies.' He gestured around him with his free hand, pointing it for a moment at Sheldrake, whose head was almost level with the roof.

He turned back to Daisy and stared at her with his flat eyes.

'I see you're wearing the necklace you stole,' he said. 'You worthless little thief.'

'It was never yours,' hissed Daisy furiously. 'It belongs to my mother.'

'Finders keepers.' He smiled an unlovely smile. 'My men took that necklace from your mother's dead body. Just like I'll take it from yours.'

Daisy swayed, unanchored by rage and grief.

'You're nothing but a murderer.'

He laughed. 'I'm much more than that, my dear. The Grim Reapers are hunting down your kind across the world. We're unstoppable.'

So it's true, thought Daisy. *Grim Reapers. All the nightmares are real.*

But Craven was still speaking. 'Hunting Botanists is only the beginning. We're going to conquer the Greenwild, one pocket at a time. Thanks to your bauble' – he waved his knife at the dandelight – 'nowhere will be safe. And when I hand over Mallowmarsh to the Great Reaper, why then –' he smiled – 'I'll be rewarded. The Great Reaper will return the magic that was stolen from me.' His eyes were almost black in the darkness. 'Leila Thistledown was nothing, and she died like a nobody. Like you all will.' He spat the words, and Daisy's fear was replaced by a terrible heat that blazed from her bones and out through her throat.

'Ma was better than you'll ever be,' she said, her voice hoarse.

She was aware of the lake below her, and beyond it the dandelion meadow shimmering against the night. Somewhere down there was a hidden garden, and inside it a sapling.

The plan arrived in her mind as if it had always been there.

Slowly, each move deliberate, she reached into her jacket and pulled out the shining dandelight. She saw Craven follow it with his eyes as she lifted it. Silently, with the fingertips of her mind, she began to gather a hundred threads of magic.

'Here,' she said, and she tossed the dandelight high into the air.

Several things happened very quickly. Craven fumbled as he tried to free his hands to catch the soaring globe. The glittering knife dropped from his grasp and the lightning seed in the hilt exploded on contact, shattering the glass beneath their feet with a noise like a thousand chandeliers exploding. And the roof began to fall inwards like sheets of ice collapsing into a dark lake.

Craven leapt as the dandelight rose and spun and hung suspended in the air above them.

Daisy felt the darkness reach out its arms for her, and with the last of her energy, she called out to every leaf and branch and vine in the glasshouse below and felt them surge upwards at her command, smashing the remains of the roof and rising around her like a giant cat's cradle. She sent out a vine to lasso the dandelight from the air and flick it towards her like a toy. And then she fell, as if in slow motion, backwards into the darkness, and into the green arms of a living rainforest.

The last thing she saw was Craven as he teetered, cried out – and then plummeted through the heart of the broken roof and towards the solid stone floor forty metres below.

Chapter 49

There was an instant of silence, and then a savage roar as Craven's Grim Reapers began to fight with redoubled fury, splashing petrol and sending up new arcs of flame into the blazing sky.

Daisy had asked the vines to fling her as far as they could from the battle, and she landed with an almighty smack on the grass beside the lake. The shock of the impact was immense. Napoleon leapt into her arms and she lurched to her feet, watching as the Mallowmarshers staggered back from a fresh attack. She didn't have much time.

Pain radiated from her wrist, and she wondered if the bone had cracked as she'd fallen. But there was no time to think of that now.

There was only time to run.

Around the lake, past the Roost, into the dandelion meadow she ran, the dandelight clutched in her hand, until she was tumbling through the old wooden door and into a warm summer night where the world was peaceful and Mallowmarsh was still safe. There were white climbing roses, and lavender and cherry trees in the moonlight. The sky swarmed with stars. And there, in the apple tree, was Hal.

He took one look at her face and leapt down to meet her.

'Is everything all right?' His voice was worried, urgent. He peered at her through his glasses and came to crouch next to her on the grass.

Daisy shook her head, thinking of Mallowmarsh burning, the Heart Oak falling and the still form of Artemis lying pale on the ground.

Wordlessly, Hal placed an arm round her, and Daisy felt a wave of comfort like being tucked inside a warm, bright house on a cold, rainy night. The temptation to stay was almost overwhelming.

She took a deep breath. 'I – I don't have much time.' She forced herself to remember that, outside the garden, a battle was raging, and every second counted. She got up and walked towards the knobbly little sapling they'd uncovered and which she had barely paid attention to, overshadowed as it was by the lustre of the silver apples. It had grown in exactly the spot where she'd tossed down her coat that first night.

The spot where Ma's shrivelled old seed had fallen out.

Now, growing from the rough, twisted little branch, was a single, perfect pomegranate. Not big and scarlet like the ones at Moonmarket, but small and the colour of sunrise and coral and watermelon, streaked with veins of silver like ore lines of moonlight.

She had staked everything on this guess, but now she felt the truth like a zigzag of lightning through her bones.

It was the pomegranate she'd read about in *The Compleat Botanist*.

Ma had brought the seed with her from Iran, and it had grown here in the garden that Daisy and Hal had worked to make together.

A tree said to take root only where a true friendship exists.

Hal was standing beside her. 'I can't believe it,' he said, and his face was wonder-struck. 'A real, live whishogg.'

'I know,' said Daisy. She understood, at last, that this tree was the heart of the hidden garden. Its power pulsed outwards like the blood through her veins, and she knew that if she picked the fruit, she'd never be able to come back.

'But . . . it's incredible!' Hal gave a sort of leap, as if he had pins and needles in his legs. 'My first discovery. Yours too. And in our own garden!' He jigged up and down on the spot, and then – 'Ow!' He cursed. He'd collided with the lowest branch of the apple tree, and it had sliced across his left eyebrow. A trickle of blood was falling from the cut. 'It's nothing,' he said, dancing up and down. 'Ow!'

Daisy laughed despite herself; he looked so comical that she couldn't help it. 'Here,' she said, handing him a dock-leaf to mop the blood. 'You'll probably have a nice dashing scar, like a pirate captain.'

Then suddenly it hit her.

She looked at his white-blond hair, his dark eyes, the cut across his eyebrow and at last she knew why he seemed so

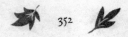

familiar; like someone she had always known. It was the face she had examined a thousand times, slightly blurred, standing beside Ma and laughing out at her from a faded photograph.

It was the face of her father.

Dizzily she sat down in the crook of the apple tree, which curled a steadying branch around her waist.

Hal was staring at her, looking concerned. 'Are you all right?'

'Yes, yes. Fine.' Daisy stared at his sharp profile in the moonlight, all her urgency forgotten.

She remembered playing on the sun-flooded wooden floors of an old house, rolling a paperweight back and forth between them. She remembered flying a kite, his hands steady over hers as they guided it across the sky. She remembered him swinging her round and round in a blur until she screamed. She remembered the rumble of his voice reading her a story and the quirk of his eyebrow when he was amused, with that funny white scar running through it.

The garden had given her more than a best friend.

It had given her the boy who would become her father.

She thought again of the wizened old seed in the crimson envelope, and the wish she had made that night at Wykhurst. She had held onto her only photo of Pa, with one thumb covering Ma's face, and wished – rashly, extravagantly – for *help*. She had wished on a whishogg seed, and because no wish could bring the dead back to life, it had given her the next best thing. It had taken her back in time to meet her father.

'What?' said Hal, and Daisy realized she was still staring. 'Nothing.'

Warning, the book had said: *be careful what you wish for.*

Hal looked at her, and with the odd dream logic that meant he always seemed to know what Daisy was thinking, he said, 'This is it. Isn't it? This is the last time.'

Daisy nodded, eyes smarting, and turned back to the whishogg. 'I need the wish, Hal. It's the only way to save something that matters a lot. But if I pick it' – her voice faltered – 'I might not be able to come back.'

Hal's dandelion hair was white-blond in the moonlight, and his thin face was smudged with dirt. 'I always knew it couldn't last,' he said, and his voice had a new firmness Daisy hadn't heard before. 'And, actually, I've decided to leave Mallowmarsh. You're the one who made me believe I could do it. I wrote to my Traveller family, like you said . . . and they wrote back. They want to meet me! They've said I can come and live with them for as long as I like – and, Daisy, I'm going to go. And one day, when I'm an explorer, I'm going to stop the Grim Reapers.' His eyes looked suddenly very grown up behind his wonky glasses. 'I'll never be good enough in Father's eyes. But you've made me see that he's wrong.'

'Your father's a fool,' said Daisy impulsively. 'Hal,

you—' What she was saying was so important that she couldn't quite look at him. 'You're the best person I know. And you're going to be the best explorer the Greenwild has ever seen.'

Hal's face was lit from the inside. 'I'm going to miss you,' he said quietly.

'Me too.'

She went on looking at him, and he rubbed his face self-consciously.

'What? Do I have dirt on my nose?'

'No,' said Daisy. She didn't have much time, but she had to say this. 'Only, Hal, promise me you will travel, and – and you'll go to Iran. I know you'll love it there. Promise me.'

'I promise,' he said. 'Nothing will keep me away.'

Daisy felt the seconds ticking away and gulped with the unfairness of what she had to do. How could she say goodbye, now, when she'd only just found him? *Her father*. The thought made her dizzy, like a punch to the jaw.

'*Courage, joonam*,' she heard the familiar voice say: the one she needed most.

At last, she looked at Hal. 'Shall we do it together?' she said.

Hal nodded and, as one, they reached out and pulled the pomegranate from its branch.

It felt cool to the touch, and when they split it open they saw a mass of silvery-pink seeds like pale gems and, set in

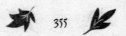

355

the centre, one that glowed brighter than all of them. The ruby seed.

'Take it,' said Hal. 'You need it more than me.'

Daisy looked at him, taking in every line of his thin face, trying to fix it in her mind forever. Then she nodded.

The next few minutes were too painful to remember, except in flashes. The silver apples on the tree, seen for the last time. The feel of the pomegranate seed in her hand. Hal's voice, as she stood at the door, his hand in hers. 'We'll see each other again,' he said. 'This isn't goodbye.'

And they would meet again, she knew, for a few short years. Years that were in her past and his future, but altogether timeless: like any time when people are truly happy.

Daisy arrived back at the battle to find a scene of desolation. The Great Glasshouse was missing its roof, surrounded by shattered glass and blasted rocks. The smell of crushed roses and smoke mixed in the air and she could see the fight raging around her.

Matron was up again and charging at Madame Gallitrop. The fox-haired man was locked hand-to-hand with Sheldrake, who was staggering with exhaustion. Artemis lay on the ground nearby, silent and still, chest barely moving.

Daisy closed her eyes and gripped the seed between her fingers.

A single wish. But for what?

She thought of Ma, and she heard Craven's voice saying once again, *My men took this necklace from your mother's dead body.* And now it was Miss Tufton's voice that she heard, solemn and firm: *The one thing that magic cannot do is bring a person back from the dead.*

She knew then with a terrible certainty that Ma was gone, and the greatest wish of her heart was impossible.

No, she pleaded. *Please, no.*

This was the hardest thing of all. It was the terrible thorny truth that bit its way through her chest. She could feel grief like an ocean, and she knew it was coming for her, inevitable as a wave that scrapes the sky before it crashes and falls.

But, first, this last task. This one wish.

Artemis needed her. Mallowmarsh needed her. The Greenwild needed her.

It wasn't too late to save the living.

Daisy dug a hole in the earth with torn fingernails, and pressed her palms over the whish-seed. She pictured Artemis, and she pictured the Heart Oak, both of them fierce and tall and whole again in her mind.

And then, with every muscle of her broken heart, she wished.

For a moment, there was only emptiness, and Daisy sagged.

Then a thin shoot rose from the earth. It hesitated, and then it thickened and twisted and rose about her.

357

It was a tree formed of her wish, a tree with glittering branches that filled the sky until it became the sky itself, scattered with bright constellations, dazzled with stars shooting and streaming endlessly up into infinity and blackness. Then the stars rained down like spears and where they fell, fresh tendrils began to sprout and curl from the ruined stump of the Heart Oak, silver and red in the dying firelight. Slowly they twined upward, growing into branches that budded with wavy leaves and tiny bright acorns, until the rich, living canopy seemed to spread itself over the whole of Mallowmarsh.

On the ground nearby, the commander of Mallowmarsh opened her bright blue eyes.

All around, Botanists looked up and they saw the Heart Oak rise.

Daisy felt the power in the earth beneath her.

She felt the tide of the battle as it began to shift.

Strangely — was she hallucinating? — Marigold Brightly was there, her long gold hair matted in the firelight, leading a group of under-gardeners against the invaders, wielding a terrifyingly sharp rake in her hands. Daisy saw the fox-haired man backhand her with a truncheon so that she fell to the ground, fighting for breath. But then there was Sheldrake taking up the charge, Brutus baying at his side, both of them flanked by snake vines that wrapped themselves around Craven's men, while a phalanx of deadly nightshade flowers spat poison into their faces.

'MALLOWMAAAARRSH!' roared Sheldrake, and the Botanists rallied to his call.

Madame Gallitrop was striding forward, lightning seeds in each hand, knocking the attackers aside with bolts of blue electricity and blasting Matron off her feet. Gulliver Wildish, his leaf-waistcoat smouldering, was directing an army of ferocious palm trees that curled their roots around the invaders, pinning them to the ground.

Craven's supporters were beginning to turn tail and run with shouts and panicked cries. They were out of ammunition. With Indigo at their head, a herd of blue horses was stampeding across the grass, tramping the invaders underfoot, while hot-pink hedge-pigs shot spines like blow darts and a battalion of parakeets dive-bombed and pecked at their eyes.

Chef McGuffin waded into the fray, laying about him with a ladle, while Mrs Marchpane followed, brandishing a pastry whisk like a cudgel. Ivy Helix had joined forces with the Prof, and was using a slingshot with devastating aim, blue eyes narrowed. And with Napoleon leading the charge, the hedge-lions gave thundering chase, and the elephants trumpeted mightily, tossing Craven's men aside with mighty green tusks, before galloping down to the lake, sucking up great trunkfuls of water and spraying it over the fire until the last flames sputtered out and died. The attackers were chased into the depths of the Sighing Forest, where the Mallowmarshers turned and left them.

'Aaaaaah,' sighed the pines, sending up pale puffs of mist. 'Aaaaaah, aaaaah.'

In the morning, there would be many new trees in the forest: each with horrible expressions etched into their petrified bark.

Daisy was in pain. She felt a burning ache deep in her right arm from her earlier fall, and she could barely raise herself with the other. She breathed, and the last thing she saw before she passed out was the quick scarlet wink of a red rose in a puddle of lake water.

As red as a ruby, or a pomegranate seed, or a burning wish.

Chapter 50

'Shut up, Indigo. Can't you be serious for once?'

'I am being serious, O dearest Prof. You look perfectly frightful.'

'Well, I can't help it if my eyebrows got burned off. At least it shows I was doing my bit.' The Prof's voice was indignant.

'Shh, children,' came another voice – a voice Daisy had thought she'd never hear again. 'Daisy is resting. I said you could visit if you were *quiet*.'

Daisy stirred and opened one eye.

Indigo and the Prof were perched on the end of her bed, one on each side, and she was in her attic room at the Roost. The morning sky shone cheerfully through the skylight, so that the air was dashed with blue and gold, like an aquarium. The sheets were cool and crisp against her skin, and there was a constant burn in one arm. She knew without looking that it was broken.

'You're awake,' cried Indigo, throwing himself at her.

'Ouch!'

'Oops, sorry!' he said as the Prof piled on. 'Ach, Daisy, we thought you were dead. When you fell like that – You *should* be dead. How could you do anything so completely

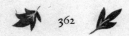

stupid?' He pulled back, blinking.

'Except those vines caught you, Daisy.' The Prof's eyes were bright. 'I've never seen anything like it. You used so much magic that you've been asleep for the last three days.'

'Lazybones,' said Indigo, rolling his eyes.

Daisy laughed and it hurt her chest. 'And Tuffy? Where is she? Is she—'

'Miss Tufton is—'

'Right as rain,' said the woman herself, bustling into the room with a steaming bowl on a wooden tray, which she placed across Daisy's knees. 'It'd take more than a little knock on the head to do away with me.'

'Tuffy!' Daisy lunged forwards, slopping soup everywhere. 'You're all right!'

'Now, now,' said Miss Tufton, quelling her with a look. 'Settle down and drink your broth.'

Daisy sat back obediently and picked up her spoon. 'And Craven,' she said, sipping, 'is he really gone?'

'Yes,' said Artemis. 'No one could have survived a fall from that height. Except you, apparently.'

There was silence in the room for a moment, and then Indigo spoke.

'Acorn will be so annoyed she wasn't here when you woke up,' he said. 'She's been sitting by your bedside non-stop – she only left to get more lettuce for Albert.'

Daisy smiled and closed her eyes. She couldn't remember ever feeling so tired before – or so wonderfully safe.

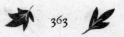

When she next woke, the room was empty. Moonlight poured through the window, and Napoleon was curled up at the foot of the bed, snoring gently. The dandelight, she noticed, was resting on the bedside table, shining softly like a nightlight. She moved slowly, swinging her feet to the floor softly so as not to disturb Napoleon and wincing as the movement jarred at her arm. She padded over to the chest of drawers and picked up the sketchbook she had found all those days ago. Now, though, it was heavy with new meaning.

It had belonged to her father.

She picked it up and smoothed the battered leather binding, tracing the indent of Artemis's writing on the flyleaf: *The Logbook of Hal White, age twelve and a half*. Before, she had raced through the pages, looking for clues about Cardew. Now, she turned them slowly, poring over each image.

Here on the first page were the gaudy scarlet flowers of the Great Glasshouse; here a speckled orchid; here on the next were three fluffy, fire-breathing chicks, with a note underneath in a cramped, almost illegible hand. She hadn't noticed the writing before. *Sawlt henn chiks*. The spelling was atrocious, and the handwriting was worse, like the scrawl of a toddler.

Daisy turned the page and saw a sprig of fat berries shaded in loving detail. Underneath was a single word in

364

the same disordered hand: *bloobrys*. A few purplish smears decorated the corner of the page, as if Hal had been eating blueberries while he drew.

On the next page Daisy recognized a group of familiar, lofty camellias, caught mid-song, and, flipping forward, a drawing of bedraggled hoopoes with black racing-stripes, looking very damp and sorry for themselves. *Flud*, said the heavy scrawl, in explanation.

The entries went on like this for pages, meticulously mapping out the world of Mallowmarsh – astonishingly lifelike stag-beetles and sun-badgers and foxgloves, snapdragons and parakeets caught with breathtaking deftness in mid-flight. Looking closely, Daisy noticed the contrast between the finesse of the drawings and the painful scrawl of the writing – the light, effortless pencil strokes against the frustrated letters scored deep into the paper. The drawings were painstaking and observant, sometimes funny, furiously big-hearted. The notebook was a portrait of a boy who was wild and imaginative and so alive that it was impossible to think of him being gone. Daisy swallowed. Then she turned to the final page, and breathed in.

It was a portrait of herself. She was sitting on her favourite branch of the apple tree in the hidden garden with one leg swinging down, looking out through the leaves and laughing straight out of the page.

Daisy shut the book and carried it with her back to bed. Her father had lived in this room as a boy, had grown up

365

in this house with Artemis and the skylight and the telescope and the larder tree and the Heart Oak down by the lake. She knew he was gone – and yet, somehow, she felt closer to him than she ever had.

She was tracing her eyes over the drawing for the hundredth time when she heard a soft knock at the door.

'I heard you get up,' said Artemis. 'Is everything all right?'

Daisy nodded, unable to speak.

Artemis's eyes fell on the notebook. 'Why, it's Hal's—' She looked at Daisy, and stopped abruptly in the doorway. 'So you know,' she said.

'Yes. Hal . . . Hal White was my father. And that makes you my—'

'Your grandmother,' finished Artemis gently. 'Yes.'

Daisy sat frozen for a long, suspended moment – and then the spell broke and she rushed into Artemis's arms. Her body was warm and she smelled of grass and rain and rosemary. It was the first time Daisy had been hugged like this since she'd said goodbye to Ma: as if she was both loved and needed.

Artemis let go of her and pretended to glance around so that Daisy could wipe her eyes with the ragged ends of her hair.

'How long have you known?' asked Daisy.

'Not long,' said Artemis slowly. 'You see –' she sat down on the end of the bed as Daisy sank against the headboard, knees drawn up to her chest, Napoleon round her shoulders –

'your father was odd . . . imaginative. Quiet, but *wild* with it: he used to go off for hours on his own, daydreaming and sketching. But he found it very hard to read, or write. He was the cleverest child I ever knew, sharp as a knife – but he said the letters wouldn't stay still. They jumped around on the page and he couldn't make them do what he wanted. Of course, now we know it's called dyslexia, but at the time . . .

'Well, I believed him, but his father had no patience for it. He shouted at Hal; he punished him. And when he didn't get into Bloomquist – he failed the written exam, the second test – Hal's father said he was a shame and a disappointment to the family name.' She snorted. 'He forgot that it was MY surname. And I didn't care what Hal was, as long as he was happy.'

'Your surname?'

'Yes. Didn't you know? Green magic is usually passed down through the female line, so husbands and children always take the wife's name. That's why Hal – or Henry, as he was calling himself by then – became a Thistledown when he married your mother.' She shifted on the bed.

'Anyway, after he failed the Bloomquist test, the arguments with his father grew worse and worse. The summer before he left, when things were bad, Hal started talking about a girl who'd come to live at Mallowmarsh. He used to tell me about her – that she had brown hair with red and gold bits in it, and she was called Daisy. I thought, always, that Daisy was an imaginary friend, a way for him

to cope. So, imagine my surprise when you turned up here, with your name, and your hair. I thought I was imagining things.'

'But it's true,' said Daisy. She opened Hal's notebook to the sketch of herself sitting careless and laughing in the crook of the apple tree in the hidden garden – only last week and thirty years ago. 'He drew this.'

'You were real after all,' whispered Artemis. Then she laughed aloud. 'My son's imaginary friend, come to life!'

Chapter 51

Daisy explained – haltingly at first – about the hidden garden. It was this, more than anything else, that convinced her the garden was gone. There was no magic left to stop her from speaking, and the words tumbled out.

'It was real,' she said. 'Mallowmarsh, but thirty years in the past. It grew from a wish – Ma left me a seed, you see . . .'

She explained as best she could, and Artemis nodded.

'Of course,' she said. 'It makes sense. And *what a wish*.'

Daisy stared fixedly at the stiff cuffs of her nightgown. They were white and embroidered with tiny green oak leaves. She tried very hard not to think of how much she missed Hal: his grouchiness, his cleverness and his bone-deep kindness.

'So,' she said, swallowing, 'what happened to Hal after he left Mallowmarsh?'

Artemis closed her eyes, and seemed to gather herself. 'Hal's father had family among the Moon Travellers – a grandfather and cousins, good people – and they invited Hal to live with them. I went to see him every month at Moonmarket, and I tried to persuade him to come home. But he was terribly stubborn; and I could see that he was

safe and happy where he was. In the end, I had to let him go.'

She drew in a breath. 'Anyway, six years after he left, Hal started sending specimens back to Mallowmarsh – the rarest and most legendary specimens in the world. The mimsy fern, the crosspatch baobab, the phosphorescent mango.'

Daisy sat up, listening hard.

'But Hal wasn't satisfied with saving plants from Darkmarket. He wanted to shut down the market itself. He decided to go undercover: changed his identity and embedded himself in a Darkmarket operation. It was the only way to find out who was running the business: to weed it out from the root.' Artemis frowned. 'His best friend, Cardew, went with him. They were supposed to keep each other safe.'

'But?' prompted Daisy.

'But . . . one day, while they were posing as Darkmarket agents in the Amazon, Hal did something impossible. He found the ghost-moth orchid. He told Cardew, trusting him to keep it safe – and Cardew betrayed him for it. By that time, of course, Cardew had gone over to the Darkmarketeers – or the Grim Reapers, as they were starting to call themselves – for real. He killed Hal . . . and everything my son had discovered about the Grim Reapers died with him.'

Daisy thought of Ma sobbing at night after Pa's funeral. She thought of her father's strong arms when she was small:

their hide-and-seek, story-time, high-holiday glory times. She knew then that he had not wanted to leave them behind. That he would have done anything to be there for them always.

Artemis went on quietly. 'Cardew killed two more Greenwilders in the struggle, before he was captured and made to stand trial. He was stripped of his magic and cast out into the Greyside. I thought he was dead. And I was glad.'

Daisy closed her eyes, and Napoleon sat himself consolingly on her feet like the world's smallest purring hot-water bottle.

Then: 'Hang on,' she said, remembering something urgent and sitting up so fast that Napoleon yelped. 'I should have told you before. Brightly was working for Craven. He was blackmailing her because—'

But Artemis was already nodding. 'I know, Daisy. I worked it out around the same time you did. It's no wonder Brightly acted as she did, with her son's life in the balance.'

'She said . . .' Daisy frowned. 'She said that as soon as Craven attacked Mallowmarsh, her side of the bargain would be done. Is that why . . .'

'Yes,' said Artemis. 'That's why she fought on our side in the battle – after freeing herself from the boat where you'd locked her up.'

'Is she all right? What happened to her?'

Artemis's forehead creased.

'I'm afraid that Brightly didn't survive the fight,' she said quietly. 'But I think, also, that she did not mean to survive it. Thanks to the ghost-moth orchid, she had no more than a few months left. She'd given more than seventy years of her own life to her son – and, this way, she went down fighting for the world Max will grow up in.'

Daisy rocked back, feeling as if she'd been walloped in the chest.

'And Max? Where is he?'

'Craven had the boy imprisoned in the cellar of his home. By the time we got there, Max had escaped. We've got Botanists out scouring every inch of London as we speak.'

Daisy sucked in a breath. 'Craven really planned everything, didn't he?'

Artemis nodded. 'With the help of Maud Daggler. She's a dangerous character – a Botanist by birth, with little magical ability and a whole lot of bitterness to go with it. She's been at the heart of the Darkmarket for years.'

'She must have taken the dandelight from Brightly and handed it over to Cardew.'

'Exactly, Daisy.'

'But . . . if Sheldrake didn't steal the dandelight, then what was he doing with Matron at Moonmarket? Who was he talking to in the Sighing Forest?'

'I can't answer that, I'm afraid, Daisy,' said Artemis, suddenly becoming very interested in a ladybird that was walking across the quilt.

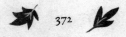

Daisy was about to protest, but the look on the commander's face told her it would be no use. Instead, she swallowed, and said, 'Craven told me he was working for the Grim Reapers. I think . . . they're the ones hunting down Botanists.'

'Good greenness, he really did talk, didn't he?' said Artemis. 'And I'm afraid you're right. For years we've been telling our children stories of the Grim Reapers: monsters who stalk the earth with their scythes. And all this time a group of human monsters has been growing into the name: a vast organization that unites the worst elements of the two worlds: an alliance of power-hungry Greysiders and corrupt Botanists like Daggler. For centuries, the Greenwild has stayed secret, but now thanks to Craven there are Greysiders who know about us. And, even though he's gone, they're not going to leave us alone.' She rubbed her temples. 'The dandelight is the missing weapon in their arsenal. It's a compass as well as a key – and it could lead the Grim Reapers to each and every door to the Greenwild. No pocket would be safe.'

'But what do they actually *want*?'

'What *don't* they want? That's the question, Daisy. For these people, cutting down every tree in the Amazon rainforest would only be the start.'

'But – but WHY? That's *evil*.'

'There's big money in destroying the earth, Daisy: pumping for oil, planting crops for livestock on pristine

rainforest land, mining for minerals, selling rare specimens for profit. Enough to make men millionaires many times over. There are Grim Reapers in every government, in every big company and organization – always pushing for more destruction.'

With a shiver of unease, Daisy remembered the photos of Craven shaking hands with presidents and prime ministers and A-list celebrities.

Artemis was still speaking. 'And if that's what they're doing in the Greyside, imagine what they have planned for the magical specimens and wonders of the Greenwild. We're talking about destruction on a scale we have never seen before.'

Daisy tried to imagine the full horror of this, but it made her head hurt too much.

'Why kidnap Botanists?' she asked instead. 'Why keep them prisoner?'

'I don't know,' said Artemis slowly. 'I've heard rumours of terrible things . . . All we can say for now is that the Botanists are more useful to them alive than dead, whether as bargaining chips, or for another purpose we can only guess at.'

'But . . .' Daisy swallowed, and her throat went tight. 'Craven said Ma . . . he said Ma was dead.' This was the shadowy thing she'd been trying not to think about: Craven's words, and the utter finality in his voice.

She looked to Artemis as if begging her to deny it. But

Artemis said nothing, and only held her hand.

After a long time, Daisy wiped her eyes and said, 'It was her necklace, wasn't it? That's how Craven knew she was a Botanist.'

'Yes.' Artemis looked pained. 'They never met, before. Your mother didn't come to Cardew's trial. I think the idea of it was too painful.'

Daisy nodded. 'And there's one more thing . . .'

'Go ahead, Daisy.'

'Craven mentioned someone called "the Great Reaper". It sounded like he was the one in charge. Craven thought that if he could hand over Mallowmarsh the Great Reaper would give him back his magic as some sort of reward.'

Artemis's laugh was bitter. 'I fear he was deceived in that hope. But he was right about one thing, Daisy. Greed is a well that never runs dry. The Grim Reapers are on the rise. And that means the attacks and disappearances aren't going to stop any time soon. We may have won the battle, but the war has barely begun.'

Chapter 52

There was silence again in the room. They sat as the moon sank beyond the window, and the pale green light of pre-dawn filled the sky, spangled with sequinned fading stars.

'How did you work it out?' said Daisy at last. 'How did you really guess who I was?'

'The dandelight,' said Artemis, nodding to where it shone on the bedside table. 'It was handed down through the White family for centuries: all the way from Francesca White, Robert Chiveley's mistress. I gave it to Hal when he left for Moonmarket so that he'd always be able to find the nearest pocket, no matter where he was in the world. You turning up with it – it could only mean one thing. That Hal had had a child I didn't know about.' Her eyes flicked to Daisy. 'And then, of course, there was Brutus.'

'Brutus?'

Artemis gave an unexpected snort. 'Yes: that absurd dog, licking you from head to toe. A Greenwild bloodhound recognizes the blood of its master, Daisy. It remains loyal to that bond through the generations.'

'What?' Daisy didn't understand. 'I'm not related to Sheldrake.'

'Oh, yes you are,' said Artemis. 'You see, he was

Hal's father. My husband.'

Daisy stared at her, dumfounded.

Artemis nodded. 'We've lived apart ever since Hal left. I could never forgive him for driving Hal away. And he couldn't forgive himself. Neither of us could leave Mallowmarsh – it's our home, our life's work. So . . . we separated. He stopped using my surname, went back to his bachelor name: Sheldrake. I stayed here at the Roost, and he moved to his cabin in the woods. He's lived there ever since.'

Daisy was struggling to take everything in. In one day, she had found and lost her father, gained a grandmother – and now incredibly . . . 'A grandfather?' She wasn't sure she liked the idea, if it meant being attached to Sheldrake. Even if he had probably saved her life in the battle.

Artemis wrinkled her nose. 'Yes – although I doubt he'd like you calling him that. He doesn't like to admit he's getting older.'

Daisy looked at Napoleon, curled up on the quilt between them. Dawn was breaking, the lemony light flooding through the round porthole window, and a blackbird was singing its heart out on the roof.

'You know,' said Daisy, 'Hal was working on the hidden garden because he wanted to do something to make you proud. He cared about you. A lot. And –' Daisy paused, realizing – 'my parents always said I was named after my grandmother.' She paused. 'My proper name is Diana: the

Roman version of Artemis. I couldn't pronounce it when I was little, so it became Daisy instead. But *he named me after you*.' She looked at her grandmother. 'He never forgot.'

'Oh,' said Artemis, and her blue eyes were very bright. The morning light was like fresh water, cool and sweet. 'Oh, Daisy.' A single tear ran down her cheek, and then she threw her arms around her granddaughter.

Chapter 53

'Hurry up!' called Indigo from below. 'We're going to be late.'

'Coming!' Daisy paused in the kitchen to get a pear from the larder tree. It fell into her hand, cool and heavy. Then, taking a large bite, she threw open the kitchen door and flew down the spiral staircase. The steps blurred beneath her feet as she ran, a bubble of happiness rising in her throat as she saw Indigo turning cartwheels on the grass, and Acorn beaming, and the Prof polishing her spectacles, which winked in the light. Shortly after Daisy had woken up, the commander had announced that their demerits had been struck from the record, and the Prof had been unstoppably cheerful ever since.

'Although,' she said, 'it's never too early to start preparing for the next test – it's in March, you know.'

Daisy spun down the final curve of the staircase, feeling the whole world still whirling around her. Ma's necklace was around her neck, and her arm was out of its cast. For the last week, Miss Tufton had forced her to drink regular beakers of bitterbone brew (made, she said, from the crushed stems of the ghostly white ossuary flower). The smell was a mixture of blue cheese and old socks, but it had worked.

Now, Daisy felt the breeze against her skin, and drew a deep breath into her lungs. The sky was periwinkle blue, and the air was as fresh and sparkling as golden elderflower cordial.

Napoleon leapt lightly down the steps beside her. Their adventures didn't seem to have affected him at all. If anything, his whiskers were finer and his bearing snootier than ever.

Indigo turned a last cartwheel and a parakeet flew around Daisy's head, twittering excitedly. She grinned at him and Acorn and the Prof. 'Let's go.'

Winter had lessened its grip on Mallowmarsh while Daisy slept. The grounds were filled with frilled white snowdrops and bright-blue irises, bottle-green frippery-fibs and great drifts of early daffotrills (sounding, as Brightly had promised, just like a pompous brass band).

They made their way around the sparkling lake beneath the waving silver birches and plum trees – and Daisy's eyes widened as the Great Glasshouse came into view.

The glass had gradually been healing itself over the last week, under the watchful eye of Gulliver Wildish and the tender ministrations of a small army of gardeners and under-gardeners. It had grown back in new and elaborately curving and ballooning panes, with domes and fanciful turrets in the heights. There was no sign of the gaping hole through which Craven had fallen to his death.

'Look!' said the Prof, pointing at the group of students

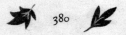

gathered around the doors of the glasshouse, where a sheet of paper was pinned on a large corkboard. 'It must be the Bloomquist test results. They always post them there.' Daisy lagged behind while the others ran ahead. Then the Prof gave a shout of disbelief, and Acorn began leaping up and down.

'Daisy, Daisy! You have to see this!'

Daisy hurried over and Indigo shoved the sheet of paper in her face. 'It's marked out of twenty,' he said.

Bellamy, Professor: 19

Bubble, Septimus: 13

Cantrip, Kalissa: 17

Helix, Ivy: 18

Podsnap, Indigo: 14

Rowan-Rajan, Ravi: 15

Rowan-Rajan, Rishi: 16

Thistledown, Daisy: 20

Daisy stared. 'But – but that's impossible. I failed. I didn't do any magic during the test.'

'Not according to Honoria Plume,' came a voice from behind them. Daisy turned and saw Artemis grinning at her. 'It wasn't her who petrified that venomous hydra,' said the commander, looking hard at Daisy. 'It was you.'

'Me?' Daisy shook her head in bewilderment. 'No. There must be some kind of mistake.' What she was hearing seemed huge and impossible, like being told that she'd swallowed a rhinoceros without noticing.

'Honoria doesn't make mistakes about this kind of thing. And in view of the magic you used during the battle, we both agreed that this mark was the least you deserved.'

Daisy watched, stunned, as a smiling Artemis strode away across the lawn.

The Grand Mallowmarsh Founders' Day garden party always took place at the end of January, and it couldn't have come with better timing. By five o'clock that evening, the celebrations were in full swing on the lawn in front of the Great Glasshouse, and it was clear that the whole event was going to go off with a bang. Wildish was seated at a shiny grand piano that had been pulled out onto the lawn, his wooden hand dancing lightly over the lower keys. An orchestra of camellias was creating music alongside him, while the topiary elephants and tigers swung their trunks and tails in time to the music. The air was soft, the trees filled with music and laughter and parakeets, and the glasshouse itself gleamed like a garnet in the light of the setting sun. The Heart Oak was hung with fresh ribbons and gold coins, and Daisy thought that the magnificent old tree had never looked finer.

Meanwhile, Mr McGuffin and Mrs Marchpane had been working for days on a grand feast – not aided by the

Littlies, who had locked themselves in the kitchen the night before the party and wreaked gleeful havoc. They'd been discovered before dawn that morning, covered in apple sauce and tipsy on plum wine, and were still in disgrace.

Despite this mishap, the three large tables on the lawn groaned under the weight of buttered potatoes and honey-glazed carrots, roasted chickens and meltingly soft onion tarts, crusty breads and hearty pies. There were lemony cheesecakes, banoffee pies and tiny starberry cakes drenched in honey syrup, cupcakes topped with marzipan acorns, and piles of honey sandwiches, flaky sugarplum pastries and jugs of fresh cream.

A flotilla of lilypaddles was crossing the lake, bringing over guests, and the grass was already full of people milling around, talking, eating and laughing.

Daisy spotted Madame Gallitrop chatting to a tall Botanist with a very impressive curled moustache.

'Who's that?' she asked. Indigo glanced over.

'Oh, that's Ivor Whelk, a famous marine botanist. He's just come back from studying piranhas in the Amazon River. Anyone who's anyone,' said Indigo, grandly, 'is invited to the great Mallowmarsh Founders' Day garden party.' He took a slice of cake from one of the tables, glanced around to check no one was watching, and dunked it into a cream jug. Daisy joined him, and spotted Artemis and Sheldrake talking quietly together in the shelter of the trees.

'I can't believe no one told us that they used to be

married,' said Indigo through a mouthful of cake. 'It's just like the grown-ups to keep something like that secret.'

Daisy nodded, watching Sheldrake's upright figure. She'd got everything so hopelessly mixed up.

The sun was sinking calmly into the lake, smooth as a mirror. The air was cool and crisp, and the sweet violets and sump-roses had a richer scent than ever before. The aerial tulips floated on the breeze like orange candles, while glasses of sweet dandelion cordial were passed around and the Prof played leapfrog with the Littlies.

'Child!' called the Prof's Aunt Elspeth. 'Come away from there. You'll tear your clothes!'

The Prof smiled sweetly at her. 'Holes are good for ventilation, Aunt,' she said.

'Why, you infuriating—' Aunt Elspeth started after her just as one of the Littlies went darting across her path with a giant ice-cream cone. The ice cream survived intact, but Aunt Elspeth tipped slowly and elegantly into the lake. She emerged with water pouring out of her nose and a strand of pondweed draped artistically over one ear, and had to go inside to change. After that, the evening suddenly took on an even rosier glow: pleasantly full of possibilities.

Kalissa Cantrip was juggling apples; Albert reposed in his matchbox by Acorn's side, feasting on a particularly juicy leaf; and Napoleon was enjoying a spot of parakeet chasing, his favourite sport. The air was filled with the screeching of indignant birds as they flapped upwards and circled back to Indigo.

For once, though, Indigo wasn't paying attention.

He was running full-tilt towards two men, one tall, one short, who had appeared beneath the plum trees at the edge of the lake. He was whooping with excitement, and then the tall man swung him into his arms while the other laughed.

'Papa! Dad! You're home!' For a moment there was only a chaos of voices and hugs and delight, and Daisy stood back, and tried not to think about Ma and all she had lost.

Then Indigo pulled away.

'Daisy, these are my dads.' They both grinned at her. The tall man had Indigo's amber eyes, kind and crinkled at the corners beneath winged eyebrows and a shock of curling hair.

'It's good to meet you at last, Daisy,' he said gravely. 'I'm Rafael Podsnap. I understand it's thanks to you that Mallowmarsh – and Indigo – are safe. Oliver and I are both so grateful.'

He gestured to his husband, a thin and bespectacled man who was enchanting a small army of pine cones to chase after a shrieking, laughing Indigo.

Daisy shrugged awkwardly. 'Indigo did a lot of it,' she said. 'What he does with birds and animals, you know – it helped win the battle.'

'The commander told us,' said Rafael Podsnap, eyes bright with pride. 'We've been talking about finding Indigo the right teacher. There's a famous Venezuelan Botanist who has the same ability, and she says she'd like to teach him.' He paused, looking at Indigo, who had arrived back at their side, wide-eyed and out of breath. 'If that's what you'd like.'

'There are other people like me?' Indigo looked stunned. Then, 'Yes!' he said. 'YES!'

Rafael grinned and glanced back at Daisy. 'The Pacific Islands are beautiful, and coral is fascinating, but there's nothing like the feeling of being home.' He took an enormous bite of profiterole and closed his eyes in bliss.

'Mmmph,' he said, sounding for a moment like his son. 'This beats six months' worth of ship's rations, I can tell you.'

Daisy turned and saw Ivor Whelk behind her.

'Excuse me,' she said to the Podsnaps. 'There's someone I have to talk to.'

She approached the marine Botanist and looked at him, gathering herself.

'You've just come back from the Amazon, right?'

'Yes,' he said, smiling cautiously. 'Why do you ask?'

'You didn't meet anyone out there called Leila Thistledown, did you? She looks like me, but grown up, and prettier . . .' She trailed off as Whelk shook his head, and she felt her chest deflate like a child's balloon.

'I'm sorry,' he said. 'She disappeared the week before I arrived. I'm afraid there was nothing to find.'

Daisy nodded. She knew Ma was gone. For a long time,

a bright, stubborn place inside her had burned with hope, like a white candle that refused to go out. But now it was dark. She had cried through the long nights following the attack, weeping not at the pain in her arm, but for the loss she knew now was real as rock, undoable forever. It hooked the breath from her lungs and cut off the blood supply to her fingers. It made her feel numb all over, as if her whole body had been to the dentist, and her heart had been ripped out like a rotten tooth.

She remembered spending one long summer day on a Scottish beach with Ma, building sandcastles and picking up sea glass. She remembered the way Ma had plunged into the icy water like every wave was an adventure, how her laugh had filled Daisy with its message of fierce delight. Now, it felt as if her love for Ma had been a bomb that she'd been carrying around in her chest, and that it had finally exploded. She wasn't sure she could survive it, except that, somehow, she was still breathing, still taking one step, and another.

'Come on,' said Indigo, glancing at her. 'Let's get some banoffee pie before it's all gone.' Daisy stood beside her friend and looked out across the lawn. Despite their naughtiness the previous night, the Littlies had been allowed to stay up late, and toddlers ran across the grass, screaming and laughing while penny-puff pods flowered and puffed rainbow powder into the air, streaking their faces with festival colours.

Acorn ran amongst them, her eyes shining. Indigo's parents were dancing a waltz to the music of the piano, and then Acorn's mother, Ida Sparkler, and various other couples joined in too, until the whole party was dancing. Artemis danced with Wildish, who executed a surprisingly energetic tango, his eyebrows joined in concentration. Indigo swung Acorn around and around, until his dad swept him into a wild two-step; and the Prof danced with one of the under-gardener's sons, who looked as though he couldn't believe his luck.

The sun had set, but a marmalade sunset still glowed above the treetops, and the ancient yew trees were hung with candles in tiny jam jars. Music drifted on the chilly air, and the whole night felt alive and full of promise. Then all at once into the dark sky soared fireworks: golden dandelion puffs unfolding and dissolving in a thousand sparkles, bright silver Catherine wheels exploding and shimmering like carbonated stars and greeny-blue ones rising like the tails of fierce young comets. Daisy thought of the night she had arrived at Mallowmarsh, and how much had changed since then.

Winter was ending, and the year ahead beckoned, unknowable. Mallowmarsh was saved, and Craven was gone – but many Botanists remained missing, and the Grim Reapers were out there, gathering their forces. They would, thought Daisy, have to be brave and braver still. But as she looked around and saw the Prof teaching Acorn how to tap-dance, and Indigo running around with bright, coruscating sparklers, and Mallowmarsh itself spread out around them like a living dream, she felt a spiky sort of protectiveness and resolve. The rescue mission would soon be setting out for the Amazon. She would be ready.

There was someone standing next to her now, and she looked up to see Artemis's sheets of silver hair and pointed chin in the darkness – a chin like Daisy's own. Artemis held out her hand, warm and dry, and Daisy slipped hers into it. Then she saw the tall, shaggy-haired shape of Sheldrake making his way over to where they stood next to a small bonfire, where Indigo was roasting marshmallows from the nearby mallow bushes. The air smelled of burnt, caramelizing sugar. The man nodded at Daisy in the flickering firelight.

'Daisy.' One word, but it held warmth in it, like a smooth stone that has been cupped for hours in your pocket.

Daisy reached out solemnly and offered him a marshmallow from the end of her skewer, which he recognized as the peace offering it was. He ate it in one wolfish gulp, yelping as the singed edges burned his tongue.

Then from beyond the firelight came another figure: one Daisy didn't recognize. His face was very thin and tanned, with lots of fine lines around his eyes as if he'd spent a long time smiling into the sun.

'Cuthbert Quirk!' cried Artemis. 'You came!'

Daisy recognized the name of the explorer who had sent the minim moss and the pigmy marmoset.

'I did,' he said gravely. 'I had a letter to deliver. One that I found on an injured parakeet trying to leave Peru. I saw the name, and then I heard about the girl who had arrived at Mallowmarsh, and I knew I had to come and find her. Are you Daisy Thistledown?'

Silently, she nodded, and Cuthbert Quirk took a small piece of paper from his pocket and placed it into Daisy's hands. Her heart cartwheeled in her chest, and she unfolded it with fingers that shook only slightly, holding it up so that she and Artemis could read it in the light of the fire. On it were scrawled four words.

My rascal, it read, in handwriting that was painfully familiar. *I'm alive.*

Artemis, reading with her, gave a cry. And in the branches of the yew trees, the candles shone and did not go out.

About the Author

Pari Thomson works as Editorial Director for picture books at Bloomsbury Children's Books. Half Persian, half English, she lived in many places while she was growing up, including India, Pakistan, the USA, the UK and Belgium.

She studied at Oxford University and now lives near the river in London, not far from Kew Gardens.

Acknowledgements

I owe the greatest thanks to so many people for the existence of this book. First and foremost, to my extraordinary agent Claire Wilson. Thank you for seeing something in this story, and for making dreams come true.

To Emma Jones, my UK editor, for kindness, humour and endless patience, and to all the brilliant people at Macmillan UK. To Janine O'Malley for invaluable advice and insight, and to the whole team at Farrar, Straus & Giroux. To Pete Knapp and to everyone at both Park Fine and RCW. To the hugely talented Elisa Paganelli, for making this book an object of such beauty.

To my parents, for everything, always. To Lily and Daniel, my wonderful siblings. To Richard: never forgotten.

To Cathy, without whom this book would not have been written. To my kind and brilliant friends, with special thanks to Amy for the champagne. And to Tom, who arrived at the end.

To the keepers of Kew Gardens, for making it a place of green magic and wonder.

And finally, to my wild and wonderful Iranian and English families all around the world.

*Turn the page for a sneak peek at
Daisy's next thrilling adventure:*

GREENWILD

THE CITY BEYOND THE SEA

Full fathom five thy father lies;
Of his bones are coral made;
Those are pearls that were his eyes;
Nothing of him that doth fade,
But doth suffer a sea change
Into something rich and strange.
Sea-nymphs hourly ring his knell:
Ding-dong.
Hark! now I hear them — Ding-dong, bell.

– from *The Tempest* by William Shakespeare

Chapter 1

It was a day like a freshly peeled orange: bright and zesty and sweet.

The smell of spring was in the air at Mallowmarsh, and Daisy Thistledown was feeling hopeful. All over the gardens, Botanists were hard at work, tending giant palm trees in the Great Glasshouse, harvesting football-sized plums from the orchards, and planting new lightning seeds in the Mallow Woods. Wild violets were blooming beneath the ancient yews, and the sky was filled with parakeets swooping from tree to tree, delivering post and screeching joyfully.

A couple of apprentices waved at Daisy as they walked past, and she waved back, grinning. After three long weeks of waiting, the expedition to the Amazon rainforest would finally be setting off tomorrow, and Daisy felt the thrill of it racing through her veins like electricity.

She was standing at her usual spot on the edge of the lake, watching the Mallowmarsh shipbuilders put the finishing touches to their work. It had taken a team of trained Botanists two full weeks to lay the living beams and grow the mast from a seedling – but at last the ship was almost ready: proud and high on the water, with a hull of polished oak wood, a great white sail furled tight as a bud, and an elaborate system of rigging that used living green vines instead of rope. The ship strained at its moorings, as if eager to be on its way.

Daisy had observed the final preparations with mounting impatience and excitement: the deliveries of mosquito netting from Moonmarket and biscuit barrels from the Mallowmarsh kitchens; the piling up of no-glare marsh lamps and crates of phosphorescent mangoes on the shores of the lake. She had tried to help (and been waved away) as everything began to be carried on board, and Botanists went staggering up the gangplank with heavy jars of healing chamomillion cream and extra-sticky binding vine, and anything else that could possibly be needed for a voyage to the Amazon.

Of course, children weren't technically allowed on the dock, but she had so far managed to ignore this instruction.

'Back again?' asked Madame Gallitrop, who was supervising the loading of a caged Venus flytrap onto the deck of the ship. Her voice was resigned.

'I thought,' said Daisy, 'I'd come and see if you needed help.'

Madame Gallitrop, the head of the Intemperate Glasshouse, was a plump and cheerful Frenchwoman with merry dark eyes and an enormous black bun of hair. 'I see,' she said dryly. 'Well, *ma chère*, the ship is stocked, the provisions are loaded, and we are nearly ready to set off for Moonmarket tomorrow night.'

4

Daisy felt her fingers tingle, and she summoned a small vine from the shore to curl around her ankles. She could feel anticipation rise up in her like sap through a stem as she gazed at the floating ship. It looked very fine, with its portholes gleaming, flags fluttering, and its mast – a living oak tree – growing straight from the smooth wooden deck.

The ship was where Daisy felt closest to her mother.

This was partly because its jaunty pennants reminded her of Ma's own devil-may-care brand of confidence, and partly because the ship was Daisy's ticket to finding the person she cared about most in the world. Her mother was imprisoned somewhere in the heart of the Peruvian rainforest, and this was the rescue mission that was going to save her.

'Isn't there anything I can do?' she asked for the hundredth time. 'Perhaps I could polish the railings? Or dust the capstan?' The vine she'd summoned coiled eagerly over her left foot.

'No,' said Madame Gallitrop, shaking her head. 'We have everything under control, *ma chère*. You know you're not supposed to be here. Leave the preparations to the experts.'

'But—'

'Watch out!' It was a Botanist from the kitchens toting a crate of ginger-root beer along the dock. 'Out of the way! Children aren't allowed near the ship.'

Daisy felt a wave of annoyance – and suddenly the vine at her ankle surged out of her control. It shot into the air, ballooned to the width of a python, and snapped the landing

5

stage in two with a great splintering crash.

Daisy leapt back onto the bank just in time, but the barrel went flying into the air and lodged in the ship's mast, showering ginger beer on the Botanists beneath. Madame Gallitrop went toppling headfirst into the water with an almighty splash and emerged glowering, a frond of riverweed draped over one ear like an ill-conceived hairpiece.

She spat out a small water beetle. 'Enough,' she said, her voice unusually frosty. 'Kindly help me out of the lake, Daisy, and then make yourself useful somewhere else. You must learn to *control* your magic. Control is key.'

Daisy Thistledown was a Botanist too – one who had only just discovered that she had green magic. As it turned out, using magic was one thing; keeping it in check was another.

'But,' she said, bracing herself against the bank to heave Madame Gallitrop out of the water, 'I want to do something. I want to *help*!' She heaved again, and the Frenchwoman collapsed onto the remaining half of the landing stage. She righted herself with dignity, straightening her sopping overalls.

'*Non!*' she said, reverting to her native French. 'That was the fourth accident this week. You can go and "help" elsewhere!'

'Oi! Get that child OFF the landing stage,' roared one of the shipbuilders, a grizzled man who was persuading the nearest mizzen-mast to grow high enough to take a sail.

'What have I said about untrained children using magic near the ship?'

Madame Gallitrop, now standing on the shore and dripping from every inch of her hair and overalls, shot Daisy a pointed look.

Daisy slunk away, her cheeks hot. But she was still close enough to hear the shipbuilder's words as he surveyed the damage she'd done to the dock.

'That girl,' he said, 'is a lost cause.'

Chapter 2

Max Brightly was a lost cause. That's what the midwife said approximately two minutes after he was born, taking one look at his furious pinched mouth and the way his small, angry fists punched the air. And people had gone on saying it all his life: 'That boy,' they said, 'is a lost cause.'

His mother's friends had said it wryly, flinching at his outraged infant roars. His teachers had said it despairingly, lifting their hands in defeat each time Max picked a fight or used a word so rude it made them feel faint. And so, finally, had the doctors – lots of them, after Max became sick and even breathing began to hurt. The tone was hushed now, but not so quiet that he couldn't hear the words from his hospital bed, where he lay with his skin very white – so pale that his birthmark stood out like a smashed strawberry beneath his right eye – and his hands resting on top of the starched cotton sheets. 'That boy is a lost cause.'

In fact, the only person who had never said it was his mother. 'There's nothing lost about you,' she told him fiercely. And she glared at anyone who dared to suggest otherwise.

Max's mother wasn't an angel, or a saint, which was what most people who knew her liked to say. After all, Max

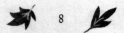

thought, angels didn't wink at you slyly when someone told a bad joke, and saints didn't wear tight jeans with silver boots or turn heads in the street with their gold hair and loud laughter.

Max turned heads too, but for other reasons. He hated the way people always seemed to glance between him and his beaming mother, wondering how she could be related to the boy with sticking-up black hair and the unrepentant scowl. The only things he'd inherited from her were his grey eyes and the deep dimple that appeared in his left cheek when he smiled, which wasn't very often. He was as spiky and awkward as the outside of a conker shell, and other people often made him feel itchy, like the feeling you get from wearing a prickly jumper that has shrunk in the wash.

There was one other thing he'd inherited from Marigold Brightly, but it wasn't something you could see from the outside. It was a sort of bone-deep, bone-headed resolve. When Max decided to do something, he did it.

Which was why, when he found himself, at the age of twelve and three-quarters, kidnapped and imprisoned in a damp cellar, Max decided he was going to escape.

It was very cold inside the cellar and Max could hear the sound of water dripping somewhere above his head. It was, he thought, the loneliest sound in the world. He had been here for a long time now – he wasn't sure how long – and hunger was blocking out his thoughts like white noise.

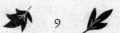

9

What he knew was this: he had been taken from the London hotel he'd been staying at with his mother ('Just for a few nights,' she had said, when they'd arrived from New York). They had been in the middle of an argument – the usual one, about Max not being well enough to start school – when a noise had sounded from the corridor. There had been a moment, stretched out in Max's memory, just long enough for them to look at each other, eyes wide.

Then the door had splintered and fallen inwards with a scream of wood, and suddenly the room was full of two men – big and tall and masked. Max's mother had shouted and then the taller of the two men had crossed the room in three steps and backhanded her across the face so that she fell to the ground and lay still. Her eyes were closed, and Max couldn't see if her chest was moving.

He roared and scrambled towards her; he tried to fling himself on the man – and then a sack was tossed over his head, and everything went dark. He felt himself being lifted bodily over the other man's shoulder. 'No,' he heard himself shout. 'Mom! No, please!' He flailed out wildly with his arms, straining to get free, and felt his fist strike something hard: the man's nose. Max's captor grunted, and then he knocked Max's head against something hard, and his brain became a firework that flared and then went dark.